I0746490

j.f.r. coates

Text copyright 2024

Cover by Chromamancer

Impossible Magic
978-1-922061-81-2

J.F.R. Coates
Queensland, Australia

IMPOSSIBLE MAGIC

BOOK 2: THE DESTINY OF DRAGONS

BY J.F.R. COATES

ACKNOWLEDGEMENTS

I don't think I could ever properly thank everyone who has contributed to this series in the ten years since it was first released. So many people have shaped my writing career and skills that I would always risk leaving someone out.

I first have to thank my parents. Not only did they support my choice to become a writer, they also fostered and nurtured my interest in reading as a child. Without that, these stories would almost certainly not exist today.

I also have to thank those other writers who have inspired me over the years. From J.R.R. Tolkien to Philip Pullman, Neil Gaiman to Robin Hobb, my work does not exist in isolation. All of these great writers and more have had some inspiration on the stories I have wanted to tell.

I would also like to thank my husband. His support over the years has provided me with the capability to continue writing these stories.

And then there are my readers. Whether this is your first introduction to the *Destiny of Dragons* series, or you have been with me across the last ten years, thank you all! Without you, the writing process would be a vastly different experience.

And finally, it would be remiss of me not to mention those who supported my Kickstarter campaign to officially launch these 10 Year Anniversary Editions of the trilogy. Your support means the world to me.

Thank you everyone!

CHAPTER ONE

Ellian

I knew I had risked my brother's fury. Inviting fifty humans to camp near the nomad's lair had invoked that rage as expected, but I hadn't thought he would go four days without speaking a single word to me. Given that Vinzent still wasn't talking to me either, most of my time was spent with the humans and Airil. The Nixan barely left my side. Though he claimed that he simply wished to make sure I was safe amongst such dangerous company, we both knew that the humans weren't going to betray us and attack.

We had learnt a lot from the humans. Their leader, James McArthur, had told us all about the war and why humans were crossing the mountains into draconic lands. The human prime minister, backed by the wealthy former soldier, George Symons, wished to expand the human nation, and saw the lands east of the mountains as perfect territory to build their new cities. Rumours whispered that George had his own agenda with the Axinstone, but we had yet to prove anything. Either way, dragonkind had not taken well to the invasion and had fought back as best we could, but our clans were broken and divided. We had not been able to repel the invasion.

A council had been called by Clan Xital, the pompous and arrogant leaders of dragonkind. They had sent my cousin, Anzig, the haeraig of our clan, to steal a Nixan artefact of magic the humans had taken many years ago. Clan Nixa claimed that if the Axinstone was returned to them, they would have the power to push the humans back across the mountains.

I didn't know if my cousin still lived. Ddraig Tsona of Xital had broken the news that my cousin was dead, and the Xital dragon had wrested control of Laxtal out of my paws. I had been banished, disgraced, for refusing to believe his words. Airil doubted the Xital ddraig too. He also believed my cousin was alive, and I looked across at the blue-scaled Nixan and smiled. Under the supervision of James, Airil was awkwardly holding a human weapon; what they called a gun.

For the last few hours, James had been showing us how to use some of their more powerful technologies. Some we were familiar with, such as the small gas lighters they used to create fire. Laxtal still possessed a few of these little glass objects; relics from years gone by when humans and dragons traded in peace. Others, like the gun, were proving to be more of a challenge. They had been designed with a human in mind, and Airil couldn't grip the metallic device and operate it at the same time.

"It's no good," the Nixan said, finally giving up and placing the gun down, taking care to follow the human's instruction by never pointing it towards anyone else.

"I didn't expect you to be able to use that," James said. He lay in the grass, ten feet away. He leaned against a tree, holding a book in his hands. I had tried to decipher the strange black markings that covered the inside of the book, but it had only resulted in giving me a headache that still hadn't gone away. It seemed to give the human some amusement though, as he had done little else for the past hour, except for occasionally giving Airil and me advice and guidance around our progress with his technology.

The rest of the human camp was not far away. Already there were signs they intended to stay much longer, to my brother's disgust. The humans had cut down many trees and turned the timber into small shelters. Unlike dragons, they preferred to live above ground, and were not content with our caves and warrens.

I was having a hard time adjusting to the smell of the camp. The scent of human was one of danger. That had been ingrained into my mind for the past few years. Clan Xital had warned us to always be on guard when the scent of humans was strong. Now it was overwhelming, but I was slowly convincing myself that there was no threat present.

Airil spread his wings and lay down beside me. He kept one eye on the cloudless sky, waiting for the hunting party to return. Mulner had flown out in the morning to hunt for the nomads, though he had made a point that he would not collect anything for the humans to eat.

All day the Nixan had been restless, and even as he lay down his wings kept twitching against his back. He constantly seemed to be on the verge of taking flight, avoiding my gaze a lot more than usual. I had already tried to ask what was bothering him, but for once he hadn't answered my question and had remained in glum silence.

While Airil looked upwards, I looked to the east, back towards the territory of Clan Laxtal. The memories of losing the clan still hurt. I knew that if I had even the slightest chance of defeating Ddraig Tsona, I would return in an instant and reclaim what was rightfully mine. With Anzig missing, and Ddraig Astar having fallen in battle, I should be ddraig of Laxtal, but I had been defeated in challenge by the Xital dragon. If I returned and failed again, the shame would be too great. I would not disgrace myself like that.

I had mulled over the idea of returning to Laxtal with the group of humans in support as a show of strength, but I had quickly discounted that. Ddraig Astar had been killed by humans. It would look bad if I wrested leadership of the clan back with human support. Whispers would lead to gossip, which would lead to accusations that I had arranged the death of our beloved ddraig, and as untrue as it was, it would only serve to undermine my authority. Until I had proof that Ddraig Tsona was working with the larger group of humans, then I would remain an exile.

I glanced across at Airil, who had closed his eyes and appeared asleep. I knew the futility of going home, but I wasn't disheartened. My time amongst the nomads had been relaxing and enjoyable, but productive too. Once Mulner forgave me for bringing the humans, I knew we would share many good experiences with each other. He was my brother, after all.

We were still playing our part in the war with the human nation; tracking and hindering the main army's progress as it gradually marched north towards Nixa. The human force, many thousands strong, made little progress each day. This worried Mulner. The army never remained stationary, but their slow advance suggested that they were waiting for something. Or searching. Reinforcements came from across the mountains almost daily, new humans joining the main force with additional equipment and food, evading our attempts to cut off these supply lines.

None of the nomads had been able to determine what their purpose was, or who they'd attack next. Their movements would suggest Nixa, but Airil was confident that the clan's magic would rebuff any attack, regardless of whether the Axinstone was in their paws or not. No invading force – human or draconic – had ever set paw within Nixa's lair, and Airil saw no reason why humans should be the first to break his clan's defences.

I sighed and looked up at James. "How would you defeat them?" I asked him.

James frowned as he placed down his book. "Who?"

"The humans. You know a lot more about them than we do, so how would you try and defeat them in battle?"

"I wouldn't even consider engaging them without equal technology or numbers. Whenever we've been at war in the past, you've always had an advantage because of your wings and scales. It was so easy for dragons to escape our reach, but things have changed. George Symons has created a swathe of weapons designed specifically to kill dragons. Older guns wouldn't have had much effect on your scales, but these were designed for that purpose. Whatever magic is infused with the bullets is beyond my understanding, but they're what has helped give us the advantage," the human said.

"So what do we do?"

"I can think of one thing. It may not work – it probably won't, but I can think of nothing else just yet. We were not the only ones who had doubts about this invasion. I know there were at least a hundred others that came over the mountains who didn't like what we were doing, but they were all set in their ways of following orders. Enough people respect George and General Summers to stay in line, but there was a lot of uneasiness. We were never told what our objectives were, and that unsettled a lot of people," the human said. He idly plucked at the grass with his hands, twisting it between his fingers.

"So if we were to challenge and defeat the two leaders, the armies should turn back?"

"Our ways are not yours. I doubt a challenge would do much to change anything, and there could be others who would step up to carry on their work. I don't know much about this Rico who advises George, but I think he could rally just as strong an army against you if necessary," James said slowly. He flicked aside the blades of grass between his fingers. "I think you might need to send a message to Kernow with bloodshed. I think you might need to kill them."

My wings fluttered in fear. I had never killed anything as large as a human before, and I doubted I would have the courage to fight one of them alone. Vinzent wouldn't hesitate. He would leap into the fray without a second thought or concern for his safety. I turned my head, expecting to see Vinzent lying by my side, only to remember that he hadn't spoken to me in two days. I no longer believed that he truly wanted to be my mate.

"Of course, if you wanted to reach either of them, you would have to confront them in battle," the human added as he leaned forward. "And to do that you will need to raise an army yourself. I heard you say before that the draconic clans are divided. You will have to find some way to unite them if you want to win this war. General Summers and George both know this, so they'll do anything they can to stop the clans uniting. They'll happily pick you off one by one."

"I don't know how that can be done," I said, shaking my head and looking to the ground. I had no authority amongst other dragons, not anymore. No ddraig or haeraig would now listen to me. It would have to fall to another dragon to unite the clans.

Wind suddenly gusted around me as the beating of wings descended. Startled, I looked up to see the silhouetted form of my brother landing beside me. His teeth were bared and there was still anger in his eyes. I recoiled from him, expecting him to berate me for spending time in the humans' company again. It never came. Mulner had instead turned his focus to James.

"You say we have to kill this General Summers?" he growled at the human. He had been listening in on our conversation.

"I'm not saying it will work, but I think it's the only way of showing Kernow that this war would cost too much to continue," James said, throwing his hands up defensively as he shuffled back slightly.

"Then I have a job for you both," Mulner said, turning to face me and Airil, who had lazily opened his eyes.

"Who said you could order us around?" I demanded of my brother. I knew I shouldn't speak to him in that manner, but resentment of how he had treated me over the last few days came to the surface.

Mulner roared at me, advancing so his muzzle touched the tip of mine. "I am ddraig in these parts. Beyond the clans my authority is everything. Are you challenging me for that, little sister?"

I bowed my head and flared my wings in submission. Of course I had no desire to challenge my brother. This small band of nomads was all he had for a clan. I would not dare take that away from him.

"What do you need us to do?" Airil asked, more diplomatically.

"You should learn from this one, Ellian. He actually talks sense." Mulner growled as he took a couple of steps back from me, his eyes never once leaving mine. "I want you to go to Nixa and tell Ddraig Krateos everything the human just told you. Any weakness we can discover and exploit, the better our chances. Take Vinzent with you. He tells me he got along well with Haeraig Zeena. If he can make the Nixans listen to you, then that's all for the better."

"I won't be able to carry them both," Airil said.

Mulner frowned and pawed at the grass. "Then fly fast. We can't afford to delay," he said.

I had to admit, I was a little disappointed. For a brief moment I had hoped Airil would be able to take us to Nixa in an instant. I wasn't worried about saving my wings, I was easily strong enough to fly to the clan of magic, but I wanted to experience the thrill of Airil's magic again. Nothing had compared to those brief moments of travel.

"If you think I can be of use, I volunteer to come too," James said, raising his hand into the air.

Mulner turned to Airil. "Do you think your clan would let a human approach?"

Airil didn't answer straight away. He kneaded the ground with his paws for a full minute before he looked up at James. "I would love to have you come with us so you could speak to Ddraig Krateos yourself, but I don't believe you'd be allowed anywhere near the clan. I think it would be best if you remained behind."

James nodded and rose to his feet. "Then I shall take my leave. If you need anything before you depart, please come find me. And Mulner, I hope this means you'll start to trust me. I mean only the best for both of us. Kernow does not need to fight this war, nor does it need to support whatever plans George and Rico have hidden from us all."

Mulner said nothing. He refused to place his eyes anywhere near the retreating human.

"I will go," I growled, taking the chance to speak before my brother. "But only on one condition."

"I already know what you're going to ask, and I can't make any promises," Mulner said quietly as he stared intently at a daisy. "I've never trusted a human before and I don't see why this one should be any different."

"He hasn't killed us yet," I said playfully.

"That's because he hasn't had chance to speak with Vinzent. Seriously, that dragonet is sending me insane. I don't know how you put up with him in Laxtal," Mulner said, sticking out his tongue in disgust.

I giggled. I was sure Vinzent had been pestering Mulner to take more decisive actions in the fight against humanity, just as he had been doing to me after our banishment from the clan. The silver dragon had been dismissive of the nomads' involvement in the fighting, a matter which Mulner had violently taken offence to. Of course, now Vinzent would get his wish. He would finally go to Clan Nixa, where he had wanted to go ever since Ddraig Tsona had sent us away from Laxtal.

I sobered up as I realised how insufferably smug he was going to be on the flight north. Mulner seemed to have the same thought, as it was his turn to laugh.

"I'm glad to be rid of the dragonet, but if he can convince Nixa to start uniting the clans, then perhaps I'll give him a little slack," my brother said brightly, his earlier anger forgotten like it had never been. He looked up to the sky, empty but for a lone eagle circling overhead. He stopped smiling. "If you fly out soon, there's a cave to the north you can rest in overnight. From there you should be able make it to the Nixan lair before sunset tomorrow."

Mulner placed his head on my shoulder. It appeared like all was forgiven. "Be safe, little sister," he said softly. "I don't want to send you away, but I know Nixa will probably listen to you and Vinzent. They might even still treat you as ddraig of Laxtal. I know they wouldn't acknowledge a clanless dragon like me."

"I'll do my best," I vowed.

Mulner pulled away from the embrace and looked into my eyes. I held his gaze for a few seconds then looked away. "Just promise me this, Ellian. You go to Nixa, do what you have to do, and then come straight back home. I'll do what I can with Cinson here to prepare for your return."

"Of course," I said.

I looked across to Airil, who was smiling with his wings already unfurled and ready to fly. He seemed eager to be off. I groaned at the prospect of telling Vinzent where we were going, but there was no sense in delaying it. I kicked off from the ground and launched into the air. Airil and Mulner followed right behind me.

We had paused only to eat our fill from the pheasants killed by the hunters, before flying out shortly after the sun's highest point in the sky. I had been surprised by Vinzent, who had glumly nodded and remained silent after I told him we were to fly out to Nixa. However, it did not take him long to fly up to my wingtip and start pestering me with questions about why we were going to the clan of magic.

I sighed and told him everything the human had told me, and gradually Vinzent's exuberance returned. He was already planning what to do once we had Nixa's assistance, already working out which other clans would be willing to back our cause. Clan Axaatl, of course, would be willing to help us, he told me. Ddraig Aranat had long been distrustful of Xital and it wouldn't take him much convincing of a plot to fragment dragonkind. I chose not to mention that at no point had James told us any dragon was involved in the human invasion. I just let him talk, his words sinking into mere background noise.

From my other wing, Airil and I shared a mischievous grin. The Nixan wasn't paying any attention to Vinzent either. We had our own wordless conversation, amusing ourselves with the antics of the impetuous dragon. Vinzent carried on talking, oblivious to the fact that he no longer had an audience.

I was glad he was returning to his normal self. I had been worried about his recent subservient behaviour, wondering if the shock of our banishment from Laxtal had done significant damage to his confidence. Now my biggest concern was getting him to shut up once we located the cave Mulner had suggested we spend the night.

I looked down at the ground slipping beneath our wings. We were passing over the expansive plains that made up most of Laxtal and southern Nixa. We could see for miles in all directions, right up to the foothills of the Sxinix Mountains in the west, and all the way to the unbroken, flat horizon that circled us completely. Though I couldn't see the human army itself as it slowly marched north, here and there I could see tell-tale signs of their presence. There were a few trees felled to provide firewood, and in the foothills I could see the swirling wisps of smoke that marked their encampment. There was no danger of us being seen, not from this height, but even so we flew no closer to the foothills than we had to.

"Ellian, are you even listening to me?" Vinzent asked.

I started. The sun was starting to sink low towards the horizon. "I'm sorry, what were you saying?" I said, hoping that Vinzent wouldn't start repeating everything I had been working hard to ignore over the last few hours.

"I said Airil's found the lair we're resting in," the dragonet replied with a huff.

I looked around, and Airil had indeed started descending, aiming for a low band of hills that diverged away from the Sxinix foothills. We couldn't have been far away from the northern borders of Clan Zantiin. I could see nothing that indicated that the humans had come this far north, but I was still a little uncomfortable at their proximity. It only looked about five miles to the south where the smoke twisted and danced up from their encampment.

The air was starting to cool as the sun sank behind the mountains. I chased after Airil, who had already landed amongst the hills. I could see the shelter now – calling it a cave was probably too generous. It was little more than a deep alcove in the moss-covered rock.

Airil beamed widely as I landed with Vinzent by my side.

"This is it?" the dragonet said dismissively, summing up my thoughts perfectly.

"These hills mark the southern boundary of Nixa. This is a Nixan cave," Airil said brightly, using a tone of voice I wasn't entirely sure I liked. It reminded me of the sadistic glee some Nixans thrived in when subjecting other clans to their displays of twisted magic.

The Nixan took a couple of steps back. His hindquarters disappeared into the rock. I blinked twice and shook my head, Vinzent doing the same. My vision didn't change. Airil was standing in the rock. Our confusion only increased the Nixan's mirth, and he chuckled as he disappeared entirely from view.

"Just close your eyes and walk forward," he called out, voice slightly muffled.

I glanced across at Vinzent. A look of abject terror was on his face, his eyes wide and mouth slightly agape. Neither of us had ever experienced a Nixan lair before. I had no idea if this was normal, but I had heard that they were protected by magical means.

Ignoring Vinzent's squeak of terror, I followed Airil's encouragement and closed my eyes. I took one step forward, then a second. I felt a brief resistance as my muzzle pushed against the cold stone, then, to my utter shock, the pressure gave way.

I couldn't help it. I opened my eyes. I shrieked as my mind twisted away from the swirling vortex that ripped through my vision. Shafts of colour and edifices of darkness assaulted me. Bursts of light exploded all around me as I forced myself to keep walking.

Out of the light materialised a blue paw. "Take it," echoed Airil's voice.

I didn't hesitate. I grabbed Airil's paw.

Immediately the lights that had been accosting my vision disappeared, and I found myself in a brightly lit chamber with a roaring fire of green flames in the centre. Airil's pale yellow eyes were staring into mine. "I said to keep your eyes shut," he said quietly, before turning away as Vinzent stumbled through the smooth rock just behind me. His eyes were still closed as he staggered forward, not stopping until Airil stepped on his tail.

"What was that about?" the silver dragon growled as he opened his eyes and turned on the Nixan.

"I'm sorry. Nixan magic can be confronting for those not of our clan to deal with. Only a Nixan can pass through into one of our lairs without any repercussions." Airil said. He looked around at the small chamber, which was completely empty. "We'll be safe in here though. No human will be able to find us."

Vinzent snarled as he turned away from the Nixan and curled up by the mystical fire.

"Is that what you always see?" I asked Airil. I was horrified to hear my voice tremble in fear. I felt unsteady on my paws, but I hid this from Airil by lying down by the fire.

The Nixan shook his head. "I can just pass straight through the boundary and not feel or see anything. Sometimes I almost wish I could see what you see, to experience what it'd be like just once. It is the same with my magic. It is just the blink of an eye to me, but from what other dragons tell me, it is anything but."

I stuck my tongue out at Airil as he curled up just beside me. "Trust me. You don't want to know what it's like," I said with a nervous giggle. "I imagine it'll be much worse at the main lair?"

"Probably," Airil admitted, eliciting a snarl from Vinzent on the other side of the fire, but otherwise the silver dragon said nothing.

I sighed and stretched my wings. We had not exerted ourselves over the course of the day, but they were a little sore and stiff. I hoped the heat of the fire would restore them as I slept. If we wanted to reach the central Nixan lair before the next sunset, we would have to push ourselves hard and fly fast and without rest. We would have to do our best to ignore the legendary hunting grounds of Clan Nixa as we flew. I hoped there would be time for hunting after we had spoken to Ddraig Krateos.

I closed my eyes. Before falling asleep my mind wandered to the other side of the mountains. I was on my own journey now, sleeping in an unknown cave, probably far away from any other dragon except for the two I travelled with. Had Anzig felt the same excited thrill as the one that had settled in my chest?

Perhaps in Nixa I would find answers to my cousin's fate. Maybe some of the seers and telepaths could tell me where Anzig was, if indeed he was still alive. I assumed that he was going to be returning with the Axinstone. Without it, Clan Nixa would not have the strength to unite the clans, but that did not mean I would back down and shy away from my duties, for to do so would be to accept that Anzig was dead.

My cousin was alive. For a moment I was convinced he was in the chamber with me, but I opened my eyes only to see Airil and Vinzent.

His presence still lingered as I fell into slumber.

CHAPTER TWO

Anzig

Whispers.

They didn't stop.

Shadows started to approach me as I tried to move.

The whispers grew louder.

"He's still alive."

"He's hurt."

A snarl. "I can see that. Get Isikian. Isikian!"

Yes, Isikian. The healer. If someone was hurt, then he would need to see to them. For a moment I wondered who needed his help. Then my world exploded into pure pain. It felt like fire was burning out my insides. Light pierced into my eyes even though they remained closed.

I couldn't even scream in agony. The pain was too intense even for that.

Oblivion was better than this. I longed to return to unconsciousness.

A cool touch on my head.

Slowly the pain receded until it was little more than a dull ache at the back of my mind. My eyes fluttered open to see the concerned face of Isikian staring down at me. Keita stood by his side. "Anzig, are you alright?" she asked.

"No," I whispered. I could taste blood in my mouth. Memories started to eke back into my mind. I remembered feeling scared. I was flying away from the great spectre. She had trapped me. "Nightwings?"

The healer shook his head as he pushed Keita away. "Azlak says he saw her fall into the sea. We haven't seen her since."

Behind Isikian other silhouettes began to move and come closer, more in to focus. Keita lingered just behind the healer, as did Azlak and Carlee. At the edge of my vision I could see Inilta's grey scales, as well as a flash of red I took to be Okazuni. I couldn't see Nataik, but I assumed she was there all the same.

The whispers persisted, though no one spoke. Slowly I turned my head, trying to find the source of the indistinct noises. My eyes were drawn to a large stone wrapped tightly in Inilta's tail. I felt a tightening in my chest, followed by a fresh wave of pain.

Isikian followed my gaze and allowed himself a shadow of a smile. "Yes, we have it. We found the Axinstone," he said. The healer's smile vanished as my head slumped back to the ground. "Haeraig?" I heard him ask in concern, but I was unable to respond.

Again I felt Isikian's paw on my chest, but this time the pain returned tenfold. It felt like my flesh was being rent apart.

I heard Isikian's panicked voice.

Then there was nothing.

No pain. No sound. No light.

Time passed. I couldn't know how long.

Was this death?

A voice cut across the void.

"Couldn't you use the Axinstone?" Keita asked. I could see desperation in her eyes, but I knew it was useless.

"It's too dangerous. He's not Nixan, do you have any idea what could happen to him?" I protested.

"But he's dead already," Keita cried. I relented at the anguish I saw in her eyes, even the one long ago damaged beyond use.

"I can try," I whispered as I stepped forward and placed an emerald-scaled paw on the haeraig's lifeless body.

Emerald? Was my paw always that vivid?

I shook my head and cleared the errant thought away. Of course it had always been emerald. I had no time to think about the momentary delusion. With the Axinstone in my mouth, I reached into my well of magic, pushing deep to reverse the terrible wounds the haeraig had received. His left wing was little more than a tattered shred of flesh and fragile bone, but it was the gaping hole where his chest had been that was the problem. I didn't know how he had survived this long.

I found the faintest spark of life, still stubbornly flickering. I gently gripped it and nurtured it, protecting it from fading away. To my eyes the haeraig's life was a tiny ball of golden light, enveloped in the blue glow of my magic. Flashes of green shouldn't have been there. There was another magic present, but it was neither hindering nor helping me. Like bellows on flame the spark of the haeraig's life grew. Willing it back to strength was easier than it should have been, and it was soon strong enough that I no longer needed to sustain it. I turned my attention to healing his body.

I glanced across to Keita, who was nervously watching on.

The healer looked back down and shook his head again. Was it not working?

I blinked several times to clear my vision, but there was something not right about my eyes. Everything was still so blurred and unfocused, my field of view so restricted. But of course, that was always how I had seen the world for many years, ever since I had been young, when that thorned branch had slashed across my eyes.

Okazuni pushed up against my side. His paw touched mine as his head rested against my shoulder. The Nyrian knew the depth of emotion that I felt for Anzig. He had been my closest and greatest friend for so many years now. My heart felt like it was beating in my throat as the Nixan healer focused on Anzig once more.

Blue light emanated out from the healer's paws as Anzig's wounds started to close before my eyes. I took half a step forward, barely daring to breathe lest I distract Isikian. I stopped at a touch on my tail. I looked back to see Carlee, her eyes staring into mine.

She looked away first, but I released her tail anyway. The young ness wasn't going to interfere with the Nixan's magic. I hung back behind Anzig's oldest friend and Okazuni, barely able to watch. I was no stranger to wounds as severe as the haeraig's, but that was no comfort. I had witnessed many a dragon's death from battle injuries that seemed trivial compared to the gaping cavity in the haeraig's side. Ddraig Astar would never forgive me if his son died here.

The haeraig spluttered back into life, his chest rising in breath.

Darkness drew me back in as my mind began to slip away. Isikian's voice whispered me to the void. "Let him rest for now."

Claws tore into my chest over and over again. I could not escape the pain.

Locked in an endless escape over the bay, I could never reach the far shore. The island remained the same distance behind me. Nightwings loomed over and around me, her great wingspan blotting out the sun. Her claws and teeth dug into my flesh, piercing between my ribs and spilling enough blood to stain the ocean crimson.

The spectre's voice boomed through my mind. "Little One. Please!"

A shriek of pain speared through me. The great shadow of the spectre flickered. I plummeted towards the churning ocean. Maznar was already there, floating on the surface, adding her blood to mine through the wounds over her eyes. She clung to a piece of driftwood, her claws scraping out deep gouges as she struggled to stay afloat.

The spectre looked up to me with blinded eyes. "Please. I don't know how much longer I can hold on."

I plunged into the water and everything went white.

My eyes snapped open as I heaved for breath. I cried in pain before realising that nothing actually hurt. My wings quivered. My heart pounded rapidly. It felt like I had just flown at full speed for hours on end. I grimaced as I sucked in deep breaths, trying to control my body as I jerked into consciousness.

Dream and reality gradually disentangled.

A cool paw rested on my forehead. "Are you alright, Haeraig?"

"I... I think so," I replied, opening my eyes. Isikian stood above me, the healer looking weary. He grasped the Axinstone in his other forepaw. I had to look away from the magical heat the precious stone gave off.

Tentatively, I rose to my paws. I glanced back to inspect my chest, where there was no longer any evidence of the terrible wound I had seen there... no. How could I have seen the wound? My eyes had been shut and my thoughts elsewhere. I must have imagined the entire thing, a part of the dreams that had confused my tired and weary mind. I shook my head, confused, and decided to focus on the Nixan in front of me.

"Are you still in pain, Haeraig?" Isikian asked. His paw moved from my forehead to feel around my chest.

I resisted the urge to pull away from the Nixan's touch. My claws tensed, scraping at the stone floor. I took another deep breath and focused inwards. Phantom aches still made themselves known, memories of the dreams and the escape from the island. But there were no lingering pains. "Nothing, no."

Isikian exhaled slowly. "Good. I was worried. The healing was too easy, especially for wounds like yours. I feared I hadn't done enough, even with the Axinstone."

I didn't have chance to question what he meant, as before I could speak, I was distracted by movement. I looked beyond the Nixan as a shadow emerged from the darkness.

Keita pushed aside Isikian as she approached me and put her head on my shoulder. "You're alive," she whimpered. "I didn't think you'd ever wake up."

"I'm here. I'm alright." I leaned into Keita, trembling slightly as though my wounds were about to reopen. I struggled to hold back tears.

For the first time, I was properly aware of my surroundings. I was safe in the mine on the mainland, in one of the small chambers beneath the surface. Inilta's fire provided illumination to the dark room, though some golden sunlight streamed in from above, coming from low to the east. It was near sunset. Again.

I swallowed, my mouth dry. "How long was I out for?"

"A full day. We got out yesterday," Isikian said. His claws tightened around the Axinstone. "We didn't know what to do if humans found us, but I don't think they've even been looking."

"And Nightwings?"

"We haven't seen her."

I lowered my gaze. I had dreamed of the spectre falling into the water, barely clinging to survival. Had that been mere dream, or was there some element of truth to it?

I rose to my paws and stretched my wings, making sure that nothing hurt still. Everything felt intact, with no evidence of the terrible injuries remaining. I didn't even have a scar. I breathed in deep. "Thank you, Isikian. I do not doubt you saved my life."

"We should have some food for you, if you're hungry," Keita said. She stepped away from me and waited in the archway that led to the next room. I could hear the murmur of my other companions through there, but none had come through to see me yet. I was grateful for that. I didn't want too many dragons around me all at once. My body may have recovered, but my mind still struggled to understand the dreams and visions that had plagued me.

With every step I expected the agony to return. Judging by how close Isikian stayed to my side, he feared the same. Silence fell as I emerged into the main chamber. The rest of my companions were all around the fire, strips of meat scattered between them. They all jumped to their paws and bowed their heads towards me. All but Azlak. The seer was curled up in the dark, shadowy corner of the chamber, his wing pulled over his face. His chest moved too rapidly for him to be asleep.

For some reason, I was compelled to shake off the healer and push through the other dragons to approach Azlak. I was right. He was not asleep, and he pulled his wing away the moment I stood in front of him.

The seer squeaked in terror as he looked up at me. "I'm sorry, Haeraig, I shouldn't have left you," he grovelled, pushing himself as far down as the unyielding ground would allow him. "I thought I'd killed you too."

I was just about to forgive the seer and tell him he was not at fault, when my mind picked up on that last word the seer had uttered. "Too?" I repeated. Who else did the seer think he had killed?

Azlak's eyes were wide as he tried to back away, but he already had nowhere to go. Keita had followed me across, as had Carlee and Isikian. They had quickly surrounded him. The seer looked between the two nesses and then towards the healer. He whimpered, before looking down at my paws.

"I Saw you die in a human ambush. If you had stayed in Laxtal instead of coming here, you would have died a couple of weeks ago, along with hundreds of others. The only way for you to survive was to come and claim the Axinstone," the seer said quickly. He took a deep breath and continued. "I never expected another to take your place on the battlefield, and in death, least of all Ddraig Astar.

"Your father is dead. You will stand at the wylax and become the ddraig of Laxtal on our return."

Instantly, my chest felt it had been torn open once more with my heart, shattered, falling in shards to the ground. My legs buckled below me, unable to support the enormity of the words I just heard.

"I'm so sorry, Ddraig," Azlak whispered.

"Do. Not. Call. Me. That," I snarled at the seer, launching myself forward and striking him across the muzzle, drawing blood from the shocked dragon. He fell to the ground and cowered, his wings covering his face to fend himself from the anticipated blows that never came. I did not care if the seer spoke the truth. I knew I would not claim that title until I returned to Laxtal and learned what had really happened. A dragon with the might of my father could not have died so easily.

I pushed past Keita and Carlee and stalked from the mine. I could hear pawsteps following me, so I took to wing in an attempt to lose my pursuer, but whichever dragon it was took to the air too.

Isikian's healing had been perfect; I felt no physical pain from the wounds I had suffered, but it was a different agony that gnawed at my insides now.

I had a sudden memory of a time long ago, when I was still a dragonet. I could remember the first time I had ever seen father in council, how much power he possessed, and how confident he was. Everything he said was right, everything he did was something to admire, especially to a young dragon who would one day have to follow in his pawprints. Now that day had come, and those prints were far too large for my paws. I wasn't even half the dragon that my father was... had been.

"Anzig!"

Carlee's warning brought me back to the present. I was glad she had called out. Without realising where I was going, I had been flying out into the bay, directly towards George's island. I halted my flight and allowed the veteran ness to come up by my side. She said nothing as we slowly descended to a small beach at the base of the cliffs, but I could hear her unspoken words rushing through my head.

There was a gentle calm to the waves folding over, gently caressing the sandy beach. Though it soothed me, nothing was ever going to heal my heartache. "What do I do, Carlee? I can't replace my father," I said, my voice cracking as I tried to fight back my grief. I had wanted to cry, to shed forbidden tears, but I could not do that in front of Carlee.

"You are Ddraig Astar's... you are his son. You can be his equal," Carlee said in a pained tone. "You will be his equal." She was suffering as much as I was, but her eyes were dry. No threat of tears there.

"I don't see how," I whispered, as she placed her wing around me like she used to do when I was a dragonet. I would never admit weakness to any dragon other than Carlee. I rested my head against her shoulder. "Why do I have no confidence in myself? Father always said it was natural for every haeraig to have confidence in themselves. I tried so hard to convince him that I had, but I was always terrified. I still am."

"I... I don't know," Carlee said.

I looked along the moonlit beach. In the distance I could just about see the twinkling lights of the human city. The sight had lost all sense of immediate danger. I knew the humans would be looking for us, but they had lost Nightwings. Without her, I doubted they would ever find us. We would hear them coming long before they could reach us, before they got into range of their devastating weapons.

"You have allies, Anzig. There are many dragons in Laxtal who will fly by your side at the wylax. They will support your leadership," Carlee continued after a brief silence. "The duties of haeraig will fall to Ellian, and she is very capable. The two of you will lead Laxtal to glory, I can tell."

"But I've done nothing to earn their respect. Father was able to control Laxtal so effortlessly because he had earned their loyalty. I won't have that," I said.

"Anzig, you are about to become a hero in Nixa. Don't you think Laxtal will see that?" Carlee pointed out. I had to admit, she had a point. Haeraig Zeena had already promised an alliance should I return with the Axinstone. We had done the hard part in stealing it from the humans, now we just needed to cross the mountains and return home. An alliance between Nixa and Laxtal? I knew I should feel excited that I was bringing about such a momentous occasion, but I could not. I had done little to accommodate the success of the mission. If anything, Azlak had been the difference between success and failure. The clan's omega had outshone me. No one was saying it, least of all Carlee, but I knew it to be the truth.

I chose not to share these worries with Carlee. I already knew what her answer would be. She would chide me for being silly and try to convince me that everything that had happened was all my doing. But that was not true. I remembered all the times I had failed to act when I need to lead. I hadn't even been the one to seize the Axinstone: I had been reduced to willing Azlak along as he took the glory of laying his paws on it first.

"You are a great dragon, Anzig. You will become a great ddraig too," Carlee said, breaking into my thoughts.

"Alright," I said, nodding my head, but not agreeing with her. For years I had convinced father that I was the haeraig he wanted me to be. I now had to convince Carlee and the rest of the clan that I was the ddraig they wanted me to be. Any mistake I made would be pounced on.

I sighed and looked down to the waterline, where the waves gently lapped at the sand. Starlight shone off the top of a glistening rock just beyond the surf, but the night was dark with only a thin moon already sinking low towards the western horizon, in danger of vanishing entirely behind a bank of thick clouds. The moon had barely been halfway towards full when we had left Xital. I bowed my head, realising we had been almost a month already. Nearly five weeks where there had likely been no ddraig or haeraig in Laxtal. I could only hope the clan had obeyed my wishes that Ellian lead in my stead. I had expected that would only have been until my father returned. Now, that would never happen.

"I want to fly out in the morning. We have wasted a day already," I said. I was still focused on the rock amongst the waves, but my mind was already thinking about how we should get home. "George will be out searching for us, so we should get as far from here as possible. I also don't think it would be wise to take the same route back. We alerted a few humans to our presence. If word gets out that dragons stole the Axinstone, they'll all be on their guard."

Carlee smiled. "See? Spoken like a true ddraig. You've a good mind for this, Anzig. What's the matter?"

I had tensed up in fright. What I assumed was a rock in the water had moved. It rolled through the waves and washed up on the beach. When the water receded, I could clearly see what it was for the first time. Though it was little more than a shadow against the sand, I could tell it was a black-scaled ness.

"Fetch Isikian," I asked of Carlee, and then as an afterthought, added, "And the seer."

The veteran ness launched into the air without questioning me. I watched her fly away before slowly approaching the prone dragon. A low moan emanated from her. She was still alive.

"Are you Maznar, or are you Nightwings?" I asked the ness. This was the spectre that had haunted us ever since we had passed into human territory: an ordinary ness who the humans had enhanced with their magic to be of enormous size. As Maznar she had helped us through our dreams, but as Nightwings she had threatened to kill us, and had nearly succeeded in killing me before I had escaped.

She spluttered and spat out a mouthful of water. "I am both," she said weakly. She started to chuckle, but this quickly descended into a coughing fit, bringing up more water from her lungs. She hauled herself a little further up the beach once she had recovered and looked up towards me. The familiar red glow of her eyes was absent. "But right now I suppose you can call me Maznar."

Wingbeats heralded the return of Carlee, and she brought with her Isikian and his brother, as well as the seer, who lagged some distance behind. Inilta summoned a ball of flame to hover above his head, throwing Maznar into the light.

I recoiled away from the sight of her and looked down at my paws. Blood poured from slashes either side of her face which cut deep through her eyes. She was completely blind, and it was all my doing. I had struck out at Nightwings as she had lunged for me, raking her across the eyes. This was the result of my actions.

Isikian made to push past me and approach Maznar, but I flung a wing out to stop him. "Can we trust her, Azlak?" I asked the seer without even turning around to face him. He knew the spectre best. That was the only reason I had summoned him down to the beach. I had no desire to speak to him after he admitted to killing my father with his actions.

"We can," the seer said timidly.

I growled and furled my wing, allowing Isikian to move forward and approach Maznar. He placed his paw over her ruined eyes, who only flinched slightly at the sudden contact. Once more, the soft blue light of Isikian's magic emanated out from the healer's paw. When he stepped back, the shine of Maznar's red eyes glinted in Inilta's flames.

She blinked several times and held her paw in front of her muzzle, her eyes tracking every movement. She then bowed her head to Isikian. "Thank you. I didn't deserve your help."

The healer smiled and backed away, allowing me to come forward again.

"You tried to kill us," I growled.

Maznar stared down at my paws. "I did," she replied.

"And how do we know you won't try again?"

Maznar's eyes were pained as she looked up at me. "I never acted of my own free will. The humans had controlled me since the day I hatched and turned me in to Nightwings. I never wanted to be that monster," she said.

"But can they still control you?" I demanded. I knew we could never trust the ness if the humans still had any influence over her behaviour, no matter what the seer may suggest. Azlak had already proved his advice was fallible.

Maznar's eyes flicked to the healer. "Not without the Axinstone."

"Then go with Isikian and the others. Lie by the fire and recover," I growled, before turning away and looking out over the bay. Many sets of wings fluttered away up the cliff. I wondered if I what I had done was wise. The ness had after all come close to killing me, and now I was welcoming her to sleep amongst us. I slumped to the sand and placed my head in my paws.

"Are you sure you're doing the right thing?"

I sighed. I should have known Carlee wouldn't fly back with the others. I could hear her paws gently crunching in the sand as she came back across to me before she sat down by my side. I kept looking out across the water. "We know the spectre is complete evil. I can't see that she would have changed so suddenly."

"She isn't that spectre anymore," I said.

"Whose authority are we taking that on? The spectre's? Azlak's? I think we just learned that you can't trust the seer," Carlee said bluntly. I pulled my wing over my head. I didn't want to think about Azlak's betrayal. I didn't care that he said he had saved my life in forcing me on this journey. His actions had led to the death of my father, and that was all there was to it.

Carlee wasn't ready to leave me yet though. "Remember what I said to you about trust, Anzig?" she reminded me. She waited for a response, but I wasn't about to give any. It didn't take long before she continued anyway. "One of the most important things about becoming ddraig is learning who you can rely on for support, to know which dragons will never tell you a lie."

I drew my wing back a little, so I was able to stare at Carlee with one eye. "Will you ever tell me a lie?"

Carlee looked away. "Only if I must," she whispered.

"Then how do I know you aren't hiding something from me? How do I know you aren't keeping a secret from me like the seer was?" I snarled.

"If ever I hide something from you, Anzig, it is because you aren't ready to know the truth," the veteran said. "Your father told me many secrets. Yes, some of them do concern you. There may come a day I may have to tell you some of them, though I hope I do not have to. But please, do not ask me what they are. I vowed never to reveal any of them unless the need was dire. I carry this knowledge to protect you, not to harm you. You must trust me on that."

"I know. I trust you," I whispered. I couldn't justify my anger at Carlee. She had been at my father's right wing for so many years now, and I knew she had my best interests at heart. At the same time, that didn't stop me disagreeing with her from time to time, and this was one of those occasions. I had spoken to Maznar through my dreams before we had even reached the humans' island, while Carlee had not. There was an honesty in her admission that she was no longer controlled by humans.

"Keep an eye on Maznar if you feel a need," I told Carlee.

The veteran nodded. "Come back to the fire Anzig. It's been a long time since any of us have slept properly. I think we all deserve the rest if we're flying out tomorrow."

I really didn't want to go back and face the other dragons. I would much prefer to stay out on my own, but it didn't take long before I relented. A cold breeze was blowing off the ocean, making Inilta's magical flames too tempting to resist.

When I returned to the mine, Azlak retreated further away into the shadows. I curled up beside Keita, who entwined her tail around mine. With her touch I felt a lot of my worries fade. With this, I also started to feel the seeds of excitement grow. In just a few days we would return to draconic lands, and I would no longer need to worry about humans ambushing and attacking us.

Instead, I would have to stand before Nixa and present them with the Axinstone. And then, after that, I would face my clan and present myself before the wylax, where I would take my place as the ddraig of Laxtal.

I closed my eyes and thought of home. Would those thoughts bring nightmares or dreams? I was almost too scared to find out.

CHAPTER THREE

Azlak

Not a moment had gone by that I regretted telling Ddraig Anzig about the death of his father. He would have known eventually, but perhaps if I had said nothing he would never have learned of my part in his father's death. He would have stood before the wylax and become the ddraig of Laxtal believing his father had died in an ambush where no dragon was to blame. That would have been a lie, and one that would have torn at my gut. It would have been a shame as great as the one that ailed me now.

My muzzle still hurt from when he had struck me. The shock of that alone had stunned me. I had never known Ddraig Anzig to strike anyone in anger before, and I had never been the target of his wrath until yesterday. I had received no apology, nor did I expect one. I certainly didn't deserve one. The new ddraig had every right to be angry and I had refused Isikian's offer to heal the scratches.

I stayed some distance off the back of the group as we flew east. It felt good to be on the move again, after spending so long trapped in the mine and on George's island. The Sxinix Mountains were still well beyond the horizon, but I could almost sense their presence, the tall peaks urging us on. They were the physical boundary between human and draconic territory, and therefore the boundary between danger and safety.

We all knew that the humans would be out searching for us in their attempts to reclaim the Axinstone. However, they had lost one of their greatest weapons. Nightwings had been defeated, and the ness they had corrupted to create the terrifying spectre now flew amongst our number. The shadowy form of Maznar flew not far ahead of me as she also lagged behind the rest of the group. The other dragons had not openly shunned her, but nor had they been keen to welcome her. Carlee had been vocal against allowing Maznar to join us, but for some reason Ddraig Anzig had rejected her pleas, instead trusting my word that the former spectre no longer posed a threat.

Isikian had exchanged a few words with Maznar earlier in the day, but that had been the extent of her communication with the group. I had wanted to fly up to her side and speak with her too, but my confidence had been shattered by Ddraig Anzig's attack. I was relieved I didn't need to fly in the position of power yet. All we had to do was fly directly east, following the directions from the map Nataik carried, the gift I had earned from two humans before we had reached the city of Trevena. Only when we were closer to the mountains would I once again need to fly ahead of Ddraig Anzig and the others.

Far below us the mostly empty countryside drifted by. We were fighting against a headwind, so progress wasn't as fast as we would have liked, but I was still confident we could make the mountains within two days. Away from the city of Trevena, signs of human settlement gradually diminished. They had still left their marks though; mostly in the winding black roads that twisted through the land, as well as the tall and thin metal poles that Nataik had said carried the electricity that powered their advanced technologies.

I noticed that while all the other dragons would occasionally look down and take in the sights, Maznar kept her eyes firmly above the horizon. Not once did she glance down. She probably didn't want any reminders of what she had once been; a pawn controlled by humanity. Now she was free to live her life as a dragon, assuming of course dragonkind would accept her. She was being tolerated at the moment, but I knew it would take some time before she was accepted.

Like me, she was a mystery. Her origins were completely unknown. She had told us her egg had hatched in George's castle, but she wasn't telling us how the human got hold of her egg – if she even knew herself. She believed she wasn't a Laxtal ness, but her appearance was a little contradictory. Her muzzle and horns were similar to Inilta's and Isikian's, but she also shared a little resemblance to Ddraig Anzig's or my own. Either way, she couldn't be the mysterious dragon from my recurring visions. The other Laxtal dragon with magic was a drake, I knew that for sure. The voice was definitely male, even if it did change a little between visions.

"You surprised me, Little One."

I looked up. Maznar had slowed her pace so she was flying next to my left wing. "I never expected any of you to survive, let alone actually succeed in taking the Dragon's Head Rune," the ness said. Her red eyes flicked around, moving from one place to another, never once settling on any one thing. No doubt a human trait she had picked up.

"I did tell you my visions were true," I replied.

"But everything I told you of George was true too. I still do not know how you managed to break his defences with such ease," Maznar said.

"What are you saying?"

"I'm saying that I don't think George was unaware of your presence there. It was almost as though he wanted..."

A large gold dragon stood over a smaller green one. The gold dragon had a shard of rock in his paws, which glowed as a dragon's head burned on its surface. A shadow stood over the two drakes. The dark form of a human knelt down and wrested the stone from the dragon's grasp, who tried to claw at the human's hand. Green arcs of lightning shot from the human's fingers as he held the Axinstone aloft. He pointed down at the cowering dragons. The gold one pleaded with the human.

The human laughed and thrust his hand forward. The green dragon shrieked as he was engulfed in magical lightning...

"...you to take it," Maznar said. She edged slightly closer to me, her wing slipping in beneath mine. "What did you See?"

"I... I don't think it's right to say," I said. I had not Seen that eventuality before. I was sure the human was George, though I hadn't seen him clearly. The dragon who had surely been killed was Ddraig Anzig, and the other I recognised as Ddraig Tsona.

"You know it would be so easy for me to find out. Once you're asleep and dreaming, I have access to every memory you have, even those you've forgotten," Maznar said, with a flash of her red eyes that reminded me of the spectre.

I shivered in fear. Had I been wrong to trust Maznar? There were many secrets I held, locked away in the corners of my mind. I certainly didn't want her gaining access to my memories. "I saw Ddraig Anzig dying again. I have seen him die three times now at the hand of George, all in different ways," I whispered. I hoped that my honesty would deter Maznar from prying into my dreams, but I still feared her reaction.

"All that means is this war is far from over. It would be naïve to think you've defeated the humans simply by taking the Dragon's Head Rune. George was harvesting magic from that stone for years. He has plans for that magic you could not even conceive of," Maznar warned. She veered away from me a little and for the first time looked down to the distant ground. I followed her gaze. We were passing over a large lake, upon the surface of which I could just make out a couple of tiny boats.

"I know you will do everything in your power to save Anzig. Quite simply, you must. I may not know the future like you do, but I have seen a truth in his past that makes him crucial to this war," the ness continued. Her eyes were now on the ddraig, about fifty feet further ahead at the front of the group.

"What?" I asked the ness, who didn't seem like she was about to reveal her secret.

Maznar snickered. "It is not for me to say. He must discover this for himself."

I growled but did not try and force Maznar to give me the information I desired. After all, it was none of my business. This was a secret of Ddraig Anzig's past, not mine. I had no right to know, and I doubted the ddraig would trust me with his secrets anymore.

"Isikian is suspicious of me," Maznar said. At that moment the Nixan healer glanced back and narrowed his eyes in the direction of the black ness. "He believes I'm hiding something from you all, something about where I come from."

"And are you?"

Maznar revealed all her teeth in a malicious grin. "I have watched George's dreams many times. My particular favourite of his was when a drake gave him a solitary egg. I hatched from that egg."

"A dragon gave you to the humans?" I could scarcely believe what I was hearing. No dragon would voluntarily give up their own egg, especially not to a human. Eggs were one of the most precious things a dragon could ever be in possession of. Only in dire circumstances were eggs passed on to another. But that was not the most worrisome thing of Maznar's revelation. There was the implication that the humans had a draconic ally.

"I always knew George was working with at least one dragon, though I never once saw them. I was never able to get their name either. George isn't a magician, but I always got the impression he had been trained to defend himself against magic. I think I only saw what he wanted me to see, and nothing more," Maznar said. We were falling further back from the others now, but I was too interested to hear what the ness had to say to try and catch up.

"Have you told Ddraig Anzig any of this yet?" I asked. Surely he would need to know this information. The knowledge that a dragon had betrayed his species could be crucial.

Maznar slowed down further, so much so that she'd almost stopped. I hovered just by her side, turning away from the rest of the group. "He doesn't yet trust me. I doubt he will believe me."

"So why tell me? He won't listen to me, especially now he thinks I killed his father," I said bitterly.

"You did," growled another voice. I almost fell out of the air to hear Carlee right behind me. The veteran had silently flown back to us. "If I had my way, I'd leave you both behind, but luckily for you that decision is not mine. So long as Ddraig Anzig wishes you to continue with us, I will honour that. But let me warn you now that if either of you threaten or cross him again, I will not hesitate to abandon you. Understand?"

I had never considered Carlee to be a friend, nor was she a dragon who was even occasionally civil towards me, but never had she been so openly hostile. She terrified me, and I couldn't bear to look in her direction. I quietly told her that I understood, but Maznar remained silent as she also looked anywhere but at the older ness.

With a strong beat of my wings I pushed forward and started to catch up with the others, flying ahead of the two nesses. Carlee snarled as she barged her way back in front, but Maznar was content to remain at the rear. How much had Carlee overheard? I doubted it would have been much. The older ness would have been quick to condemn Maznar for suggesting there was a traitorous dragon somewhere in the clans.

Carlee had rested well in the time it had taken to steal the Axinstone. There was colour in her brown scales again, which had worryingly started to fade as we had been approaching the castle. I no longer feared her imminent death, and the resulting reaction the ddraig would have to that, but I still wondered if my last vision of her passing had been averted. That was one of the hardest things about my magic: I was rarely sure how far into the future, and in what order, my visions would come to pass. Some happened within seconds of the vision, but a few had taken years.

I did not speak with Maznar again during the flight. Instead, I flew just off Isikian's tail. In the distance, the Sxinix Mountains started to rise from the horizon as a tiny, distant smudge, though I knew there was no chance of reaching them this day, or even in the next two. I had not Seen anywhere for us to rest for the night, so I left that responsibility up to Ddraig Anzig. I was glad. I didn't want to advise the ddraig. He wouldn't trust me. In fact, I no longer trusted myself.

Before long we started flying over a massive forest that, as far as I could tell, didn't end until it reached the foot of the mountains. Here and there the green expanse was broken by a rocky outcrop or a lake. The path of several rivers and streams sliced their way through the forest, and once or twice I could see a small human village.

As the sun started to sink down behind us, Ddraig Anzig occasionally glanced back. He kept doing so until he finally managed to meet my eyes. I whimpered. He gestured with a small flick of his tail to join him at the head of the group.

I flew beneath the others to join the ddraig, keeping just below his right wing. "Why did you hide it from me?" The ddraig's voice cracked as he spoke. I was alarmed. I hadn't expected this.

"I was scared. I'd killed your father. I thought you'd throw me out of the clan," I said.

Ddraig Anzig laughed nervously. "If you'd actually have been responsible, then I may have done so. But I've been thinking... you acted to save me. You couldn't have known that your actions would result in my father dying," he said slowly, like he had been rehearsing those words for a while now.

"But I should have known. What's the point in being able to see into the future if I can't even know what the consequences of my actions will be?" I protested. I didn't know why I was arguing against the ddraig, who was defending my actions, but it had brought up a common shame. I had no control over my magic. It was unreliable.

"Once we cross the mountains, I'll get Isikian and Inilta to train you. I'm sure they'll be able to help you to control your magic better," the ddraig said.

I ducked my head in thanks. Isikian had already suggested that he would be willing to help me train my magic, but I wouldn't have been surprised if the healer had forgotten the promise. "That would be most appreciated, Ddraig Anzig."

"Do one thing for me in return, Azlak. Never keep a secret from me again," Ddraig Anzig said, a touch of harshness returning to his voice. He had been hurt by my betrayal, there was no doubting that, and yet he appeared willing to forgive me.

"Of course," I said. At the forefront of my mind was the image of Carlee lying in the bloodstained grass, whispering her dying words into the ddraig's ear. That was followed by the ddraig himself dying, engulfed in human magic. Then there was the death of Ellian, who I assumed was now haeraig. There were so many secrets I kept from Ddraig Anzig, and I already knew I would never be telling him most of them. If ever he were to unlock my mind and somehow read my thoughts, he would only find heartbreak.

"Have you Seen where we must rest tonight?"

I shook my head and lagged a little further behind the ddraig. "It is remote here. I doubt we'll be disturbed by humans, no matter where we sleep."

"Alright then," Ddraig Anzig said after a slight hesitation. "I'm sure we'll find somewhere to rest."

The ddraig called Nataik up to his side next, as I slowed to the rear of the group, just ahead of Maznar. A few moments later, Nataik descended into the forest by herself. Ddraig Anzig angled down soon after, aiming for a small lake surrounded completely by trees. The water was stained brown by the trees that encroached right onto its banks, except for a small area on its southern boundary, where there was an open grassy patch. It was here that we landed.

Keita and Carlee went straight for the water and drank their fill. Ddraig Anzig told us we would be waiting here for Nataik to return, and she would lead us to a suitable refuge for the night. There were fish in the lake, and once Inilta had caught one for himself, the others all started hunting for themselves with varying degrees of success. Just the two of us, Maznar and I, remained behind.

"Not hungry?" I asked her as I spread out my wings, catching some of the speckled sunlight that filtered through the heavy canopy of leaves. My wings were already weary from the day's flight, fighting against the headwind had been tough.

"I... I have never hunted for my own food," the ness said, pawing at the ground. "I was always given all the food I needed."

I had never heard of a dragon who couldn't hunt their own food, but I quickly realised I should have known Maznar would never have learnt. Dragonets were taught how to hunt at a very young age, but Maznar would never have had that opportunity, having been given to the humans as an egg.

"I could show you if you like," I said, wearily furling my wings again.

"Another time, maybe. I shall watch the others for now. I have eaten recently," the ness said, much to my relief. Though I did want to help Maznar, I was exhausted, and I was thankful to settle back down in the grass. I closed my eyes, just to rest them for a few moments.

Thunder rumbled and lightning flashed. A storm was building in the east as black thunderclouds rolled in from the distant ocean. The smell of blood was in the air. A great battle had just taken place. Three dragons stood on the top of a hill bisected by a narrow gorge. Two nesses, one lilac, the other crimson, stood next to a small gold-scaled dragon. They looked around the plains, where a dozen humans were walking, occasionally stooping to pick something up from the sparse grass.

The red ness and the gold dragon took to wing and flew away to the north just as the rain started to sweep in. The lilac ness quickly took shelter from the storm and disappeared into the gorge, moving with a strange, limping gait.

I stirred uneasily. A shadow passed over my wings.

A voice I didn't recognise spoke. "My son? You're my son?" A bronze dragon stared down at another drake...

...Okazuni stood before Vinzent. The Laxtal towered over the smaller red dragon, but that hadn't deterred Okazuni, who advanced on the larger dragon, teeth bared as he hissed. Ddraig Anzig dived in, putting himself between the two feuding dragons...

...A shadow moved in front of me. "I'm a Laxtal, but I have magic too."

My eyes snapped open. A shadow stood over me, mirroring my vision. For a moment my heart surged in hope, but then I glanced up and saw the red eyes of Maznar. She had a fish in her mouth and looked absurdly pleased.

"You caught that by yourself?" I asked.

Maznar nodded fiercely and dropped the fish at my paws. "I caught two. That one's for you," she said brightly.

"I'm not hungry, thank you though," I said, averting my eyes and backing away.

In an instant, Maznar's eyes turned cold. She trod on my outstretched wing with both forepaws, pinning it uncomfortably to the rough foliage. My shoulder popped painfully as the joint pulled back.

"That hurts," I hissed. I tried to escape from her paws, but she only pushed down harder until I cried out in pain. Her claws started to pinch the thin membrane of my wings, threatening to tear through the vulnerable skin.

"Alright, alright, please, just stop," I gasped, hoping she would relent. The fragile bone and sinew stretched too far. My jaw locked open as I whimpered and tried to resist writhing too much.

Maznar snarled and pushed her claws in harder for a moment, before releasing me and pulling away. Her eyes glared into mine. Without saying a word she turned away and left me alone with the fish she had caught for me.

I whimpered, not daring to move my wing yet. Blood leaked from the small pricks her claws had left behind. My breath came out in short, sharp gasps. The pain was intense, but it didn't feel like any significant damage had been done. This time.

Still breathing quickly, I looked at the retreating back of the ness. What had caused that?

Behind her I could see the rest of the group together. At some point Nataik had returned, and the Xigax dragon was in discussion with Ddraig Anzig. I must have closed my eyes for longer than I realised, it had only felt like a few moments. I hadn't even had chance to think over the visions I had Seen. Other than the recurring vision of the unknown Laxtal with magic, I had never seen any of the others before. It had been some time since I had seen the dragonet Vinzent in any of my visions. I wasn't overly surprised. Now we were on the return to Laxtal, I expected to See more from my clan.

It wasn't much longer before Nataik led us back into the air. I growled and gritted my teeth together as the movement stung the puncture holes in my wing. The cold air felt like ice against the thin membrane. I said nothing about it. If I went to Isikian to heal the wounds, he would ask how I got them. If Ddraig Anzig learnt of Maznar's actions he would start to doubt her loyalty, which would in turn cast further doubts over my belief that we could trust her. It would be better to remain silent.

Nataik took us on a short flight to a small cliff over the top of which poured one of the many rivers that meandered through the forest. I landed on the top of a damp rock, the spray from the waterfall coating my scales. I was the only one who took to paw, everyone else stayed in the air, waiting for Nataik to make the next move. Just visible behind the waterfall was a dark hole leading into a cave. Ddraig Anzig followed the Xigax ness inside, darting through the torrent of water and into the darkness beyond. A few moments later I was all alone as the others followed the ddraig.

I stayed outside a little longer so that I had more time to think over the visions Maznar had interrupted. It didn't take me long to realise I recognised all the dragons in the first vision. Ellian was the one who had remained behind. Haeraig Zeena of Nixa was the other ness, and the dragon that had left with her... it had been me. Why would I have a need to fly away from the central lair of Laxtal with the Nixan? I didn't understand it.

I sighed and turned away from the cave. I was scared of what was coming. There was a shadow over my visions, a threat of some major revelation that I was still to learn. It was the shadow of Nightwings every time. She was going to play a significant role in this war, but I just didn't know what.

I took to wing and slowly glided downstream. I had no desire to go into the cave just yet, and I hoped that some water could help soothe the stinging pain in my wing. Sunset was still about an hour away, so I had no reason to rush. The stream was hemmed in on both sides by the forest, the trees encroaching to just a few feet from the banks, covered by masses of reeds growing out from the fast-moving water.

The water bubbled over the stony bed, and the wind gently caressed the leaves of the trees. They were the only sounds I could hear. It was so peaceful here; I found it hard to imagine that less than a day's flight away was one of the largest human cities we knew of. Though most of Laxtal was barren and dry, there was one small part of our territory that was as lush and green as this, but I had only been there twice.

The dappled sunlight played tricks with my eyes, making me believe that the shadows between the trees were moving. Every time I turned to look, there was nothing but falling leaves and a few calling birds. Nothing to be concerned with.

I turned a corner where the stream angled away to the left, and I almost fell out of the air. Just ahead was a stone bridge crossing the stream. A dirt road ran down the bank on the far side of the river, before cutting straight across and continuing on the opposite side, then curling away deeper into the forest to my right. My alarm quickly subsided as I realised there was not a human around.

I fluttered down and landed on the bridge's wall, looking into the stream. The reeds were thick here, growing almost to the height of the bridge. There was a faint scent of human in the air, but it was an old smell. I was sure there was no danger. The cool water looked inviting, but I settled onto the stone wall, glad of the silence and time to compose my thoughts. I doubted any of my companions would come out and find me; I doubted they would even have noticed my absence.

With one leg dangling off the edge of the bridge, I closed my eyes and thought wistfully of Laxtal. There was nothing really waiting for me there; no dragon who would welcome me home. My father barely acknowledged my presence in the time before we left. I doubted it would be any different now.

A low rumbling caught my attention. I jerked upright and looked down the road. I could see a column of dust downstream, rapidly coming closer. I didn't stop to think and dived off the bridge, landing with a gentle splash and disappearing into the reeds. The water came almost to my neck. The cold water stung my wing, and I had to bite down hard to resist a whimper of pain. One of the great metallic beasts the humans used for transport – a car I'd heard Nataik call them – pulled up and stopped just before it got to the bridge. Barely daring to move, I listened as I heard metal slamming and the heavy footsteps of two humans, plus the lighter movements of two smaller ones.

Hidden in the reeds, I looked up at the bridge as two elderly humans came up to lean against the stonework. Two of their young came up beside them, one male and the other female. Both were blonde haired with eyes wide and innocent.

The two children each held a strip of reed, which they must have taken from the other side of the bridge. On a count of three, they threw their reeds into the water. They then darted back from the wall. I could hear them cheering from the other side of the bridge as the two fragments of reed floated down the stream. One of them yelled, "Mine won, mine won!"

One of the older humans also disappeared from the wall, leaving just the one that I could see. She continued to lean on the wall, looking out over the stream. I was not a good judge of human character, but as I looked upon the old woman's face, I could only describe her as kindly. Just from looking at her, I could tell that she would never willingly cause harm to any living creature. This human was no threat to me, of that I was certain. Her presence soothed me so much I almost found myself emerging out of the reeds and into her plain sight.

I resisted and held firm. The human may appear gentle, but she could still be able to warn other humans that we were here, and those may not be so accommodating of us. These humans didn't seem like they were going anywhere soon, and I certainly couldn't get away without alerting them to my presence. I couldn't even move without making a noise, standing in the cold water and covered by the damp, clinging reeds.

I heard movement right behind me. I turned my head back, trying to keep my body still and avoid creating any ripples. There was a gentle incline in the embankment leading right down to the water's edge. The two young humans had both ran down the slope, several pebbles in each hand. They started throwing the stones into the stream, shouting with glee as the water splashed.

The younger of the two children looked up to the bridge and waved. "Grandma, Grandma, watch this," she yelled, before throwing her pebble as far as she possibly could. The stone hit the opposite bank, sinking into the soft mud with a loud squelch.

The child crowed in delight, and the woman watching on laughed and clapped. "Oh, well done."

I shivered. The humans had me surrounded now, though I doubted they knew I was here. The two children were so close they could almost reach out and touch me. They didn't seem threatening, and I doubted any of the four would cause me any direct harm. Even so, I didn't want any humans to know where we were as this would risk George discovering us.

One of the children ran back up the embankment to join the two adults, leaving the young girl alone by the waterside. She was still quite content throwing pebbles and bits of reed into the water, which she was stripping from the stalks that grew right by her. Her grasping hand met some resistance as she pulled. She turned to tug at the stalk. Her eyes widened as she stared directly at me.

I tried to back away without making any noise, but the child just giggled and carried on throwing bits of reed into the water. She didn't even care about my presence. I kept a wary eye on her before glancing up at the bridge to see if anyone else had noticed me, but the woman had turned around and was looking in the other direction. I couldn't see the other two, but I could hear their voices not far away.

The young girl threw the last of the reed she had plucked out from the ground and ran up to the other humans.

"Do you know what they call this bridge?" the old man was saying. I couldn't hear any response, but I assumed neither of the children knew, for the man continued, "They call it Robber's Bridge because once upon a time, robbers would hide in the reeds and jump out at travellers and take their money."

"I saw one, I saw one," the little girl crowed out. "I saw a robber in the water."

I shrank down into the reeds, glad my golden scales would help a little in blending in against the dull yellow stalks, but I needn't have worried, for the human didn't approach. "I'm sure you did," the human said with a laugh. "Come on squirts, or your mum and dad will be wondering where we are."

The two children groaned, but it wasn't long before I heard them get back into their car and start driving away, crossing the bridge and disappearing into the forest. A cloud of dust lingered long after they had gone, and it wasn't until that had been dispersed by the wind before I had the courage to emerge from the reeds. I shook dry my wings and quickly took to the air. I flew back upstream before any other humans happened to stumble upon the remote bridge. My paws and wings ached from the cold, and though I had been scared, I couldn't help but feel happy about witnessing the humans. They weren't all out to harm us, and that was a pleasant thought to carry back to the cave, where I rejoined my companions.

None of them even questioned my absence as I slipped in behind the waterfall and into the darkness. It was a small cave, and there wasn't much room left, forcing me to lie in the entrance. I tucked in my tail so it wasn't caught up in the torrent of water, and for a while I just lay there with my eyes open, looking out into the forest. This was the sort of peace we would strive for.

CHAPTER FOUR

Ellian

Clan Nixa was a beautiful land with wide open meadows fed by three large rivers that flowed through the clan's territory from west to east. Even from the great height we flew, it was easy to see why the Nixan hunting grounds were famed across the draconic territories. Vast herds of deer roamed the lush landscape, as well as multitudes of rabbit and other smaller creatures. Wildcats and eagles also hunted in Nixa, but there was always plenty to feed all, even in the winter months. The sky had been clear all day, but as evening started to approach a thick bank of clouds was rolling in from the eastern horizon.

We were still some distance from the lair when a messenger came out to meet us. She introduced herself as Newita, and that she was to take us down to the central lair.

The Nixan ness didn't say much, except to exchange a few words with Airil, who then retreated to us, looking a little uncomfortable. I remembered then that he had never been given permission to leave Nixa and help my brother and his nomads. I hoped he wasn't going to be punished for his actions, as he had been a great help to us on the borders of Laxtal.

There was nothing to identify the Nixan lair from above the ground. Only a few low mounds were visible from the air. Newita took us down to the top of one of the mounds, on the summit of which was a large rock standing upright and partially embedded in the dirt. Vinzent and Airil landed by my side, with the dragonet looking as perplexed as I felt. There was nothing to distinguish this as the entrance to the lair. Where was Newita leading us?

The ness placed her paw on the rock, and the granite started to glow red.

Vinzent took a few steps back as the rock started to slowly spin and descend into the hill. The ground started to rumble and shake as a glowing passageway began to emerge in the ground. It was nowhere near large enough for a dragon to walk down, but that didn't deter Newita, who confidently walked forward and down into the passage. I shook my head and closed my eyes a few times, trying to work out how the ness had done it.

"Just don't think about it," Airil said, noticing my confusion.

I looked across at Airil, mouth agape. How was I meant to just ignore what I had just seen? A ness had managed to fit into a gap that I knew for a fact was not large enough for her.

"Take a step forward and try not to think about what you're doing. Close your eyes if it helps," the Nixan said.

I tried to follow Airil's advice, squeezing my eyes tight and moving forward. A red glow pierced through my eyelids, but I refused to open them, not until I nosed into the ness who had gone in before me. She huffed as I opened my eyes and nervously looked around. A red glow continued to permeate everything, providing more than enough light to see by, but I was perturbed by what met my eyes. I found myself in a small chamber with no points of exit or entry, but even as I looked Vinzent and Airil emerged from what had appeared to be solid rock.

"Are we ready to go on?" Newita said.

"Where to though?" Vinzent asked. He was shaking as he stood by my side.

Newita grinned widely. "Onwards," she said, before promptly disappearing into the opposite wall.

"Just follow her. It's alright," Airil said, nosing my side.

This time I didn't stop to question how. I just walked forward and accepted that I would just pass right through what my eyes told me was solid stone. I met only the slightest resistance before I found myself in another glowing red passageway. I couldn't see Newita ahead of me, but I could hear her pawsteps. The passageway twisted and turned, in the shadows I was sure there were other pathways shooting off into the darkness. I didn't dare step away from the light. I had no idea where I would end up if I strayed from the path before me.

I kept on walking, but I couldn't shake the feeling that I was barely moving at all.

Finally, a stone wall rose in front of me. I didn't hesitate and pushed through the barrier as though it wasn't there, emerging blinking and half blinded onto a small ledge. I gasped at the sight that greeted my eyes, once they had adjusted to the light. A massive chamber of smooth white stone that dwarfed the Laxtal lair spread out an impossible distance in every direction. The size was too great to fit beneath the few low mounds I had seen from outside. I could barely see the far distant ceiling, though I was sure the magical passage had not sloped down too much. Light streamed in from several large holes that had also not been visible from the surface.

I wrinkled my nose. I couldn't place what it was that irritated me, but something about the smell of the lair was unsettling.

"Welcome to Nixa," Newita said dryly as Vinzent and Airil emerged from the hidden passageway. The silver dragonet shrank back, but the wall had solidified behind him and he was unable to retreat through the passage. Newita barked in laughter. "Shall I take you straight to the ddraig's chambers? He is expecting you."

"It's alright, I'll take them," Airil said. "I imagine Ddraig Krateos will want to see me too."

Newita nodded and flared her wings. "If you wish," she said, before flying away. I soon lost her amongst the hundreds of other dragons soaring through the expansive chamber. Some flew to similar ledges located all around the lair before vanishing into the rock.

"Shall we?" Airil said, unfurling his wings and steadying himself, ready to launch into the air. I mimicked his actions, though behind us Vinzent was a little more reluctant to take to wing.

The Nixan led us almost directly up, towards the very top of the great lair. Just beneath the domed ceiling was the entrance to a small antechamber. Smoke drifted out on a small breeze. My nose twitched at the smell. It was not a wood fire that burnt within, but one powered by coal. Only the richest and most powerful clans used coal for their fires in the best of times, but now it was scarce. Humans mined coal in the far noth, in regions too cold for any dragon to comfortably live. Since the war had started, coal and other luxuries traded from humans had become rare indeed.

No one was present as we entered the antechamber, carved from the same unblemished white stone as the main lair. There was no other discernible exit, but Airil told me this was the entrance to Ddraig Krateos's personal chambers. I took his word for it. It was pointless arguing with a Nixan in their lair. Nothing was normal here.

A roaring fire in a small alcove to the side warmed the little chamber. Thick rugs adorned the floor. I recognised the patterns typical of the northern clans, who used the pelts the native creatures there to craft the thick rugs that kept away all but the worst chill. It took a bit of effort not to lie down and curl up in them. Instead, I sat down in front of the fire, spreading my wings a little and taking in the heat.

Vinzent sat by my side, his paws nervously clawing at the thick rug.

"Looks like you got what you wanted after all," I said quietly to the dragonet.

Instead of boasting about his victory, Vinzent just bowed his head. "I shouldn't have gotten angry with you. I know you were doing what you thought to be the right thing. Can you forgive me?" he said.

"There's nothing to forgive," I assured Vinzent. Not that long ago I would have rested my head on his shoulder, but he was sat just too far away for me to do that, and I didn't move across to him.

"All the same, I'm sorry Ellian. If Nixa provide their support, then I will follow you back to Laxtal with an army in our wings. We won't let Ddraig Tsona control our clan any longer," Vinzent said.

"We still don't know Ddraig Tsona is helping the humans, Vinzent," I reminded the dragon, but he ruffled his wings and didn't respond.

Wings fluttered by the entrance, and I turned to see Haeraig Zeena join us in the antechamber. Her eyes widened as she saw us. "Vinzent? Ellian? I wasn't expecting you. Are you waiting for my father?" she asked. She never even looked across at Airil, sat just a couple of feet away.

"We have some information for him," Vinzent said brightly, accidentally flicking his tail into my side as he spun around to face the Nixan haeraig. "We've been spending time amongst the nomads, and..."

"We'll tell Ddraig Krateos first," I growled, cutting across Vinzent, who I knew had been about to tell the haeraig everything. "He is expecting us."

"I'll go see if he's ready to see you," Haeraig Zeena said, darting past us and straight through the opposite wall with a burst of red light.

"I wish they'd stop doing that," Vinzent muttered as he approached the offending wall. He placed his paw against it, but it was completely solid. Though he pushed his whole weight to the stone, the wall did not allow him to pass.

Airil chuckled and stood up. "It won't let you through," he said. He placed his paw over Vinzent's and a red glow emanated out from the rock where the dragonet touched it. His paw started to sink into the wall before he recoiled in shock. "Only a Nixan can pass through these walls. Other dragons can only pass through when a Nixan places a paw here to allow them passage; otherwise it's just solid rock."

"How does it work," I asked, coming up to the side of the two drakes.

"I wouldn't know," Airil admitted. He backed away from the wall to look into the fire. "It was all done so long ago now. No one knows what magic was used to create this lair, for it seems far beyond the magic of any dragon here. It must have been a great effort by the entire clan. I doubt we'll ever create anything this grand ever again."

"It puts our lair to shame," Vinzent said, lowering his head.

I growled, unhappy that Vinzent was so quick to dismiss our clan. Any slight against Laxtal could diminish our standing in the eyes of the other clans. Laxtal desired to be allies with Nixa. We wanted to be their equal, not inferior to them. No, our lair was not grand and magical, but it was beautiful in its own right.

Airil shook his head. "I loved Laxtal. I think I preferred it to here. It's the smell, mostly. Laxtal smells like a real place, but here... the lair has no scent," the Nixan said.

He was right, and I realised that was what had annoyed my nose. Other than the coal smoke, there was no underlying scent I could detect. There was no smell of moss or plants like those that pervaded the caves of Laxtal, or anything else for that matter. It was sterile.

I didn't have chance to respond to Airil though, as the wall behind us started to glow red again, and two dark forms stepped out. They resolved into the shapes of Haeraig Zeena and her father, Ddraig Krateos of Nixa. I bowed my head to the small bronze-scaled drake, with Vinzent and Airil doing the same behind me.

"Ellian, what do we owe the honour? And Vinzent, am I right?" the ddraig rumbled.

"We have information, Ddraig Krateos. Something that could help us fight the humans," I said, looking down at the Nixan's paws.

The ddraig looked down at me with a hard glare. "What kind of information?"

Stuttering a little, I told the ddraig about the humans we had tracked on the edge of Laxtal, and how we had gained their trust. A human village had sprung up on our side of the mountains, but these humans were allies to the draconic cause. They were able to provide us with information. I was allowed to speak without any interruption from the haeraig or the ddraig. Neither showed any reaction until I had finished, when Haeraig Zeena glanced up at her father.

"Your bravery has to be commended, Ellian," Ddraig Krateos said. He held out his paw. "Come into my chambers and we can discuss this further. Zeena, if you can see to Airil and Vinzent."

I looked across to Vinzent, suddenly worried that I was about to be parted from him. He had only come along because he had been familiar with some of the Nixans before, and I had hoped that he would have been able to convince Ddraig Krateos to make a decisive action in the war, but now it looked like it was going to be all up to me.

Vinzent made no protest though, and he allowed Haeraig Zeena to guide him away, along with Airil. I turned back to the ddraig and briefly met his eyes, but I couldn't hold his gaze for long. Though his physical stature wasn't that impressive, there was a force behind those eyes that alarmed me. I had heard tales of the strength of his magic, and I caught a brief glimpse of it in his eyes.

Ddraig Krateos placed his paw on the wall of the antechamber, making it glow red once more. "Go through, Ellian. I shall join you in a moment," he said.

I tried to hide my surprise at being invited into Ddraig Krateos's chambers. I was not representing any clan, so there was no need for him to treat me with the honour and respect a visiting haeraig or ddraig deserved. I highly doubted that he hadn't heard of Ddraig Tsona's push for leadership of Clan Laxtal, and the Nixan assumed I was still in control of my clan.

I pushed through the wall and into the ddraig's chambers. They were much more luxurious than the ones in Laxtal, where Ddraig Astar had resided. Just like the antechamber, thick rugs adorned the floor, and a fire blazed away in one corner, again feeding off a massive pile of coal. The smoke from the fire drifted up through a natural fault in the rock, leaving the room clear and warm. Hung on almost every wall were many decorations and adornments, ranging from human-made artworks to sculptures of ivory and gold. High up in an alcove was a small silver statue of a serpentine dragon, similar to the one in Ddraig Astar's chamber. I was sure it was sculpted of the same ness, though there were a few little differences in her posture.

Whereas the caverns in Clan Laxtal were lit by torches and flame, Ddraig Krateos's chambers were kept alight by several glowing orbs of light hovering near the ceiling. Though they gently moved as though caught in the ebb and flow of a gentle tide, the light they gave off was constant, never flickering; a source of unwavering light. Just like the lack of smells irritated my nose, the light hurt my eyes; it was almost too perfect.

A red pall to the chamber announced Ddraig Krateos's presence, and I turned and bowed my head to him as he settled down beneath the silver ness. "So you gained the trust of some humans?" he rumbled. I nodded my head. I had already told him everything the humans had told me, there was nothing more I could say on the matter without repeating myself, so I stayed silent. "And what do you expect us to do with this information?"

"I do not expect anything, Ddraig Krateos, but I hope it will allow you to devise a strategy to help defeat the humans," I said, looking down at the Nixan's paws.

Ddraig Krateos snorted in amusement. "I appreciate your faith in Nixa's strength, but we alone cannot take on the human army. We would not be able to get close enough to this General Summers to challenge him. While we have many dragons with powerful magic, few of us are acclimatised to battle. We are not a clan of warriors, like Clan Xigax, or even Clan Laxtal," he said with a nod of his head, acknowledging the strengths of my clan.

"But if we were to get every clan united, surely then we could outnumber the humans so greatly we couldn't lose," I said. I tried to meet the ddraig's eyes, but once more I was intimidated by the great power I saw there and had to divert my gaze, this time toward the silver ness directly above his head.

"Yes, we could unite the clans, but there is one thing in our way," the Nixan replied.

"Ddraig Tsona," I whispered.

"A Xital dragon," Ddraig Krateos corrected. "We have no evidence to suggest it is Ddraig Tsona who is helping the humans, and I personally think it unlikely. His actions in taking control of Laxtal could be used as evidence either way. We haven't heard any stories of destabilisation from your clan, nor of any further human incursions, so we have to say the Xital ddraig has the best interests of dragonkind at heart. Your suspicions of him may be ill-founded."

I fluttered my wings at the reminder that I may have made a mistake in challenging Ddraig Tsona and losing my place in the clan. "Surely we can unite the clans without alerting Clan Xital," I said, but I already knew such an action would be hopeless.

Ddraig Krateos agreed with my private thoughts. "No. There are few clans who would be willing to act without explicit permission from Clan Xital. Any move we make will quickly be made known to the Royal Clan and the traitor within their midst. We need to neutralise, or at the very least expose, the traitor before we can make any action."

"What can we do?"

Ddraig Krateos sighed and turned away, looking into the fire. "I do not know," he admitted in a strained voice. It was probably a rare occasion indeed that the Nixan ddraig conceded defeat in anything, and I chose to remain silent until he spoke again. After all, I was not his equal, not anymore.

"I think the first thing is to know what is going on in Laxtal," the ddraig said eventually. He stared into my eyes for the few seconds I could hold his gaze. "I have no direct authority over you Ellian, so you don't have to obey my commands, but I think it is for the best that you return to your clan. Speak to Ddraig Tsona about your meeting with the humans. Use his knowledge to work out who the traitor in Xital is."

"But what if Ddraig Tsona is the traitor?" I whispered, feeling a tight clench in my chest at the prospect of returning to Laxtal. I couldn't work out if it was excitement or fear that gripped me, or even a little of both.

"He is not," Ddraig Krateos growled. "Ddraig Tsona has nothing to gain by siding with the humans. It will be a dragon in Xital who desires more power. Ddraig Tsona already is the most powerful dragon. He can't gain any more."

I exhaled slowly and tried to convince myself to believe Ddraig Krateos. I had to trust his judgement on the matter; he had been involved in politics with Clan Xital for many years now. He would know Ddraig Tsona much better than I did.

I thought of the promise I had made to my brother. That I would return straight to the nomadic lair. It took a couple of moments for me to break that promise. "I shall go back," I said.

"Excellent. We will not be idle here. We shall do all we can to prepare before the Axinstone is returned to us," Ddraig Krateos said with a slight nod of his head.

A flare of hope burned in my heart. "You really think Anzig is still alive?"

"We are certain of it. We felt a surge of power two days ago that could only mean one thing. A dragon is in possession of the Axinstone," Ddraig Krateos said. "That it should happen under the face of the thief was a sign that it was always fated to be so."

"Two days ago? Then they could already nearly be at the Sxinix Mountains by now," I gasped. Surely it wouldn't take them long to cross the mountains and return home.

Ddraig Krateos nodded. "That's what we're expecting, which makes it imperative that we're ready to act as soon as we have the Axinstone. We don't want to give the humans and the Xital traitor any time to react to our power."

"Then I shall leave in the morning, Ddraig Krateos," I said. I knew it was too late to make any worthwhile distance in what little remained of the day. I would be better off waiting until morning and getting a full day of flight, which would take me almost all the way to Laxtal.

"We shall provide shelter for you and your companion tonight, and I shall see you off in the morning if you return here," Ddraig Krateos said, before his voice took on a harsher note. "But you will not be able to take Airil with you this time. If we are to be ready to defend our lands, we need every dragon in the lair."

"I understand, Ddraig Krateos." I bowed my head. It annoyed me that the ddraig seemed to be blaming me for Airil's choice to help the nomads when I had nothing to do with it, but I hid this from my posture. I was in no place to argue with the Nixan, not when he had opened his clan to me for the night. Rarely were visitors permitted to stay within the lair; it was an honour usually reserved for visiting ddraigs. All others needed to find a place to rest in the moors, though there were plenty of suitable caves and burrows to take refuge in.

Ddraig Krateos dismissed me after that and opened the portal through the wall for me to leave. Haeraig Zeena was already waiting for me on the other side, though there was no sign of Airil or Vinzent. The Nixan sat reared on her hind legs, and between her forelegs a ruby floated. I cleared my throat, and the ruby fell to the floor and disappeared into the rug as the haeraig lost her concentration.

"I'm sorry Ellian, I didn't expect you to be so quick," she said as she searched for the ruby. She eventually found it and returned it to a ledge just behind her. In a behaviour most unusual for a haeraig, she didn't look right at me. "Vinzent told me everything about the humans. You're a brave ness, Ellian. There aren't many that would do what you did and approach humans like that."

"I just did what I thought was best," I replied, bowing my head and keeping calm, though inside I was glowing at the haeraig's praise.

"You deserve better than living with the nomads," the Nixan added.

I glanced back at Ddraig Krateos's chambers, wondering if our discussion was meant to be private. Surely the ddraig would be informing his daughter of the proceedings though, so I felt confident enough in telling Haeraig Zeena what we had planned.

The Nixan was startled, but not overly surprised that I would be returning to Laxtal to try and discover the identity of the Xital traitor. "I think Ddraig Tsona would be more willing to listen to you now you've spoken to the humans," she said after a little pause, by which time she had started to lead me through the lair. We were descending through the great central chamber: down towards the far distant floor that never seemed to get any closer.

"I certainly hope so," I said. I knew I was risking my reputation in this. If Ddraig Tsona refused to listen to me then I doubted I would ever be able to return to Laxtal again, regardless of who was ddraig. My standing would be completely destroyed if I failed.

The Nixan banked away to the right, and as I followed her, I caught a glimpse up at the ceiling. It was so far away now, but the floor below didn't appear to be any closer. She led me into a small cavern that had no magical walls; it was open to the rest of the lair but for a thin sheet of fabric that hung over the entrance. A second, smaller chamber branched off the first, also shielded by a veil.

Vinzent was already waiting for us, and the dragonet bounded up to his paws when he saw us come in. Haeraig Zeena didn't stay for long, though Vinzent protested when she prepared to leave. The haeraig just smiled and said, "I have duties to attend to."

As the Nixan flew away, Vinzent sighed and lay back down in front of the coal-fuelled fire that was burning in the corner. For all his eagerness in coming to Nixa and urging Ddraig Krateos to summon an army to reclaim Laxtal, the dragonet now seemed disinterested in what the ddraig had said. He didn't even ask me what had gone on in the ddraig's chambers, instead just lying in front of the fire with his eyes closed.

"I'm leaving for Laxtal in the morning," I said eventually, but even that barely drew any reaction from the dragonet.

"Already?" Vinzent asked, opening one curious eye.

"Ddraig Krateos is expecting Anzig back soon. We need to be ready to act with the Axinstone, but we can't do that until we know who the traitor is within Xital. Ddraig Krateos thinks Ddraig Tsona could be able to work out who is feeding the humans information," I explained.

"That's it? That's all the help Ddraig Krateos is providing?" Vinzent scoffed. "We already know the traitor is Tsona."

"We have no proof of that," I growled. I thought we had ended this argument, but Vinzent seemed quite keen to pick it up again.

"No proof?" the dragonet snarled. He pushed up against me, pressing his muzzle against mine and glaring into my eyes. "Ellian, he forced us out of our clan, and for what? Because we dared question his mighty self?"

I took a step back and swiped across Vinzent's muzzle, making him recoil in shock. "He banished us because we challenged him and failed. The same happened to us as would happen to any dragon who challenged the authority of the ddraig and failed to defeat them." With his mouth open, Vinzent turned away to stare into the fire. I almost approached him to place my wing around his body, but I held my ground. "If Ddraig Krateos trusts Ddraig Tsona still, then so do I."

"So you're flying to Laxtal alone?" Vinzent asked sombrely.

"Alone? What happened to you following me back to Laxtal no matter what?" I asked with a hiss.

"I said with an army behind our wings. If we fly back alone, we'll be killed. We need to take Laxtal back with force," the dragonet said with a sinister growl. His pale blue eyes glinted red in the firelight.

I had to take a few steps back from the silver dragonet. I had never heard him speak like that before, and I was scared by the look in his eyes. "I will not condone an attack on our own clan," I whispered, but I don't think Vinzent heard me.

"You keep saying we need to act in this war to help Anzig, but every time a chance comes along you always take the easy option," he snarled. Again, he advanced on me, and once more I had to step back. "You fled Laxtal when we should have stayed and fought. You supported Mulner when he was doing nothing to stop the humans roaming our land. And now you'll return to Tsona with your tail between your legs and just to try talk to him, to beg him for mercy. We should be going back to rip out his throat for what he is doing to our clan."

"He's not doing anything to our clan, Vinzent. Ddraig Krateos has heard nothing from Laxtal. No unrest or misdirection. There is nothing to prove he's trying to fragment dragonkind by taking control of Laxtal," I protested, but Vinzent just shook his head and growled.

"You have no ambition, Ellian. You'll never reclaim our clan if you're afraid to take risks. I thought you were better than that," he snarled. I was backed right into the corner now. I had nowhere to go and nowhere to look but right into Vinzent's eyes. Staring me down was not the dragon who had agreed to become my mate. This was a rival who desired the power I had once claimed.

I felt utterly numb. This was a drake who had been at my side and beneath my wings since we were both hatchlings. He had supported me all the while, never once crossing me. Every word he spoke now was agony to my heart.

"I thought I could trust you to help me," I said, barely forcing a hoarse whisper out of my constricted throat.

"I thought I could trust you to be a decisive leader," he retorted. "I thought you could be a mate I would be proud of.

"What are you saying?"

Vinzent didn't answer for a few moments. He seemed almost ashamed as he turned away from me. "You've always been my closest friend, Ellian. I hope you always will be. But, as a mate... I can fly higher."

A growl built from the back of my throat before I unleashed it as a vicious snarl. I couldn't believe what I was hearing, but Vinzent was unapologetic as he calmly faced me down. He made no attempt to try and ease the pain that was tearing through my body. I couldn't even think properly, certainly not well enough to formulate a response other than a savage snarl.

"I'll stay here and see if I can convince the Nixans to get an army to follow you to Laxtal," Vinzent said, but I barely even heard him. I wanted to lash out and strike him, but I forced myself to hold back. He would easily overpower me if it came to a fight, and deep underground I didn't have the space to employ any of my tricks I had learnt from Carlee over the years. The fact I could not lash out frustrated me further.

"Are you even listening, Ellian?"

"No," I replied bluntly. I curled up in the corner of the cavern and pulled my wing over my body in a clear sign I didn't want him to disturb me. With my eyes still open, I could see Vinzent's shadow moving through the membrane of my wing. He started to approach, before changing his mind and turning away. I could hear him muttering to himself, but I wasn't able to catch the words.

He fell silent, before retreating into the small antechamber.

I remained awake for a long time. I was hurting too much to relax my mind enough to sleep. Truth be told, I was tempted to take to wing and leave Nixa immediately, but I doubted I would be able to escape the lair without the assistance of a Nixan dragon, which I knew I would not be able to obtain. The only dragon I could trust was Airil, but I knew I would have no chance of finding him. I was trapped here with the drake who had betrayed me.

I would leave for Laxtal at first light, and I would be flying alone.

I did not see Vinzent the following morning. I awoke early and flew directly to Ddraig Krateos's chambers and waited for the Nixan to rise. He did not keep me waiting for long, and he rumbled a greeting before guiding me out through the clan's defences. I tried not to show my fear to the ddraig as I walked through the glowing walls. Not once did he question the absence of the silver dragon.

I emerged squinting into the sunlight, stood atop of one of the many low rises that marked the Nixan lair. I unfurled my wings and looked up to the clear sky. Conditions were almost perfect for flight; I would even have a tailwind to push me along my way. A storm had raged overhead throughout the night, but apart from a few damp patches of grass, there was nothing to show the lair had been victim to the violence of wind and rain.

"Send a messenger as soon as you reclaim your clan, or if you are able to determine who the traitor in Xital is," the ddraig said. "The moment the Axinstone is returned to us we shall be in contact with you to make a plan of action."

"I shall do my best, Ddraig Krateos," I said, bowing my head towards the more experienced dragon.

"Good. Your best will be needed. You will need to convince Ddraig Tsona that it is in dragonkind's best interest that you lead Laxtal again. Once he understands that Anzig still lives and will return to draconic territories soon, he should relinquish control without the need for a formal challenge," the ddraig said.

I nodded my head again. I was relying on Ddraig Krateos's belief that we could still trust Ddraig Tsona. If the Xital ddraig was the traitor we were trying to find, then I knew to fear for my safety. Given the dragon who was most vocal as Ddraig Tsona's aggressor was Vinzent, I was happy to put my faith in the Nixan. I no longer believed Vinzent's opinions were in my best interests.

"May the wind fly under your wings, Ellian of Laxtal. Prove yourself worthy of being a child of Nixa. I trust we will meet again soon," Ddraig Krateos said, with an almost imperceptible bowing of his head.

I acknowledged the ddraig's respects, before kicking into the air. I hoped to leave many of my worries behind in Nixa. The only thing that mattered now was the clear blue skies before me, and the rolling plains of Laxtal beyond the distant horizon.

I was returning home.

CHAPTER FIVE

Anzig

Three days after leaving Trevena, we were relieved to see a physical marker of our progress. The Sxinix Mountains loomed high above us, rearing up to block out half the sky. Those great heights were all that separated us from the draconic territories. Our only worry now was crossing them. There were no issues of humans finding us; we had seen no evidence of any settlement within miles, and they had no reason to cross the mountains this far north. They were using the much easier Gota-Sxinix pass on the southern borders of Laxtal. I would have loved the opportunity to take the southern pass, but it would have been crawling with humans, so our only option had been to stay in the north. Of course, this pass also had the advantage of taking us fairly close to the northern borders of Nixa. Isikian believed we would be at the Nixan lair within another three days.

Azlak had taken the lead of the group once more as we flew up the side of the mountains. I still couldn't really see our destination, but the seer had assured me he knew where he was going. He had not answered me when I had asked if it would be anything like the ordeal we had suffered on our last trip across the Sxinix. That had been an arduous walk over a narrow path buffeted by icy winds. It had not been pleasant, but I knew I would be willing to endure much worse as we returned home.

Inilta flew just behind my wing. In his paws he clutched the Axinstone. The Nixan had not let the glowing stone out of his grasp ever since leaving the old mine. I could still feel its power pulsing; a rush of magic that manifested into a prickling heat on my scales. I felt invigorated by the energy that I was getting from the Axinstone, but I was trying to hide its effects from the Nixans. Isikian especially was quite concerned that I was so strongly affected by its magic.

We halted for a brief respite at the summit of a sheer cliff, giving us the opportunity to prepare for the mountains proper. I sat with Keita, looking back down at the forest we had emerged from. Here and there were the little signs of human activity. Small villages dotted the edges of the forest, the closest of which was still many miles away, too far distant to cause us any concerns.

The only worry I had on my mind now was whether the humans would retaliate for the theft of the Axinstone. It was something I hadn't considered until now. There hadn't been any consistent fighting between our species in the war so far, just sporadic outbreaks of violence and the worrying advance of their army. Their presence stole territory and forced us closer to our lairs, but they had not yet been seeking us out to eradicate us.

Usually.

As irregular as the violence had been, human soliders had still taken both parents from me. How many other dragons would lose their lives before we could reclaim our territory?

The human George would know that dragons had stolen the Axinstone. What measures would he take to retrieve it? I was sure Nixa would be aware of the dangers, but I knew I would have to discuss the matter with Ddraig Krateos. I needed to know that the other clans would be safe from human retribution. Every clan that bordered the Sxinix needed to be alert: Laxtal especially. I trusted Ellian to have the clan prepared for anything, but she would have had a struggle to control the clan following the death of my father. We needed to hurry back before the clan descended into chaos and confusion surrounding its leadership.

My restlessness must have been evident, as Keita gently placed her wing over me. "We're almost there. We just need to cross the mountains and we're safe," she said.

"For now," I replied. These lands looked so peaceful, but I knew my future would not reflect that. My clan would be looking to me to help guide them through this war, but I didn't know if I could soar to those expectations. I had seen what humans were capable of, and I wasn't convinced we could be victorious. As ddraig of one of the ruling clans, it would be expected of me to devise some brilliant scheme.

Of course, some dragons would point out the successful theft of the Axinstone, which could be considered my idea, but we had been lucky. I had also had little to do with the success of the attempt, and once more I doubted my ability to lead Laxtal. My father had left pawprints too big for me to ever hope of filling.

"We can win," Keita said softly. I looked across to her. She was staring down at the great forest, but I knew she wasn't able to see the details I could see.

"What makes you say that?"

"Because Azlak says we can, and you have put your faith in him. I doubted him. We all doubted him, all except you. Now look at us, we've come this far," she said.

I allowed myself a small smile. She was right. Azlak had been our guide for so long now, and he still seemed to believe we had a chance to defeat the humans. If Keita had decided to place her trust in the seer, then anything was now possible. She had been Azlak's most vocal critic at the start of the journey, and had even refused to acknowledge his existence when we had been dragonet's and the seer's magic had first started to manifest.

Keita growled as Maznar approached us. Whilst she had been able to finally trust Azlak, trusting the spectre had been another matter entirely. She disagreed with me in allowing Maznar to travel with us, but had reluctantly accepted my decision for the time being.

Maznar bowed her head as she approached, deferring to both myself and Keita.

"Azlak says we should be taking to wing soon, Ddraig Anzig," she said quietly.

The ness had spoken little since we had left George's castle. Everyone was nervous in her presence, whilst she was reluctant to acknowledge the silence that surrounded her. I still saw the shadow of the spectre in her red eyes, and that unnerved me. Every time I saw her, I relived the pain of my shattered wing and mutilated tail and chest.

Azlak was the only dragon who'd had a lengthy conversation with the spectre, but neither of them had revealed what they discussed. I got the feeling they were hiding something from me, but at the same time I could convince myself that I was simply being paranoid. Maznar would hold many secrets after spending so much time amongst the humans, and I trusted her to reveal the information she knew when the time was right. As for Azlak, he had every right to look away in guilt when he caught my eye. I knew he still considered himself responsible for my father's death. There had been a brief moment when I had hated the seer with every thought, but over time I had relented to the degree that I was able to forgive him. I acknowledged that he had saved my life, and that he had been unaware that his actions would result in the death of someone most precious to me and the clan.

Keita pulled me aside before we rejoined the others. "Are you certain about the spectre?" she whispered.

"It's been a long time since I've been certain about anything," I replied. I spread my wings, eager to get into the air once more. I just wanted to get away from human lands. On the other side of the mountains, maybe I would start feeling surer of things again.

"I thought so," Keita said, looking down at the ground. Her voice was dull, almost sorrowful.

She took to the air before I could question her meaning, and she didn't approach my wing again as I took my position just behind Azlak. Instead, the ness hung back with Okazuni, delighting the Nyrian dragon with her presence.

Azlak led us further still up the mountain. Initially, there was no sign of a route through the mountains, but the more we flew, I started to make out the outline of a steep valley that seemed to cut right between two gigantic peaks, piercing into a bank of thick cloud.

The valley looked like something had taken a swipe at the solid rock, leaving behind a thick gouge that was over a hundred feet wide. Even from this distance I could see a few mountain goats leaping from rock to rock, before scampering into some of the toughened shrubs and trees that clung to the rockface as we approached. It was not the narrow path that meandered above a great precipice like we had used to cross into human lands, but it still looked like we would have to make the journey by paw. I could see from the patches of snow that had fallen into the valley how the wind gusted and swirled, making flight risky.

Sure enough, Azlak led us down to the edge of the great ravine and allowed me to take the lead from him. I could see no detours to lose our way on, so his guidance was no longer necessary until we reached the open plains beyond the valley, which we would have to do before nightfall. I doubted we would find anywhere to shelter between here and the far side of the mountains.

I was left alone to furrow a safe path through the valley, having to negotiate loose stone that had accumulated over the years. Snow swirled down from the high peaks either side. In some places it had built up to form a thick layer, in others it had already started to melt and form large murky puddles. We walked around them, not knowing how deep any of them were; would I just splash through them or fall down a hidden abyss?

It was cold in the valley, with a piercing wind whistling between the two walls of stone. It howled and shrieked as it pushed against me, trying to tease my wings open and force me back down the valley.

I emptied my mind and focused on putting one paw in front of the other to keep moving forward. If I weakened for just a moment, mentally or physically, the results could be dire. I simply couldn't allow my wings to unfurl. The wind was too strong to take flight. I could easily find myself dashed against the rock.

Occasionally, I could hear grunts and snarls from behind me as the others suffered a little difficulty, but I couldn't look back. I had to keep my eyes firmly on the ground just before my paws. I trusted Isikian would assist anyone who fell and injured themselves. The healer had been sent to the back with the Axinstone, prying it from his brother's protective grip, so he would be able to see anyone in trouble and quickly tend to them.

Here and there I could see signs that this valley was not as abandoned as I had initially thought. Worn and faded stone structures emerged beyond ridges and peaks overlooking the valley, too rigid and angular to be wholly natural, yet they looked nothing like the buildings the humans liked to construct. They were certainly not dragon-made, for no dragon would dare live so high up, in this cold and bitter wind.

Then I saw the first pawprint. Gigantic, bigger even than a human, and entirely the wrong shape. I hurried on, put in the mind of a great bear or some other predator. None of the others seemed to notice the print, and I said nothing about it. I didn't want to put fear into them. Not when I didn't know how old the tracks were. I could smell nothing fresh on the air, just snow, ice, and the oncoming storm.

As the many steps trudged on, my fear began to abate. I had almost forgotten the prints before I started to hear something. There was an echo in the wind. I was sure I could hear voices in them, softly speaking to each other, though I was sure that none of the dragons behind me were saying anything. Like me, they were too focused on treading carefully to carry any conversation. I couldn't hear what the mystical voices said. Every time I tried to listen to what they were saying, they faded away until I could barely hear them over the howl of the wind. I shook my head and tried to ignore them. It was no use listening to phantoms in times like these.

It was difficult to judge time as I pushed ever onwards. The sun was almost completely obscured by the sheer cliff walls that rose either side of us, as well as a thickening bank of clouds we climbed towards. The light was rapidly fading, but I was sure nightfall was still some way off. I had received no warnings from Azlak that progress was too slow.

As the light faded, so did my vision. Shadows seemed to leap out of the rock as the darkness engulfed the valley. The ground underpaw was starting to get slippery as the clouds descended, blanketing the rock in moisture. I stumbled a few times but just managed to keep my balance. I called to the others to follow in my pawprints where I knew the ground was sure and firm.

I heard Keita cry out in pain as she fell to the ground. I gritted my teeth and forced myself to keep pushing on, though I wanted to turn and see that she was alright. I had to trust Isikian that he would see to the ness.

I felt the ground ease downhill slightly beneath my aching paws. I took heart with this, hoping that it meant the end of the ordeal was near. Claws scrambled against the rock to my side, and I caught a flash of gold as the seer moved towards me, clambering over the loose stones to lope at my side.

"A storm is approaching, Ddraig Anzig. If we keep this pace I don't think we'll get off the mountain in time," the seer warned.

"We can't go any faster," I snarled, once again stumbling on the slippery rock as Azlak's instruction broke my concentration.

"We must though."

"What do you expect me to do?" I growled. Keita had already fallen once; I knew that if we moved any faster others would start to struggle. We would be testing Isikian's abilities too much by risking more injuries.

The seer didn't say anything as he dropped back behind me once more. I could still hear him muttering to himself, barely audible over the howl of the wind. I glanced up at the clouds, and had to agree with the seer in one sense: it did look like a storm was brewing. The clouds were blacker than any I had seen before, and we were not far below them. If a storm were to break, we would suffer the full force of it, exposed in the narrow valley with nowhere to shelter.

A flash of searing lightning lit the sky, followed almost immediately by a deafening crack of thunder.

"I warned him," I heard the seer say. I knew I had to turn around and berate him for his insolence, but as I did, I slipped on the uneven ground, only just keeping upright. I growled quietly and made a mental note to speak to Azlak later and turned my focus back to the damp rock beneath my paws. We needed to get off the mountain before the storm released its ire upon us all.

I shivered as the temperature dropped further. There was no longer even a hint of the sun behind the clouds, and against my best reasoning, I started to push harder. Maybe Azlak was right, and it was worth the risk trying to move quicker rather than get caught up in the mountains at night, during an oncoming storm.

Finally, we emerged onto open ground. The valley walls flattened and widened out, until all that was left of the deep cleft we had traversed through was a shallow bowl looking out over the wildlands that lay to the north-west of Nixa. Though it was covered in shadow with patches of rain falling already, never before had I seen a more beautiful sight than the draconic territories; land unblemished by humans.

I did not hesitate before taking to wing. I could hear Azlak doing the same just behind me. Through the wild, gusting wind I fought to control my flight down to the far distant ground. Without any clear destination, I aimed for the banks of a narrow stream at the edge of a large forest, much like the one we had just left behind in the human lands.

We were just in time. Large drops of rain pelted my wings as I descended, threatening to unbalance my flight and fling me out of the sky. With great relief, I landed safely on the soft ground, revelling in the feel of the dirt and mulched leaves beneath my paws. I couldn't relax yet though. We needed some shelter from the rain that was rolling in from the east – a great curtain of water that was slowly approaching.

Azlak was the next to land, and he came to the ground by my side. "Where next?" I asked him, hoping he already knew a place to shelter.

"I... I don't know," the seer said, looking around with despair. He hadn't Seen anything. I growled. His magic had failed us.

The others all came to land soon after. My mood lifted in seeing Keita amongst them, looking unscathed from her fall in the valley. Everyone looked toward me, but their focus was down at my paws, all waiting for me to explain our next move. Once again, I had nothing. I didn't know these parts at all, and I had no idea where to find any shelter.

I turned to the two Nixans. "Do you know of any caves or nomadic lairs near here?" I asked them.

Inilta didn't hesitate before shaking his head, but Isikian pondered the question a little longer. The healer stared at the mountains with intent, holding his muzzle high as he sniffed the air. "I think I might know of one, Ddraig," he said after his contemplations.

"Then lead us, Isikian," I said. The healer unfurled his wings, resulting in a few groans from the others of having to take to the air again so soon after landing.

Isikian led us back towards the mountains, but stayed low to the ground. The wind pushed us onwards, keeping us ahead of the worst of the storm, though we surely only had five minutes at most before it hit us.

There was a gaping cave at the foot of the mountains, much taller than Nightwings had been and at least three times wider than her extensive wingspan. There were strange symbols carved into the rock around the edges of the cave mouth, but I had no time to study them now. We all dived into the darkness that awaited us inside, and not a moment too soon. The torrent of water drenched the ground in moments.

Inilta wasted no time in producing a fire. The light from his flames didn't reach the far walls. The cavern was massive.

"I've never seen anything like this. Is it an old lair?" I asked Isikian.

The healer shook his head. "I don't know, Ddraig Anzig. Our clan has known of this place for a long time, but we've never been able to understand it. We do know it's not a natural cave, and a lot of strange artefacts are found here."

"Is it safe?" Carlee growled.

"As far as we've ever been able to determine," Isikian replied.

I looked around, trying to penetrate the inky darkness without any success. Beyond Inilta's fire, the blackness was near absolute. I noticed something. A crimson glow in the distance. I nudged Carlee to get her attention, and she growled again. When she turned her focus to me, I nodded in the direction of the glow. Her eyes widened slightly, either adjusting to the gloom, or in surprise at what she saw. I whispered to her to take Okazuni and investigate.

They quickly faded into the gloom while we waited nervously for them to return. We had all seen the strange glow now. Keita and Azlak waited impatiently by my side. The seer was looking down at his paws, his eyes shining white. I resisted the urge to ask him what he was Seeing.

"Ddraig Anzig, come quickly. There's something here you must see." Carlee's voice shattered the silence, piercing the darkness. I could sense fear in her voice, or was it excitement? I immediately plunged into the void before me. I was not alone. I felt Azlak's and Nataik's presence alongside me as I went deeper into the nothingness before me.

Almost imperceptibly, a deep red hue replaced the black of nothing. I began to make out familiar shapes, as though bathed in blood. It seemed everything that came into vision was. The cause of Carlee's consternation was a large stone tablet with a crack down the middle. I glanced up to a shelf high above our heads. It was from up there that the crimson light was shining, but Carlee directed my attention to the slab at her paws. There were strange markings around the edge of the stone, just like the ones at the entrance to the cave.

"It looks like human markings, but I can't read what it says," the veteran said. She looked expectantly across at Nataik. The Xigax ness had proved in the past that she could read these strange, human-crafted symbols.

It took but a few moments before Nataik shook her head firmly. "This is no language I recognise," she muttered.

I glanced back, searching through the darkness for the red-eyed shadow. "Maznar, what about you? Can you read what these say?"

I got no response. I couldn't even see her in the darkness outside of Inilta's magical light, which had followed us across the cave as the Nixan reluctantly joined us.

"That one there says 'Nixa'," Azlak said, looking over Nataik's shoulder. He traced a claw across some markings that had no meaning to my eyes.

Nataik growled as she looked at Azlak's marks. "I think you're right," she said, before we were all distracted by a noise high above.

In the light of the red glow, I could just make out the bloodied shape of Okazuni's head leaning over the shelf's edge. "There's another one up here," he called down.

Nataik was the first to take to wing, and she had cried out in excitement before I was able to join the Nyrian on the shelf. The source of the light was a large blood red stone set into the wall. It illuminated dozens of carvings of differing shapes and sizes. Some were the elegant markings of human writing, while others seemed to be small images. I thought I recognised one as the head of a dragon.

"Look at this," Nataik was whispering. I didn't glance over, knowing I wouldn't be able to recognise whatever it was she was excited about. Carlee and Azlak didn't show the same restraint. I was instead focusing on the glowing orb in front of me. I reached out with a paw, a claw's length from the stone. It felt cold, but at the same time I sensed a slight tingle of magic.

"The Eight thank the dragons of Sxinix for their assistance in reclaiming Kyte's rune," Azlak said slowly as he read from the stone slab. "You will always find a powerful ally in Ehran."

"Ehran? I've never heard of it," Carlee said with an annoyed snarl. I understood her frustration. Any ally would be useful now in the fight against the humans, but if Carlee did not know where this place was, or who dwelt there, then we had no chance of finding them before humans swept aside our defences.

I placed my paw on the stone. There was a pulse of magic that flowed through me, but then dissipated as quickly as it had appeared. Whatever magic there had been in this place had long since gone, as had whoever had once lived here.

"I know of Ehran," Maznar said. She melted out of the shadows, perched atop the shelf. "George spoke of it to me several times. It is a mountain, far away to the south."

"Could they help us?" Carlee asked.

Maznar showed her teeth. "Ehran no longer has the same power it once did. They will be of no use to you."

I growled softly and pulled my paw away from the orb. For a moment I had dared to believe we might have found some way to win this war, something more than promises from Nixa.

"Is that what I think it is?" Azlak's awed whisper pulled my attention away from the brief flutter of hope. The seer's focus was on a small scrap of ancient parchment, decorated with elegant images inscribed on it. This wasn't human text, but a picture of a bird nestled in red flames. "It's a firebird."

"A firebird?" Carlee scoffed. "A tale told to dragonets and nothing more. They aren't real."

"Then what is this?" the seer asked, not deterred by Carlee's scepticism.

The second image was of a creature I had never seen before. Its front half was like some sort of hunting bird – a hawk or an eagle perhaps, but it had the hindquarters of a wildcat.

"What manner of creature is that?" I asked. Azlak shook his head, unable to provide any answer, but Nataik pointed out a small squiggle of blank ink the seer had missed.

"The humans call it a gryphon," she said. "You might know it as a skycat."

Maznar growled. "Pompous and arrogant creatures." She spread her wings and soared away, vanishing into the darkness before anyone could question her.

I had never of such a creature as a skycat, not even in stories. I couldn't bring myself to believe it was real. Like the firebird it had to be a creature of myth and legend. Disappointed, and shaking my head, I believed that there was nothing here to help us.

I turned from the small shelf and looked out into the darkness. It never seemed to end. I could not tell how deep the cave went, and there was a strange prickle of magic that tickled down my tail. There was something powerful here, something that rivalled the Axinstone.

Though the fire tempted me, I took a few cautious steps deeper into the darkness. Pawsteps sounded behind me. I glanced back to see Azlak. I was tempted to tell the seer to leave me alone, but I was glad of the company. I bared my teeth at him, but did not chase him away.

"You feel it too, Ddraig?" the seer asked. I did not answer him.

There was no echo to my pawsteps. The firelight seemed so small and pitiful behind us. The shadows clung close to my eyes, obstructing vision even to the end of my muzzle. Nothing could breach that darkness.

Soot covered the ground beneath my paws. My nose wrinkled at an unpleasant scent, but I did not turn around. Had I been alone, I might have given up the search in the darkness, but Azlak's presence forced me to keep moving. Phantoms returned to my mind. Whispers plagued my every thought.

My muzzle bumped into something solid. I yelped and fell back, striking my tail against Azlak's legs. My eyes watered. I angrily wiped away the forbidden tears before the seer could see the glistening moisture in my eyes. "Inilta!" I called out, half-turning to look back to the distant fire. "I need your magic over here."

As I waited for the Nixan, the whisper at the back of my mind grew louder. It came from somewhere in front of me. Only one word repeated. *"Father?"*

"Can you hear that?" I asked, but the seer did not respond.

The grey-scaled Nixan slouched closer. His eyes flicked through the darkness. He seemed as apprehensive about the shadows as I felt. At my command, he summoned his magic to illuminate what lay ahead.

Nothing could have prepared my eyes for what I saw. A dragon made of stone rose from the floor. The statue was bigger even than Nightwings, perched on his hindlegs with his wings partially unfurled as though ready for flight. His distant face was twisted in pain and terror.

A voice boomed through my mind.

"Father? Father, is that you? Father, I'm so sorry!"

I yelped in fear and cowered back, no longer caring about any display of power. My eyes were locked onto the statue, expecting it to move, but it never did. And all the while that immense voice pleaded inside my head.

"What do you think it is?" Azlak whispered, his voice barely audible over the screams of that desperate voice.

"I don't know," I whimpered. My claws scratched against the stony ground. "But that voice… it's hard to think."

"Voice, Ddraig?" Inilta asked. The Nixan dragon stepped forward, his bright magical light lifting to illuminate more of the statue. Though I barely dared to look, I could see the craft that had gone into the statue was exquisite. Every scale was beautifully carved.

"Father! Father?"

I tore my eyes away from the statue. "Can't you hear it? He's pleading for his father."

"I hear nothing, Ddraig," Inilta said. The Nixan glanced towards Azlak, who shook his head.

I couldn't believe they heard nothing, but I kept my mouth shut and my wings furled tightly to my sides. I shuddered. "Come on. There's nothing else back here."

I did my best to ignore the look of worry on Azlak's face as I pushed past him. The screams from the statue slowly faded to silence, but their echoes reverberated throughout my thoughts for so much longer.

We found nothing else in the cave, though none of us were willing to explore more given the terror we felt when approaching the statue. None of us knew what the statue was in the cave for, or what it meant. No one else mentioned the voice I had heard, so I spoke no more of it. The night had been uneasy, but our exhaustion had been enough to overwhelm our fear and unease.

We left the massive cave at first light, eager to put the place behind us, and to be travelling south towards the Nixan borders. There was not much flying left now; we were close to the claimed draconic territories. We just needed to keep the mountains at our right wing and we would be at the Nixan border by nightfall.

There was no trace of last night's storm: the sky was a beautiful, pristine blue. It was perfect flying conditions, and we were all glad for the relatively easy flight south. I was left alone for most of the day, but behind me conversation was light and playful.

Towards the end of the flight, Isikian had come to my wing to inform me of a good refuge for the night. I eased back to allow the healer to take the lead, and once more the Nixan guided us towards somewhere to rest.

It soon became clear where the healer was taking us to; a towering mountain that rose high above any of the other peaks around it. Below the snowline, the ground was green undulated grasslands, punctured by claw-like shards of rock. Dotted around the mountain, I could make out what appeared to be networks of interconnected caves. These caves were inaccessible to anything without wings, as the first few hundred feet of the mountain consisted of sheer vertical cliffs, without even the hint of a cleft or fold to provide any purchase to climb.

In the gathering gloom, we landed high above the grasslands below, upon the northern slopes of the mountain, near a cave entrance. Exhausted, we stumbled into the mountain. A cold wind had started to blow, and we were grateful for its shelter. I paused for just a moment at the threshold of the cave to look back out over the surrounding land. To the north and east was dense forest, though beyond that I could just make out in the distant haze, the undulating plains that led into northern Nixa and Turaxa.

Inilta quickly lit a fire again – his flames erupting from the dusty rock floor of the cave. It looked as though our shelter for the night was occasionally used by nomadic dragons, though none were present at the moment. The charred remains of a fire was visible on the floor. The smell of charcoal lingered; it had only been a few days at the most since it was last occupied.

"What is this place?" I asked Isikian as the healer moved to settle down near his brother. Lying nearby, Carlee kept an interested eye open.

"This is Kxisila. It's been known to Nixa for many years as a refuge if our lair is ever compromised," the healer explained.

"Kxisila?" Maznar said slowly, the ness sidling up close to us. "I have seen this place before, in the dreams of a human. They called it Dragon's Haven."

Isikian sucked in his breath. "The humans shouldn't know about this place. Unless they learn how to fly, they have no way of scaling the mountainside," he said.

"They were not up this high. In the dream they were looking at the mountain from the bottom of the cliffs, but they knew what was up here. They remembered being told... by a dragon," Maznar explained.

"A dragon? Do you know who?" I asked, worried by this. Of course, the dream could have come from a long time ago, before the war between dragon and humans, but I doubted this. Even then I doubted Nixa would have made the location of Kxisila known to humans.

"I'm afraid the human didn't know the name," Maznar said. She looked me right in the eye for a moment. "But I can tell you that there is a dragon colluding with the humans. I don't know who, but I believe it's the same one who told them of this place, and they have good influence within their clan. He also gifted my egg to George, though he is not my father."

"Why haven't you told us this before?" Carlee growled.

"Because it wasn't relevant until now. There's nothing anyone could have done with the information, even if I had told you," Maznar said, flaring her wings slightly in protest at Carlee's accusation.

The veteran ness snarled, but chose not to respond to the spectre, instead turning away and pulling her wing over her head. I had no doubt I would hear more about this later, but for the time being Carlee was willing to let the matter rest.

I chose to focus on something else Maznar had said. "How do you know this dragon isn't your father if you don't know his name?"

Maznar grinned a wide, toothy smile. I suppressed a shudder as I was reminded of those gaping jaws reaching for me, ready to devour me at the first opportunity. "You forget, Ddraig Anzig, that I can see dreams. George often dreamed about the time he was given the great prize he so coveted: the egg of a dragon. He also remembered he was told by this dragon that the egg was found abandoned in the wilderness. The dragon didn't know where my egg came from, but given my magic I would suspect Nixa," she said, with a nod towards Isikian.

The healer exhaled slowly. "That would take a worry off my mind, if I could be sure you were a Nixan," he said.

"I still search dreams every night to find who my father is, but I've never been able to reach into the sleeping minds of those in Nixa," the ness said mournfully.

"You wouldn't. No magic can penetrate the boundaries of the lair. You would have to be within the lair to see into the dreams of those sleeping there," Isikian said. The healer looked around, his head drooping as he looked to curl up on the floor. "If you'll excuse me Ddraig Anzig, I must rest now."

"Of course, Isikian. We should all get some rest. Do you expect we should arrive in Nixa tomorrow?"

Isikian smiled, lifting his seemingly heavy head up towards me. "Nothing will stop us," he said, before bowing his head and backing away. He wearily crossed to the far side of the fire, his shadow dancing around over the uneven floor. His departure left me alone with Maznar.

"I may have told one untruth," the spectre said quietly. She pawed at the ground, her claws easily gouging the dirt that covered the cave floor, creating a trio of slashes. "There wasn't just one egg found by the dragon. There were three. Three eggs, Ddraig Anzig. Only one was taken by human hands. You would do well to remember that."

Before she gave me chance to question her, Maznar slunk away into the shadows, her black scales rendering her near invisible in the darkness; almost as well as Nataik's chameleonic scales. Only her glowing, piercing, red eyes gave away her chosen spot.

Three eggs? I had no idea what that meant, so I pushed it to the back of my mind in the hope that the spectre would explain further in the morning. I was tired of so many evenings throwing up mysteries and riddles. The dragon statue of the previous night still bothered me.

I turned away and picked out the sheen of Keita's red scales in the darkness. She was lying near Okazuni and the tips of their tails were almost touching. I felt a pang of jealousy strike my heart. She opened her eyes and looked at me, and for a moment I thought she was about to rouse herself to come over, but she just shifted her wings and curled into a more comfortable position.

With a strange sensation of light-headedness, I spiralled down onto the ground, alone by the fire. I squeezed my eyes shut and tried to ignore the sinister thought running through my mind that I was losing the one ness I had ever loved, all because of my inability to take action. The voice was wrong, I tried to convince myself. Keita knew I loved her. Didn't she? I thought back, trying to find some indication that Keita had given, some sign that told me that she loved me in return, but my mind drew a blank. She had always been there for me, but only ever as a friend.

Carlee had warned me of this. I had made a promise to the veteran that I would be open and honest with Keita, that I would tell her my feelings. But I never had. I had delayed and put it off, always coming up with some reason why she already knew, why she didn't need me to state it so explicitly. Why I could succumb to the coward within me.

I looked across at her with one eye, and I tensed up as I saw her tail slowly inch across to Okazuni's. The tips entwined as their breathing slowed as they fell into slumber. I shut my eye again and suppressed a pitiful whimper, trying to forget what I had just seen.

Keita was mine. She had to be.

I could not lose her.

I would not lose her.

But what would I do to keep her?

CHAPTER SIX

Azlak

I woke before the sun had risen, but I had not been the first. Okazuni and Keita were not in the vast cavern by the time I roused myself and left the cave to greet the first rays of light as they breached the horizon.

There was a strange hollowness in my chest I had never felt before, but instinctively I knew what it meant. A significant future had died here last night and it didn't take me long to realise what it was. The future I had once seen of Ddraig Anzig standing over a clutch of eggs had gone. Those had been his eggs, I knew now, and his mate must have been Keita. But she was gone, and Okazuni with her. I bowed my head in dismay. If the ddraig and Keita had been destined to become mates, then the ddraig's feelings for the ness must have been strong indeed. Now she would never be his. He had lost his future mate to a rival drake. I could only hope that because the relationship had all been in the future the effect on the ddraig wouldn't be so severe, but I knew in my heart that he would take the news badly.

Now I had something else in common with the ddraig. Neither of us had any prospects of a mate. Of course, the ddraig still had power and respect – there would be no shortage of nesses wishing to be his mate. However, there was no chance any Laxtal ness would give me a second glance, perhaps not even a first. None would agree to be my mate, not that any of them had taken my fancy. My desires lay elsewhere, but that did not matter. I would always be alone, with only the Laxtal drake endowed with magic for company, whenever he deigned to reveal himself to me, but I did not believe we were destined to be mates.

I sighed and looked out over the expansive forest that encroached on the mountain, a hundred feet below. In the far distance I thought I could see the glimmer of water. That had to be the river that marked the northern boundary of Nixa; there were no other bodies of water anywhere near here, if my memory was correct.

A dawn chorus started to erupt from the forest as the birds began to wake. Two dark forms flew out from the trees, ascending almost vertically to the sky. At first I thought it was two birds, until I saw them appear to entwine and start spiralling back down to the forest. I turned away, embarrassed at what I had seen. I covered my eyes with my wing, giving Keita and her new Nyrian mate some privacy.

Wings rustled as another dragon emerged from the cave. Timidly, I uncovered my eyes, but the sky was clear and devoid of any dragons. I glanced back to see who had joined me, and was a little surprised to see the dull brown scales of Carlee. The old ness was normally one of the last to rise. Of course, she didn't even acknowledge my presence as she stretched out in the sun, spreading her wings as she took in the morning warmth. I expected nothing else from her. I may have been successful in guiding Ddraig Anzig to retrieve the Axinstone, but I knew my standing was unlikely to rise within the clan.

I couldn't help but feel a little bitter at that. I had risked much, and I felt I had given a good account of myself throughout the ordeal. Only rarely had we been in any sort of danger I had not foreseen, and I thought I deserved some respect from my clan. Carlee though, was never going to give me that, but I hoped that Ddraig Anzig would be more forthcoming.

The two Nixans and Nataik soon joined us. The ness emerged from the cave looking ready to fly. Inilta carried the Axinstone with him, just as he had ever since we had reclaimed it. He had relinquished it just the once, and then only to his brother. The healer lay down not far from me and spread his wings out to catch the morning sun, while Inilta and Nataik spread out closer to the edge of the cliff.

Ddraig Anzig followed soon after, although he appeared confused and unsteady on his paws as he came out from the cave and approached us. His eyes were unfocused as he looked up towards the clear sky.

"Have you seen Keita?" the ddraig asked before taking a seat on the grass by my side, forcing Isikian to shift away.

"N-no," I stammered, not wanting to reveal what I had seen Keita doing. I had already been the bearer of too much bad news for the ddraig. I was not about to burden him with more.

Beyond the ddraig, Isikian frowned. "We shouldn't delay here. It won't be long before Ddraig Krateos is aware of our presence. It is not wise to keep him waiting," he said.

"I'm sure Keita will be back soon," I said, hoping that the ddraig wouldn't notice that Okazuni was also absent. I wanted to avoid having to tell the ddraig myself.

The missing couple weren't much longer. They returned just as Maznar was the last to emerge from the cavern. Okazuni was the first to land, with Keita taking to the ground just by his side. Her wing remained unfurled as she held it over the smaller Nyrian drake in a manner that almost dared someone to comment on it. I heard a sharp intake of breath from the ddraig as he glanced up to see them. His whole body convulsed in such a way that I feared the wound in his chest had somehow reopened.

With what looked like a gargantuan effort, the ddraig rose to his paws. "We're all here then," he said weakly, averting his eyes from Keita and Okazuni. "I think we're eager to leave." At his words, the small group gathered close. Slowly, the ddraig's head rose until he looked strong and confident again, but I could still see the shadow of agony in his eyes.

"We've been through so much together. We did the impossible and took the Axinstone from the humans. That challenge is over now, but another one is set to begin. I hope I can count on you all to stay and help," he said quietly, but with everyone gathered so close, we all heard every word.

In turn, every dragon pledged their support to Ddraig Anzig. His relieved smile briefly flashed a grimace when Okazuni and Keita spoke, but he quickly managed to hide the pain. "We're from different clans. That unity is what we need. If we're to win this war we must act as one. Dragons of every clan must fly in unison to defeat the humans. We have already shown dragonkind that is possible. Just one short flight and we can begin in earnest."

It was so different from Astar's roaring speeches, but I was no less inspired by his son's quieter approach. If there had been any doubts in Ddraig Anzig's ability to lead and inspire, it was quelled in that short speech. I knew he had the quality in him: the quality of his father.

We took to wing a short time later, with Inilta taking the place by Ddraig Anzig's wing. Okazuni and Keita flew together a little way from the main group. As normal, I flew at the rear along with Maznar, but this time Isikian joined us. I had expected the healer to stay near the front, guiding the ddraig on the quickest route to the Nixan lair, but that job seemed to have fallen to Inilta.

"My offer of training you to control your magic is still valid. If we are given the time, I will spend as long as you need to help you. The same applies to you too, Maznar," Isikian said.

The spectre scoffed, but I was grateful that Isikian hadn't forgotten his promise, made what felt like so long ago. "Will I get to see others with the same magic?" I asked. I had never actually spoken with another seer. They rarely left Nixa, and I had never been to the clan of magic's lair. It would be interesting to know how the other seers controlled their magic, and if we had shared any visions of the future.

"I'm sure that can be arranged," the healer said, baring his teeth in amusement.

"I just want to spend one night there. So long as I learn who my father is, I'll be content," Maznar growled.

"You'll want to spend more than one once you get there," Isikian replied, seemingly unperturbed by Maznar's apparent dismissal of his clan's home. "If you learn who your father is surely you'll want to remain with him?"

Maznar growled again. "He abandoned me when I was just an egg. Why would I want to stay?"

"Then stay for the wonders of the lair. You are a Nixan, Maznar. I'm sure my clan will forget your history with the humans if you want to be part of dragonkind," the healer said. "I won't waste words trying to explain what Nixa is like, because it is utterly beautiful, but, at the same time, indescribable. Only a Nixan can truly appreciate that. Dragons from other clans experience the lair in different, lesser ways."

The spectre stayed silent, but whether ignoring Isikian or mulling over what he had said, I was not sure.

"What do you expect me to see?" I asked Isikian.

The healer hesitated and dropped lower in the air. "I don't know. You have magic, but I don't know if you'll see the lair as a Nixan, or as a Laxtal. I suppose we'll just have to find out," he said uncertainly.

I was suddenly nervous. What if I did see the lair as a Nixan does? Would that mean anything? Would Isikian and the rest of his clan see that as proof that I wasn't a Laxtal dragon after all? I wished I hadn't brought it up with the healer. It would have been easier on my mind if I didn't have to worry about what I would see.

I fell back from the healer and Maznar as we flew south, following the line of the mountains on the edge of the great forest, flying ever closer to Nixa. There was no vision to confirm it, but I had a feeling something momentous was about to happen, something more than the return of the Axinstone. I tried to cast my mind out to See it, but nothing happened. It remained just an ominous expectation.

We crossed over into Nixa just before noon. The boundary was marked by a raging waterfall gushing out, and down the side of a mountain. The border then followed the river until it reached a small lake about a hundred miles to the east, where Nixa bordered Clan Reneza. The river hadn't always followed its current course. It had snaked through the plains some way further to the south. Many years ago, Nixan dragons had changed its course to mark their boundaries and leave a lasting reminder of the great power at their disposal.

Just a few minutes after crossing the border into Nixa, Ddraig Anzig sent Nataik away. The Xigax ness quickly disappeared into the blue sky as she flew off to the south as we started to angle away from the mountains. As I followed where she had gone, I saw what must have worried the ddraig. Several wisps of smoke rose from near the mountains, though what was causing it was hidden behind the foothills. It didn't look like a natural blaze, which although rare in these parts at this time of year, could have been started by the lightning storms of the last few nights.

We eased to a slightly slower pace while we waited for Nataik to return to us, much to the consternation of the two Nixans, who just wanted to keep flying on as quickly as possible. Our caution was well rewarded, as she returned just a few minutes later with one breathless word. "Humans."

Immediately, the ddraig led us lower to the ground where we would be harder to spot from the foothills. I felt a familiar fear grip my chest as we descended. I had hoped we'd left the humans behind us, at least for a while. We needed the chance to return the Axinstone so Nixa could develop a strategy to defend our land. I knew this couldn't be a group of humans sent out to reclaim the Axinstone. We were able to cross the mountains in places the humans couldn't reach, so they couldn't have got to Nixa quicker than us. These humans had been here a while, deep in draconic territory. It worried me. No doubt it concerned the ddraig greatly too.

I didn't hear what Nataik had to say to Ddraig Anzig about the humans, but they seemed to be far enough away that they didn't pose us any immediate threat. I noticed the ddraig kept on glancing back though, in the direction of the mountains. He was definitely unnerved by their presence. Even when the wisps of smoke had faded into the horizon the tension remained.

After another few hours of nervous flight, Isikian moved up to the head of the group to fly at the ddraig's wing, with Inilta flying just behind. It was a Nixan guard of honour for the Laxtal ddraig as we finally approached the Nixan lair.

A tingle ran through my spine as a dark dot in the distance started to come nearer. A Nixan messenger was coming to meet us. I was not surprised to see the red scales of Haeraig Zeena. Nixa would want to honour us on our return.

Haeraig Zeena flew straight up to Ddraig Anzig and shared a few quiet, but excited, words with each other, before the Nixan haeraig inspected the Axinstone, which Inilta still fiercely clung to. Even now, Inilta did not surrender his hold on the precious stone, and I doubted he would, except to give it to Ddraig Krateos and none other.

Under Haeraig Zeena's guidance, we flew right for the Nixan lair. From the air, all that I saw of the lair was five low hills in the shape of a dragon's paw. On the top of each hill I could see a rocky shard that formed the paw's claws. It was to the nearest of these that the haeraig led us.

She waited for everyone to land near her on the summit of the hill, then bowed her head towards the ddraig. She lifted her head to address us all. "You're to stay close to myself, Isikian, or Inilta," she warned. "Our lair is a dangerous place for those not of our clan. Stay close to us. Don't wander and you'll be safe. Stray from the path and we may never find you again."

Okazuni hissed under his breath, but otherwise there were no objections to Haeraig Zeena's grave words. We had all heard stories of the dangers of Clan Nixa and their lair. It was heavily defended by magic and was designed to prevent any enemy force from ever gaining access to the inner caves. Even Carlee, a veteran of many wars and the vanquisher of countless lairs, showed a flash of fear at Haeraig Zeena's warning.

The Nixan haeraig waited for a few more moments to let the true importance of her words sink in, before placing a paw on the shard of rock wedged into the hill. In an instant it shone with a crimson glow and started to spin, digging down and creating a large passageway as it descended. It looked just about large enough to fit Carlee, the largest in our group.

Once again, Okazuni stepped back, disconcerted. He hissed as he took a few steps away from the new passageway. He wasn't the only one. Keita also seemed troubled, and she squawked in fright as Haeraig Zeena led the way into the glowing tunnel. Ddraig Anzig followed right behind. If he was afraid, then he didn't show it as he kept close to Haeraig Zeena's tail. Keita, Carlee, and Nataik were coaxed in by Inilta, before Isikian followed Okazuni in, leaving me alone with Maznar.

The spectre smiled at me. "You see what I see," she said knowingly, before diving in after the others.

"What do you mean? What do you see?" I asked, scrambling in after her before Isikian got too far ahead, but the ness just chuckled and didn't answer.

The tunnel sloped heavily downhill and was mostly made of dirt, though ribs of stone supported it every few feet. It was perfectly straight, with not a kink or deviation down its entire length. The walls shone with a consistent red glow that neither wavered nor flickered, providing a perfect light to see by.

Magic assaulted me. There was so much power, just out of reach. It almost felt as though I could tap into the latent magic embedded in the very walls of the lair, if only I could touch it. I had to resist stopping and reaching out with my paw, knowing that the magic wasn't anywhere close physically, but was pushing only against my mind.

After about one hundred feet, the tunnel broadened out into a small chamber just large enough for our group of dragons to fit comfortably. There was only one exit to the chamber, other than the one we had just emerged from. Haeraig Zeena waited for me to come into the chamber, before quickly counting to make sure everyone was still present. Once she was satisfied no one had been left behind, she plunged onwards into the opposite tunnel, again drawing a squeal of fear from Keita. As before, Ddraig Anzig followed the haeraig without hesitation, and the others all fell into line once more.

This second passage was much the same as the first, but it ran flat. It was also much shorter, coming to an end after half the distance when it flared out into a massive cavern, far larger than anything I had ever seen before, even the pitch black cave with the mysterious statue.

The Nixan lair stretched almost as far as the eye could see in every direction, with the white walls of the far side a seemingly impossible distance away. The far distant floor, speckled with many different colours, looked to be at least a mile distant from the rocky ledge we found ourselves on, the ceiling almost as far too. I could just make out several large holes glowing with light, that punctured the cavern roof – whether natural or magical I could not tell. This lit the entire...

The great ceiling erupted in an explosion of flame and smoke, showering the lair with jagged shards of rock. Many dragons died instantly, with many more dragged down to the floor under the weight of the falling stone.

Sunlight streamed down from the gaping hole and shadows swarmed in from the light.

...lair with a steady white glow.

I shuddered. Never before had Nixa fallen to an invading force. Not once had an enemy even laid a single paw inside the lair. What manner of sorcery will be able to destroy the ceiling like that? It would have to be an immense power to be able to overcome the magic of Clan Nixa that held the lair secure.

Maznar bared all her teeth as she grinned at me. "You'll See all sorts of things in here you were never able to See before," she said. She raised a single claw and pressed it against my wing. I didn't move, for fear of tearing the vulnerable membrane against her claw. Her meaning was obvious. "Make sure you tell me all the good ones."

The spectre looked around the empty ledge, then down into the great cavern, where the others had already started descending to the floor. In the aftermath of my vision, I hadn't noticed them leaving. "I think we'd better catch up," she said, removing her talon from my delicate wing membrane. A quick glance revealed my wing was not damaged. This time.

I didn't need to be reminded of Haeraig Zeena's warnings of staying close to the Nixans, and I dove after them, quickly catching up with Maznar right at my tail. A low rumble was emanating from the floor, and it wasn't until we were about halfway down that I recognised it for what it was. It was the welcoming roar of thousands of Nixan dragons. The floor was packed with what must surely have been every single dragon in the clan, turning it into a writhing mass of colour. To one end was a raised podium, upon which stood Ddraig Krateos, flanked by four other dragons.

Ddraig Krateos reared up onto his hind legs, spreading his wings for balance, and roared to his clan. In an instant, they were silent.

Haeraig Zeena landed on the podium first, and she bowed her head to her father. One of the dragons standing beside Ddraig Krateos moved aside and allowed Haeraig Zeena to take his place.

Ddraig Anzig was the next to pay his respects to the Nixan ddraig, though he did so with barely any movement of his head. The two drakes were equals; the leaders of two of the ruling clans. The only dragon they would contemplate deferring to would be Ddraig Tsona.

One by one, the rest of us submitted to Ddraig Krateos. Maznar had hesitated when she looked at the intimidating eyes of the Nixan, but once she bowed her head towards Ddraig Krateos, he turned to Ddraig Anzig.

"Have you what you set out to retrieve?" he rumbled. I knew he would already have seen the Axinstone, clutched in Inilta's paws, but the ddraig wanted to make a show of it in front of his whole clan.

Ddraig Anzig nodded once. "Inilta, if you would," he said.

Inilta needed no further encouragement. He moved forward and placed the Axinstone on the ground next to Ddraig Krateos's paws. There was absolute silence. It seemed every dragon in the great hall had stopped breathing. The silence was deafening, shattered as Inilta spoke. "I present you the Axinstone, Ddraig Krateos. Taken from the human George Symons and returned to its rightful place."

Suddenly, there was movement. The Axinstone began to rise, seemingly of its own accord until it hovered in front of Ddraig Krateos's muzzle.

"You have done well, child of Nixa," the ddraig said to Inilta, before meeting the gaze of all of us individually. No one but Ddraig Anzig could meet his eyes for more than a second. Each head in turn bowed in deference. "All of you have done this clan a great service, and for that we will always be beholden to each of you."

The Axinstone rose higher still, until it was visible to every dragon in the chamber. The fiery head on its surface shone brightly as it fuelled the magic of thousands of dragons, bathing all present in a red light. A low hum touched my ears, eerily similar to the machines in the human laboratory where they had been experimenting on the precious artefact.

I couldn't help but gaze in wonder as the Axinstone continued to rise and glow ever brighter, liquid magic dripping from the surface like searing lava.

"Our power has returned!" Ddraig Krateos had to raise his voice over the hum. "The world shall tremble at the onslaught of our magic, restored to its full strength once more. All those who cross Clan Nixa shall be crushed by our fire, by our minds, by everything our clan can muster." His great voice boomed ever louder, until he was shouting, his words bouncing off the cavern walls and ceiling. So loud were they, I had to resist covering my ears with my wings. "The humans who stole the Axinstone, who threaten our land and that of our neighbours shall be the first to feel our wrath. Children of Nixa, feel the power returning to you. Our enemies shall burn and we shall prosper."

Ddraig Krateos's chest heaved as he tried to draw breath. His wing bones were shattered, the membrane torn and tattered. He struggled and ground his teeth in pain and anguish as he tried to drag himself forward with broken legs. The shadow of a human streaked across the ground towards him. The ddraig was helpless to see it dancing and bouncing over the uneven surface. He knew what this meant. He knew to whom this dancing black shape belonged to. The dragon looked up with fear in his eyes as it towered over him.

"Clan Nixa, this is our time!" The ddraig's climactic conclusion and the ensuing, almost deafening roar of his whole clan cleared my vision. I shuddered. I had never Seen Ddraig Krateos in a vision before, and it was unusual that the first time he had appeared had been his death. That didn't normally happen. I shivered and tried to hide my discomfort from the thousands of dragons, though I doubted I was the focus of anyone's attention. Most eyes were still on their ddraig; the remainder upon the Axinstone as it circled above our heads.

Ddraig Anzig had been speaking, but my ears still rang with the subsiding roars and shrieks of joy to hear what he had said. I looked across at the two ddraigs. They were almost the exact same height, with the Nixan being slightly taller. I had Seen them both die at the hands of humans now. Dragonkind needed a strong Laxtal and Nixa. The damage done losing both ddraigs in this war could be massive. I didn't know what I could do, but I knew I would need to do everything within my power to save their lives.

The collective noise in the cavern diminished enough for the spectacle to continue for some time, with Ddraig Anzig speaking more of our adventures. Prompted by the Nixan ddraig, he told the assembled clan a little of what we had seen in human lands. He spoke of the experiments the humans were running with the Axinstone, though I noted with interest that he made no reference to Nightwings or Maznar. No explanation had been offered for the additional ness in our ranks, but no questions had been asked.

Finally the clan was dismissed, and Ddraig Krateos addressed Ddraig Anzig directly as the clan began to disperse. A few simply vanished from where they were standing, but most took the conventional route and took to wing, creating a thunderous applause of wingbeats. Isikian and Inilta took their leave and joined the mass exodus up into the higher reaches of the clan's lair.

"You have exceeded all expectations, Ddraig Anzig," the Nixan ddraig said. His head dipped almost imperceptibly. "By coming back with the Axinstone so soon you have given us a good chance to strike back at the humans before their defences are prepared."

"You honour me, Ddraig Krateos. We were just doing our duty," Ddraig Anzig replied.

"Come with me. Let us discuss matters further in private. We have a war to win, and you need to be brought up to date of all the latest developments this side of the mountains," the Nixan said, before he turned to the other Nixans who had remained by his side. "Zeena, take the others to the guest chambers so they can rest. Take them up to hunt if they wish it."

"What do you wish us to do, father?" one of the other dragons asked.

"Scout out this human army on our borders. Their presence unnerves me, especially as they have evaded our scryers. I want to know what they're doing there, and what their plans are," the ddraig rumbled. "They should never have been able to get so close."

Nataik took a tentative step forward, drawing the gaze of the Nixan ddraig. The ness dipped her head to the ground. "With respect, Ddraig Krateos, I know more about humans than any other dragon here. Allow me to scout out with your sons. I can interpret the enemy's movements more than they can. Again, I mean no disrespect to your clan nor kin."

Ddraig Krateos growled as he pondered over this before nodding his head once. "I agree. Nataik is it? If you feel you do not need rest, then yes, my sons will be glad to have you," he said. All it took was an almost imperceptible swing of the ddraig's head towards his sons for the request to be granted and so ordered.

"Stay close to us," one of Krateos's sons warned the Xigax ness as he unfurled his wings.

The four sons of Ddraig Krateos took to wing, closely followed by Nataik. The two ddraigs did not linger long either. Barely had the air settled before they took flight. I watched their progress as they spiralled ever upwards towards the far distant ceiling. It was such a long way, I imagined it would get quite tiring trying to get anywhere within the lair.

"Would you care to hunt this evening?" Haeraig Zeena asked of us.

Without Ddraig Anzig, we were devoid of a clearly defined leader, and no one answered the Nixan.

"I believe we'll be alright until morning, thank you." I surprised everyone, even myself, by speaking first. We had eaten in the forest on the other side of the mountains. I knew I could wait another day before hunting again; I imagined the others would feel the same. However, I was rather surprised that the others deferred to my response, as no one else spoke.

"Then I will escort you all to the guest chambers. I wouldn't recommend straying from them without a Nixan to guide you," Haeraig Zeena said. Her eyes lingered on me for a moment. "You'll have company in there. Perhaps you will be able to control the dragonet; he is from your clan after all. He's barely left me alone for the last few days."

A Laxtal dragon in Nixa? I wondered who that could be. Other than us, there was no reason for any Laxtals to be within the lair of the clan of magic. I doubted Ellian would have sent any dragons away from the clan in the absence of Ddraig Anzig. Something was amiss. I didn't need to see the flash of silver scales as Haeraig Zeena led us into the guest chambers to know that things were not going as they should. There should be absolutely no reason for Vinzent to be here. Ellian would not have sent him from her side if she was still in control of Clan Laxtal.

The dragonet didn't approach us while Haeraig Zeena remained. The Nixan reminded us once more of the dangers of the lair and how we needed to remain in the safety of the guest chambers. If we needed anything, there would be a guard stationed nearby.

Haeraig Zeena snarled at Vinzent, deep in the room's shadows before she moved to leave. She paused in the entrance and exchanged a few words with the guard stationed outside, her voice raised for all our benefit. "The dragonet doesn't leave, Kaz. The others may do so if they wish, but not that one," she said disdainfully, with a flick of her head towards the corner. Then she was gone, a fluttering of wings fast fading into the great chamber.

Only then did Vinzent emerge from the shadows, and he slinked towards Carlee. His belly almost touched the ground as he moved forward. He was met by a vicious snarl from the ness. "I think I have made a massive mistake," the dragonet said, staring down at the veteran ness's paws.

"Why are you here?" Carlee growled. There was a hostility in both her voice and eyes that was usually reserved for me.

Vinzent whimpered as he started to answer.

"I allowed Ellian to leave. She went back to Laxtal alone when I should have remained at her side and returned with her," the dragonet said.

"Why was she even here?" Carlee snarled. She approached the cowering Vinzent, who was not the self-assured dragon I remembered from before we left. This was a dragon stripped of all self-confidence.

A shadow of his former self. A shadow from the shadows. He reminded me of myself.

I couldn't make out any of what Vinzent had to say for himself, such was the quietness of his voice, but he kept on repeating one name. Ddraig Tsona. What did the Xital ddraig have to do with this? I had Seen nothing to place him in Laxtal at this time, and now I was sheltered in Nixa, I was not sure whether I would be able to See anything outside of the lair.

Whatever it was that had involved Ddraig Tsona, I was not to know yet as Carlee dragged Vinzent away into another chamber to speak with him privately. She warned us all with a glare not to follow.

Keita glanced at Okazuni for a moment, before turning her attention towards me. Her usual disdain towards was absent, and to my surprise she approached me. "You've been looking at me strangely all day," she said quietly.

I tried to avoid her gaze. I didn't want her to know what I had seen that morning. It had been a private matter between her and Okazuni. I didn't want it to look like I had been prying. It was bad enough that I knew secrets of her future without knowing the secrets of her present too. I sighed. I needed to say something.

"There was a future. One that is no longer possible. He would have been your mate." I whispered.

"Who?" Keita said, with a sharp glance back towards Okazuni, but the Nyrian wasn't paying any attention to our conversation. No one was. Maznar's focus was on the distant, muffled echoes of Carlee's tirade upon Vinzent.

"Ddraig Anzig," I said.

Keita shook her head fiercely. "No. You're wrong. He has never loved me like that. He's only ever been a friend and nothing more. I learned that and got over it a long time ago."

"No, Keita. He has loved you for years. I had a vision... You were to have two eggs with him. But that future is dead now," I said. I didn't know why I was telling Keita this. I didn't want her to suffer for the choice she had made. Okazuni was her mate now, and that had been her decision.

If Keita felt any grief over my revelations, she hid it well. "If he really felt that way, he should have told me. I was not prepared to wait for something when I couldn't be sure it was ever going to happen. It's his own fault," she said bluntly, no emotion on her face or in her posture. I had no response, remaining silent as she returned to Okazuni and lay down by his side. The Nyrian spread his wing over his mate's body, and they started quietly talking to each other.

There was a fireplace in the cavern, but it was unlit and I couldn't see any fuel for it. For now, we didn't need any fires, as the walls emanated sufficient warmth, providing a comfortable heat to lie in. Maznar turned away from the antechamber where Carlee had taken Vinzent, and for a moment it looked like she had something to say before turning again, settling and closing her eyes instead. She didn't look tired, but she seemed desperate to sleep, probably longing to peer into the dreams of the Nixan dragons around her. There were still several hours until the clan started to sleep. The spectre would have to wait a little longer.

Unlike the others, I could not settle. I was too restless to think about lying down and doing nothing. I put my nose outside the chamber to have another look around. There was only a small ledge separating the guest chambers with the sheer drop of the great cavern below. We had flown up so high from the floor, but the ceiling still stretched upwards a great distance still. Lying on the ledge, looking rather bored, was a blue-scaled drake. This must have been the dragon assigned to guard us, who I had heard Haeraig Zeena address as Kaz. He turned as I walked out to join him, and when he didn't demand I go back inside, I settled down by his side.

"What did the dragonet have to say for himself?" Kaz said in a voice laced with venom.

"I don't know. Carlee is speaking to him now. Why is he here?" I asked.

"He arrived a week ago with Ellian and my brother, who had been helping out with the nomads on the border of Laxtal," Kaz explained, but that answer only raised further questions. Why would Ellian have been with the nomads, when Ddraig Anzig had tasked her with leading Laxtal in his and Astar's stead?

"Ever since then the dragonet has been annoying Haeraig Zeena, trying to convince her to raise an army and fly on Laxtal. He believes Ddraig Tsona is a traitor and is trying to fracture the clans by taking command of Clan Laxtal. Ddraig Krateos believes Ddraig Tsona is trying to strengthen dragonkind by ensuring all the ruling clans have an experienced dragon leading them," the Nixan continued. I hissed softly as I pondered this, but there were still two questions I had to ask.

"Ddraig Tsona is controlling Clan Laxtal? Why? And where is Ellian now?"

"I don't know the answer that. You'd have to ask Airil – my brother – that one. He spent a lot of time with the nomads. He was there when Ellian and Vinzent joined them. As for where she is, I would imagine she should be in Laxtal by now. She left four days ago. I understand she had information that could be important to the war, something that could help Ddraig Tsona and the other ruling clans fight back against the humans."

"Could it not have waited for us to return?" I asked. It was strange that Ellian would fly out alone, only for her cousin to return with the Axinstone so soon after her departure.

Kaz shook his head. "No one expected you to return so quickly. We were aware a dragon had reclaimed the Axinstone, but we thought it would be another few days for you to cross the mountains at least. I assume Ddraig Krateos and Ellian thought the information too important to delay until the Axinstone's return," he said.

"Someone should fly after her," I said. I couldn't help but feel a little uncertain about the ness flying back to Laxtal on her own, but until I knew all the circumstances regarding her departure, I couldn't be sure of myself. I just had a feeling I was missing something I had already Seen, but not understood at the time.

"She'll have made it to Laxtal by now. There's nothing we can do to call her back," Kaz said.

I pawed at the rock and looked up. There was a lot of activity as dragons flew back and forth across the chamber. Most of them were little more than specks of colour glinting off the light that poured in from the ceiling. "Would I be able to see your brother? There's something not right about this."

"Ddraig Krateos wouldn't have sent Ellian alone if he thought something was wrong," Kaz said, but all the same he unfurled his wings and prepared to fly. "I can trust you to stay here, right? Just sit here and don't let the dragonet out, or Haeraig Zeena will never forgive either of us."

As the Nixan flew off I glanced back into the chamber. I could not see or hear any stirrings from inside, so I returned my attention on the great chamber, watching the myriad of movement going on above and below me. I couldn't explain it to myself why I was so desperate to learn the answers to what was going on around me. I had no business in knowing why Ellian hadn't been in Laxtal, but I felt like I was missing some crucial piece of information. As I waited for Kaz to return with his brother, I tried to remember every vision of Ddraig Tsona I had Seen recently, but the only one I could recall was of him dying at the hand of a human.

There had to be something I was missing. It was moments like this I longed for better control over my magic. I needed to be able to control what I Saw. Had Vinzent been right to doubt Ddraig Tsona? It seemed absurd that the dragonet would be correct when the vastly more experienced and knowledgeable Ddraig Krateos believed he knew otherwise, but... something nagged at my mind. What had I Seen that I had overlooked?

Thin columns of powdered rock continued to tumble as hundreds of dragons plummeted to the ground. Vicious snarls, shrieks, and cries echoed down from above in response to the crack of human gunfire.

One voice boomed through the chaos. "The lair is taken! Fly, Children of Nixa! Retreat to Kxisila," cried the voice of Ddraig Krateos. He then screamed in anguish and pain. His voice silenced. A shattered body fell to the black depths.

The destruction of Clan Nixa was close at hand.

I trembled in fear. If Nixa fell, dragonkind would crumble soon thereafter. Quickly. Completely.

CHAPTER SEVEN

Anzig

I hissed and turned away from Ddraig Krateos.

The Axinstone was in its rightful place in the ddraig's chambers in the highest point of the lair. A statue of a serpentine ness; nothing like the terrifying statue we had seen in the cave, sat in an alcove above Ddraig Krateos's head. She held the precious stone in her mouth. The Nixan ddraig had finished informing me of the happenings in Laxtal, and I was worried by Ddraig Tsona's presence there. I did not doubt Ddraig Krateos's trust in the Xital, but I was concerned that he would not relinquish control of the clan once I returned.

"Ddraig Tsona is honourable. He will not keep you from your rightful place as the leader of Clan Laxtal. He will allow your clan to hold the wylax," Ddraig Krateos said, seeming to understand what my concerns were. "I told Ellian the same thing. Ddraig Tsona has nothing to gain from betraying dragonkind. There is a traitor within Xital, but it is not from the head of the clan. That we have not received word from your cousin does not confirm Ddraig Tsona's guilt."

"I thank you for your words, ddraig, but I cannot tolerate a Xital leading Clan Laxtal." I couldn't recall such a situation ever happening before in times of peace between two clans.

"I know. I do not approve of the situation either," the Nixan ddraig replied. *"But it's the best option we have right now."*

"I trusted Ellian to rule the clan. I know she is a capable leader. There was no better option to rule Laxtal than her," I countered. I knew I was bordering on disrespect, but I was annoyed by the Nixan's comment, laying doubt at my choice of Ellian to rule in my stead.

Ddraig Krateos shifted in discomfort. "I do not doubt her as a future leader. She lacks the experience now, which is required to rule in times of war. She will make a fine haeraig if you choose to reinstate her into the clan and if she can win back the trust of the Laxtal dragons."

I growled, somewhat appeased for the moment. We had more important things to discuss than petty squabbles over the competence of my cousin. Ddraig Krateos had sent out his four sons and Nataik to scout the human army we had seen on our way into Nixa. They were a long way north of the Gota-Sxinix and the western border of Laxtal where most human activity had been over the past months. Though the Nixan didn't fear an attack on the lair, he was worried that they might restrict movement of dragons in the area, picking off those who travelled the wildlands, and posing a constant threat towards the nomads.

Above the head of the Nixan, the Axinstone pulsed with crimson light several times, the molten dragon's head upon its surface constantly in flux. I could have sworn I heard some whispering emanating from the stone, but Ddraig Krateos didn't react and there was no one else in his chambers with us. One word repeated itself over and over again, different to what I had heard from the statue in the darkness. It sounded like a name, but not one I was familiar with. *"Bri'An,"* the stone was saying. *"Bri'An."*

"So, Ddraig Anzig," the Nixan said, pulling my focus away from the Axinstone. Even still, my eyes drifted towards the fiery insignia on the precious artefact. "We are to discuss the terms of this alliance, as well as to plan what we can do to rid our lands of this human army. I understand you must be tired from your flight, but I would be interested to know your thoughts on the matter. Did you learn anything of their behaviour while you were in their lands?"

It took everything I had not to bow my head. The Nixan ddraig oozed power and strength, and every instinct within me wanted to submit to him, but that would be foolish. I was his equal now. We were both ddraigs of ruling clans. The only dragon I needed to bow to was Ddraig Tsona.

"I didn't hear much from the humans," I said slowly, trying to cover my immediate silence by furrowing my brow in thought. I scratched my claws against the floor and looked away from the Nixan, looking up to the alcove above his head. I realised that the statue was the twin of one in my father's chambers – in my chambers, as they were now. "I did hear that they moved into our territory to claim new land for their lairs, for their cities, but I find this difficult to believe."

"Last time I crossed the Sxinix, I saw they had a lot of unused land," the Nixan mused. The tips of his wings fluttered as he settled into his nest of rugs and blankets. "I agree with you. More territory for their lairs should not be high on their needs. There must be some other purpose to this invasion. Unless we know this reason, turning them away without violence is a remote chance."

"But they still have the advantage should it come to violence," I said, but immediately wondered if I should have admitted such a thing. As ddraig, I needed to be on my guard when it came to showing weakness. I did not want to look vulnerable to my Nixan counterpart.

To my relief, Ddraig Krateos inclined his head. "We must rely on Clan Laxtal's efforts for physical strength so that we can match the humans. Clan Nixa has many strengths, but claw and tooth combat is not one of them," he said, before pausing. His smouldering eyes held my gaze. "I understand Laxtal has recently suffered some heavy losses. Your cousin informed me you lost many dragons in the attack that claimed your father's life. Even still, any hope of survival requires you to muster a strong army. You may need to rely on your neighbouring clans for reinforcements, but I doubt they will listen until you have been formally declared as the ddraig of Laxtal. It must be imperative that you hold the wylax as soon as you return home."

"We have good relations with our neighbours. They will answer our call, whether or not the wylax has been held," I said, trying to inject confidence into my voice. If I were to be the equal of the Nixan ddraig, then I needed to sound it. This was no place for a weak and scared dragon. "But I must ask, Ddraig, what would we do with this army? We cannot defeat the humans with tooth and claw alone."

"You are right, of course," Ddraig Krateos replied. He toyed with the corner of a rug between two claws. "It will take more than strength to win, hence why you have us. But loathe as I am to admit it, even the power of the Axinstone is not enough to defeat these humans. We need both. Magic and might."

"Laxtal will uphold our end of the agreement, you have my word," I said. I curled the tip of my tail. The Nixan had not promised much, still giving just vague hints and suggestions at what he might do with the might of his clan. My breath caught in my throat. Never before had I pressed a ddraig to speak more than they wished, even to one of the minor clans. As a haeraig, I had never felt comfortable with that authority, but those times had changed. I struggled not to stutter. "What does Nixa intend to do with its magic to help us defeat these humans?"

Ddraig Krateos did not answer at first. His eyes glinted in my direction, but he didn't fully meet my gaze in an official challenge. He stretched out his forelegs, splaying his paws. I half expected him to yawn.

Just when I thought he was going to ignore my question entirely, Ddraig Krateos finally spoke. "Your father would have asked the same question," he said slowly. "Clan Nixa will shape the battlefield with our magic, literally and figuratively. We will guide the humans to where your army can best face them, and our magic can then harass and kill just as effectively as tooth and claw. We just can't do it without the protection of Laxtal. We would be vulnerable to their weapons otherwise."

"We're to be your protectors?" I asked, tilting my head to the side. My eyes narrowed as I looked back up to the silver statue, a whisper at the back of my mind catching my attention for a moment.

"There is no shame in being a shield when you give the sword a chance to strike, should you wish to use a human analogy," Ddraig Krateos replied. "There are many valleys in Laxtal and Nixa that would make for a good site to ambush. A place where the humans will think they have the advantage, but we can turn that against them. Let Nixa scout out an appropriate site for our magic, while you gather the army that will win this war."

Though something prickled at the back of my neck, I was glad that a more experienced drake was able to take command of the situation. I had found myself unable to devise a plan of action in the attempt to steal the Axinstone. Yes, we were successful in the end, but it was not due to any great display of leadership on my part. In the Nixan ddraig, I could see a dragon who believed every choice he made. In many ways, he was similar to my father, but the Nixan's strength came from a different source. He dominated through the force of his mind and his magic, whereas my father had been an imposing figure of tooth, claw, and muscle. I knew I could never command the same respect as my father through physical presence alone. I needed to develop my mind like Ddraig Krateos had done, to outwit and outsmart opponents without a situation ever becoming physical.

"But will that be enough?" Ddraig Krateos said quietly.

"It won't be easy, but I think it could work," I replied. There wasn't much else we could do.

Ddraig Krateos looked a little startled, but he quickly recovered his composure. "We would need you to act fast in Laxtal. You will need to work quickly to generate enough support in the surrounding clans."

"I can leave tomorrow if I must," I said. I had hoped for a little time to rest first, but I understood the necessity of acting urgently. Hopefully I would have time to rest my wings in Laxtal.

"I think that would be for the best," Ddraig Krateos agreed. The Nixan then surprised me by bowing his head in an obvious display of respect. "You have done great service to my clan. You and your kin are always welcome within this lair. You may not be of our clan, but you are certainly a child of Nixa. Send us an envoy once you have stood for the wylax, and then we shall truly fly together as ddraigs of equal strength."

Another flash of ruby light burst out from the Axinstone, followed by another tirade of whispers. *"Bri'An, Bri'An."* Again, Ddraig Krateos was quite unmoved by the outburst. I twitched my head, trying to clear my mind without alerting the Nixan to anything amiss.

"The honour is mine Ddraig Krateos," I said, ensuring I bowed my head lower than my ally had. "I hope the two of us can work together when the war has passed." I had already done something my father had never achieved as ddraig of Laxtal. There had never been a close bond between Laxtal and Nixa, just a cordial and mutual respect and nothing more. I had no illusions that one great accomplishment would not be enough to transform me into a great leader, but it was a lift to my confidence to know I had achieved something that my legendary father had not.

I departed Ddraig Krateos's chambers soon after. The Nixan had placed his paw on an alcove in the wall before I passed through the archway that divided his personal chambers with the small antechamber beyond. He didn't explain why he felt the need for such an action, but nor did I question it. I had noticed him perform the same motion as we had entered his chambers too.

Haeraig Zeena was awaiting my return, ready to take me back to rejoin the rest of my group, down in the bowels of the lair. She didn't seem overly interested in what conversation had taken place between me and her father, and if anything looked a little annoyed by something.

"...show... Laxtal dragonet... he wants to... mate..." I heard her mutter.

I didn't know if those words were meant for me to hear, but I felt obliged to ask her, "Is everything alright?"

"What? Oh. Yes, of course," she said. She tilted her head as she looked across at me, respectfully avoiding my eyes as my rank required. Then she exhaled heavily and scratched at the rock beneath her paws. "Ellian's companion seemed to have gotten it into his head that I want to be his mate. I've spent much of the last few days trying to rid myself of his attention," she said, grimacing with distaste.

"Vinzent?" I asked in shock. I had thought the youngster was utterly devoted to my cousin and wouldn't consider anyone else to be his mate. I couldn't believe I could have been so wrong. But then, I had already received one harsh reminder that I knew nothing of the devotions of other dragons. The one ness...

I stopped myself. Purge the memory. I knew it wouldn't do to dwell on that.

Haeraig Zeena nodded her head mournfully. *"I should never have shown him friendship."*

I had to blink and shake my head. I was certain the Nixan's mouth had not moved when she had spoken. Was she a telepath and able to put thoughts into my head?

"What is your magic?" I asked the haeraig.

Haeraig Zeena responded by lifting an emerald from the rock behind her without touching it. "I can move things with my mind, just like my father," she replied. *I must have been mistaken. "Why's that I wonder?"*

"I thought I saw… that I heard… never mind," I said, shaking my head again.

"Are you alright, Ddraig Anzig?" the haeraig asked, tilting her head slightly to the side, and taking a hesitant step forward. With her concentration broken, so did the invisible thread to the emerald break, causing the forgotten stone to fall to the rug beneath her paws.

"I'm fine," I said, though in truth I felt I had been chilled to my very core by an unseen icy blast of frigid mountain air. I could still feel the warmth of the walls and especially the scorching heat of the Axinstone behind me, but neither warmed my body.

"He's not alright. I should get…"

"I'm fine," I said, firmer this time and cutting across Haeraig Zeena. This time she didn't question me, but I could see she was puzzled. "I think I just need to sleep."

Haeraig Zeena sucked in her breath as she thought over that. "If you're sure, Ddraig Anzig, I'll lead you down to the guest chambers. Kaz will be guarding you tonight. He's a healer, so if you feel unwell, please approach him," she said quickly.

I growled at the implication of weakness in needing a healer, but the haeraig didn't apologise. She silently took to wing, and I followed suit as she dived out of the antechamber and into the great cavern.

There were a lot of dragons flying through the cavern, though they took evading paths in respect of our ranks. I doubted few recognised who I was, having only seen me once from a distance, but they knew Haeraig Zeena and they knew to get out of her way. One dragon knocked into my tail as he flew past, but by the time I could react and turn to face him, he had already disappeared into the crowd.

That moment of hesitation almost caused me to lose Haeraig Zeena, but I chased and caught back up as she trimmed her wings and steepened her descent. The warnings of staying close to a Nixan lingered in my head. I focused solely on the haeraig so I wouldn't lose her again, keeping her just a few feet in front of me.

I glanced behind me for a moment and saw the green dragon keeping close to my tail. Before me was a clear descent now that we were out of the busier upper half of the lair. Down here was only really used for rare visitors and when the ddraig wanted to address the whole clan. I looked back again. He was still close behind, but I knew he was lying when he said he was feeling fine. His eyes were pale and glazed as he flew, as though his mind was far away. He was definitely more confident than he had been the last time we had met, at the Council of Xital, but something was certainly ailing him.

I flattened my flight as we approached the guest caverns, dreading getting close to the silver dragonet again. If he dared...

The ddraig shot right past me, not even adjusting his flight as he descended further and further.

"Ddraig Anzig?" I called after him, trimming my wings once more and chasing after him. He was getting close to the ground and still he didn't alter his wings. He was going to...

The ground came up so quickly. I pulled my wings up as hard as I could until every sinew and tendon felt like it was being torn out, but it was not enough. I hit the ground with a sickening crunch. I was conscious for long enough to register the dust in my mouth mingling with the blood, the agony, and then the humiliation before my mind went mercifully blank.

"He wasn't feeling well. He didn't admit it, but I could tell something was wrong."

The voice of a concerned ness returned me to consciousness. I recognised the voice, though it took a moment to place it as Haeraig Zeena. I was lying on a stone floor, but beyond that I knew nothing of my surroundings. I was aware of nothing beyond my closed eyelids, and I kept it that way in an attempt to sooth an ache at the back of my mind.

"I could find nothing wrong with him, other than the damage to his wings and legs," an unfamiliar voice said. "A few cuts and scrapes as well, but nothing else."

"I'm telling you Kaz, I looked back at him and his mind wasn't there. Something is troubling him," Haeraig Zeena said again.

"Did anyone else see him fall?"

"No, I don't think so."

I heard one of the two voices come closer but kept my eyes closed as I tried to piece together what had happened. I knew I had hit the ground hard, but every time I went over the sequence of events leading up to the impact I became lost in my tumbling, swirling thoughts. Something had happened between leaving Ddraig Krateos's chambers and the impact that escaped my recollection.

"I don't think we should tell anyone about it then," Kaz was saying. I could hear his paws scuffing against the floor and his tail dragging behind. He was quite close to me now. "I think he'll be grateful if this embarrassment wasn't made public."

"Of course," Haeraig Zeena replied.

A paw touched against my forehead. "He's awake," Kaz said.

I opened my eyes to look into those of a blue-scaled dragon. Kaz averted his gaze but moved no further away. "I've healed your wounds, Ddraig Anzig, but I don't know what caused you to fall. It was nothing physical," the healer said.

My paws were shaky as I pushed myself up to a sitting position. "I think I just... lost concentration," I said, my voice as uncertain as my paws. I tried to smile wryly at Haeraig Zeena, but it came out more as a pained grimace. "I think sleeping would be a good idea."

"Are you sure you can fly?" the haeraig said.

I wasn't convinced, but I flared my wings anyway, wincing at the slight pain that still lingered. It wasn't far we had to go, and I wasn't about to shame myself a second time. "I'll be fine," I said, knowing that once again the Nixan would not believe me. "The healing was a skilled one. You should feel proud of yourself, Kaz."

"It was... surprisingly easy," the Nixan healer admitted, dipping his head in acknowledgement of the praise. He scuffed his paw on the ground. "Perhaps we can help him up together, Haeraig."

I didn't know whether to snarl at Kaz for his insinuation that I was weak, or to thank him for his help. The healer seemed to know the position he had put me in, for his ducked his head in apology.

"After you, Ddraig Anzig," Haeraig Zeena said with a little reluctance.

I nervously took to wing, desperately trying to maintain my focus this time. The two Nixans stayed right below me, ready to block my fall if I were to drop from the air again. If anything, their presence made me more afraid of failing. I had never thought so hard about each individual wingbeat before. Flight was normally such a natural movement, but now it was laboured and clumsy as I fought to stay aloft.

After what felt like an age I was instructed to land on a small ledge on the side of the great cavern. I looked down to see how far we had come, shocked to realise it was barely a hundred feet.

"Kaz will be just out here if you need him," Haeraig Zeena said.

"I know," I said, bowing my head away from the Nixan. I didn't want her to be so concerned for me. It was setting a bad example for the strength of my clan.

Without another word, I walked unsteadily into the chamber to rejoin the rest of the group I had travelled with. At first, I thought everyone was asleep; Keita, Maznar, and Okazuni were all curled up and gently breathing. Keita and Okazuni were lying together, tails entwined and wings overlapping. I ignored that corner and turned away. Then I noticed Azlak and a second dragon. I had to double take and look back out to the ledge just to make sure Kaz was still out there, because the dragon Azlak was talking to was identical.

Azlak looked excited as he bowed his head towards me. "Airil here has been planning how we might start to train my magic," the seer said quietly, respectful for those already asleep.

"He is already quite proficient, given how little training he has had. I would have feared he could have lost his mind to the future," Airil said.

The seer glowed with the praise. *"Hopefully I'll get a few days to practice here."*

"We'll be leaving in the morning unfortunately. We don't have any time to delay," I said, much to the disappointment of the seer.

Airil took a tentative step forward. "If I may, Ddraig Anzig, I would like to ask permission to join you. Not only will I be able to help Azlak more in Laxtal, but I'm concerned for Ellian. If there is a traitor in Xital, they could already have some influence in Laxtal through Ddraig Tsona, even if the ddraig himself isn't aware of it," he said.

The decision wasn't mine to make. It was up to Ddraig Krateos whether or not he would allow one of his dragons to leave the lair, but I had been told Ellian had trusted and liked Airil. That was enough for me.

I gestured upwards with my wing, towards the distant chambers at the top of the lair. "You may come if your ddraig permits you."

Airil nodded. "I shall ask him in the morning. I imagine my brother will want to come too. He didn't like me leaving him behind last time."

I nodded, looking towards the shelf outside. I presumed that Kaz was Airil's brother, hence the similarities between the two. It would be good having the two Nixans with us, especially if Isikian and Inilta remained as I expected. They had been away from home for a while now. I didn't blame them if they wanted to stay. I wanted to be back at Laxtal and was looking forward to leaving in the morning.

Nataik still hadn't returned. I wondered if she too would be remaining behind in Nixa, providing the clan of magic some information on human behaviour as they tried to develop an effective strategy in countering their movements. Until the fighting actually began, she would be bigger asset to Nixa than to Laxtal. She had been a strong, reliable companion during our time on the other side of the mountains, and though I couldn't call her a friend, I would miss her company.

I left Airil and Azlak to their practice and lay alone in the middle of the room. I had a lot to think about, and that was even after trying to forget about my embarrassing crash. It had been a long time since I had lost control of my flight in that manner. I was grateful that only Kaz and Haeraig Zeena had seen it, and they had decided to keep it amongst themselves.

I settled down and tried to think over what still needed to be done, but I was distracted by another voice running through my mind. It was like someone was whispering in my ear, but the only ones talking were Airil and Azlak, and this voice belonged to neither of them.

I squeezed my eyes shut but the voice only got stronger. I could barely think as the voice dominated my thoughts. Before I realised what I was doing, I was on my paws and ready to approach Kaz, when the voice suddenly stopped. The silence was wonderful, and I collapsed back to the ground in relief, drawing a curious glance from Airil in the process.

"Twitchy as a ferret that one."

What was wrong with me?

Come the morning I had no time to think about the voices, and mercifully they had stayed away and not disturbed me. We had been summoned early to meet with Ddraig Krateos, as he wanted to see everyone who was making the journey to Laxtal. We had gathered in the entry to his private chambers, and with Haeraig Zeena present as well, it was a tight fit for so many dragons. Kaz and Airil had joined us also, hanging around near the back of the group as though they hoped their ddraig wouldn't notice or question their presence.

Maznar had been restless, and she had not stopped moving since landing in the antechamber. At times she had tried to push her way to the front, before a sharp glance from Ddraig Krateos had sent her scurrying away to the back again. I tried my best to ignore her, wrinkling my nose at the scent of humans that still lingered wherever she went. It took all my concentration to keep my thoughts my own. I couldn't allow any distractions.

Nataik hadn't joined us. She had briefly spoken to me earlier that morning, advising me that she wished to remain behind and help monitor the humans. We would miss her company, but I knew her skills were better needed here.

"I have already told you what needs to be done," Ddraig Krateos said, looking around at those gathered before him. He had spent a few minutes placing his paw on the head of every dragon, whispering something in their ear. He had not placed his paw on me, that would have been inappropriate to a fellow ddraig, but he had still spoken to me, quietly, so no one else could hear. He had told me I was a credit to my clan and my father's name. I had said nothing in return but felt my heart swell in pride. That was all I wanted, to know that I was acting honourably and giving a good representation of my clan, that I wasn't failing my father.

"All that's left for me to say now is good luck to you all. Fly strong and true. Our clans will lead the offensive against the human invaders, so I am sure we'll talk again soon. May the wind be strong at your backs."

Haeraig Zeena led us away after the ddraig had dismissed us, though Kaz and Airil remained behind with Maznar. I glanced back at the two Nixans, who after a few words with their ddraig, also took to wing and chased after us. Evidently Ddraig Krateos had allowed them to join us. Maznar lingered around the ddraig for a few more moments before she dived out of the antechamber without uttering a single word.

The stay in Nixa had been short; I had hoped for a longer rest in the clan of magic, but at the same time I was relieved to be flying home. It was less than a two day flight between the Nixan lair and Laxtal, though we would pass over the territory of Clan Pyrulus along the way. I wondered what sort of reaction I would receive. I had achieved the glory of reclaiming the Axinstone for Clan Nixa, but Laxtal was under Xital control for the first time in the clan's history, and this had come when I had been absent from my duties. There could well be some dragons that would resent that.

As the son of Ddraig Astar and the nominated haeraig, the position of ddraig should be mine by rights, but until the wylax secured that, I remained vulnerable. Being absent from the clan, and with Ddraig Tsona taking control from Ellian, I feared what I might find in Laxtal. Another dragon could already have stood for the wylax, making me a usurper and pretender to the heritage I had hatched into.

We made good progress that morning, leaving Haeraig Zeena behind just outside the lair entry. Airil and Carlee took up positions by my wings as we flew over the famed hunting grounds of Nixa. Our hosts had provided us with food before seeing Ddraig Krateos, but a few covetous eyes were cast down at the rich plains below. The grass was lush and green, even this late into the cooling season, and herds of grazing animals roamed in great numbers.

As the land rolled by beneath us, I started to feel nerves building. The might of my father had always protected me in Laxtal, but now that was gone. I would be judged solely on my actions from here on out. I had made a good start, but I would always need to prove myself further. My first act would be to convince Ddraig Tsona to relinquish control of the clan to me. He had already deposed Ellian for being too inexperienced, but she was not the true leader of the clan, and nor had she been the designated haeraig at the time. I had true claim to the clan's leadership. Ddraig Tsona could not justify remaining on as leader of Laxtal upon my return.

We rested for the night in an empty nomadic lair on the border between Nixa and Pyrulus. It was only a small cave, but it was the only one for quite some distance. There was evidence of dragons recently staying here too, as the wood storage had been quite depleted and the smell of smoke still lingered. I thought of Ellian, who had made the same journey a few days ahead of us. She would be unaware that we were so close behind, but she would be in Laxtal by now. I could only hope that Ddraig Tsona had received her with the respect she deserved.

Without Inilta or Nataik, we struggled to have a fire lit. Most of the nomadic lairs used human technology to light fires, and it took almost twenty minutes for Azlak to work out how to operate the small glass firelighter. Finally, flames burst into life, and we were able to lie down in comfort and prepare for the day ahead. Azlak and Carlee had both tried to comfort me and assure me that we would run into no problems, but I couldn't help but feel that it wouldn't be easy.

All day I had been picking up fragments of voices in my mind and I had struggled to maintain my focus and keep a level and consistent flight. I was terrified by it as I had realised what they were. I was listening to the unspoken thoughts in the minds of my companions. I had tried to hide myself away from the others, lest they discover this new secret. It was magic, I was sure. I looked across at Azlak – the only Laxtal with magic, the enigma Nixa had never been able to explain, and the omega of the clan. That would be my life too if this ever got out. No one could ever know that I could hear the hidden thoughts of those around me.

"Someone should tell the ddraig."

I lifted my head and looked around the small cave. Was that voice or thought? I couldn't even be sure who it was who had spoken – if indeed they had spoken at all. I put my head in my paws and suppressed an agonised whimper. This was not what I had wanted my return to Laxtal to be.

CHAPTER EIGHT

Azlak

Ddraig Anzig appeared to be highly stressed as we approached the Laxtal lair. We had passed from the lush plains that covered Nixa and Pyrulus and into the more barren Laxtal. We were just a couple of hours away now, and the ddraig's flight patterns were getting more erratic. Carlee flew by his side to try and calm him, but he kept shaking his head and trying to fly further away from the old veteran. I had never seen him so scared before.

I looked across at Maznar, who had been flying at the ddraig's side for most of the journey, but she had fallen back to fly with me as we made the approach to the lair. She had been quiet since leaving Nixa and had refused to tell me what she had uncovered in the dreams of the Nixan dragons. I could tell she had discovered something, but she coyly evaded the question anytime I asked, and I doubted I would learn anything she did not wish to reveal.

Keeping pace just behind Maznar, and at the back of the group, was Vinzent. The dragonet had not spoken since leaving Nixa, and he looked almost as afraid as the ddraig did at returning home.

Of all the dragons, the only ones who really looked excited to be arriving in Laxtal were the two Nixans, Airil and Kaz. They had been weaving through the group, trying to engage in conversation but generally finding their incessant chatter falling on deaf ears. No one was feeling talkative, and they had eventually given up trying to interact with the others around noon. They had promised me they would help train my magic once we got to Laxtal as I had left Nixa before Isikian had the opportunity to fulfil his promise. I looked forward to having some sort of control over my wayward magic.

The beacon fires did not light. We flew over several pyres, which seemed to have been abandoned by their keepers. The Nixans and Nyrian dragon cast envious eyes towards the outposts. The chemicals and powders that allowed the beacon fires to be so diverse were a closely guarded secret, held by our clan for generations.

Despite the lack of beacons, a scout soon came out to meet us. It was a dragon I didn't recognise. They didn't even appear to be a Laxtal, and I noted Ddraig Anzig's hastily hidden concern as the dragon approached us.

"Identify yourself," the scout barked as they came near. She was a Xital, clearly identified by the crown of horns on her head.

"I am ddraig of this clan. Who are you?" Ddraig Anzig replied firmly.

"Ddraig Tsona is ddraig of this clan. Identify yourself or we treat you as hostile. We have you surrounded," the scout said. True to her words, several other dragons flew up from the ground to back up the scout.

By now Ddraig Anzig and the scout were directly in front of each other, hovering in the air as they both bared their teeth. All around us nearly twenty dragons flew close and slowly circled us. We weren't going anywhere without the permission of the Xitals.

"I am Ddraig Anzig, son of Ddraig Astar. I am the rightful leader of this clan."

"Anzig is dead," the scout replied. Her eyes flicked away from Ddraig Anzig's. I couldn't be sure what she saw there, but I doubted it was anything good. The fear and nervousness had vanished from the ddraig's poise, replaced by barely contained anger. The Xital was hesitant as she spoke. "You should leave these lands."

"I will do no such thing," Ddraig Anzig growled. "You will take me to see Ddraig Tsona. Immediately."

The scout looked towards the ddraig for just a moment. Then her eyes flicked around the rest of us, lingering on me. Her wings faltered, and she dropped lower in the air. "Very well. I know you are not who you claim to be, but I will let Ddraig Tsona decide your fate. Understand now that he will not be happy for your disturbance. Should you wish to fly away, we will not pursue. This is your last chance to leave peacefully."

Ddraig Anzig snapped his teeth, but he allowed himself to follow the Xital scout. We all fell in line behind the ddraig, stunned at what we had just seen and heard. We had believed Ddraig Tsona could have been trusted with passing power of Laxtal back over to Ddraig Anzig, but that looked unlikely now.

Flanked by over a dozen Xital dragons, we returned to the Laxtal lair with the feeling of prisoners. We were not to receive the welcome back to Laxtal we had hoped for.

Another Xital came out to meet us as we flew down the gorge at the entrance to the lair. "Who are these?" the newcomer asked. She was a large dragon with dark copper scales.

"He claims to be Anzig," the scout growled.

The copper ness stared into Ddraig Anzig's eyes for almost a full minute before looking away. "I'll take them to Ddraig Tsona right away," she said. She seemed uneasy by what she had seen in the ddraig's eyes.

We were led through the familiar tunnels of the lair, with the copper ness in front of us and three other Xitals behind. Along the way I saw eyes shining out from the shadows as Laxtal dragons cowered and shied from the Xitals. Whispers started to follow us down the tunnel. At least these hidden dragons recognised Ddraig Anzig for who he was, even if they were too afraid to come out and greet him.

There must have been at least one hundred Xital dragons present throughout the lair, stationed as guards to quell the Laxtals. Though they were easily outnumbered, their status as the Royal Clan had intimidated the Laxtal dragons into submission. No one came forward to offer the rightful ddraig support. I could see fear in every pair of eyes we passed. Something had to have happened for them to be so scared and subservient. I dreaded what had happened to Ellian. I should have Seen this. I should have known what to expect.

The central chamber was almost deserted. On the podium to one end was a small gathering of dragons. I focused on just the one; the largest of the ten there. Ddraig Tsona was deep in discussion with one of his companions and didn't look up as we emerged out from the tunnels. The dragons around him tensed, spreading wings and keeping their eyes firmly on our group.

The copper ness landed by Ddraig Tsona's side, and only then did the large dragon look up to acknowledge our presence. He took one, quick glance over at Ddraig Anzig and hissed in shock, eyes wide. "Not possible."

"You have a lot to answer for, Ddraig Tsona." Ddraig Anzig growled as he barged past our captor and approached the Xital dragon.

"And you should be dead," the Xital spat, his voice full of venom and spite. He stepped away from his clanmates, drawing Ddraig Anzig's path closer to the centre of the great podium that overlooked the chamber. The eyes of every Xital and Laxtal dragon present turned towards the feuding ddraigs. I eyed the Xitals nervously.

"Then you were misinformed." I had never heard so much vitriol in Ddraig Anzig's voice before, not even when I had revealed to him that I had been responsible for his father's death. Even Ddraig Tsona seemed intimidated enough to take a step back from the furious Laxtal dragon.

"Misinformed?" Ddraig Tsona snarled. His muzzle pulled back into a sneer, glaring at Ddraig Anzig. The Laxtal dragon did not waver.

Anzig barked in humourless laughter. "George never told you what happened, did he?"

A hush fell across the chamber. I could hear every pinched breath, every rustle of a wing. The accusation Ddraig Anzig made was sudden and inflammatory. Every sense strained as I half-expected the Xitals to leap to the defence of their ddraig. None did. None moved.

The poise and confidence fled Ddraig Tsona. His eyes flicked around the darkened cave, suddenly unable to meet the fierce gaze of the smaller dragon before him. His wings flared as he took a hasty step backwards. Whispers circulated the great chamber. Laxtal dragons prowled in the shadows. Xitals shared worried glances. "I don't… I don't understand your meaning."

Ddraig Anzig smiled. "Of course it's you. It's always been you, hasn't it? You started this war so that dragonkind would lose. What has George promised you? What do you gain out of the destruction of your own species?" The ddraig's voice had risen to a booming crescendo, echoing around the chamber. A few muted whispers dared to respond, coming from the cowed Laxtals.

"You've got it wrong," Ddraig Tsona said, taking another step back.

"Power? Is that it? What more can you gain? But oh, of course. You want more than just power over dragonkind. You want a place of high status with the humans too, don't you?" Ddraig Anzig said, causing Ddraig Tsona to back up even further. There was something strange about the Laxtal ddraig's eyes, but I couldn't place what was amiss.

"Let me explain," Ddraig Tsona said.

"There is nothing to explain. I have been threatened by Xital dragons in my own territory. I have been treated as a prisoner," Ddraig Anzig said with a fierce snarl. He suddenly dropped the volume of his voice. The words came out ominously quiet, but the power, confidence and not-so veiled meaning were all the more potent. "You are to leave now and stop interfering in my clan's business. You are to fly away and have nothing more to do with dragonkind. Live amongst the humans if you wish. I'm sure they'll be happy to have a new pet."

Ddraig Tsona blinked. He stood his ground, and the sneer slowly came back to his muzzle. He started to pace around his adversary once more. A few of the Xitals closed around us, claws scratching against the stone ground, confidence returning to their poise now that their leader had recovered his. One of them glared menacingly at me. I tried to return his gaze with some confidence. I didn't need my magic to know what was coming. I wasn't sure Ddraig Anzig was aware of the danger. His focus was solely on the Xital ddraig.

"I suppose you'll want to learn the fate of your cousin," Ddraig Tsona drawled. All his prior concern had evaporated as he straightened his poise. Now it was Ddraig Anzig who missed his step, almost stumbling.

"What have you done with Ellian?" Ddraig Anzig asked, his voice dropping even further to a strained whisper.

"Oh, nothing. Yet," the Xital replied.

"If you lay a single claw on her, it will be an act of war against Clan Laxtal. We are stronger than you think," Ddraig Anzig snarled.

A couple of the other Xitals shifted uncomfortably. I took advantage of their confusion to take a small step forward. Like my ddraig, I had to be ready to fight the Xitals if it was necessary. Keita and Carlee had also stepped forward to defend the honour of Clan Laxtal. Even the Nyrian and two Nixans stepped forward. Vinzent remained in the shadows with Maznar. All around the great chamber, dragons emerged from the darkness, muttering in quiet conversations, but they did not yet come close. I saw my father amongst them. He did not meet my eye.

Ddraig Tsona laughed. "War? Do you grow tired of fighting humans that you must kill a few dragons too?"

"We will fight anyone who is a threat to this clan," Ddraig Anzig growled. He dug his claws into the rock beneath his paws as he stood his ground, refusing to step back as the Xital advanced on him. They pressed muzzles together as Ddraig Tsona tried to intimidate his younger foe without success.

The Xital dragon pulled away. Ddraig Anzig relaxed slightly, but was surprised as Ddraig Tsona spun back around and cuffed him across the face. Unprepared, Ddraig Anzig was powerless as the older, larger, and more experienced dragon slashed across his face twice more, drawing blood.

Carlee roared and lunged at one of the other Xitals, and she was joined by Keita and Okazuni as the other Xital dragons joined the fray. I struggled to deflect the aggressive intentions of the copper ness as she tried to bite and claw at me.

I had no time to focus on Ddraig Anzig's fight. It took all my strength to push away the ness and keep her snapping teeth away from my vulnerable wings. She pushed me onto my back. All that was keeping her away from me were my outstretched legs, but I was beginning to weaken. The ivory points of her teeth snapped closer and closer.

The Xitals had numbers, but we had one of the greatest warriors ever to live. Carlee may have been old, but she overpowered three of the Xital dragons and forced them to retreat within seconds. Trickles of blood splattered down from their wounded flanks as they flew away to the tunnels. The fleeing Xitals were chased from the lair, pursued by other Laxtals roused from their submission.

I shrieked in agony as the copper ness finally found her target. Pain coursed through my wing as her teeth shredded through the thin membrane. My legs collapsed, allowing her claws access to my chest. She tore at my scales and ripped open many deep gashes as she wrenched my wing aside, snapping one of the brittle bones. I screamed and weakly tried to push her away, before she was thrown off. She screeched as Carlee snapped at her tail before she fled with her clanmates, evading the veteran's attempts to pin her down.

Snarls continued to reverberate through the massive chamber. I gritted my teeth and turned my head to see the two ddraigs still in combat, with Ddraig Anzig sprawled on the floor. No one dared to intervene in the fight. This was no mere scuffle. This was a fight between two ddraigs. No one was permitted to interfere in such a duel for the pride and honour of two clans was at stake.

Ddraig Anzig struggled to rise. His wing trailed uselessly along the ground, the membrane torn in several places, and a great gash in his right shoulder stained his green scales a deep red. His legs splayed wide as he forced himself to four paws.

I closed my eyes as pain threatened to overwhelm me.

"You still haven't given up?" a regal and proud voice said. Ddraig Tsona was shocked and surprised, although it sounded like he was also in a lot of pain. "I'll give you that, you have courage. But you are also a fool. I didn't want to kill you Anzig, but if you persist in fighting, then I have no choice."

I knew this part. I squinted my eyes open as the Xital threw himself forward, always keeping to Ddraig Anzig's injured side. Fresh wounds tore into his scales as blood soaked the sand on the stony floor.

Ddraig Anzig stumbled on his outstretched wing and collapsed to the ground at the same time his opponent crashed into his side. The two rolled and thrashed as though caught in a maelstrom. Purely by chance, Ddraig Anzig's teeth found the neck of his foe. He bit down hard, choking the life out of the gold dragon in his clutches.

The Laxtal ddraig was weakening fast though, and his adversary was able to break free of the death grip and fled the fight. Vinzent launched into the air and gave chase to the Xital, following him towards the surface.

Ddraig Tsona fled in fear.

I closed my eyes again as Ddraig Anzig slumped back. I could hear his whimpers of pain as Carlee spoke to him. "Get Kaz."

"I'm not leaving you here," Carlee said.

"Go," Ddraig Anzig said, his voice strained by pain. "Please."

This time, Carlee obeyed the ddraig and I heard her wingbeats slowly fade away as she flew out of the chamber. I groaned as I struggled to roll onto my side, but the pain was too great. I struggled to hold back shameful tears.

My eyes slowly opened as Ddraig Anzig struggled to his paws. I could only see his silhouette as he rose.

"Azlak?" he whimpered.

I didn't answer. I recognised this pain, but the impossibility of the situation gripped my agonised chest. I couldn't even breathe as the ddraig limped closer.

How? I couldn't believe it. This must be a vision.

"Azlak, how do you do it? How do you control it? I'm like you. I'm a Laxtal, but I have magic too. How can that be?"

This couldn't be happening. This... this was the moment I had been waiting my whole life for, and it was Ddraig Anzig?

"It is happening though. This is real," the ddraig said mournfully. He grunted in pain as he tried to move his wings.

I found myself completely unable to speak. He had broken into my thoughts. He had heard what I had been thinking. I saw the ddraig nod slowly in confirmation.

"How can I control it?" he whined. I could tell he was desperate. I remembered how hard it had been to control my magic when it had first emerged, but I still had little control over it. I was not the dragon to ask. We had two Nixans with us. They would be able to help the ddraig in honing his fledgling magical abilities.

Ddraig Anzig shook his head vigorously, only to yelp in pain at the movement. "No, you can't," he said, once he had recovered. "No one can know about this. Please, this has to be secret. I don't want... I don't want..." He bowed his head and turned away.

This time I could read the ddraig's thoughts. He didn't want to be like me, the omega of the clan. My magic meant the clan shunned me. Even as the ddraig, he feared the same would happen to him.

"I'm sorry," Ddraig Anzig whispered.

"I won't tell anyone," I gasped, forcing the words through teeth clenched in agony as Carlee returned into the chamber. The two Nixans and Vinzent flew with her.

Kaz landed by Ddraig Anzig's side and placed his paw on the wounded dragon's chest. An orange light emerged from the Nixan's paw and spread over Ddraig Anzig's body. I closed my eyes and leaned my head back as I waited, gritting my teeth together as every movement and twitch of my wings lanced pain through my entire body.

"Tsona has fled," Carlee growled as Kaz performed his magic. "The Xitals have all flown off with him. Okazuni and Maznar are guarding the entrance in case they return, and Keita is ensuring everyone hears of your victory. She is to send her father here when she finds him. You have done well."

"We have another threat to our clan now though. We need to be on our guard against Xital and the humans," Ddraig Anzig said. He sounded stronger now, and I could hear him getting to his paws. "I should have killed him when I had the chance."

A cool paw touched my scales and the pain faded. I could feel the gashes in my chest knit together. There was a dull snap as my wing jerked back into position, the broken bone mending into one. I grunted in discomfort as the pain began to recede into an unpleasant memory. My eyes opened in relief. The healer gazed down at me. He smiled.

Carlee had taken Ddraig Anzig away from the rest of us as she continued to give him advice and guidance on what to do from here. High above us, a few dragons were starting to fly back into the chamber. They were all Laxtal. Carlee was right; the Xitals had fled with their defeated leader. Surely they wouldn't suffer this dishonour for long. No one stood up to Clan Xital and got away with it.

An army of dragons stood on the hills surrounding the Laxtal lair. The ddraigs and haeraigs of many clans stood at its head, as well as a single human. Facing them was another army. Humans and Xital dragons stood side by side as Ddraig Tsona and the human George advanced alone on the draconic force.

"Surrender now or be destroyed," the gold-scaled dragon yelled.

Snarls of derision from the Laxtal army met his words.

Of course they would be back. Now I had finally Seen Tsona's treachery. Ddraig Anzig had been right. Vinzent had been right. It was the Xital ddraig who was the traitor and was conspiring with the humans against his own species.

"Azlak? You made it back?"

I turned at the familiar voice and stared into the brown eyes of my father. He then surprised me by lowering his eyes first. He had never shown any respect to me before.

"You doubted me, father?" I asked, already knowing what the answer would be without having to See it.

"Every second," my father whispered. He looked away, ashamed. "I could barely believe my eyes before. You stood up to the Xitals when I could not. Keita told me what you did across the mountains. I am so pleased you have proved me wrong. You have made me proud, my son."

Slowly, awkwardly, he placed his wing around me. "I won't deny I feared the worst when Ellian told us you'd convinced Anzig to chase the Axinstone. But you have showed me an ability I did not know you possessed."

Out of the corner of my eye I could see Saya land and approach her son, Vinzent. She did not appear quite so impressed at Vinzent than my father was with me, and she took the dragonet away to one side and appeared to scold him. Vinzent was gradually getting lower and lower as his mother's tirade continued.

Amongst some of the other dragons to return to the chamber was the albino dragon, Yalle. He had been Ddraig Astar's closest friend and one of his most formidable allies, despite his physical weaknesses that were a result of his albinism. Yalle's target now was Ddraig Anzig, and the albino interrupted the conversation the ddraig was having with Carlee.

"Are you even listening, Azlak?" my father asked, breaking into my curious observations. What was it that Yalle had to say to Ddraig Anzig? Whatever it was, I could tell it was urgent. I apologised to my father and edged closer to the ddraig.

"They have Ellian," Yalle was saying.

"Where?" replied Ddraig Anzig. His wings flared in distress, ready to fly off at a moment's notice to go and help his cousin.

"Xital, I believe. She only got here four days ago. The beacons were still working then, so we knew she was coming. We tried to warn her to stay away, but she was infuriated at how Ddraig Tsona was leading the clan. She tried to challenge him again, but he did not obey the usual rules. They outnumbered her. She fought valiantly, but they quickly subdued her," Yalle said, shuddering in disgust. The traditions around combat were clear. That was just another betrayal from Tsona against our ways.

Carlee curtailed the ddraig's vicious snarl. "I know what you're thinking, Anzig," the veteran ness said. "You are needed here. We must hold the wylax to secure your position. It would not do to go off on another mad quest when Laxtal needs you to rule." Her paw tapped the ground as she spoke. "This is another's task this time."

"No. Tsona knew what he was doing by taking Ellian. He's made this my responsibility," Ddraig Anzig replied, quickly reducing the loudness of his response, ignoring the fact that Tsona thought him dead when Ellian had been captured. His wings were still unfurled and he tested the ground beneath his paws, getting himself ready to fly.

"All the more reason to stay behind. Tsona wants you there and not here. He's trying to trap you," Carlee said, but I could tell the ddraig was not convinced. He was going to Xital, and no one was going to tell him otherwise. Carlee sighed as she relented. "Then you take me with you."

This time it was Ddraig Anzig's turn to protest. "No, I need you here to lead the clan."

"Me?" Carlee scoffed. "I couldn't lead this clan to save my scales. If you insist on this madness, then I'm going with you. I'll be of no use here."

Saya lifted her head and looked across to the ddraig. "Under my guidance, the clan flourished before Ellian returned," she said proudly.

"Your guidance?" my father growled, taking an interest in the conversation again. He stood by my side and snarled at the ness. "Funny, I don't remember that happening. I seem to recall it was all Yalle and myself."

"Of course you would say that," Saya said. She advanced on my father and stared up at him, trying to make meaningful eye contact. However, my father had a massive advantage in size and was not at all intimidated by her. His chest swelled out as he took in a deep breath.

Then Ddraig Anzig was standing between us, snarling at Saya. "Enough of this. You will not be leading the clan in my absence, Saya. If Carlee is accompanying me, then the only dragon I trust who is to remain behind is Azlak. Yalle and Marin will assist him," the ddraig said.

For the second time I was stunned by Ddraig Anzig's words. I couldn't believe he was going to be making me the leader of the clan in his stead. I had no belief in my abilities to lead. It had been hard enough leading the small group of dragons as we travelled to the human territory. Now the ddraig expected me to lead the entire clan? My legs started trembling where I stood. I feared they would give out on me, sending me crashing to the floor like felled prey. The slight dizziness in my head did not help me stay upright and dignified.

"I believe you can do it." I heard Ddraig Anzig's words, but I could tell he hadn't spoken. He looked into my eyes and I felt a touch against my mind. I couldn't explain how, but I knew it was the ddraig. His words eased me enough to be confident of staying upright at least.

There were a few muted protests, but they were quickly silenced by a slow, deliberate sweep of Ddraig Anzig's head. It was obvious there was nothing else to be said on the matter. Ddraig Anzig had spoken and decreed. I was the appointed leader of Clan Laxtal until he returned from Xital.

I straightened my neck and tried to make myself appear as tall as possible, a difficult feat given my father, standing right next to me, was almost twice my height. Ddraig Anzig's words had done a little to allay my fears, but I was feeling a little light-headed as I thought about what was beginning to unfold before us. I was surprised I had not Seen these events. Perhaps it meant nothing of significance was going to occur? I could only hope.

Ddraig Anzig rose to his paws and addressed the clan at large, which had slowly been filtering into the chamber and were now all gathered, expectantly waiting for their new ddraig to address them. Most of them showed signs of suffering. Some were injured and most looked like it had been a long while since they had eaten. Great changes were coming to Clan Laxtal. I just hoped I could deliver them.

"I am sorry I could not be here to prevent your pain," Ddraig Anzig said, speaking loudly so all present in the great chamber could hear his voice. "When I left for Xital, I could not have known what was to come. I was not to realise that I would be saying farewell to my father for the last time. Laxtal has suffered in my absence, in the absence of its true leaders. I wish I could return now and say all will be healed, but we fly into dangerous times.

"Clan Xital has allied itself with the humans who live on the far side of the mountains, the same humans who harass our borders and have killed Ddraig Astar. Individually, they are formidable. Together, they make a dangerous foe. But we do not face this storm alone. As reward for recovering the Axinstone, Clan Nixa have pledged their support to us as an ally in this coming war. The clan of warriors and the clan of magic will fly wingtip to wingtip, no matter what winds these humans and traitorous dragons hurl at us."

A powerful roar echoed Ddraig Anzig's words as the dragons of Laxtal opened their mouths and beat their wings. Paws thumped against the ground. If Ddraig Anzig had feared what reception he would receive, then he need not have worried. I was sure the dragons of Laxtal would have tolerated anyone of their clan to lead them — even me.

Ddraig Anzig flicked out his wings. The clan fell silent in stages, the roars fading and then one by one the stamping paws and voices dripping to silence.

"One of our own has been taken by Clan Xital," Ddraig Anzig said. He began to pace, his tail lashing out a fitful movement behind him. "I will fly out there myself to rescue Ellian, who will stand as my chosen haeraig. If there is any other dragon taken prisoner by these traitors, inform me, and I will ensure they are brought back home safely. You are to follow Azlak's rule until then."

I resisted the urge to shrink back as attention rippled to me. A thousand pairs of eyes all looked in my direction, and I struggled to keep my head held high. I would not embarrass the faith of my ddraig so soon.

"I trust Azlak," Ddraig Anzig continued, mercifully drawing much of the focus back to him. I exhaled slowly. "I know that he will oversee the recovery of the clan while I deal with Xital. On my return we will hold the wylax, and I will speak my commitment to rule Laxtal with the same strength and honour that my father did. I will follow his wingbeats. I will prove myself the leader he always was."

A lone voice shouted. "Ddraig Anzig!"

Another voice followed. And then another, and another. Before long, the entire clan shouted the name of their new ddraig. It might have been a trick of the firelight, but for a moment I was sure Ddraig Anzig's eyes were wet. Then he moved, retreating towards the shadows, and the moisture was gone.

When Ddraig Anzig spoke next, after the raucous cheering had subsided, his voice was softer. "Azlak, if you would follow me. Carlee, Vinzent, Airil, and Kaz, I would like you to join us as well." He swept his head around, looking over the thousands of gathered dragons, no longer cowed, no longer afraid. "Yalle and Marin, I would like you to ensure there are no wounded. I want to know what food we still have, and to arrange hunts if we need it. Winter approaches, and I would not have the clan starve during the cold months."

I hesitated for a moment. I turned to face my father, who would be leading the clan by my side. Before leaving for the Xital council I could never have believed that this could be possible. Nor could I have believed I would be looking forward to it. I was excited by the prospect. Terrified at the same time, but thrilled that I was no longer the omega of the clan. I couldn't explain where the confidence had come from, but I wondered if Ddraig Anzig's revelation that he was the drake I had been looking for had anything to do with it.

At a gentle nudge from my father, I spread my wings and followed Ddraig Anzig up towards the chambers behind the great firepit, where the rulers of Clan Laxtal resided. Only once before had I been in those caves. There had rarely been a reason to summon me to see Ddraig Astar or any of the other dragons who ruled the clan. Until now.

We left behind the clan, buzzing with activity already. I heard my father bellowing out commands, ensuring that Ddraig Anzig's orders were carried out.

Ddraig Anzig led us all into the small series of caves set aside for the haeraig of the clan. They had always been his personal chambers, so it was probably habit alone that had led him in there. The walls were bare, but the floors were covered in thin rugs from the northern clans, which helped retain some of the warmth in the caves. There was evidence of recent occupation, and the ddraig growled as he readjusted some of the rugs. It appeared that the Xitals had helped themselves to the nests of the ruling dragons of Laxtal.

"You know what Ddraig Krateos said needed to be done. I trust that you will do whatever is necessary to defend the clan, as well as the preparations for the wylax," Ddraig Anzig said, looking at me as he spoke. I tried to meet his eye, but the fury I saw there was intense. He was seething at Tsona's intervention in the clan, as well as Ellian's capture. I glanced down to look at his paws, unable to meet his eyes any longer. "Vinzent, you'll join us, and we'll take Maznar as well. If Tsona has humans with him she'll be able to help us."

Vinzent looked less than thrilled at the prospect of flying to Xital, but he didn't vocalise his complaints. Judging by the frown on Ddraig Anzig's face, he had heard the dragonet's misgivings anyway.

One of the Nixans took a tentative step forward and bowed his head. "I wish to come too, Ddraig Anzig. I blame myself for not trying to stop Ellian leaving Nixa on her own. I would like to help rescue her," he said.

Ddraig Anzig considered the offer for a moment before he nodded his head. "Of course you can join us, Airil. We may have need of your magic," he said. He turned to the Nixan's twin. "Kaz, I hope I'm not requesting too much of you, but there are a lot of injured dragons here. Please do what you can to help them."

"I would be honoured to help," Kaz said.

In truth I knew he had little choice in the matter. He may not be of Clan Laxtal, but he was still obliged to carry out the requests of the ddraig. There weren't many ddraigs though who would so graciously request the assistance of a dragon of another clan, rather than ordering them. In my mind, that was something that would set Ddraig Anzig apart from other clan leaders. He had an aura of humility about him that some would consider a weakness, but would make him well liked throughout the clans. I could only hope that weakness would not be exploited. I had not Seen it happen, but I feared it.

"We should leave right away," Ddraig Anzig said, but Carlee cut across him.

"It's evening already. We won't get anywhere overnight. We may as well rest properly before leaving in the morning," the ness said. She stared down the ddraig, who had looked like he was about to argue, but under the stern glare of his mentor, he relented.

"Yes, you're right. One night at home, then we leave at first light. Please start getting everything prepared," Ddraig Anzig asked the old ness. "Use as many dragons to assist you, as you see fit." Carlee nodded, and left along with the Nixans, leaving me alone with the ddraig. He looked around the chambers, which would be so familiar to him. His eyes found mine again. "Azlak, stay near me tonight. I want you to see how things are done. Yalle and Marin will be able to help you whenever you need it, but it would be best you know as much as you can."

I vowed to stay close to the ddraig and pick up as much information as I could. There would be a lot I had to learn, and only a couple of hours to do it in. I knew I would never be able to know but a small fraction of what I needed to know about leading the clan. I was sure Ddraig Anzig wasn't expecting that of me, but a newly found sense of honour and pride demanded that I do the job to the best of my ability. I would become the ddraig's shadow until he had to leave for Xital.

"If you leave me for now, I'll join you in the central chambers soon," the ddraig said. He had already turned away and sat facing the far wall before I had even bowed my head.

The ddraig must have thought I had already gone, but I had hesitated for just a moment.

I lingered too long.

I knew I would never forget Ddraig Anzig's scream of anguish.

CHAPTER NINE

Anzig

The passion of anger carried my wings a long way. It wasn't until I saw the lone spire of Xital's mountain did it finally falter. I had fulfilled my promise of taking to wing almost as soon as dawn's first light, and we had flown hard ever since. Two impatient nights had been spent in empty nomadic caves, where I had spoken to no one, only growling and snapping when someone got too close. Even Carlee gave me space, but the whispers of their thoughts still crowded my mind.

We landed far enough away from the lone mountain to avoid being spotted by any patrolling sentries. We couldn't be sure if Ddraig Tsona had warned his clan that I might follow him. Any advantage we could gain would benefit us, as now we had arrived at the royal clan's lair, I began to wonder the wisdom of this foolish mission. Clan Xital had declared themselves with the humans, making them our enemies. Carlee had reminded me of this whenever she could, in speech or in thought.

Our temporary shelter was a small woodland, raised up on a low hill that overlooked the mountain. There was a scent on the wind that made me uncomfortable, but I couldn't place it. I kept my eye on the sky, sure that there had to be a trap somewhere. Ellian was surely the bait. We had to be aware not to set the trigger.

"What now?" Vinzent said. He tightened his wings to his back and hung his head low.

I looked to the summit of the mountain. From this angle I couldn't see the entry into the largest natural cave known to dragonkind; the audience chamber of Clan Xital. Through that entrance was a way into the network of tunnels that was home to the Xital dragons.

"We get Ellian out of her prison," I said, keeping my eyes fixed on the distant mountain. "We fly away before Xital knows we're here."

"First we must find her, Ddraig," Carlee said. Her eyes narrowed as she scanned the horizon. Her tail quivered. "There are usually scouts and patrols protecting the lair. I don't like how quiet this is, and there is that smell on the air…"

Maznar scoffed. She lifted her head as attention snapped to her. Only Vinzent turned his head away. "Have you really forgotten it already? Or are your noses so weak you can't work it out?" the ness said. She laughed and dragged her claws through the soft soil, digging up a few brown leaves. She shredded them and let the small fragments disperse on the wind. "There are humans here. Lots of them."

I hissed in dismay. Now that it came to my awareness, I recognised the scent for what it was. It had blown across the bay towards us when we had taken shelter in the mine. Xital's treachery was now out in the open if humans were so close to the central mountain.

"That might complicate matters," Carlee said slowly. Her tail curled around her hindlegs. "It was difficult enough when I thought we faced just Xital dragons. To have humans as well? This is looking less like a mere trap and more like a suicide flight."

I shook my head and let out a small growl. "We need to find out where they are holding Ellian. Has anyone gone down into the Xital lair before?" I asked, sweeping my gaze around my companions. They all looked away, unable to meet my eyes. Whispered thoughts teased at the back of my mind. I struggled to ignore them.

"I have been beyond the main chamber once," Airil said. "Not far, though. Certainly nowhere to keep any prisoners."

"Then we start searching," I said, ignoring the frown on Carlee's face. "I expect she'll be held somewhere beneath the mountain, but we should also check the surrounding caves."

Beyond the central lair were several independent networks of tunnels used by the many visiting clans. There was almost always a representative of every clan present in Xital, but now there appeared to be none, the Xital territories abandoned. What had happened here to banish away all the visiting emissaries? Clan Laxtal hadn't had a dragon present in Xital since we had left after the council, so no information had come to our clan. A quick glance to the north gave me a likely answer; that was where the human scent was stronger. It was likely that no dragon would want to be anywhere near them.

Carlee clicked her tongue. "Ddraig, let us think about this first."

I shook my head. "We don't have time to sit and think about it. We're not just in danger here, but back home as well. The longer we stay here, the more chance of being spotted, but we also risk a dragon in Laxtal deciding they should take the wylax themselves. We need to act now."

Carlee slumped, her shoulders and head dropping down almost to Vinzent's level. "Very well. What would you have us do?"

"We should split up and start searching for Ellian," I said, not wanting to hesitate before my companions. "Carlee, you should take Vinzent and begin your search around the central mountain. I shall take the others and hunt through the visitor's caves. Meet us back here in one hour, whether you find her or not."

"Very well, my ddraig," Carlee said. She dipped her head and flung out her wings. "Come, Vinzent. Stay on my tail."

The silver dragonet lingered a moment, staring beseechingly at my paws. I said nothing, waiting for him to take to wing. He reluctantly did so, chasing after Carlee who had not once looked back. I watched them until I could no longer make them out against the pale blue sky.

"We fly south, to the Laxtal chambers. Ellian might have broken free from her captors," I said, glancing back to Airil and Maznar. I spread my wings, ready to take flight. There still wasn't a single Xital dragon in sight. No patrols or guards. That was most unusual.

Maznar grinned, her white teeth showing bright against her dark scales. "Optimism. I like it. Fly on, ddraig. We shall follow."

For some reason, I shuddered. Maznar's words did not sound genuine to my ears. Her use of my title rang hollow. But I could detect nothing sinister her thoughts. Just like Vinzent, I hesitated. But I did not do so for long. I forced myself to take flight, ever wary of any Xital presence.

The familiar rise of the Laxtal caves soon rose from the low hills. Every time I had come to Xital, I had resided in those caves. Each of the ruling clans had their own small network, while the other thirty-one clans had to cohabit in one larger group of connected caves. I was unfamiliar with these clusters of caverns, having never set paw inside them, as there had never been a need on my three prior visits. I knew that if Ellian was not in the Laxtal caves, then it would take a long time to search through all the others.

The empty sky continued to unnerve me as we soared over the ruling clan's territory. There should have been someone. It was like Xital had emptied. Ddraig Tsona couldn't have faced such a total rebellion. Fear began to worm into my gut. Was the clan empty because its army had already taken to wing, launching a campaign against the surrounding clans?

"Look, there." Maznar's voice broke into my thoughts.

I followed the point of her foreleg, beyond the mountain and towards the plains in the east. A dark smudge spread out across the land, too far away to properly see.

"Is that what I think it is?" Airil asked, the Nixan flying close to my left wing.

From my other side, Maznar laughed. "If you think it's a human encampment, then you're correct."

"I wouldn't have thought they would be so obvious about it," the Nixan said, so quietly I couldn't be certain if he spoke the words aloud. I chose not to answer, just in case.

"You would be surprised about many things, little dragon," Maznar replied. She tilted her wings, almost soaring directly into my path. "Be glad that I don't believe Tsona would hold Ellian amongst them. If we are careful, we don't have to deal with any humans today."

"Then where do you think they might be keeping her?" I asked, the question from my mouth before I could stop it. I doubted I should be asking the spectre her opinion. I was glad only Airil was around to hear us.

"I wouldn't know," Maznar said, smirking. "I've never been here with waking eyes before."

"Then we search everywhere if necessary," I said, trimming my wings to drop closer to the ground. The other two followed right behind as I swooped into the familiar caves that housed any Laxtal visitors.

I knew right away that they were empty. The torches were cold and unlit, shrouding everything in impenetrable darkness. There were no recent scents, not even the faint ones lingering from our last visit. No dragon had been in these caves since we had left for the Axinstone, over a month ago.

My shoulders slumped as I landed at the farthest reach of the light. I had known it couldn't have possibly been that easy, but still I had hoped. Perhaps Ellian had escaped the clutches of the Xitals, but surely she would have come here first.

"What is that sound, Ddraig?" Airil asked, stepping forward to my side. He tilted his head, eyes narrowed as he faced the darkness ahead of us.

My heart pounded. For a moment, I dared to believe again. Then I realised that it was not the sound of a lone dragon Airil had heard. This was something bigger than that, and it did not come from the Laxtal caves. It echoed through them. It was the sound of a thousand dragons or more, all shouting at once. We had found the Xital clan. They were underground, likely in the audience chamber of the central mountain. Where I had sent Carlee and Vinzent.

I took a step back and started to turn, but only bumped directly into Maznar. I snarled. She did not let me past.

"They are smart," the spectre said, standing her ground despite my growl. She smirked. That infuriating partial reveal of her fangs. "Well, the old one is. The little welp I'm not so sure about, but Carlee won't fly into a trap. She'll be fine."

"She's right, Ddraig," Airil added. The Nixan stared into the darkness, then swung his head around and squinted as the light fell across his eyes. "Ellian isn't down here. I doubt she would have stayed for long if she had escaped. She'd have flown away as quickly as possible."

"Perhaps you're right," I admitted. I clenched my paw and thumped it against the ground. I had committed to this plan, wanting to do something, but now I realised I was chasing a shadow. If Ellian had escaped by herself, then she wouldn't be in Xital. There wasn't much I could do to change that now. I would not find Carlee and Vinzent if I chased after them. All I could do was keep to the plan and fruitlessly search the empty chambers surrounding Xital.

At the very least, there might be some clue as to why the lair was so empty. I forced myself to ignore my worries for Carlee and Vinzent. I had to trust that the veteran ness would keep them both safe. There had never been a reason to doubt her abilities before.

I emerged into the light once more. I heard the wingbeats immediately. A shadow flicked overhead, and a voice called down. "Are you lost?"

I tensed, freezing in panic as a dragon swooped low. She clattered to the ground just in front of me, kicking up a cloud of dirt. A crown of horns circled her head. She was a Xital dragon. She did not bow to me.

My tongue plastered to the bottom of my mouth. I was unable to speak, sure that she knew who I was and why I had come. Maznar and Airil remained silent behind me, warily waiting for me to say something.

The Xital wrinkled her nose. "You should not be here today. We certainly weren't expecting anyone. Your ddraig didn't send any message through to us. You should remind him to do so next time."

I sucked in my breath, the correction almost bursting out before I could contain it. She didn't recognise who I was. I scratched at the ground and allowed my head to dip. "My apologies. I shall be sure to inform the ddraig when I return home."

Maznar stepped to my side. I resisted the instinct to snap my teeth at her and push her behind. For the moment, I could not be the ddraig. I was an ordinary dragon, just like her. "May I ask what is happening here?" the spectre said, boldly speaking the question that had been on my tongue since our arrival. "I would have expected to see patrols. Guards. Anything, but your clan appears empty."

The Xital dragon narrowed her eyes. "Ddraig Tsona has gathered the clan in the lower chambers for an important speech. I understand he seeks new allies in the coming wars, but there are also new enemies," she said, staring intently at each of us in turn. "What is your clan to be?"

"That is something to be decided by our ddraigs," I said hesitantly.

"Of course. You would not have come if your ddraig was not willing to negotiate with us," the Xital dragon said. She flicked her tail and lifted her head. "It is good to learn that some of you western dragons have seen some sense. We were beginning to worry that we would have open rebellion against us."

"We would like to avoid that necessity," I said, the words true. I did not want to fight Clan Xital, but I would not side with them along with humans.

The Xital ness smiled. "Good. I am glad to hear it. But while I am sure you are eager to see Ddraig Tsona, he will not be able to meet with you just yet. Let me take you to your clan's shelter, where you can rest and eat. Clan Xital will still look after you, don't you worry about that."

I frowned and glanced back, confused. Why would this dragon need to take me anywhere? My mouth hung open, but I said nothing. Maznar's red eyes twinkled in amusement. I swallowed my pride and confusion, allowing myself to turn back to the Xital. "If you could, thank you."

"Then follow me," the Xital said, flaring her wings and launching into the air, battering us with a gust of downdraft.

I bit down on a growl.

"Curious, don't you think?" Maznar said quietly. She nudged a paw against my side.

"We shouldn't leave her waiting," Airil said, ignoring the ness, or not hearing her.

I reluctantly agreed with Airil. I spread my wings and kicked off the ground, beating hard until I was able to close in on the Xital ness, who had not slowed down at all. She did not fly towards the central mountain, instead following the ring of low hills and caves that surrounded the lone peak. We soared over the Axaatl caves, which looked as empty and deserted as those for Laxtal. Other than the one ness we followed, I could see no evidence of any other dragon in the air. Our guide did not mention the human encampment, visible on the outskirts of the great lair.

To my surprise, she led us to the northernmost outcrop in the lair, which I knew contained the Nixan chambers. A chill ran through my body, and my wings faltered. There was no way this Xital ness could know what went through my mind. But there could be no other reason to lead me here if she didn't know about my magic. Why else would she come here? I was not Nixan. Only Airil was. Had the ness seen him and assumed we were all from the clan of magic?

We touched down just outside the cave entrance. Inside was dark, and I could already tell Ellian had not come here, not that I truly expected that. Only faint scents lingered on the air, none fresher than a couple of weeks old.

"I trust you know how to operate the lights, and where the food stores are?" the Xital ness said, turning to face us as we landed behind her. Her eyes lingered on me. I resisted the urge to keep her gaze, instead dropping my head.

"I know how," Airil said.

The ness lifted her head higher, looking down on us with haughty eyes. "Good. Should anyone give you trouble, tell them Grazta brought you here."

"Thank you, Grazta. I appreciate it," Airil said. The Nixan stepped ahead of me and bowed low, sweeping his wings wide.

Grazta's hindlegs tensed against the ground, but she didn't launch straight away. She hesitated. "Do not leave these caves. Our clan is holding important business. Interfering with that might jeopardise your clan's alliance with Xital. You would not wish to do that."

"Of course not," Maznar said, a wide smile on her muzzle. Once again, she bumped against me. I kept silent, my head down.

The Xital dragon said nothing more. She sniffed and shook her head, before launching hard and fast into the air, once more buffeting us with her downdraught. I fought back a sneeze as a cloud of dirt wafted over my head. She was soon out of sight, disappearing back onto her patrol around the lair. I had to hope that Grazta wouldn't alert the Xital ddraig to our presence just yet. If he knew we were here, he would immediately move to challenge me again, and this time I knew he would make sure he didn't lose.

"That was exciting, wasn't it?" Maznar said, her teeth all in display as she leered towards me.

"What was that about, Ddraig?" Airil added. The Nixan peered into the dark cave, but quickly seemed to come to the same conclusion as me. No one had come here for a couple of weeks. He turned back to me. His eyes wandered, lifting up, towards my horns. "Why did she bring us here?"

I couldn't answer. Fear brought a bitter taste to my throat and mouth. I didn't trust myself to even open my jaw, let alone speak. I simply shook my head and barged past Maznar, climbing the low hill on paw until I stood at the summit. The rolling terrain of Xital opened out beneath me, with only the great spire of the lone mountain rising higher, reaching almost impossibly towards the thin clouds.

To my relief, I was left alone. There was little point in searching the remaining caves that encircled the lair. Ellian would not be in any of them. Our only hope was to somehow find our way into the lone mountain undetected and to hunt for Ellian there. With almost the entirety of Clan Xital in the way, I could think of no way we could achieve that.

I became lost in my thoughts, struggling to work out how we would get Ellian out once we found her. If we found her. Ideally, we'd be able to get away without Ddraig Tsona even knowing we had been here, but I knew that might not be possible. We would likely have to fight again, and this time he would be able to call upon the humans who were staying close by. Perhaps it was a bad idea bringing so few dragons with me, but nor would I have wanted to bring a full army at my wings. If outright war could be avoided with Xital, then I would choose that route. This was a time when dragonkind needed unity, not division.

Ellian was close by, I knew that. Whether or not it was a facet of my hated magic, I could sense her not too far away. She was down there, hidden beyond the thousands of Xitals who had gathered below the surface to listen to their ddraig speak, a rally against Clan Laxtal and me. Somewhere beneath my paws was my cousin.

Before I realised what I was doing, I had started to cast my mind outwards. I began to pick up the occasional stray thought from underground. Distorted voices ran through my mind, though the words were never clear enough to understand. I gritted my teeth and squeezed my eyes shut as I tried to block out the thoughts. My tail thrashed as I struggled against the magic as it threatened to overwhelm me, but every effort I made to slow down the trickle of thoughts only increased the flow.

I could barely distinguish my thoughts from the others.

I couldn't believe what I was hearing. How could Clan Laxtal be so reckless to throw aside the long peace there had been between our clans? Ddraig Tsona was right. Their inexperienced leader had doomed them. It would be easy to overwhelm Laxtal, especially after their recent losses in battle. Soon, their territories would be ours, and no dragon would dare challenge our might again. Our ddraig looked so strong and regal up there, his wings wide. His voice powerful...

...This should have been a proud and mighty moment. I stood before my clan, roaring them into a powerful fervour. They would fight for me. Dominate these lands for me. With allies of both dragon and human, I would be unstoppable. And yet my thoughts were with Selane. Where had I last seen her? I couldn't recall. Did they have her, like I had one of theirs? Was she...

...Someone would be along to rescue me soon. Someone had to. Surely. I placed my head in my paws, knowing that such thoughts were futile. No friendly dragon even knew I was here. I was alone, and at the mercy of the treacherous ddraig. No. If I was to get out of here, it would have to be my doing, but there was no way out of this cell. Not with those wretched creatures keeping watch close by. They had no right to be here. This was our land, not theirs. And yet that traitorous ddraig had let them take up camp here...

...This place was irking me. It was so primitive, nothing like what we had at home. Why did we have to be out here anyway? Why did we have to suck up to this dragon? Why was he so important that he got to say what we could and couldn't do?

"Ddraig Anzig, should we check the other caves?"

The words pierced the alien thoughts like a claw through wing, breaking my magic's hold on my mind. Back in control, I looked up to see Airil cautiously approaching, his head tilted.

I swallowed down the bile in my throat. Each breath came sharp and shallow. A convulsion ripped through my body. It felt like my mind frayed around the edges.

"Are you alright, Ddraig Anzig?" Airil asked. The Nixan crept closer. His mind brushed against my mine. I recoiled and shook my head.

My eyes locked with Maznar's. Those red orbs burned through my fear. For a moment she was the terrifying spectre of Nightwings again, the shadow of her wings spreading wide to obscure all light. She saw right into me, her eyes perceiving everything. She couldn't know, could she? Unless she had invaded my dreams. Could she have pried into my sleep to see my secret?

"Ddraig Anzig?"

I realised I hadn't answered Airil yet, and he was still looking across at me, concern etched across his face.

"I'm alright, Airil," I lied, just as I had done to his brother in the Nixan lair. The words were bitter in my mouth. I knew the Nixan would not believe me. At least he didn't question it any further, but I knew he would bring it up again. I didn't need magic for that.

I glared at the mountain as I struggled to formulate a new plan. My paws twitched and scratched at the ground, digging parallel grooves through the loose dirt. It felt a great effort just to keep my thoughts my own, with the edges of my mind looser than I had ever known it to be. I was sure that if I tried to expand my awareness again, I could lose myself in the minds of those around me. I could not let that happen.

"Ddraig Anzig?"

My muzzle wrinkled into a snarl, but the quick retort that I was alright died in my throat. Airil didn't look towards me. The Nixan's focus was beyond me, towards the mountain I stared at. I recognised why a moment later. The same dull rumbling we had heard earlier started to make itself known again, and it was getting louder.

Thousands of wingbeats roared as the Xital dragons poured from the interior of their mountain home. I stumbled backwards, then turned to flee towards the mouth of the Nixan caves.

Airil let out a startled squawk as I pushed past him. He hurried behind, with Maznar lazily following us both.

Not a single Xital dragon looked down as the fearsome army emerged from their mountain. They were a never-ending horde, all following a single dragon at their head. I was surprised it was not Ddraig Tsona leading them, but instead a dragon with grey scales. At their leader's command, the head of the army began to wheel around to the east, thundering directly over my head.

I struggled to think of which clan's territories lay to the east of Xital. If my memory served me well, it was the minor clan of Fentra. They had not achieved, nor contributed, anything of significance for dragonkind in recent memory. If Ddraig Tsona wanted to add more land to Xital and more might for his army, then they would meet little resistance in Fentra.

"What are you doing back here?" Maznar asked dryly as she caught up to me. She peered into the darkened cave and smirked.

"Our presence won't be questioned in the Nixan chambers," I said, hating the truth behind the statement. Airil would be in his rightful area, and Grazta had seemed to think I belonged there too. Unless Ddraig Tsona joined his army and saw me, then we would be safe if we masqueraded as Nixan visitors.

"A bit strange, isn't it?" Maznar said.

I whirled around and snapped my teeth right in front of her muzzle. "What do you know about it?" I snarled. She went to move back, but I put my paw on hers. "You never even saw another dragon until a few weeks ago. You know nothing about what it means to be Laxtal or Nixan or any other clan. Don't try and make it sound like you know more than you do, because you know nothing. Do you understand me?"

Maznar ripped her paw from beneath mine and mantled low, her wings spread wide. "Of course, Ddraig."

My growl faltered at the sincerity of her words and the depth of her bow. I found it hard to maintain my anger, but the fear still lingered. Were these innocent words from the former spectre, or did she really know too much about my growing magic? My muzzle wrinkled as I turned away from her. My eyes briefly slid over Airil, who watched on with tilted head and partially lifted paw.

The army of dragons seemed to never end. They emerged from the great chamber with thundering wings and a roared cry of passion. Their many voices all melded into one cacophonous noise, the individual words lost amongst it all. I watched for Ddraig Tsona, but he was not towards the head of the column, and I doubted his pride would allow him to fly anywhere but the front. He remained in Xital, though I could not imagine the purpose.

This added urgency to our need to return to Laxtal. We needed to get back so we could start sending out emissaries to our surrounding clans. Xital had the advantage over us. Not only did they have the humans backing them, they were already swaying their neighbours to their cause. They were the Royal Clan. They would not find it difficult to influence the minds of the ddraigs from the clans that bordered

Xital. It would not be long until a horde of warriors descended on Laxtal. We had to be ready. We needed allies, and we were fast falling behind. We had to rescue Ellian and escape Xital before nightfall. There was no time to waste.

Once the last of the dragons came from the mountain, I spread my wings and waited a few moments longer, just in case any late stragglers were to join the force. None followed, and the thunder of several thousand wings slowly faded as they flew east.

"We should return to the rendezvous to wait for Carlee and Vinzent," I said slowly, still with my eyes on the back of the horde of dragons. They showed no sign of splitting apart into smaller groups, with none staying behind in Xital. Occasional flutters of movement closer to the ground betrayed the positions of the guards who continued to patrol Xital's territory.

"I don't think that will be necessary, Ddraig," Airil said. The Nixan peered towards the base of the mountain, where there was some more movement.

I had caught the movement out of the corner of my eye, but had dismissed it as another Xital guard, but Airil's attention made me look towards the base of the mountain again. I squinted, and sure enough I caught a flash of silver scales glinting in the sunlight. Vinzent flew low to the ground with Carlee by his side. They must have seen us, for they flew directly towards the Nixan caves.

I lifted my head as Carlee fluttered to the ground a short distance away. Both the veteran and the dragonet by her side bowed to me as they approached.

"What are you doing here, Ddraig?" Vinzent asked.

Before I could answer, Carlee snarled and bumped the silver dragon aside. "We think we might know where she is being kept, Ddraig Anzig."

"Where?" Hope blossomed in my chest. Xital's army had largely emptied the clan's territory, leaving the lair almost deserted for us to explore. Fortune favoured us, though it also reminded me of how little time we had to waste.

"There is a new network of caves to the east of the lair," Carlee explained. "I did not think Xital had enough new dragons to expand the lair, and nor do I know how they are constructing these new caves.

Xitals don't like getting their claws dirty to rip through rock in such a way."

"East, you said?" I looked in that direction, eyes narrowed. I could not see the encampment from this low, but I could still pick up the faint scent of humans on the air.

"You think the humans might be helping them expand the lair, Ddraig?" Carlee said. She blinked and followed my gaze.

I flicked my wings. "I imagine they are. Why else would they be here? They must be staying back to protect Xital while Tsona goes out with his army to control the surrounding clans. They wouldn't leave this place undefended, not when Tsona knows we fly against him. If they're giving the humans the chance to settle here, then it makes sense that they're needing to make the lair bigger."

"If that's true, Ddraig, then it might make it difficult for us to find where Ellian is being kept," Airil said. The Nixan wandered towards us, keeping a respectful distance away from me. He avoided my eyes as he pawed at the ground. "I know some of the ways down there, but if these caves are new, then I will be unfamiliar with them."

"And you're wrong to say Ddraig Tsona is leading that army," Vinzent added. The dragonet hissed and ducked his head as I glared at him. The youngster looked away. "He has stayed behind to look for someone called Selane. We overheard a conversation between a couple of Xitals. This dragon has gone missing, and Ddraig Tsona is worried about her."

"That's no concern of ours," I said. I took a deep breath and assessed what we had to do. It had sounded so simple in Laxtal. Get to Xital, find Ellian, and free her. Now we were here, I was at a loss of what to do. She was somewhere beneath us, probably in the new caves to the east of the mountain. Those new passages had to connect to the main caves directly below the mountain, but even getting into those would be challenging.

"If Tsona is distracted with this Selane, then it might keep his eye away from us," Carlee said.

"Is there another way down, or do we need to go through the council chambers?" I asked, looking up at the gash in the side of the mountain. That entry was still guarded, and though the flow of dragons coming out had ceased, we still wouldn't be able to get in undetected.

"I think there might be," Airil said with a laugh. He had a slightly mischievous gleam in his eyes. Given what his magic was, I knew what he suggested. He would be able to transport us directly in, avoiding the guards in the process.

"Surely there's another way?" Vinzent said uncertainly. His head was jerking from side-to-side, his wings slightly unfurled. "Couldn't Airil just go straight down himself and get Ellian out?"

"Not without knowing the way. There's too much rock down there to risk it," Airil said, raising his forepaw up. I noticed he was missing a toe. "That's the price I paid for a slight misjudgement. Unless I know exactly where Ellian is being kept, I can't get to her."

Vinzent ducked his head and looked away. His paws were absently playing with the grass as he thought. I could feel his mind trying to come up with another suggestion, as well as his frustration as his realisation grew that there was no other way.

"So where can you take us?" I asked the Nixan.

"I was here a few years ago with Ddraig Krateos. We were taken into the tunnels beyond the council chamber to speak with Haeraig Ilibela. I can still recall the layout perfectly, and I can take us down directly into one of the antechambers," the Nixan explained.

"What if there's someone in the chamber? What if they have altered the underground layout in some way?" Carlee asked, raising her paw off the ground. This last question made Vinzent groan out loud and spin himself down into a tight ball, covering himself with his wings.

Airil's tail wrapped around his hindleg. "I never said it was perfect. There is always that risk, but what is the alternative?"

Carlee snorted, but she didn't protest any further. I took this as an acceptance that we had no other option. Airil would teleport us into the lair, and then Carlee could guide us down to these new tunnels. The lair would not be deserted, but hopefully enough dragons had departed that we wouldn't bump into anyone once we were inside.

"You first, Ddraig Anzig?" Airil said, reaching out with his paw and placing it on my muzzle.

I blinked, and I was standing in a dark cavern. The only source of light came from the tunnels, around a sharp corner in the rock a few feet away. I could only just see Airil in the gloom. I looked around in shock, stunned by the sudden change in scenery.

"That was..." Airil said, before trailing off into thought. "No, never mind."

"What do you mean?" I asked, but the Nixan wasn't enthusiastic in answering.

"No, it's nothing, Ddraig. Sorry. Just forget I said anything," he said, before disappearing with a whiplash-like crack, leaving me alone in the dark. What had the Nixan meant? I was sure something had disturbed or worried him, but we seemed to have appeared right where he wanted to, and what was more, the cave was empty. I couldn't even hear the echo of a dragon passing nearby.

I was not alone for long, as just a few moments later, Airil reappeared with Maznar. Again, the Nixan frowned as he removed his paw from Maznar's muzzle, but this time said nothing before vanishing once more.

All I could see of the spectre was her red eyes, reminding me of the first time I had seen her, in a shroud of smoke and darkness in a dream on George's island. She snickered softly to herself. "Do you know what I'm thinking?" she asked.

"No, of course not," I replied. I tried to keep my voice calm, but a cold shiver passed down my spine and my tail twitched in response.

"Why not?" she said. Her teeth shone in the soft light as she smiled. She knew, but before she could say anything further, Airil returned with Vinzent. The Nixan stumbled as he materialised, but he was gone again in just a moment.

Vinzent immediately fell to his side and just lay there, cowering with his paws covering his eyes. He moaned softly until I hissed at him to be silent. Just because we couldn't hear anyone didn't mean no one would be able to hear us. Ddraig Tsona could not know of our presence here. Everything relied on getting out before the Xitals discovered us down here.

Airil returned for the last time with Carlee. The veteran ness was more composed than Vinzent, but I could tell she was a little bit rattled by the experience in the way she couldn't keep her wings still. The Nixan meanwhile had collapsed to the ground. His chest was heaving as he struggled to draw breath.

"Just... give... moment," he panted. He forced a few deep breaths and squeezed his eyes shut. "Sorry. Takes a lot of effort. To move someone who isn't Nixan. Even short distances."

"We can't linger," Carlee said. She had gone to the entrance, where the cavern led out to the tunnels. She peered out in both directions before sitting down. Her whole body was quivering, eager to move.

I allowed Airil a few minutes of rest before I got him back up to his paws. He still looked tired, but Carlee was right. Every moment we stayed here increased the chance of detection. We had to move on.

"Never again, Boss. Never again," Vinzent whispered to me as he passed, falling into line just behind Maznar.

I shoved the dragonet forward as I let Carlee take the position of power at the front. I lingered, letting Airil go ahead of me, leaving me to bring up the rear. It was not a position I was used to, but Carlee and the Nixan were more familiar with these caves than I was. It would be my duty to ensure we were not caught unawares from the rear. I could hear nothing behind us. The lair was quiet.

Moss and lichen glistened on the walls, wet with moisture. Clinging to the ceiling were large stalactites that regularly dripped droplets of water. The floor was damp with this constant drizzle, leaving the rock slippery underpaw. We must have come deep below the surface, into the lesser used parts of the lair, for I had expected Xital to look better than this. Strips of glass bars screwed into the rock provided light, glowing with an even white illumination. I recognised the human technology, but these were old caves, carved naturally eons ago.

I kept glancing back. Something prickled at my neck, crawling over my scales like an itch I could not reach. My wings fluttered as I strained my ears for any sound behind us, but I could hear nothing. This part of the lair seemed utterly deserted.

I couldn't shake the feeling that our presence was known; that someone tracked our progress. No one watched us, I was sure of that. Nothing moved in the few shadows between the light. No claws tapped or scratched against stone but for our own.

A pressure grew against my mind. It was a sensation I had never felt, but I was immediately able to detect it. I closed my eyes. Without knowing what I was doing, my mind pushed back at the touch. I felt a soundless grunt and the contact was gone.

My unseen struggle had gone unnoticed by the others and had left me lagging behind. I hurried to catch back up to Airil's tail just as Carlee paused at the junction of a side passage. This one delved sharply down and was almost completely unlit. The walls looked smooth, certainly in comparison to the jagged passage we crept down. The slight smell of something like coal lingered on the rock.

"This must be the way," Carlee whispered. "We should hurry. Come on."

There was no way this new passage was natural. The walls were far too straight and even, though there were some imperfections on the surface. Strange parallel grooves ran perpendicular to the gradually sloping floor, marks left behind by whatever tool had crafted the rock. No dragon could have wielded such tools.

Seeing the evidence of human occupation within the caves of a draconic lair created a sick feeling in my gut, a far greater reaction than merely hearing the rumours of such an act. We had traded with humans for generations before the outbreak of this latest war, but never before had any of their species been allowed into the heart of a draconic lair. Xital had broken that ancient law, possibly even many years ago.

Carlee hissed in warning. Wings fluttered, somewhere ahead of us. We all froze, but the sound died away. No shout of alarm came.

I glanced back and took in a deep breath. Nothing fresh reached my nose, but for the scent of my companions. No one else was close by. No dragon or human.

Underground, it was impossible to know which way we travelled. I had no reference to the surface, especially after Airil's magic had brought us into the lair. But I was sure we travelled east, towards the human encampment we had seen from the air. Why else would the humans have made this passage?

There were no answers coming, for the walls of the tunnel were completely bare, but for the strips of lighting that illuminated the way. There wasn't even a curve or corner to deviate from the perfectly straight line, further reinforcing any belief that this was artificially made by human hand, not by dragon paw or nature. Dragons had developed great skill in expanding the natural caves of our lairs, but not to this level of precision.

Looking ahead, the tunnel appeared to end abruptly, but as we got closer, I realised that there was finally a bend in the passage. Carlee rounded the corner and paused, letting out another hiss. I quickly saw why. Just ahead of us was a blockage in the tunnel; a human-style door bolted into the rock. The wood looked thick and sturdy, with a small, barred window towards the top.

I flew over the heads of my companions and grabbed onto the door beneath the window, my claws finding grip there. The gap was too small to squeeze through, the bars too close together. On the other side was a much larger passage, tall enough that shadows obscured the distant ceiling. It stretched out both left and right, again to a great enough distance that I could see no end to them. There was no natural light, with the entire cave illuminated with human technology. Their scent was stronger down here, but I could see none of them with my small vantage point. There was no movement at all.

As I fluttered down again, Maznar fumbled with the locking mechanism halfway up the door. Her paws worked quickly, and the door soon swung open. There were marks on the other side. I ran my paw over three gouges in the wood, my claws matching them almost perfectly. I lifted my muzzle and sniffed the air. There it was. Faint amongst the human smells was a familiar one. Ellian had been here.

"Let's go," I said, following the tantalising scent, turning left from the door. I now took the lead, returning to the position of leadership as I followed my nose.

We could have been in the dungeons below George's castle. Everything was almost the same as that hateful place. Dark corridors branched out with small rooms on either side. A thick door barred each room, though some were partly open. I could almost imagine that we were back over the mountains, but this was beneath the lair of dragonkind's most powerful clan. How had Ddraig Tsona allowed this to happen?

Every sound amplified into loud echoes. I struggled to keep my claws from tapping against the stone. Others were not so cautious. I resisted the urge to snarl at them, for that would risk making further noise. Instead, I bristled silently and bit down on my tongue.

In the distance, far behind us, came the sounds of humans. Though I glanced back a few times, I could see nothing of them, but I could hear their heavy pawsteps and echoing voices. They were somewhere close by, but where? And why? My mind burned with the questions, but those answers could wait. For now, all that mattered was finding Ellian and escaping with her. I could start worrying about the reasons for Xital's betrayal once we were safely back in Laxtal.

"Hey, Boss," Vinzent called out nervously. I whipped around, ready to berate him for not keeping his voice down, but he'd placed his paw on a closed door. "I think she's in here."

I pushed the dragonet out the way and put my muzzle against the wood. He was right. Ellian's scent was much stronger here. I looked up at the locking mechanism, then back at Maznar. "Are you able to open it?" I asked the ness. I thought I heard muffled movement on the other side of the door.

Maznar reared up onto her hindlegs so she could pull on the metallic lever, but it didn't move. "Locked," the spectre said with a hiss. "We'll need a key to open it."

"Where will we find one of those?" Vinzent whined, making little effort to keep his voice quiet.

I opened my mouth to berate the dragonet, but my demands for stealth were quickly rendered irrelevant as a burst of heat prickled my scaled, followed by a loud crack that shattered the silence in the tunnel. Airil vanished from where he stood, and a muffled yelp came through the thick door we could not open.

A second crack echoed through the tunnel, reverberating several times as it sounded back. The Nixan returned, exactly where he had stood moments earlier, but now he held a startled lilac ness in his forelegs. Moisture sizzled under his paws, revealing some of the enormity of power he wielded. The exertion showed as he stumbled away from Ellian, almost collapsing to the ground before he managed to regain his balance.

Ellian staggered forward towards me. She placed her paw on my muzzle, as though not daring to believe the evidence of her eyes. "Ziggy? You're really here?" she whispered.

I placed my wing around Ellian's shivering body, a difficult feat given her five inches of extra height over me. She crouched as she leaned against me, making it easier for my wing to settle over her back.

"I wasn't going to abandon you here," I said. Maznar was assisting Airil back to his paws, while Carlee had scouted along the tunnel to check for any humans. Vinzent hovered nearby, unable to even look at Ellian.

"You shouldn't have come. Ddraig Tsona, he... Oh you should have seen what he's done," Ellian said. The anguish in my cousin's voice was worrying.

"I already know, Ellian. I challenged him in Laxtal, and he fled like the coward he is," I growled, but Ellian shook her head and moaned.

"No, no, what? No, I mean here. There must be thousands of them, all waiting for his command," she said. She tried to pull free of my embrace, but I held her tighter with my wings, standing on her tail to stop her moving away. "He showed them to me. I don't know why. Maybe to get me to see how hopeless it is for us, maybe wanting me to join him? I don't know. We can't beat them though, not even if we had every clan united."

"A few thousand humans against Clan Nixa and Clan Laxtal?" I asked, trying to sound nonchalant to ease Ellian's worries, even though I was terrified about the prospect myself. I forced a laugh. "They don't stand a chance."

"You got it then? You got the Axinstone?" Ellian asked. She had given up trying to break free now and had placed her head on top of mine.

Carlee growled to get our attention. "I apologise, Ddraig, but we may wish to save this until we are safe. I find it hard to believe no one heard the Nixan's magic," she said sternly, but there was a softness in her eyes that betrayed her joy at finding Ellian again. Ellian didn't share the same relationship I had with the veteran, but Carlee had been involved in her upbringing too. She had been a mentor to so many of the younger dragons in the clan.

Reluctantly I released Ellian from my wings and walked towards Carlee. "How do we get out then?" I asked her, looking back as Ellian rubbed heads first with Airil and then Maznar. She may not have known who the spectre was, but she still recognised that the ness had come to rescue her.

She hesitated in front of Vinzent. She bowed her head. "You were right about Tsona. I…"

Vinzent growled at her and turned away. His claws scraped at the ground.

Ellian lifted her quivering paw. Her face then hardened, and her wings tightened against her back. She retreated towards Airil.

"The Nixan doesn't look capable of taking us out again," Carlee said. She had also looked back at the small group. She was right. Airil was barely able to remain standing, and certainly didn't look like he'd be able to use his magic to get us out.

The Nixan slowly shook his head and shuffled his wings, using Ellian for support. He had nothing to be ashamed of. His assistance had already been invaluable. He had gotten us down here; we would just have to find another way back up.

"Then we fly out. The humans must have some way of getting into the caves without passing through the lair," I said. There was the slightest hint of a breeze passing through the tunnels, carrying with it air that wasn't saturated with the scent of humans. There had to be another exit.

With some gentle encouragement and a firm nudge or two from Ellian and Maznar, Airil was able to take to wing behind Carlee and me, while Vinzent took up the position at the rear. I led the way, trying to follow the movements in the air to their source.

Shouts echoed behind us, melding together into a wordless cacophony that I could not decipher. There was urgency to the voices. Sharp, shouted commands mingled with the heavy thud of pawsteps. No wingbeats joined the raucous pursuit, but I could not tell if that was because they were absent, or merely drowned out by the larger humans.

I followed the sensation of breeze on my face, hoping to find the exit to the new caverns, all constructed recently, and all empty with few signs of habitation. If the humans planned to live here, then they had not yet moved in.

Finally, I saw natural light in the distance, a welcome relief from the artificial lights the humans had placed all along the walls of the cave. We were nearly there, and still there was no sign of threat ahead of us. The sounds behind us grew louder, but when I glanced back, the tunnels were empty. Their chase was too far back to have any hope of catching us.

I squinted my eyes as we approached the mouth of the cave, the light almost blinding and obscuring what lay outside. Two loud clicks caught my attention. Something whistled through the air.

I yelled in shock and pain as a heavy net entangled around my torso and wings. I immediately fell from the air, unable to even brace myself as I struck the rocky floor hard. Pain burst through my shoulder as I crashed and slid across the ground, rolled up inside the net. Three more thuds told me I had not been the only one ensnared in the trap to stop dragons escaping.

Carlee landed by my side, the only one of us to escape the nets. She tugged at my bonds as an alarm began to blare. The sounds of pursuit grew louder behind us. In the bright light from outside, dark shapes began to emerge. We were surrounded.

The ness struggled to release me, but neither tooth nor claw had any effect on the net. I tried to help her, trying to stretch my legs and free some space for her to work. The net was so tight, pinching against my scales. I could barely move.

Carlee managed to free one of my wings just as the first human turned the nearest corner. In one hand he held a knife, and in the other a small black device which he held up to his mouth.

"Fly Carlee, just go!" I yelled at the veteran, hoping she would save herself at least, but she refused. She stood over me and held her ground, wings flared as she hissed at the human.

"Get George, we have them," the human said, speaking into the little box in his hand.

I whimpered, my struggle falling slack. How could George be here?

"You'll have to get through me first," Carlee snarled, leaping at the human with her claws outstretched.

The human slashed at the ness with his knife.

Carlee screamed and collapsed to the ground, holding her paws over her eyes. Blood splattered the rock wall and dripped from the human's knife. She tried to back away, but a few moments later seven other humans arrived. They all approached us cautiously before they started lifting us up. We were powerless to resist. The nets had trapped our wings and legs, and the humans were careful to stay away from the reach of our teeth. One human slung me over his shoulder, giving me the chance to look back at the others. They were all there: Airil hadn't even had the strength to teleport himself away. They hadn't even needed a net to restrain Carlee. She was motionless as they carried her, leaving a trail of blood behind.

"Up to the mountain cave?" The human carrying me spoke to the others.

"No, they're not ready," his female companion answered. "Lock them into the caves down here for now."

Nothing else was said as the humans carried us all away from the light, retracing our wingbeats back down through the dark tunnels they had carved out beneath the Xital lair. A few royal dragons followed us now. I could see on their faces a mixture of curiosity and fear. I allowed myself a brief moment to wonder why they would be afraid, before realising that if they were scared, we should be terrified about what was going to happen.

The humans were going to kill us. George would probably want to slay us himself.

The knife sliced through the net that bound me. Before I could react to my freedom, they tossed me into a dark cavern. My companions tumbled in behind me and a door slammed shut.

Our escape had resulted only in our capture. We were trapped, imprisoned by the humans who had taken control of Xital.

I had failed Ellian. We had not been able to free her.

I had failed Laxtal. There would be no wylax to confirm my rule. I would be an embarrassment to my father's legacy.

I had failed dragonkind. Ddraig Tsona and his human allies would defeat us all.

Every shred of belief fled my wings as I stared forlornly at the sealed door, barely a scrap of light peeking through the cracks around it. Lost in the darkness, it was all I could do to keep the forbidden tears from springing to my eyes.

If the humans were to kill us, then I hoped they would make it quick. It would mean I no longer needed to live with my shame.

CHAPTER TEN

Azlak

Tsona's time in Laxtal had proven to be violent and disruptive, and I was the dragon to repair the damage caused. It had only been two days since Ddraig Anzig had left for Xital, but already I longed for his return. It would be at least a five-day round trip for him though, and that was if he was able to rescue Ellian without any trouble. I had Seen nothing of him, but I had not had the time to properly focus my magic on the ddraig.

Almost every moment had been spent overseeing the recovery of the clan, with the list of tasks seeming to grow by the minute. It had taken Kaz most of the first day to go around the clan and heal the worst of the injuries. He had exhausted himself in the process, only stopping when my father had dragged him away and told him to rest. I hadn't seen Kaz since then, but I had been told he was still sleeping. I had not even begun to put my mind towards the wylax that I knew must follow, for there would always be doubt over Ddraig Anzig's authority to rule until he had undertaken the ritual ceremony.

To my surprise, no one had yet protested my leadership of the clan. It was almost as though they saw me as a different dragon to the one who had left almost two months ago. Dragons who had once taken any opportunity to belittle me now bowed their heads as I passed.

Taking advantage of a brief pause, I settled in the main chamber close to the firepit, the smoke tickling my nose. I attacked a salted deer haunch, eager to settle the hunger in my belly. So many of the clan had suffered with hunger under Tsona's command. For three weeks, the clan had been largely idle in the time when activity was most important. Winter approached, and the clan's food reserves were too low to get through the harsher months. Now, hunters scoured the clan territory, bringing in as much meat as possible so that it could be preserved and stored.

I was left alone to my meal, giving me a rare opportunity to be alone with my thoughts. There was a wariness about the clan, a sense of unease that I wasn't able to fully understand. Whispers filled the silences, coming from the shadows between the lights. This was a clan whose pride had suffered, and one who had been leaderless for too long. We needed Ddraig Anzig to return, and quickly.

"Azlak, if we may?"

I suppressed the sigh that came immediately to my nose. I turned from the scraps of venison left between my forepaws, then blinked in surprise. I had not expected to see Keita approach, with Okazuni by her side. The ness and her Nyrian mate had not spoken to me once since we had returned to Laxtal.

I scrambled up to my paws, but I did not bow my head. "Keita. Okazuni. What may I do for you?"

To my surprise, Keita lowered her forelegs, sweeping her head low. After a moment of hesitation, Okazuni mimicked the gesture. "I'd like to apologise, firstly," the ness said. "I always doubted you, always disrespected you. I should never have done that."

No small part of my mind cynically saw the reason for Keita's apology. I had become more powerful within the clan. Now that I was no longer the omega, dragons saw me not as someone to ridicule, but to respect. I took no pleasure in Keita's apology. It would have been so easy to growl and snap at her duplicitous nature, but I put aside that bit of petty revenge. "Your apology is accepted," I said instead.

Keita smiled, her eyes unfocused as she looked in my general direction, avoiding my gaze fully. "I would also like to discuss Anzig," she said quietly.

I froze. I didn't like the softness of her voice, clearly intended not to be overheard by any dragon but Okazuni, The little Nyrian kept guard, facing away from me and glaring out towards the rest of the great chamber.

"How so?" I asked, a touch of a growl coming into my tone.

Ketia's half-blind eyes flicked towards her mate, then back to me. "Are we sure he is the right dragon to lead Laxtal now?" She lifted a paw to stall my angry growl. "You told me he always wanted to be my mate, but not once did he share those feelings with me. Was he never confident enough to approach me? Does that speak of a strong leader?"

"I have never had any reason to doubt him as a haeraig," I snarled, just about managing to keep my voice down. If Keita wanted to keep this conversation private, then I would do so as well. It would not do to make obvious that there was already dissent against Anzig's leadership of Laxtal, especially before he had the opportunity to go through the wylax.

"Have you Seen that?" Keita asked.

Her question stole the snarl from my mouth. The tip of my tail flicked, cracking against the floor. "You believe my magic is worth something now?"

"Ever since you kept me safe in those caves in Trevena, yes," the ness said softly. She looked down at her forepaws. "Have you Seen Anzig succeed as ddraig? If you tell me he will, then I will not doubt him."

I sighed. I turned back to my venison and pawed at the meat, my hunger lost for now. "My magic is difficult to understand, even when I'm careful. Taking us across the mountains to reclaim the Axinstone was a risk, but one I thought was worthwhile because I was saving Anzig's life." I looked across to Keita, meeting her eye. She knew like I did the consequences of that action. She did not look away. "I have had hundreds of visions of Anzig. Many of them contradict each other. Some futures I know can't come true anymore. Others still might. My interpretation of my visions is that Anzig will be a powerful and strong ddraig for this clan."

"Then I shall believe that will be the case," Keita said, her voice getting a little stronger again. "I have pledged my heart to Okazuni, but Anzig is still my oldest and closest friend. I will do everything I can to ensure he is as great a ddraig as his father was."

Okazuni turned his head. "He will face resistance."

"It has already started," Keita whispered. She scuffed her paw and looked around. "Saya has long wished for her son to become ddraig. I doubt she will pass over this opportunity, but I think there might be others."

"Who?"

Okazuni hissed in warning before Keita could answer. Wings fluttered over our heads. I looked up to see a familiar dragon coming down to land. My father swooped to my side and dismissed Keita and Okazuni with a low growl. They both fled without a word.

"Anything to report?" I asked, speaking before my father had the chance to say anything. I had learned that from Anzig. Speak first. It projected authority and leadership.

My father sighed. "The ddraig of Clan Zestra will only speak with our ddraig or haeraig. She refuses to treat with anyone else," he said, his wings drooping a little. He had gone to visit our closest neighbour to the south of the lair, one of the smallest clans in the region. I had expected little else from them. Our great alliance could not form without a ddraig to lead the negotiations.

"We must try again once Ddraig Anzig is back," I replied. We needed to get everything prepared, but there were some things that only the ddraig or haeraig could do.

"Then he should hurry," my father muttered. He looked down at me, brow furrowed. "How has the hunting been?"

I grimaced. "Difficult. I think the Xitals raided our winter stores, so not only do we have a hungry clan, we're also short for winter. It will take a lot of work to fill the cold caves. Especially if we're intending on hosting a larger army."

"Tchh. Humans on one paw. Starvation on another," my father snarled. "This is going to be a hard winter for us all."

Blood dripped from high above, falling in rivulets down the cliff and splashing in little puddles on the valley floor. A whimpered cry of pain filled the silence. A dragon, with a broken leg and shattered wings, tried to crawl to the safety of the lair. A shadow flew overhead.

I shuddered. Yes. This winter would be difficult. Battle and bloodshed would come to Laxtal. I doubted there would be any way to avoid that.

I worried about my visions. They were getting bloodier and more violent. I struggled to find peace in them anymore. My head hurt at just the thought of trying to pick through the dangerous futures to find safety for us all. Without control over my magic, I felt powerless to protect anyone, no matter how much authority I wielded within the clan.

Before I had much chance to think about my magic further, I realised a sudden hush had fallen around the lair. The beacon fires had been lit.

A fearful murmur ran through the clan as more and more eyes turned up to the fire, waiting for any change to the bright orange flames. The fire turned purple and began to spark, a controlled reaction to pass message on from beacon to beacon, and finally to the lair. I took a moment to work out what the specific colour and behaviour of the fire meant. Purple meant a Xital dragon. The sparks indicated they were alone.

My father was the first to react, calling out across the chamber for one of the other experienced dragons. "Yalle, get a messenger out there to see who is coming. It might be a scout they sent out and has not yet realised Ddraig Tsona has been driven home."

Yalle dipped his head and moved to obey my father right away. There had been no hesitation. Neither of the older dragons even looked to me, let alone waited for my confirmation to follow those orders. I only remained silent because I knew that my father's commands were correct. This Xital dragon needed to understand that Laxtal was no longer under the rule of the royal clan.

The chosen messenger flew quickly towards the surface. I watched him depart, before looking back towards the albino who had dispatched him. Yalle sauntered towards my position, beneath the tunnels where the leaders of Laxtal lived. Those caves were empty for now, waiting on the return of Anzig and Ellian. Instead, Laxtal had me as a representative. I would be the voice for the clan. Flanked by my father and Yalle, I shivered.

My father leaned close and whispered, too quiet for the prying ears of the rest of the clan. "I will understand if you're unable to do this," he said quietly.

For a moment my old self almost came to the fore – the scared dragon that shied away from the smallest of responsibility. But then I remembered again that Ddraig Anzig had placed his faith in me. I would not back away from that. I lifted my shoulders up and stood as tall as my diminutive frame would allow me.

"I can do this, father," I said. I wasn't offended that he had doubted me. I could feel hundreds of eyes on me. They would all be judging me, and I knew many of them would doubt me too, just like my father. But Ddraig Anzig had chosen me to lead the clan, and for now that was enough to keep them silent.

My father nodded his head once. "I'll be right at your side if you need me," he said.

"This cannot be in retribution to anything Anzig has done," Yalle mused. "Our prospective ddraig would only just have arrived in Xital. It is almost certain they do not know what has happened here. We might be able to get some information about Tsona's plans, if we manage this correctly."

I looked up to the two dragons. Their experience and knowledge would be crucial. I would be foolish to ignore them. "We still have a little time. Teach me whatever you can so I can do our clan proud."

"Proud?" my father said. The tips of his teeth poked out from his lips. "I never thought I'd live to see the day you would do this clan proud, my son. Listen to what we have to say, and we may yet see it today."

I ignored the barely veiled insult. There were more important matters to deal with. I settled down, one wary eye on the clan, and listened to everything the two dragons had to say.

It took an hour before the messenger returned. As the beacon fire had warned, a lone dragon returned with him. The burnished copper ness glared around the chamber as she landed as directed, close to the base of the raised dais and the firepit. I did not immediately recognise her, but her clan lineage was obvious with the crown of horns around her head.

"Where is the dragon who called himself ddraig?" she asked haughtily. Her eyes didn't linger on any one dragon as she searched for the leader of the clan. It took me a few moments to remember that I was the dragon she sought.

I took a few tentative steps forward, moving from the shadow of my father and into the firelight. The Xital's eyes immediately met mine. I resisted looking away. This was no haeraig or ddraig of Xital. They may be the royal clan, but as the chosen representative of Laxtal, I had no obligation to submit or show deference to her.

"Ddraig Anzig is not here. I am Azlak, and I control the clan in his absence," I said, trying to keep the nervous quaver out of my voice.

"Where is he?" the ness asked. Her tail thrashed from side to side as she glared at me. Even though she stood lower on the chamber floor, she still managed to give the impression of looking down her muzzle at me.

"That is none of your concern," I replied. I met the eyes of the much taller ness and refused to look away. I could see the ness's surprise as she glanced away first. If she had expected to come to our clan and have her way, then I knew I would disappoint her. The days of Xital holding domination over Laxtal had passed.

Though the ness betrayed her displeasure by growling, she did not press me for more information on Ddraig Anzig. Instead, she eased back onto her haunches and shook her wings. Her eyes stayed focused on my paws and didn't stray higher than that.

"I am Selane, the youngest daughter of Ddraig Tsona. I fled with my father when your ddraig bested him, but I slipped away and turned back before we made it home," the ness said. She lowered her head, dipping her eyes lower and showing off the ring of horns that ran around the top of her skull. It was not a display of aggression.

I tilted my head to the side, intrigued by her words. She had turned back by her own will. "Why did you come?"

Selane looked away. Her claws kneaded the rock beneath her paws. She seemed embarrassed – ashamed by her actions. "I have seen what my father has done, and what he has become. I do not agree with it." Her voice dropped down to a whisper. "He has betrayed the draconic way, but no one will speak out against him. I came seeking Ddraig Anzig to beg for asylum amongst your clan."

Silence met her words, with barely a breath passing through the great chamber. It felt like this ness had the entire clan craning to hear her every word.

"What caused you to turn against your father?" I asked. It must have taken an incredible act of bravery from this Xital ness to fly away from her father, the most powerful dragon in existence.

Selane swung her head back to search through the gathered crowd of watching Laxtals. "There was a drake..." she said quietly, before turning back around to face me. Her voice grew in strength once more and her posture recovered slightly, but she didn't look in my eye. "I have turned my back on Xital and I will not be allowed to return. If Ddraig Anzig is not here, I must ask it of you, Azlak of Laxtal, will your clan grant me refuge?"

My body tensed. This was no mere question put forward. This was a decision for a leader of the clan. A choice that could have massive consequences if I got it wrong.

There were so many things to consider. Was this a trap from the Xital ness? Was she truly being honest about doubting her father? I already knew Ddraig Tsona had lied about his true intentions. The Nixans had been quite adamant that we could trust Tsona, but that faith had been betrayed, like we had. Could I trust the word of the treacherous dragon's daughter?

I quickly stole a glance back at my father, who shook his head. Whether he was advising me not to offer refuge to the Xital, or that he couldn't be the one to answer, I wasn't sure. Behind him was Yalle. The albino dragon held his forepaw aloft and had clenched it tight like he intended to strike someone, though no one was even close to him. Then he relented. He nodded his head slightly as he lowered his paw back to the ground. I took this as approval. I turned to look back into the eyes of Selane, searching for something, anything.

"Selene of Xital, you are welcome to stay in Laxtal, for now, until Ddraig Anzig returns. Beyond that time, it is his decision," I said. I tried to inject an air of authority into my voice. To my ears it just sounded oddly false but, to my surprise, the Xital ness bowed her head.

"I am most grateful for your generosity," Selane said.

A single dragon stepped forward from the hundreds that had stopped to watch our exchange. None had spoken and barely any had moved until now. "If I may, Azlak. I would take Selane under my wing, to protect and watch over her until the ddraig returns," the brown scaled dragon asked. I knew immediately that this dragon, presenting himself before me, was the reason for Selane's defection from Xital, or at least a part of it. I still didn't know if I'd done the right thing, but the actions of this dragon comforted me. I couldn't place his name, but I knew I had seen him on occasion. I couldn't recall a time though we had ever spoken, or if he had been one of the many who had mocked me over the years. For now, at least, he was civil and polite.

"Until Ddraig Anzig returns," I repeated, before turning back to Selane. "Was there any other reason you came to Laxtal for? Is there anything at all you can tell us about your father's plans?"

Selane looked down into the ground and tightened her wings against her back, making herself look as small as her sturdy frame allowed. "You must understand he is still my father. I... I don't think I could betray his secrets. Not here. Not now," she said.

"I understand," I replied. I had to admit I was a little disappointed. I would have enjoyed revealing some of Tsona's secrets to Ddraig Anzig once he returned, but I genuinely understood Selane's reluctance. No matter what my father had done to me in the past, I would never have been able to betray him. The bond of blood was a difficult one to break.

"By your leave Azlak, I would like to retire with Ravet," Selane said, shifting slightly closer to the drake at her side.

I allowed the two dragons to leave, and they immediately flew away to the deeper parts of the lair. With their departure, most of the other dragons lost interest and turned away, but there was one who remained fixated with my every move. I could feel the burning of his eyes from behind me. I slowly turned and looked at my father. I could tell from the glare that he was not impressed with my actions, but I stood as tall as I could and attempted to face him down.

"Why did you trust her?" my father questioned. "It was only a few days ago we finally got rid of the last of her wretched clan from this place." He still hadn't turned away from me, but I wasn't going to back down.

"I did what a ddraig should do," I replied, trying to keep my voice even. My hind legs wanted to back away, but I managed to keep them still. I could do little about the flutter of my wings.

"You allowed a Xital ness into our clan. They are the enemy," my father hissed. His back arched upwards, and for a moment I thought he was about to attack.

"I did what Ddraig Anzig would have done," I growled. My hind right paw shifted back, almost conceding to my father. I stayed strong.

The green dragon before me snarled, showing off his teeth. He lowered his head, dipping his long, sharp horns towards me. Unlike the similar gesture from Selane, I knew this one to be a threat, a show of aggression. "Is that so?" he rumbled. A dark light shone in his eye.

A dragon moved to stand between us, positioning himself so that my father couldn't reach me. "Enough of this, Marin," Yalle growled. He faced down my father, who was quick to look away from the albino dragon. "You were quick to trust Azlak before. Has that faith gone so soon?"

Yalle was one of the most experienced dragons in the clan, who had long been one of Astar's powerful friends. His support buoyed me. Few of the clan had remained behind to witness the short exchange, but those that had would surely have been swayed by the opinion of the respected albino. But it was just one dragon that mattered now. My father's aggression failed to subside.

"He would side with Xitals over us," my father snapped, flicking out his wings. His aggression showed no sign of abating, despite the albino's presence.

"Side with her? I did nothing of the sort," I spluttered. I didn't care how much noise we made, how much attention came our way. I ignored everything around me with my focus fixed firmly on my father.

My father ignored me entirely. As did Yalle. They had eyes only for each other. I might as well have not spoken at all.

"Until the wylax, there will be no final decision made on the Xital's future," the albino said slowly. He lifted a paw, gesturing down to calm my father.

Only then did my father look over Yalle's shoulder to glare at me again. "You believe that if Anzig were here, he would make the same choice as you?"

I did not hesitate. "Yes. I don't need to use my magic to know that," I said, ignoring the customary wince my father made whenever reminded of my magic. "I learned a lot about him over the mountains. He is a strong leader, but he also looks past clan and history. He would not judge Selane for being a Xital. Not even for being Tsona's daughter. If she came here for refuge, then he will give it to her. And so will I."

"So be it," my father hissed. He took to wing and flew off without another word.

His words and anger didn't upset me too greatly. I had endured years of my father's disappointment before today. For a brief moment he had admitted he was proud of me. Though it hurt to see that discarded so soon, I hoped to restore that pride once Ddraig Anzig returned and proved my decision correct.

With the excitement of Selane's arrival ending, the clan had returned to normal. Or at least, as normal as it could be in a time like this. Laxtal had a lot of recovery before any semblance of normality could resume. The plundered reserves of food and supplies still needed replenishing, and hundreds of dragons were hard at work. They salted and preserved meat, dried out herbs, and prepared the fuel that kept alight the torches and fires throughout the caves. I had done nothing to instigate this. The clan knew what we needed to survive the winter.

There was one dragon I had not seen amongst the activity, one who I had expected to see. Kaz was not present, even amongst the Laxtal healers who tended to those still wounded and sick.

"Have you seen Kaz?" I asked, looking up to the albino dragon who had remained by my side.

Yalle rumbled softly, a deep noise that wasn't quite a growl. "I believe he is still resting in the lower chambers. I intended on inspecting the cold caves, so I can take you down to him if you like."

"Please, if you would," I said.

Yalle took off without a word, flying quickly through the chaos of the main cavern. I struggled to keep up with him, my shorter wings unable to maintain the same pace as the albino. With my increased authority, a few dragons swerved out of my way as I swooped past. A few even lowered their heads and dipped their wings mid-flight.

It was a most unsettling sensation, having so many dragons respect me so. It took all my willpower to keep my head up high and try to exude the confidence I didn't feel. I recognised most of the dragons, and almost without exception they had hurled abuse and insults at me just a few short weeks ago. Now they were respecting me as their leader. What had I done to deserve such an increase of power within the clan? Nothing had changed. I was still the lone Laxtal with magic... Only... I wasn't now, was I? I shared that curse with the ddraig of the clan. Was Ddraig Anzig trying to increase my standing within the clan so that if someone discovered his magic, he didn't fall so far? Whatever Ddraig Anzig's intentions, I wasn't going to complain that I no longer appeared to be the clan omega. Whether that would last when the ddraig returned to regain leadership of the clan, that was another matter entirely.

I was glad when we left the main chamber, leaving behind the strange sensation of respect. We flew down through the many branching passages that made up the bulk of the lair. The light was less consistent in these tunnels, with a torch every few wingbeats providing a circle of light with dark shadows between them. Small caverns and chambers opened off on either side of the tunnel, where the dragons of Laxtal lived.

There were few dragons down here, though a few faces did peer up at us as we flew by. Most of the dragons were up in the main chamber or on the surface, restoring the clan to survive through the oncoming winter. I wondered where Kaz rested. All the chambers close to the surface were claimed, but there was still plenty of space further down, towards my home in one of the darker corners of the cave network.

Even so, we flew much further and deeper than I expected. We passed the cold caves, where a few dragons worked on storing the meat and other supplies that would get us through the winter. Beyond those, the darkness grew stronger. Fewer torches were lit, leaving long stretches of shadow. We came towards the end of the lair, though a few narrow tunnels did wind deeper, but there were no more torch sconces in the walls. Ahead of us was only darkness.

The chambers this far deep below the surface were rarely used for any purpose. The clan's numbers had never swelled so much that they were necessary, and nor had we received so many visitors. These caves were damp and icy, every bit as chilled as the cold caves. Even my chambers were not this far underground, and this was all for a dragon who had expended a lot of energy, helping to heal hundreds of Laxtal dragons.

I glared sharply at Yalle, though I didn't know if he was responsible for this. He shifted uncomfortably, angling his wings and sinking deeper into shadow. "We can spare some caves closer to the central chambers if you'd prefer," he said, his voice echoing off the rock that loomed close and dark around us.

"Get some prepared immediately," I growled, surprising even myself with the ferocity in my voice. "You wouldn't have allowed this if Ddraig Anzig was here. Why should it be different because I'm in charge?"

"It was an oversight, nothing more," Yalle said. He looked ahead, avoiding my gaze. "We are here now."

There were so few scents on the air that I could clearly smell Kaz nearby. The scent of my father also lingered, but no other dragons had come down this far in a long time. I suppressed a snarl of frustration. At least I knew who to blame for bringing Kaz down here.

I landed by Yalle's side at the entrance to a small chamber. A single torch inside provided flickering light, the strong scent of the oil used to fuel the flame drifting through the air. There wasn't much breeze to carry the smoke, but it mostly rose and filtered through cracks in the stone ceiling.

The chamber was empty. Were it not for the strength of his scent, I would have believed Yalle had taken me to the wrong place.

"He was here before," Yalle said slowly. He lifted his muzzle and sniffed deeply, then turned his head to gaze into the pitch darkness that extended deeper below the lair. "He went down there."

My blood ran as cold as the air around me. "Find somewhere better for him," I snapped at the albino. "I'm going down there to fetch him."

Yalle scuffed at the ground, dislodging some grime and lichen with his paw. "Is that wise, to go on alone? You know the stories."

I met the albino in his pale eyes. He looked away. "Yes, I know about them," I growled. I flicked out a wing, gesturing to the dark passage. "Kaz doesn't. Go. Find a more suitable chamber for him, and while you're doing so try to remember what he has already done for this clan."

The albino didn't move. I snapped my teeth. "Go!" I barked.

I waited for Yalle to take to wing. He quickly disappeared beyond the ring of light, swooping up through the caves. I shivered, feeling the weight of the rock pressing down on me. The albino's wingbeats echoed back down the passage, but soon that passed beyond the range of my hearing. Instead, I could hear only the sputter of the fire behind me, and the steady drip of a trickle of water. Kaz's scent lingered in my nose, but through no other sense.

I grabbed the lone torch in my mouth and pulled it from the sconce. I had to squint with the fire so close to my eyes, but only like this would I be able to see anything in the darkness beyond. I hesitated. It had been many years since I had gone beyond the confines of the lair, into the empty and isolated tunnels beneath where no dragons dared to tread. None but the Nixan healer who had gone into places he did not understand.

Gathering all my courage, I delved into the darkness, taking my light with me. There were no sconces on the walls. Nothing to indicate any dragons used these caves. I doubted any had, not since I had been a tiny dragonet with emergent magic.

The shadows danced and flickered in the light I carried, making it seem like the cave was alive. Grasping tendrils of darkness reached for me. Icy cold water dripped on my scales. I cowered low. My teeth sunk deep into the wooden torch. The taste was bitter and laced with a little oil from the fuel.

I followed Kaz's scent. His tracks were fresh. I was sure he had come down here less than an hour ago, but it was hard to be precise.

I wanted to call out, but with the torch in my mouth, I couldn't speak. My pawsteps echoed, but that was not the only sound I could hear. A deep roar began to grow, putting my mind to the stories of the darkest caves beneath Laxtal. Stories of spirits and strange creatures that haunted the shadows. It took me a few paces to remember that what I heard was nothing scarier than an underground river.

A flicker of light pierced the darkness ahead. I hurried forward, relieved to see Kaz standing in the light. He had brought a torch with him as well, resting it against the wall so he had full use of his paws and mouth. The Nixan focused on the rock in front of him, not turning at all until I got close. His eyes widened and he smiled when he saw me.

"Have you seen anything like this before?" he asked, forgoing any greeting. He placed his forepaw on the wall, beside some strange markings that gleamed in the light. It looked like writing of some sort, in a language I did not recognise. The words appeared to have been carved by a dragon's claw. As far as I could tell, it was only two words repeated over and over. They reminded me of the stone tablets we had seen in the cave north of Kxisila, but I had never seen anything similar in Laxtal before. What else lurked down here, in the caves we had never explored?

"Nagyrz zavrat," Kaz read, tracing the words with a claw.

I carefully put down my torch next to Kaz's, ensuring I knocked neither of them over. I had no desire to find my way back to the illuminated tunnels without being able to see.

"What does it mean?" I said, tilting my head to the side as I struggled to make out the words.

Kaz held his paw still, one claw scratching at the engraved lettering. "It's draconic. This is the ancient draconic language," he said, his voice rising as his excitement grew. "I spent some time in Clan Vatrea recently. They're trying to recover our language, the language spoken by dragons hundreds of years ago. I was keen to learn, so they taught me as much as they could."

"And do you know what it means?" I asked, my voice barely a whisper.

Kaz turned back to the draconic words, his tongue protruding from his mouth as he thought. His eyes darted back and forth over the rock as though trying to absorb clues as to the meaning. Just when I thought he was going to give up in frustration, his eyes widened and he gasped in shock.

"Of course, that's it," he whispered. "It means 'never forget'."

"Never forget? Never forget what though?" I asked, running a claw along the grooved words. There were no other words engraved here to give us any answers.

Kaz shook his head. "I don't know. The ddraig of Clan Vatrea, Ddraig Boruc, believes we have lost a lot of our ancient history. We know hardly anything beyond six hundred years ago, beyond a time that he called the cataclysm, but there is evidence to suggest dragons have been in some lairs for much longer. Something terrible happened back then. Maybe that's what we were never meant to forget."

"But we did," I said. My paw fell away from the mysterious words engraved in the wall. I rarely dwelt on the past, and whilst I was intrigued by this lost history, I quickly lost interest in the unknowable draconic words. I turned and walked away, waiting for the Nixan to lose interest as well, but he still frowned in thought.

"There's nothing like this anywhere else in the lair?" Kaz asked, finally tearing his eyes away from the writing.

"Nothing I've ever seen. The caves down here are said to be haunted," I replied. I sat down by the edge of the light, staring into the darkness that shrouded the way to the river. Despite being so far underground, there was quite a strong breeze that blew through the passageways. Something in the dark caverns below kept the air moving, though no Laxtal dragon had ever explored them. I shuddered at the memories of being down there once before, many years ago. I had sought refuge there to escape the taunting of the clan, but there was something much more terrifying down there than mere name calling. There was a presence in the darkness. I had felt it before.

"All the same, I would like to explore…

The Nixan slowly approached the great edifice. An amber glow emanated from near the top of the rocky protrusion; it was the only light other than Inilta's flame that hovered over the heads of the three dragons. Kaz, Inilta, and the small golden dragon, hesitantly crawled closer to the strange new light source.

…your lair and see if I can find anything new. Who knows what secrets are kept in the rock here?"

I jumped as Kaz placed his paw on my tail, his eyes bright with intrigue.

I shook my head. "It isn't my permission you need. You'll have to wait for Ddraig Anzig to return first," I said as a cold chill spread through my body. I glanced down to the right, where I could just about see the fissure that led down to the underground river. Surely I wouldn't follow Inilta and Kaz down into those depths?

Kaz caught the direction of my gaze. "What's down there?" he said, nosing forward and peering down into the gloom. He gasped in shock. "Can you feel it? There's raw magic down there. Something of immense power."

"I can, but no one else here has ever felt it," I said, coming up to the Nixan's side, though I would much rather flee as far away from the underground river as I could.

"Of course they wouldn't. They wouldn't be able to feel magic like this," Kaz scoffed. He continued to edge further forward until the passageway dropped off sharply, falling into the darkness at an alarming rate. His tail trembled in excitement. I knew what he was going to say from the moment he turned back to face me, his eyes gleaming in the firelight of our torches.

"We should go and see what's down there," he said. He immediately dived forward, but I was able to leap and grab hold of his tail before he was able to disappear completely into the darkness.

Kaz growled as he pulled his tail from my grasp, but he didn't try to escape down to the river again. "What's down there?" he asked again with a small snarl.

"I don't know. Ghosts. Spirits. Evil," I replied. This time I wasn't able to keep the fear out of my voice. I dreaded having to go down there again, but I knew that Kaz wouldn't be deterred. "You can't go down there in the dark. I Saw us with Inilta, so he must be coming to Laxtal soon. We should wait until he's here."

Kaz grin was wide as he asked, "You're coming as well?"

I nodded glumly. "I don't know what's down there, but I think it's important enough to find out. Whatever it is, it might help us defeat the humans," I said slowly. It didn't make me feel any better about the situation, but I was sure it was something that would help the clan in the war against the humans.

"Oh, very well," Kaz said with a sigh. He peered around the narrow tunnel, but if he searched for any other traces of engraved writing, then he found nothing. "I will wait until your ddraig returns to give us permission, and I will hope that Inilta arrives so your vision can be accurate. But I will not wait too long. There is something strong down here. Something very powerful. It is strange that your clan has sat on this and done nothing with it."

"My clan is scared of anything to do with magic," I muttered. I turned my head away. "They would much rather ignore it and pretend it doesn't exist. Magic is Nixan, not Laxtal. So therefore it must not be important. Why else do you think I've always been the omega of this clan?"

"But Ddraig Anzig is different?"

"He always has been, yes," I said with a sigh. "He's never mocked me and always listened to my visions. He's one of the few dragons in Laxtal to treat other clans with respect, great clan or not. That's why he'll be the perfect ddraig, especially in a time like this. As strong a leader as Astar was, I don't think he would have allied with Nixa without trying to weaken your clan in the process."

"Perhaps fortune has put the right dragons in control at this time," Kaz said. He lightly bumped against my side, the contact lingering just long enough that I was sure it had not been accidental. "And those dragons have the right voices in their ear to guide them."

I stared at Kaz, but he ignored my gaze. The Nixan seemed aware of it, though. He smirked as he approached the two torches, the tip of his tail brushing against my cheek.

"If we're not going to explore today, how about we hunt instead?" the Nixan suggested. His eye glinted with mischief and a strange look of desire. "I hear Laxtal provides everything a dragon could ever want or need."

"Not compared to Nixa," I muttered. The scales beneath my horns felt a little warm as I flushed. Did Kaz really mean me? Did he think I was a good voice in the ear of the ddraig? And what of this contact? I shivered as his tail came very close to my neck. No dragon had ever done that before. My mind raced with possibilities before I could control them. Why would this drake, a Nixan at that, be interested in me?

Kaz turned around in the narrow confines of the tunnel. The tip of his muzzle bumped against mine. He grinned. "Let me be the judge of that. Come on. I'm hungry."

Before I could question him any further or protest that I had recently eaten, Kaz grabbed one of the torches in his mouth and leaped away. With no desire to be alone so close to the river and the spirits that might haunt it, I had no choice but to take the other torch and hurry after the Nixan.

I was relieved to return to the occupied caves again. We restored our torches to sconces and continued upwards by wing, though Kaz always stayed that little bit too far ahead of me to ask him any more questions. He glanced back occasionally, making sure I followed.

He looked back again as we emerged into the central chamber. The Nixan squawked as a green dragon slammed into his side.

I yelped in alarm, my wings beating faster. Kaz struck the ground hard, the larger Laxtal dragon pinning him down with a paw to the throat. My father.

"What are you doing?" I cried out. I landed and hurried across to them, but another dragon moved to stand in my way. Yalle. The albino's lips parted in a silent snarl.

"I should have known," my father hissed. He kept Kaz pinned beneath his paw, ignoring the Nixan's attempts to free himself.

"Known what?" I spat.

Yalle stood aside, allowing my father's glare to bore into me. I rolled my shoulders and tried to stand a little straighter.

"That you would take the side of a Nixan over your clan," my father snarled. He stomped his paw to the ground, tightening his grip on Kaz's throat with his other.

"Sided with...? I never did any such thing! I objected to the way my clan has treated Kaz. Especially after all he has done to help us. That does not mean I sided with him over Laxtal," I snarled, but my father wasn't even listening to my protests.

"I should have known this day would come, given –"

"Marin!" Yalle's shout was so forceful that it echoed around the whole chamber, attracting the attention of most of the dragons around. The albino turned his back to me as he squared up to my father.

"Why should I keep this fantasy up any longer?" my father spat. He released Kaz as he flared his wings, taking a step back from the albino.

Kaz rolled away and scrambled up to his paws, keeping his body low to the ground.

Yalle barged past the Nixan and closed the gap between himself and my father. "Because now is not the time for such matters to be discussed," the albino rumbled.

I pushed my way between the two arguing dragons, asserting my position as the acting ddraig, and glared up at my father. "Not the time for what? What are you keeping from me?" I growled. My father's eyes continued to seemingly bore right through me, as though he was focusing on the chamber wall behind me. It was as if I was invisible to him. I turned to Yalle, but the albino averted his gaze. Both held their silence.

"Have it your way then," I snarled when it became evident neither dragon was going to speak. "I am taking Kaz out to hunt. This dragon needs to be afforded some courtesy. Be sure to contact me if anything happens. Just remember that Ddraig Anzig appointed me to lead the clan in his absence. Not you. Not either of you," I spat out the last sentence, trying to enforce some of the power and status Anzig had given me. I may only be akin to a ddraig for a short time, but I intended to behave as one.

Before giving either dragon a chance to offer a retort that never came, I took to wing and flew out of the higher entrance from the central chambers. Kaz stayed close to my tail as other dragons swerved to avoid us. I didn't pause to consider what had just happened until there was grass beneath my paws and the open wind in my face. To think that such a short time ago my father had been proud of me, but now...

A green dragon stood in front of a smaller, bronze dragon. The green dragon had bowed his head in respect. "He is your son. Not mine."

"What was that all about?" Kaz asked as he landed by my side, his eyes on the distant herd of deer.

I was numb. "I don't know Kaz. I don't think I want to know," I whispered.

CHAPTER ELEVEN

Anzig

Ellian pounded her paw against the door, giving no care to the noise she made or the pain she clearly suffered. I ignored her, staring at the back wall of the cramped prison cell, my shoulders low and my wings draped around my body. I didn't know how long we had been imprisoned without word from our captors, but I knew it had to be several hours already. Possibly even a full night. It was difficult to tell without any natural light.

Maznar stood over Carlee, the veteran forced to lie still, whimpering in pain from the deep gash running through her eye and marring her face. Whenever Carlee tried to move, Maznar put pressure on her neck with a paw, forcing the veteran to remain where she lay. This was all done with a few growls and snarls from both nesses, but the spectre always won.

Vinzent sulked in one dark corner of the cell. I would have growled at him, but I knew I acted just the same way. Several times that almost roused my shame into overcoming my lethargy, but even so, I could never summon the energy to do anything.

Of us all, only Airil and Ellian made any attempt to escape, though they had not come close to succeeding. Airil's magic had failed to work whenever he had tried to leave that way. My magic had also been silent, with no errant thoughts of others drifting into my mind. That meant I was alone with my thoughts. I wasn't sure which was worse. I didn't need to know the scorn of those around me when my own mind reminded me of my failures over and over again.

"At least send us a healer, damn you all!"

Ellian smashed both forepaws against the door one last time. She snarled and turned away, her fury softening when she looked down at Carlee. Her tail still lashed, the movement in the corner of my eye distracting me.

"They won't waste a healer on us," I said. I turned around to face the other dragons. Only Carlee did not return my gaze. No one dropped their eyes. I did not deserve a show of respect. I flicked out a wing to gesture at the door. "They have us in here so they can kill us at the right moment. They won't give us any opportunity to escape."

"I don't believe that," Carlee said, her voice laced with pain. Once more she struggled against Maznar's paw. Once more, the spectre refused to let her move. The veteran coughed, blood on her scales. "I don't believe that." She closed her one good eye as she repeated her declaration, as though that would change matters.

Ellian growled at me. I couldn't even summon up the energy to growl back. I simply turned away and lay down, drawing my wing across my face. At least she didn't try to argue. Nor did she resume her futile attempts to escape.

But for Carlee's occasional gasp of pain, we waited in silence for our doom to fall. More time crept by, passed only by ever darker thoughts crowding my mind. I could see no way out of this one. No chance to escape. Not even in the dungeons of George had I felt so hopeless.

When something pounded on the door, I pulled aside my wing, a fresh snarl on my lips to unleash at Ellian. But she was not at the door. No one was close enough to strike it. The sound had come from the other side.

The snarl died on my lips as I cautiously approached the door. "Who's there?"

No one answered, but the door opened. Before any chance of escape could flit through my head, a pistol aimed directly for me. I yelped and leaped back. A human followed the pistol into our prison and the door slammed shut behind her.

The pistol lowered. The human who carried it was pale faced with shocking red hair. She carried a heavy bag around one shoulder.

"Who are you?" Ellian demanded, taking a step forward while I took one back.

The human did not lift her pistol. Instead, she crouched by Carlee's side. "You can call me Leah. You asked for a healer, did you not?"

I narrowed my eyes. "Why would you offer to heal her? Aren't you our enemy?"

The human, Leah, looked up and met my eyes. Unlike most other humans I had met, her eyes remained locked onto mine and did not look away. "There is no such thing as an enemy for a healer. We offer our services to any who are in aid."

"How can we trust you?" I asked.

Leah put her hands gently on Carlee. Neither the veteran nor Maznar made any attempt to stop her. "I don't think this one has much choice," the human said softly. "This wound is badly infected. It should have been dealt with much earlier."

Though I let out a small growl, I took another step back from the human. "If Carlee will let you, then do what you can for her."

Carlee did not resist as the human's fingers gently worked over her cheek and muzzle, taking care not to go too close to the ragged wound that still oozed blood and pus. She then slipped her bag off her shoulder and sifted through it for some supplies.

"Here, you should take this for the pain," the human said, holding out a couple of dried leaves for Carlee. Though the ness wrinkled her nose at the offered leaves, she took them into her mouth and grimaced as she swallowed. Almost immediately, Carlee noticeably relaxed. She took a deep breath and closed her remaining eye, the rise and fall of her chest slowing a little. Her tail tip languidly flicked back and forth.

Under the watchful eye of four dragons, the human got to work. She gently used a wipe to clean away the partially dried blood from around Carlee's ruined eye. Once clear of detritus, it became easier to see just how bad the wound was. There was little left of the eye, just a deep wound that exposed cracked bone and severed muscle. Behind me, Vinzent gagged. I wasn't far from doing the same.

As the human worked, she made small noises in the back of her throat. I wasn't sure if she intended to be comforting, but I could work out no other purpose for them. The scent of the liquid she used with the wipe stung at my nose. Once she was satisfied that the wound was properly cleaned, she methodically returned the bloodied wipes to a transparent pouch within her bag, then wiped her hands clean.

Leah then placed her palms over Carlee's head. Each hand could almost have engulfed her entirely, but whether it was the leaves, or because the veteran trusted the human, she barely reacted to the touch.

I crept closer, curious to know what the human was doing. Heat blossomed out from her palms. I stared wide-eyed.

"Healing magic requires knowledge of anatomy and biology," the human explained as Carlee's scales began to knit together beneath her fingers, seeming to notice my attention. "Dragon biology is quite different to a human, but thankfully for your friend, I have studied extensively."

I wasn't sure I wanted to know how Leah had gained that knowledge. I suppressed a shiver and kept my eyes on her progress.

"How is it you can use magic?" Airil demanded, watching from over my shoulder.

"Let me finish first, please," Leah said. She put one hand between Carlee's long horns, gripping tight. The veteran ness let out a quiet whimper as the heat intensified, the human's magic growing stronger. Her tail curled.

Maznar circled around the human and veteran, her blazing red eyes watching with interest. She showed no fear in front of the human, entwining between Leah's legs with ease.

The human's jaw tensed. A burst of light emerged from her fingers, engulfing Carlee for an instant. When the light faded, there was no blood on her scales. A pale scar ran from her chin to the base of her horn, running directly through the empty eye socket.

I gasped in shock. "I thought you were going to heal her?"

Leah shook her head. "I am sorry, but I cannot heal what is not there. The eye was already gone, but she will no longer need to fear infection or blood loss. Once she has recovered from the bitterleaf, she will be fine."

"And what of your magic?" Airil asked with a growl.

The human spread her hands. "There are charms placed around the cell to prevent dragon magic, while still allowing ours to work. I'm sorry, but your magic will not work here."

"Then how else can we get out?" I asked, standing in front of Airil, putting myself between human and Nixan. "If we can't use our magic… if Airil can't use his, I mean, how can we escape?"

The pistol appeared quicker than I could blink, the muzzle aimed for my head. I yelped and stepped back.

"Do not mistake my healing generosity for assistance in escaping," Leah said sharply. She narrowed her eyes, finger resting on the trigger of her pistol. "You are a prisoner of George, whether right or wrong. You will be taken to him in the morning for whatever judgement he has to give. Should you escape now, then it will be obvious who set you free. I will not put myself into that risk, but were you to escape later, well that would not be my fault, would it? Just know that escaping won't be easy, as you won't be able to use your magic even outside of this cell. George carries a god-touched charm to annul draconic magic with him at all times."

I lowered my eyes, trying my best to ignore the pistol. My mouth was dry. "What does this charm look like?"

"A jewel around his neck. A red ruby in a silver otter's head," the human replied. "Not that you heard it from me. But destroy the charm, and your magic will work again."

"Thank you," Ellian said. She dipped her head towards the human healer.

"For what?" The human's question was sharp, her tone pointed.

"For healing Carlee," Ellian added.

Leah smiled, returning the incline of her head. "You're quite welcome." She sheathed the pistol and took a step towards the door. "Forgive me if I say I hope we don't cross paths again. You will be picked up in the morning and taken to George."

The door opened and the human slipped out. Before any of us could even consider leaping for the opening, it slammed shut once more. She was gone, as quickly as she had come. I stared at the closed door, then turned to face Carlee. The veteran remained still, breathing slowly. I tentatively approached her and reached out with one forepaw, gently cupping against her chin. The white scar was jagged against her brown scales, but the blood was cleaned up. She would recover.

I didn't know how long we had until the humans would come for us. But just maybe, we now had a way of escape. I slowly turned to face the others, my tail lashing as I struggled to lift my shoulders high enough to stand to the same height as Ellian. "I think we have a way out. If we can destroy George's charm, then Airil can take us to safety."

The Nixan sucked his breath in. "I will struggle to carry us all, Ddraig."

"It is our best chance," I said, meeting the Nixan in the eyes.

Airil lowered his head. "Then I shall do my best."

Ellian moved to his side, placing her wing over his body. "We should all get some rest," my cousin said. "We will need to be ready."

A tiny hope blossomed in my heart. Perhaps we could escape this after all.

Maznar's eyes met my own. Her fierce red gaze burrowed deep into my mind and soul. In their depths I almost lost myself again, and in that moment I knew the most horrific fear.

Then she smiled and the emotion vanished. "Yes. Let's rest," the spectre said. Her laughter echoed within my mind.

A dozen humans came for us, guns raised and voices loud. They grabbed hold of us roughly, pinning our wings to our sides so we could not fly away. They wore thick gloves and sleeves to protect them from claw or tooth.

A few Xital dragons watched on with curiosity, though none approached or even spoke. I allowed the humans to carry me away, my body limp in his grasp. None of the others resisted, though Carlee and Vinzent both let out a frustrated growl. Our only chance of survival relied on the humans believing we had no hope for escape.

They took us up through the angular, man-made caves to the natural ones above. The clan still felt largely deserted following the departure of the great army. More and more draconic eyes watched us, a scaled guard surrounded the humans as they carried us to the great audience chamber. There, a dozen more humans waited for us, all carrying guns.

Of all of those waiting for us, my attention moved to the podium, upon which was one dragon and one human. Tsona moved gingerly as he stepped forward. One wing was bound to his side.

"Brave Anzig, come to free his clanmate. Such a good job you've done too. I hear you almost made it outside," the Xital traitor taunted. "You would have been a good ally, Anzig. Now we're just going to have to kill you."

The humans threw my companions to the ground with me. For a moment I considered flaring my wings, but then I saw just how many weapons the humans carried. If I took flight, they would shoot me down before I could get anywhere. Our plan was looking ever more unlikely.

"Is this the one who stole the Dragon's Head Rune?" Tsona's human companion said, stepping forward. Maznar hissed as she saw him, but the human paid no attention to her. This had to be George. He looked like he was carved from cold, hard stone, not from warm, living flesh. Even his black hair, speckled with white, looked chiselled and still. He wore an amulet around his neck, a ruby embedded in a silvered otter head. The charm that annulled our magic.

"That is the one," Tsona growled, one paw pointing towards me. His eyes burned with hatred. I did not look away.

George gestured down with his hands. "Lower your weapons."

"Is that wise?" Tsona asked in surprise.

The human grinned wolfishly. "They are no threat to us. Not here." His fingers lightly teased around the edge of his amulet.

There was a strange sensation in the back of my mind that intensified whenever the human's skin came in contact with the amulet, like there was something missing from my thoughts. A numbness in my mind. I shuddered, my claws digging into the stone ground.

Not long ago, I had stood in this chamber, scared of standing before the forty-two clans of dragonkind. Now humans desecrated this prestigious arena. I didn't know which was worse, but the one constant through it all was Tsona. I kept my eyes fixed on the Xital traitor, doing my best to ignore the humans.

Tsona struggled to meet my eyes. The Xital wrinkled his nose and shied away, keeping his injured wing positioned away from me. "We should just kill them while we have the chance," he spat.

George kept smiling. He gestured with his hands again, fending away the human guards who surrounded us. "Not yet, my little dragon. You are in no danger here. In fact, leave us," the human said, snapping his fingers. At his command, all the guards shouldered their weapons and started to move away, towards the entrance to the tunnels beyond the podium.

I stared in surprise. Tsona's shocked whimpers amused me, but most of my focus tried to rationalise why the human had just sent away his guards. Was it hubris or over-confidence? Or was there some other play here? I could see no other humans around the great chamber. Scent was more difficult to judge. So many humans had been present that it was difficult to differentiate them.

As I quickly looked around the chamber, I realised that we weren't completely unguarded after all. There were still Xital dragons watching us, perched high above us at the main entrance to the council chambers. Their silhouettes stood before the bright light of outside. Four of them. A daunting foe.

"What are you doing?" Tsona growled, turning on his human ally, evidently unaware that they were still under the protection of some guards. For a moment, he exposed his injured flank. Several long scars still marred his scales, and there were a few tatters in his wing membranes. I hadn't realised how badly I had wounded him. His flight back to Xital must have been a painful one. I found some satisfaction in that.

George ignored Tsona. Instead, the human sat on the edge of the podium, his legs dangling down. I saw that he was not unarmed. Not only did he have the amulet around his neck, but he also had a sharp knife strapped to his belt, and a pistol at his other hip. I did not want to test his proficiency with those weapons. Not yet.

I could feel the tension and impatience behind me. I hoped no one would do anything rash and attack the human. Even with six of us, one prepared human would be a difficult challenge.

"You know, I don't have to kill you," George said. Even sat down, he was still taller than me. I struggled not to feel intimidated by his height and clear strength.

My mouth was dry as I stuttered my response. "Why… why would you leave us alive?"

"Because you have the potential to be so useful to us," George said, his smile ever wider. His dull, flat teeth had none of the danger of a dragon's jaw, but I was somehow even more terrified of it than I was whenever a dragon opened its mouth.

"How?" Ellian growled, when I realised my fear had stolen away my voice.

The human laughed. "You took something I want back. Where is the Dragon's Head Rune?"

"Back where it belongs. In Nixa," I replied. I knew he would never get it there, but to my surprise he laughed again.

"Good, I'm glad you said that." He looked at a small device bound to his wrist and tapped it a couple of times. A rainbow array of colour swirled across the surface, before forming into something new, at too flat an angle for me to properly see.

Tsona placed his paw on the human's leg. "I have told you already, that place cannot be attacked," he said, but the human pushed him aside with a sweep of his arm.

"Surely you of all little dragons don't doubt me, Tsona?" George said with a sigh. He twisted his wrist and showed the dragon something on the small device. "You forget Rico's ingenuity."

Tsona's eyes widened. "Yes, that just might do it," he hissed in admiration.

Though most of what Tsona saw stayed hidden from my view, I caught a brief glimpse of bizarre lines and shapes on the black surface. It reminded me of the map the humans had given Azlak across the mountains, now carried by Nataik. The strange markings were beyond my understanding, and the human seemed to know that as he smirked again. A shiver ran down my spine, all the way to the tip of my tail.

George dropped his hand. The surface of his wrist device burst back into rainbow colours, which then retreated to create a colourful border around the edge. The main bulk of the surface turned to matte black.

"But now we've resolved that question, I have another for you, dragon," George said. He looked me right in the eye. Like the healer Leah, his gaze didn't flick around like most humans tended to do. I refused to look away, but so did he. His irises were the same pale blue as ice. "What did you do with my Nightwings?"

Only the strength of George's gaze stopped me from glancing back to Maznar. There was movement behind me, but I could not look away from the human to see what it was. No one spoke out. Maznar did not reveal herself. I was glad for that. If George didn't realise that she was alive, if he failed to recognise her standing just in front of him, then I wanted to keep it that way. If they thought she was dead, then there was no way they could attempt to control or manipulate her again.

"I killed her," I said, keeping my eyes fixed on the human. "She attacked and I fought her off. Her body fell into the ocean."

"Is that so?" George said without emotion. I wasn't sure if he didn't believe me, or just didn't care for the ness. "Such a shame. She was always so good at fetching things for me. At keeping things in order. I guess I'll have to find someone else."

I narrowed my eyes. There was something strange about the human's words, but I couldn't place what it was. He confused me, not speaking straight and clearly.

"What do you want with us, George?" I growled.

By the human's side, Tsona smirked. He flicked out his one working wing and leered at me.

George rose to stand, towering over us all. I skittered back, wary of his feet. "You specifically, or dragons in general?" the human asked, almost sounding like he had no interest in the conversation.

I chanced a quick look back at my companions. They gathered close to each other, keeping watch on our guards high above at the entrance. There was no sign of the humans who had left us, though I was sure they were not far away. "Both."

"I dream of a better world, little dragon," George said. "Whether you become a part of it is entirely up to your actions and choices now."

"Is that a threat?" Vinzent snapped, stamping his paw.

I flicked my tail, hoping to keep the dragonet quiet. I didn't work, and Vinzent stepped up by my side, his wingtips quivering. He lowered his head, angling his long, sweeping horns towards the human.

"Of course it's a threat," George replied. One hand toyed idly with the handle of his knife. "Either submit to my command and volunteer dragons to our experiments, or stand against us and face Rico's extermination. The choice is entirely yours."

The breath caught in my throat. "Experiments? You mean like Nightwings?"

The human's teeth showed again. "Trust me, dragon. You do not understand the true importance of Nightwings. She was more than an experiment. She was a development into something... greater. A fragment of history restored. Rico assures me that this is a necessary step. You would do well to join us, rather than stand in our way."

Cold fury began to burn within me. My focus narrowed until all I could see was the human. Even Tsona vanished from my attention, the dragon not important. All that mattered was George, this human who had stolen from dragons and experimented on us. And he openly bragged that he needed more dragons for this.

"I will never allow a Laxtal dragon to be submitted to your torture," I snarled. My claws scraped against the stone of the podium. That was probably a desecration of the council chamber, but Tsona had destroyed any thought of this place being sacred to dragonkind. Simply allowing a human to stand on the podium was a violation of every rule and precedent that had lasted for centuries.

My whole body shook with anger. My thoughts burned white hot. I longed for my teeth to rip into human flesh, but I knew I could not attack alone. I flicked my tail, sweeping it forward, hoping that my companions stayed alert.

"A shame then," George said with a sigh. His hand moved towards his face, twisting his wrist so the device strapped to his arm closed on his mouth. A communicator. He would be able to speak to humans not present. Summon them back. This was our only chance.

I thumped my tail again. Then I pounced. I gave the human no warning, leaping faster than he could react. My teeth closed around his wrist. I wrenched my jaw, ripping the small device apart by the strap. I grazed against his flesh, the slight tang of blood in my mouth as I opened his skin.

Then his other hand struck my side. His fist cracked against my ribs, sending me thudding to the ground and rolling, wings wrapped tight around my body to protect them.

A purple-hewed shadow whipped over me as Ellian charged. I struggled to my paws, chest aching.

Tsona whined as he backed away, single wing flaring. "What are you waiting for?" he yelped, his head turned to the Xital guards keeping watch high above.

I jumped for the cowering ddraig before the guards had a chance to react to the sudden fray. Even injured, Tsona was fast. He dodged and ducked, constantly retreating from my claws.

George screamed in anger and pain. I chanced a glance to him. His right wrist poured hot blood where my teeth had sunk in. Ellian snapped and swiped, wings flared and reared up on her hind legs. But the human held her at bay, knife in blood-soaked hand.

The Xital guards joined us, three of them landing between George and the other dragons. Carlee growled, her one eye narrowed as she glared at the large Xitals. Vinzent bared his teeth, standing slightly ahead of Airil and Maznar.

The fourth guard swooped me, claws outstretched. I threw myself to the ground, all thought of attacking Tsona forced from my mind. My bronze-scaled attacker was large and powerful, big muscles bulging at the scales around his shoulders and forelegs.

It was my turn to retreat. I barely dared to blink, lest the attacker gain an advantage on me. I evaded the fierce swipes from the Xital, feeling the air move against my scales. My heart pounded, legs shaking with adrenaline. I already felt weak, hunger gnawing at my belly, my scales cold. This was not a fight I could win.

All around me were the snarls and growls of dragons, but still the only human was George. Wherever his guards had gone, they could not hear the commotion. That gave us a chance.

Something clinked as it fell to the ground, bumping against my hindpaw. I didn't dare look, but Ellian's voice screamed out.

"Anzig, the amulet!"

I glanced down. Light shone off the silvered surface of the otter head. George shouted in anger. He had a scratch mark around his throat as Ellian shoved him back. He stumbled and fell off the podium. The other dragons scattered as he tumbled to the ground.

I had been wrong. The red bauble in the amulet wasn't a ruby. It was glass, swirling with magical light within, sparkling with an unnatural glimmer.

There was no chance to think further. I slammed my forepaw down on the glass bauble. It shattered, and my mind ripped away.

The little green dragon spasmed as though suffering from a seizure. I stayed my paw, raised ready to strike. Blood leaked from the puncture wounds where he had shattered the amulet, but that could not account for his sudden condition. He tottered and swayed, eyes blank, as though already dead. I glanced back to my ddraig in alarm, unsure what to do next. Enemy though he might be, there was no honour in slaying a dragon in this condition.

My thoughts twisted. My paw lowered.

I blinked and my perspective shifted.

Claws slashed across my muzzle. I gasped and leaped back, the silver scaled Laxtal dragon barging into me. My distraction lost me the advantage. Claw and tooth scraped against my scales.

I jumped back, stumbling over George as he struggled to rise. I fell against him, the Laxtal snapping for my throat. My head thumped against the ground. My vision swam. The green Laxtal draped over the edge of the podium, his wings and tail dangling limply.

Jaws latched on to my throat. I kicked up, but I couldn't get a proper grip on the dragon pinning me down. The world started to fade.

Light burst in my eyes as I struggled to my feet. I grunted, my arms crossed over my chest as I struggled for breath. The dragon had winded me. I moment of weakness I could not let happen again.

I ignored the throb of pain in my hand to reach for my pistol. This had gone on far too long. I had taken a stupid risk, and for what? I had learned nothing from these dragons that I had not already known. Foolishness. That's all this had been. Rico would not be amused with me.

With the other dragons occupied, I drew my pistol and aimed for the creature that had started all of this. The green male was lying prone on the ground, his chest fluttering with quick breaths.

Two dragons shrieked. I fired. Lilac and brown streaked towards me.

I jerked back. Blood splattered against me.

My gorge rose. Errant thoughts tugged at my mind, threatening to rip me away from my body again. The shattered amulet pained my paw.

My thoughts were sluggish as they caught up. George was on the floor again. Ellian lay on her back by his side. She grasped the human's gun in her forepaws. She struggled as she stood, reared up on her hindlegs. She couldn't lift the gun high, nor hold it still. It waved around wildly, with Ellian almost toppling a few times. She managed to fire it again and George collapsed with a scream as the bullet pierced his leg. Ellian tumbled back to the floor.

As I struggled to regain my balance, my paw trod down on something wet and hot. The scent of blood assaulted my nose.

A strangled yelp escaped my mouth as I recognised Carlee beneath me. Her chest heaved for breath. Blood poured from the open wound in her gut.

"No, Carlee. Please," I whispered. I put pressure on her wound with my paws. Blood soaked my scales, staining my dull green with crimson. She didn't move. She barely responded to my touch.

"We don't have time for Airil to take us individually," Ellian bellowed. She fired the gun once more. A dragon screamed in agony. "Just fly! Get out of here before they send more!"

Maznar and Vinzent took to the air immediately, quickly escaping the reach of the two uninjured dragons, flying out of the chamber. Airil crawled over to Carlee and gently shook her.

The veteran couldn't fly. She couldn't even move. Desperation gripped me. I pushed my mind inside Airil's. *"Take her to Laxtal. Get her healed."*

The Nixan's eyes widened, transfixed on me. "But Ddraig, I can't carry her so far."

"You must! Go!"

Airil struggled against the force of my thoughts. He resisted, then gave in. He put his paw on Carlee's wounded body and they both disappeared. The crack of air rushing into the space they had occupied echoed another gun shot.

"Ziggy, what are you waiting for?" Ellian cried. Two of the remaining Xitals closed in on her. Another was wounded, and the other tended to Tsona and George. She was running out of space. She was running out of time.

I flew at the Xital dragons with as loud a roar as I could manage. It did enough to distract them, giving Ellian the moment she needed. Instead of firing the gun, she threw it at the two dragons as hard as she could. They scattered.

I didn't bother to chase them. I looked back for a moment. Tsona lay bleeding on the podium, George kneeling by the dragon's side. Both wounded. Both defeated, for now.

At the far side of the cave, human reinforcements were finally beginning to arrive. They hurried into the audience chamber, guns already drawn.

Before they had chance to stop me, I turned and flew out of the cavern, wings pumping hard to keep up with Ellian.

We burst out into the light and sucked in the air, as though it was my first breath in a long time. The sun's warmth seemed to heat right to my bones. We needed to get away quickly. It wouldn't be long before the Xital dragons and their human allies would start to pour out from the lair. We flew west, following the distant specks that were Vinzent and Maznar.

They did not fly far. To my surprise, the two dragons began to descend. Ellian followed them. I recognised we had come to the meeting point on the edge of Xital's lair.

I was horrified to see a dragon meet Vinzent and Maznar. Airil.

I landed with fury in my blood. The Nixan cowered as I confronted him. "You were meant to take her to Laxtal, not here!"

Airil bowed his head. "Ddraig, I couldn't. I can't even carry myself that far alone, let alone with a dragon who isn't Nixan. I'm sorry."

"Where is she?" Ellian asked. Her sombre tone cut into my anger. Grief flooded in to replace it.

Airil looked away from us all. He pointed lower beneath the roots of a nearby tree, where the grass had grown long.

I barely dared to follow Airil's paw. I was the only one who moved as I pushed aside the grass. Carlee lay there. Her chest lifted and fell ever so slightly. But it was moving. She was alive. But she was weak. She was pathetically weak. Her teeth were stained red with her own blood. It oozed from her many wounds, but especially from the one in her belly. It turned the grass scarlet, and where it was already drying, to black. I lay down beside her, just enough contact for her to know I was there. She spluttered as she opened her one good eye.

"Anzig. My Anzig … you … are here. Looks like… like this is it," she said weakly. There was a faint hint of a smile on her mutilated face.

"No, no, you can't die," I said, desperately willing her to survive, as though my sheer willpower could keep her awake and well. I couldn't live without her. She had always been there, from the moment I had hatched. I knew it was naïve to think she would outlive me, but not once had I ever thought she would die. She was a constant of Clan Laxtal. She was my constant!

"No, it's my time," she said, her voice pitifully weak. "You listen to me now, Anzig." She coughed, the pain wracking through her frail body, red foam glistening on her lips. "Ignore what any dragon may say. You are… and always… will be, the true ddraig of Laxtal. You will be a good leader. You will defeat the humans. Do it in my honour if you need a reason." A cough rent through her broken body once more, the effort of a few sentences too much for her.

I nodded almost to myself, unable to think of anything to say. How could I possibly say goodbye to Carlee? With a great effort, she rolled her head to one side, nuzzling against mine, lowering her already pitiful voice to barely a whisper. These words, these last words, were for me alone.

"But…" Carlee said, her chest barely moving. Her eye glazed over as she tried to speak one last time. I kept my silence. "You... are not..." She struggled to draw breath. "… not Astar's son..."

"No..." I breathed, as Carlee's head tipped ever so slightly, pressing just a little harder against my shoulder. Her eye half-closed and her chest stopped.

I slumped to the ground. Carlee was dead.

And she had ripped apart my whole life.

My tears mingled with her blood.

CHAPTER TWELVE

Azlak

"There has still been no word from Anzig. We must assume that he has been captured by Ddraig Tsona or killed in this foolish mission."

I stood before Yalle and growled. "It has only been a week. Even if everything had gone perfectly, he would struggle to be back by now," I told the albino. Were it not for the presence of Kaz standing just behind me, I doubted I would have had the courage to confront the respected elder. "We must give him at least another few days to return."

Yalle scoffed and looked away, towards the horizon. He had asked me to meet him outside the lair, on top of the cliffs that overlooked the plains of Laxtal's expansive territory. But for Kaz, we were alone, free to speak without risk of anyone overhearing us.

"If you choose to delay too long, then you will find the decision is taken from your paws," the albino explained. He paced back and forth slowly, trampling a rut through the long, dry grass. "There are several here who would see themselves as ddraig. More if Anzig is truly gone."

I didn't want to admit Anzig might not be coming back, even to myself. I had to believe he would succeed in rescuing Ellian and return home to lead our clan. It had been five days since the ddraig had left for Xital. As I had told Yalle, with a two day journey each way to the lone mountain, he would have struggled to make it back so quickly. Sunset approached, and there was still nothing on the horizon, no indication from the beacon fires. It would be another day, at least. Another day of unrest in the lair.

Yalle sighed. His wings drooped. "I know you're loyal to Anzig. I know how much you care for him. But the needs of the clan must come first, Azlak. We are threatened from too many sides to soar without direction. We need someone to guide us through these turbulent winds to safety. If you are seen to stubbornly cling to the idea of a ddraig who is not coming back, then you will quickly find yourself abhorred by those vying for power."

I clicked my tongue against the roof of my mouth. "These last few days have been the first time I haven't been despised by almost everyone in the clan. I'm used to it."

"I'm talking banishment and expulsion from Laxtal, Azlak. If you are loyal to Anzig and some other dragon becomes ddraig, then I can't see you being permitted to remain," Yalle said. His words and tone were harsh, but there was no anger or aggression in his eyes. He purposefully avoided my gaze.

I held my tongue as I thought things through. Laxtal had always been my home. I belonged here, in this lair, even though I had never really been welcomed by the rest of my clan. Would banishment really be such a terrible thing? I didn't know where else I could go, but there would be somewhere. My trip across the mountains had told me one thing. The world was a bigger place than just the draconic clans, with much to learn about what lay beyond our borders.

Of course, the better option would be for Ddraig Anzig to return home and take his rightful place in his father's chambers. I looked again to the horizon, but still there was nothing. I had Seen nothing from Xital, no futures that might give some indication of what was happening to the absent ddraig.

"I have no more council for you," Yalle said, interrupting me before I had the opportunity to cast my magic out. The albino flared his wings. "The choice is still yours, Azlak. You have the opportunity to decide who the next ddraig of Laxtal will be. There are many dragons who would give their wings for such a chance."

The albino gave me no time to reply. He took to the air with a powerful gust of downdraft from his wings. He did not return to the lair, but instead swooped out towards the plains, likely to join with the hunters who still worked hard to replenish the cold caves.

That left me alone with Kaz. The Nixan had been my shadow ever since he had received better dwellings away from the depths of the Laxtal caves. The constant attention had been both a pleasure and unnerving. I was not used to it. I didn't know how to react.

For now, at least, Kaz's attention was nothing too forward or close. "What do you plan on doing?" he asked.

I let out a weary sigh. "I don't know. Yalle is right. Someone needs to be the ddraig, and if Anzig really isn't coming back? It would be foolish to wait too long, but I just feel like we haven't given him enough time. If I could just See something of him, something that tells me he's coming home. But I can't. I haven't."

"You never were taught to use your magic, were you?" Kaz said. He moved around to sit in front of me, blocking my view of the plains. "About how to summon it at will and to control what you did with it?"

I shook my head. "No one in Laxtal knew how. No one in Nixa wanted anything to do with me."

Kaz pawed at the ground, scraping up a few blades of grass and shredding the roots between his claws. "That was not right of us. A dragon with uncontrolled magic could be a danger to everyone, let alone themselves. We should have put aside these petty clan disputes so that you could have learned what to do."

I kept silent. For too long had Nixa refused to believe I was Laxtal, and for my own clan to refute my undeniable heritage. Ever since I had been a dragonet, others had shunned me because of my magic. The deaths of so many dragons plagued my visions and dreams. Some of them had come true. Others I feared still might. Sometimes I believed they were right to shun me.

Kaz lightly touched a paw to the underside of my muzzle, his grass-stained claws pressing gently to my scales. This close to him, it was hard not to meet his gaze, his yellow eyes framed perfectly by his vivid blue scales.

The Nixan had all my attention. "Let me guess. Your magic would flare when you were stressed, or some other spike of emotion. It would focus on whoever you were thinking about at the time."

I was so lost in Kaz's eyes that I nearly didn't answer. "Y-yes, that's exactly it," I stammered. My heart thumped loudly as I…

The blue scaled dragon bowed low, his muzzle practically bumping against the ground. By his side, the golden dragon repeated the gesture. Their wingtips touched.

Before them stood a human, resplendent with golden light that seemed to shine from her very being. The light was so strong that her features were completely obscured, with nothing visible of her face.

…felt a fierce burn pass through my mind. Magic ripped out before I could hold it back, and I was left panting in front of the Nixan as I struggled to contain it.

"You Saw me, didn't you?" Kaz asked. He took a step back.

"I don't know if I can understand what I Saw just yet. The future is difficult to interpret. But yes, I saw you there," I said, furrowing my brow and flicking my wings. Who would that strange being be? They looked human, but even through the veil of time I could tell there was something unusual about her.

"Fortunately, that's what we're here to resolve," Kaz said brightly. He hopped up to his paws and looked around, though for what I couldn't be completely sure. His eyes soon settled on a small rocky outcrop, a few dozen feet away from the edge of the gorge. A couple of trees stood over the outcrop, most of their leaves turning to burnished gold. "Come over here and lie down with your eyes closed. We're going to run through some mental exercises that helped to teach me how to control my magic."

"Did anyone care when your magic got out of control?" I asked with an amused snort.

Kaz chewed on his lip and hung his head. "Healing isn't some benign skill. It can be used to harm as well. An understanding of anatomy is needed, because fixing a broken leg wrong could lead to a permanent limp. Easing a headache can result in a bleed on the brain. I need to be careful with my magic, just as much as any Nixan."

My humour vanished in a moment. "I'm sorry, I didn't know. Have you ever… lost control like that?"

Kaz nodded. He managed a weak smile. "That's why control is important. Come on, let me show you."

I felt a little foolish as I found a place to settle down, my legs beneath my body. Kaz remained standing, pacing around me.

"Your magic should be treated just like any of your other senses. To a well-trained Nixan, magic is as instinctual and natural as sight or smell," Kaz explained. I ignored the usual implication that to wield magic, a dragon must be Nixan. "To properly get in tune with your magic and get a good feel for it, you should try blocking out your other senses. Ignore everything your nose and mouth and scales are telling you. Keep your eyes closed and focus only on what is within."

I did what Kaz asked, closing my eyes and doing what I could to ignore everything around me. The wind on my scales. The scent of grass and the slight acrid smell of the leaves as they fell from the trees and began to rot. I allowed myself a moment to take it all in, then tried to shut it away.

"Focus inward," Kaz said. "Try to reach with your mind to the heart of your magic. There is a well of strength and power within you. It feels different for every Nixan, but once you find it, you'll know."

Vague instructions didn't help me much. I put aside a moment of irritation and tried to do what he asked. I focused inwards, trying to ignore my senses. My tail twitched. I slowed my breathing and tried to find that inner magic. Rarely before had I ever tried to seek out a vision. Normally I did my all to avoid them.

My thoughts swirled around. Despite my eyes squeezed closed, I could find nothing within me. The breeze distracted me, carrying with it a hundred and more scents. Not only the smells of autumn, but a herd of deer not too far away. The dust and dirt of the land. Other dragons. Kaz, nearby. How was it I could so easily recognise his scent?

No visions came to me in the darkness behind my eyelids. No sudden discovery of a source of magic. I began counting heartbeats instead of searching for something I had no way of finding. Many minutes passed by. Nothing happened.

My wings slumped. "I don't know what I'm looking for."

"Just focus on what's inside," Kaz said. He was close to my left, but I didn't open my eyes. Nor did I turn my head. "Magic is a fundamental part of you, as important as your heart or lungs. You can't exist without it, just as it can't be without you. The trick is recognising that feeling. It is one you've felt for every moment of your life without realising it. No other dragon can know what that feeling is."

I took a deep breath, paying close attention to how my chest swelled and contracted as air filled my lungs. I focused on the beat of my heart, how I could feel that powerful thump and thud in my chest. I felt my pulse in my extremities. My toes twitched ever so slightly with each pump of blood.

My lungs and heart sustained me. If my magic did the same, then what did it feel like?

I thought back to my most recent vision. I recalled the feeling of magic swelling up within me. Where had that come from?

Or, if not where within me, when? When had that vision come from?

A strange, spicy tang filled my nose. I breathed it in deep. The roar of air in my lungs overwhelmed the sound of the breeze. My heartbeat thundered louder than any storm. Golden light shone from the inside of my eyelids. Seconds upon minutes upon hours danced in my mind with a branching eternity stretching out far beyond what any eye could hope to see.

I gasped. I recognised the feeling. It was a taste of what the Axinstone had given me. A sense of eternity playing out before me, but with the Nixan artefact in my paw I had been aware of all branches at once. This was but a fragment of that power, but it was still there. It was still within me.

The scent of the air around me returned, but the sense of eternity did not fade. With my surroundings came the smell of Kaz. Thoughts of the Nixan suffused into the golden light of my mind's eye. No visions came with it, but flashes of thoughts and sensations tugged at me. Emotions swelled and filled me, reaching me through time and feeling every bit as true as my own. Adoration. Respect. Love. Were these my thoughts from a future version of me that I could not See?

The more I tried to focus on those thoughts, the more slippery they seemed to become, until I lost them entirely. The many branches of eternity began to splinter as my focus failed. The heat of magic began to fade.

"I think I had it," I said, my voice trembling.

"That's good," Kaz said, speaking around a yawn.

I opened my eyes. It was night. When had it become dark?

I blinked a few times and looked to the horizon, where the moon peeked above the plains. Night had not fallen for long then. It still surprised me. Hours had passed since we had started.

The chill night air immediately made itself known. I shivered and wrapped my wings a little tighter around my body. The mental heat of my magic faded to nothing, and the sense of eternity drifted until it was nothing more than a dream-like memory.

I rose to unsteady paws, stretching my legs and letting my joints pop back into comfort. "We should have gone inside a long time ago."

Kaz had curled up close by, but he had nothing to keep himself warm. He slowly rose to his paws and gave his wings a few beats. "You seemed to be making good progress. I didn't want to disturb that," he said, stifling another yawn. "Though I was thinking about doing so soon."

My eyes lingered on the Nixan. Memories of emotions and thoughts I had not yet had lingered in my mind. Was this dragon to become someone important to me? Someone more important than any other dragon in my life? I, of all dragons, knew how changeable the future could be, especially if spoken aloud. I said nothing of my fragmented visions, but internally I allowed myself to feel a little hope.

It wasn't until Kaz shuffled his paws and stepped away that I realised I had been staring at him for quite some time. I flicked my tail and wrenched my head away. "We should go and get warm," I said, speaking a little too quickly to be wholly natural.

"I had forgotten how cold it can be this time of year," Kaz said. He stretched out his wings, almost brushing them against me. He looked up to the moon.

I caught myself staring at the Nixan again. I flicked my eyes up to the source of his focus. The face of the thief clear upon the moon's surface. "I have some spare blankets if you wanted to share them. Borrow them. Share," I stammered.

Kaz turned his head. He smiled. "I think I'd like that."

He didn't need to say which option he preferred.

We returned to my chambers with another new warmth in my chest.

chapter thirteen

Anzig

I recalled little of the flight back to Laxtal. Ellian had taken lead, and the others were wise enough not to talk to me, not even when we stopped to rest. Two nights passed by; nights when I barely slept, staring out into the starlit darkness with a fire at my back. Two nights when I had openly wept the moment my companions had gone to sleep.

I had told no one of Carlee's last words. If I was not Astar's son, then what right did I have to be the ddraig of Laxtal? It had been Carlee's secret, and now it had become mine. If knowledge of that spread, then I would not be able to take the wylax. My claim to be ddraig was solely because I was Astar's son and nothing else.

Yalle and Marin were there to meet us at the top of the gorge, above the rockfall that blocked off the entrance to the ravine from the ground. The beacon fires had roared to life as we passed over the territory. They would have known we were coming hours ago. I could not see Azlak with the welcoming group.

I struggled to bring forward a mask of calm and power. This was a time when I needed to be a ddraig for the clan. It could be a moment of triumph, returning with a freed captive from Xital. I had never felt further from celebrating. A hole in the air flew alongside me, right where Carlee should have been.

Marin stepped forward, flaring his wings in greeting as we landed. "It is a pleasure to see you back, Anzig."

Ellian let out a little growl. "That's Ddraig Anzig. Or have you forgotten already?"

The elder dragon flicked his eyes to Ellian. A sneer came onto his muzzle. "Ah yes, Ellian. Twice defeated by Ddraig Tsona. Do you think you have any authority here after that?"

"Enough of this," I snapped. Grief threatened to crack my voice. I took a deep breath and forced myself to remain strong. "I understand I am not truly ddraig yet. Not until the wylax. We shall begin preparations right away."

Marin's sneer remained, but he said nothing. Instead, Yalle stepped forward and bowed his head just slightly, enough to show some respect. "I agree. It is imperative we hold the wylax as soon as possible," the albino said. He showed the tips of his teeth as he pulled his lips back. "As Ddraig Astar's son and chosen haeraig, tradition dictates that you are the expected dragon to undertake the wylax. Do you intend to do this?"

The breath stole from my lungs. The first lie needed to come. I was not Ddraig Astar's son, but Laxtal could not know that. "Yes," I said, barely able to whisper. I breathed deep and tried again, putting the force back into my voice. "Yes. I will go through the wylax. I will be the next ddraig of Laxtal."

Once more, Yalle bowed. "Of course. I needed only hear you say it."

If Marin's sneer was anything to go by, then I doubted this would be the last I would hear about my claim as ddraig. I would need to be alert if I wanted to fend off any challengers, but I couldn't bring myself to care too much. Not now.

I knew the clan would want to see me. Though I wanted nothing more than to slink away through the shadows and escape to my chambers, I pushed past the two elders and swooped into the caves. The whispers that followed me weren't entirely in my ears. Errant thoughts strayed into my head. Whispers of surprise, of shock, of elation. The dragons of Laxtal rejoiced, but it was not my arrival they noticed. It was Ellian.

There was already a crowd waiting for us in the central chamber; a roar of dragons that I had no desire to face. I froze with fear and shame, standing still on the precipice. I felt every bit the scared dragon that had looked down on the council of dragons in Xital, those fateful weeks ago. This time I didn't have Carlee by my side to give me the confidence I needed.

Ellian was the dragon beside me. My cousin lightly touched her paw to mine. "Do you want to speak to them, or shall I?"

I choked back the immediate response of relief that Ellian would take my responsibility from me. I couldn't retreat. Not yet. If Marin's threats were true, then I was far from safe as ddraig. I needed to show I was a strong leader, no matter what grief gnawed at my heart.

I lifted my head and puffed out my chest. "Laxtal!" I bellowed, managing to cut across the clamour and noise below. I opened my wings again and soared down to the podium by the firepit. The shadows danced around the cave, making the audience look like it constantly moved, though I was sure they actually stayed quite still.

A hush fell as I touched down. Ellian and my other companions all came down behind me, including Yalle and Marin. I suppressed a little growl at that. They had played no part in rescuing Ellian, and while I knew the clan was aware of that, their presence with me still gave wind beneath their wings. I could do nothing to change that now. I did my best to ignore them.

"Twice now I have stood against the traitor Tsona. Twice now I have defeated him," I said, keeping my head high and my voice strong. "He stole Ellian away to hold her captive, but she stands with us once more. That I took her back from Xital shows Tsona that we are not a force to be ignored. We are strong, and we will not be cowed."

A moment of hesitation followed, but a roar slowly trickled into life. A familiar voice led the vocal reply. Though I couldn't see him, the golden seer had been the first to shout. Azlak was somewhere nearby.

When the roar faded, I allowed my voice to weaken. "We did not take this victory without cost. As much as this is a celebration, it must also be a time to mourn. It is with regret that I must say that Carlee lost her life in Xital. She died protecting us. She died fighting, as she would always have wanted."

She died ripping my life into shreds. I bit down on those words. I would never share them. Not to Laxtal. Not to any dragon. Already the secret weighed heavily on my wings.

"I will not allow Carlee's life to be squandered," I said, voice trembling. "She gave her life for this clan. It is right that we honour her by defeating this threat to Laxtal. We will stand against Xital and win. With me as ddraig and Ellian as your haeraig, I promise you that this victory will be assured."

The response was somewhat muted, with only a few shouted voices roaring their approval. It certainly wasn't the powerful chant of adoration my father always received. I didn't understand it. Didn't they want victory over Xital? Or did they not believe I could do it? Perhaps they were still in shock that Carlee was no longer with us, that we could no longer seek her advice and experience.

My throat tightened. No longer would the veteran guide my path. My breath quickened as the full force of Carlee's death hit me anew. Not only had she torn my life apart with her secret, but she wasn't even around to guide me through the turbulent wind that revelation had created.

A familiar ness pushed her way to the front of the crowd. Saya's vivid red scales were unmistakeable. She lifted her head high, horns gleaming in the firelight. "Are you really the dragon to be our next ddraig? Are you the one who can lead us to victory, with a haeraig who has twice tasted defeat by the enemy? An enemy only you claim is truly our foe?"

I did not like how loud the murmurs were as they spread through the cave. I stamped a paw, but the mutters did not stop. "I am the... I am the son of Ddraig Astar," I hissed, hiding the lie behind my anger. I spoke only for Saya, but I was sure that much of the clan could still hear me. "I was his chosen haeraig. If there is any who challenge my right to succession, then they have until the wylax to make their intentions known. Do you challenge me, Saya?"

Saya's eyes flicked past me, to where I knew Vinzent stood. She said nothing. Nor did her son. No one spoke, the murmurs finally ceased.

My voice cracked as I tried to continue. "I know you don't want Xital to be our enemy. For generations, they have held our best interests at heart, but that time is no longer. They have betrayed dragonkind and invited humans into their lairs. Only Laxtal, together with our allies in Nixa and the western clans, can resist them. I vow to be the ddraig to bring about this greatest of alliances."

"Alliances? Pah, is Laxtal not strong enough?" Saya spat.

"Alone? No. We are not strong enough if we are to survive," I said. I pawed at the stone. "This is not something we can do by ourselves."

"Ddraig Astar wouldn't have believed that," Saya retorted. She narrowed her eyes. "Carlee would never have accepted that weakness. Our ddraig should do the same."

"Then challenge me!" The words roared from my muzzle. I slammed my paw to the ground.

Once more, silence met my words. Saya refused to meet my eyes, and she backed down from her challenge. She melted back into the crowd, slinking away without another word.

I panted heavily, trying to diffuse the anger that burned through me. I wasn't even sure what the target of my anger was. It might have been Saya and her obvious machinations against me. It could have been Carlee for telling me this terrible secret. It may also have been against my father for hiding such a thing from me. Any or all of them might have stoked my fury, but I simply couldn't be sure where to aim my rage. There was no outlet, and I risked unleashing it on the dragons of Laxtal. I knew then that I needed to escape.

My shoulders slumped. "If there are no challenges, then please excuse me. I would like some time to grieve my friend and mentor."

There were no objections and no challenges. I spread my wings and turned to take flight. In doing so, I briefly caught sight of Ellian. A look of concern was on her face, her wings twitching as though ready to open. I feared she planned to follow me. I shook my head, hoping to dissuade that. To my relief, I heard no wings chasing after me as I flew to the narrow tunnel above the firepit.

With my father dead and Ellian not officially the haeraig, the high chambers would offer privacy for my grief and anger. After facing the scrutiny of the clan, privacy was exactly what I needed. I doubted I could have put on much worse a performance as ddraig. Any longer and I might have lost any chance of avoiding a challenge.

Habit almost took me to my usual chamber, but I stopped before pushing aside the veil. It was no longer mine. They belonged to Ellian, and soon I would need to take my personal belongings from inside. I had no desire to do so now, but I knew I would need to familiarise myself with the larger chamber further down the passage. My father's chambers. The ddraig's chambers. Now mine. For now.

Little remained of Astar's scent. It had been a month since he had died. I doubted anyone had come into these chambers since then, not even Tsona and his Xital occupiers. The air was stale and cold, with the only light coming from the single torch outside the chamber.

I found a firelighter in an alcove close to the entry. Astar had always left one there. After a few moments of fumbling with the traded human technology, I managed to get the fireplace lit, with coal still in the brazier from when my father had last used it. When Astar had last used it. I knew I needed to stop thinking of him as my father, but it hurt my heart to do so.

As the fire grew, with smoke naturally pulled up through tiny vents in the ceiling, the light fell upon his possessions, left exactly where he had last touched them. He would have expected to return to this chamber after dealing with the human incursion on our borders.

Everything reminded me of the dragon I had called father. The trinkets and jewels that had once been his prized possessions. The blankets that had kept him warm through the cold nights.

Every time I had come to this chamber in the past, I had been believing a lie. I had thought I had been visiting my father, a dragon who I could trust and believe, no matter what. He had been my idol, the rock in my life. But he had lied to me every day since I had hatched.

Fury raged, sudden and fierce. I knew who it was I could blame. Astar. If he had not lied to me, if he had told me the truth and said he was not my true father, then he could have spared me all of this. Every last bit of anguish and pain.

I had no control over my actions as I hurled down any trinket or artefact that reminded me of him. I spared nothing from my rage, not even the silver statue that smugly looked down on the scene of destruction. The ness crashed against the far wall and slipped behind a pile of thick rugs. I did not rest until there was nothing left to throw, no damage left to cause.

I felt no remorse as I stood panting in the middle of the ddraig's chambers, surrounded by the wreckage of my father's vast collection of gold, silver, and gems. It was only then that my blind anger was sated and I was able to calm my mind. A great void filled me, leaving me incapable of feeling any emotion. No anger, no hurt.

Numbly, I pushed aside a couple of gems from beneath my paws, before curling up in the thick rugs that covered the floor. More than anything I wanted a dragon to talk to, but I no longer knew which one I could turn to. Carlee had always been the dragon I could go to for advice, no matter what. That certainty was gone now, stolen away. Even if she was still alive, I doubted I could trust her. She had told the same lie as Astar.

I couldn't even rely on Keita to stand by my side. She had already torn out my heart by choosing the Nyrian Okazuni over me. I whimpered and closed my eyes, holding my paws to my forehead. I had always known that one day, I would become ddraig of Laxtal, following on from my father. But I had never expected it would be like this. I had lost my father, my mentor, and the ness I wanted to be my mate. Worst of all I had lost my identity. If I wasn't Astar's son, then who was I? And why did I have magic?

There were no answers to my questions. I shed many tears before I was able to sleep.

When I woke, I suffered a brief moment of confusion as I tried to work out where I was. Then my memories came trickling back. The destruction of the previous night laid bare before me, the scattered treasures of Astar's life across the floor.

I held my head in my paws, groaning. A headache threatened. Not a good start to the day.

The fire had burned low during the night. I crawled up to my paws and took care to pick my way through the wreckage. There was a fresh store of coal and kindling by the fireplace, beneath the alcove containing the statue of the silver ness.

It didn't take long for the fire to return to its strength and power. The heat warmed my cold scales, flooding through my body and helping to thaw out my frozen thoughts. I wiped away the lingering tears that stuck to my scales, gazing into the flickering light. Something nagged at the back of my mind. Something wasn't right. Something was different.

"Keep thinking. You'll work it out."

I froze. I knew I was alone. Apart from the crackling of the fire and my heavy breaths, there wasn't a sound in the chamber. Yet I had clearly heard a voice that wasn't in my mind. There was a metallic ring to the voice, but definitely feminine. For some reason it sounded familiar, though I knew I had never heard it before.

Though I couldn't be sure where the voice emanated from, my eyes shifted up towards the silver statue, back in its rightful place in the small alcove over the fire. Hadn't I thrown it against the wall in my rage?

"Yes, you did. And it hurt."

The statue moved. Somehow, this statue was talking to me. I held my head in my paws, fearing my latest plunge into insanity.

"You haven't lost your mind," the voice said, but her metallic tone failed to reassure me. "I am quite real."

"Then what are you?" I asked, immediately regretting my decision to encourage this creation of my failing mind. Keeping my eyes shielded by a paw, I lifted my head away from the fire and to the statue above it.

"I am a guardian," the statue said. I glanced out from behind my paw. It was as though the statue was absorbing all the light from the fire, magnifying it somehow, and projecting it back out into the chamber as a blinding flash of silver. The searing light emitting from the statue was too much too bear. To save my burning, watering eyes, I shut them, and covered them behind a paw once more. When she next spoke, the statue seemed a lot closer. I was going mad for sure. "I am a remnant of a long-forgotten magic, sworn to protect the leaders of dragonkind."

I took a stumbling, three-legged step back, as I felt a movement of air on my muzzle. I dropped my paw from my eyes but kept them squeezed tightly shut. She was close. I could feel breath on my muzzle. "Why have I not heard of guardians before?" I asked. Surely my father... Astar would have mentioned them to me, or had he deliberately withheld this secret from me also, knowing that I wasn't his son? I took another step backwards, my tail pressing against the wall behind me. I felt trapped.

"Our power isn't as great as it once was. It takes a great deal of strength to talk with dragons who are not a ddraig, and you dragons are restricted by the same magic," the guardian explained. Again, I could feel her hot breath on my muzzle, meaning she had moved towards me again, but how could she be breathing? How could a statue be moving? Was she real?

I could feel the conflict subsiding, and a small part of my mind was willing to accept that this guardian was real, and that she was really talking to me. I slowly opened my eyes, already shying away from the sight I anticipated. The statue was just a few inches from my muzzle; her silver, featureless eyes staring into mine. For a moment she was perfectly still, and I almost convinced myself that the statue was indeed just that; a statue, just as she had been all my life; but then she blinked. Involuntarily, I lurched backwards, rearing half up onto my hind paws and flattening myself up against the wall, convinced that any moment I would push myself into the rock.

The statue's mouth twitched with amusement as I relaxed slightly, embarrassed at my reaction, and dropped back onto all fours. Her scent was as I remembered, and other than her new positioning, she appeared no different. I gently reached out with a paw and placed it on her scales. It felt hard and unyielding like solid metal should, but at the same time warm like flesh. What suddenly occurred to me, something I hadn't ever noticed before, was a reflection. There wasn't one. Although the statue's surface was shiny, nothing reflected off the glistening metal. I couldn't see my reflection. I was within a paw's reach of her, but I couldn't see myself.

Her serpentine body coiled up tightly, making her seem shorter than her true size. She was wingless, and her head was a different shape than mine, with a more pronounced brow and two long tendrils emerging from either side of her muzzle. Though she had many scales on her back and sides, her underbelly was smooth and scaleless. There was no doubting that this was a ness though, despite her unusual appearance.

"Are you convinced I'm real now?" she asked.

I wanted to shake my head. I wanted to put this down to a strange dream, and that any moment now I would wake to find the statue discarded on the floor where I had thrown it. But I knew this was no dream. I had to accept that this statue was not a figment of my imagination, though I could scarcely believe she was standing in front of me as though alive.

"You are real," I said, struggling to force the words out. My mouth felt like I had stuffed it with fur from the blankets. "But I am not yet ddraig of this clan. There hasn't been a wylax since Ddraig Astar died."

"A mere formality of tradition," the statue scoffed. Her voice rung out and reverberated, like a paw had crashed against a thin metal surface. "My knowledge of the ddraig happens the moment a transition occurs. The wylax is merely a way for a clan to know who is the new ddraig, not a guardian."

I hung my head. Shame welled within me, manifesting as tears that threatened to spill out of my eyes, no matter how tight I squeezed them shut. "I cannot be the ddraig of Laxtal. You have this wrong."

The guardian growled. With vision blurred by tears, I watched as she started to uncoil her body. She must have been twice my length at least, and she pinned me against the wall, ignoring my forbidden tears. "When a ddraig dies I am immediately aware of their true successor. The moment Astar perished, our minds, yours and mine young Anzig, became entwined. Not until you chose to sleep within the chamber of the ddraig would I be able to reveal myself to you. No matter what secrets you have learned, you were Astar's chosen haeraig. That, and with the death of Ddraig Astar, makes you the successor. You are ddraig now," she said.

"But I am not his son," I protested.

"So?" the guardian said, pushing her muzzle against mine. I recoiled from the touch of her metallic scales, turning my head only to have it press up against the wall. The pressure on the side of my muzzle from her pressing against it was immense, and felt any moment now, either the wall or my jaw would give way. "It is no concern of mine, young Anzig that you are not the blood son of Astar, nor of Zhara." Her mouth constricted as she pressed against me, causing her words to come out as a foreboding rasping, and although her breath was hot on my face her words chilled my bones. "Your mind and my mind are now entwined, and that alone makes you ddraig of Laxtal."

I froze. I had not even considered that Zhara might not have been my mother. A horrid thought crossed my mind. Was I even a Laxtal dragon?

The statue stared into my eyes, her cold and lifeless orbs burning deep into my being. "Listen to my words, Ddraig Anzig. Carlee was right. Astar is not your father. Zhara was barren. She was not your mother. Where exactly your egg came from, I do not know. Astar made me swear never to search for that information in his mind, and I honoured the vow I made," she said quickly.

"So, it's true then? I'm not Laxtal?"

The guardian shook her head. "You may not be. But of that, I cannot be certain. I will though, say this young dragon; you do not look like a Laxtal dragon. Your horns and tail are too short," she said, with too much mirth in her voice for my liking.

I spluttered and choked over my words, unable to form a proper response. I had tried to ignore that fact ever since Carlee had died, but now the strange statue had said it aloud I could no longer avoid it. If Astar and Zhara were not my parents, then I had no way of knowing my true lineage. It wasn't like Azlak, who knew without a doubt that his parents were Laxtal. He knew he belonged in this clan, even if his magic did make him somewhat of an anomaly. I no longer knew where I belonged, because surely it was not here.

"The clan... they won't accept me if they know," I finally said, the words sounding distant to my own ears.

The guardian hissed. "They will not. It is for this reason, and this reason alone, young ddraig, that Astar kept the truth hidden from you. Your clan is not to know." The rasping voice seemed to intensify into a snarl as she spat out those words.

"Then I live a lie?"

"If you believe to withhold the truth is an untruth, then yes, you live untruthfully," the guardian muttered, with a sudden lessening of the pressure against me. She eased back, moving away a step and allowing me to ease a little from the wall. Her blank eyes fixed on me, although without actual pupils, it was hard to tell where she was looking. The constant, empty stare unnerved me. "Now, young ddraig, we have matters to attend. Humans are proceeding unhindered through draconic land. This intrusion into ddraggn gaeth, into our territory set aside by the treaty six hundred years ago, is to be halted or risk dire consequences. You are to stop the incursion, but know this Anzig; you have little time."

"What do I do?" I sighed. I knew we were already so far behind our rivals. Humans were swarming through our land, and Clan Xital was gaining considerable support from the surrounding minor clans. I knew we would have to do the same, but I couldn't see how that would be enough. The clan had already suffered so much; we wouldn't be able to hold off the humans for long.

The guardian backed away and started pacing the chamber. Her paw clinked against the strewn gems and jewels as she walked. "You must think of nothing else but the wylax first. You are already ddraig of Laxtal, but your clan do not believe that to be so until you have undertaken the ritual. This must be your first priority.

"Secondly, secure the allegiance of neighbouring clans. You need to raise an army, Anzig. I believe that Ellian will be suitable for that task. I have seen her grow from a little dragonet, to what she has become now. I believe Anzig, and I feel you know too, that this ness is destined to become your haeraig. She will overcome the setbacks inflicted by her defeats at Tsona's claw."

I nodded. There hadn't been any other dragon I had even considered to become my haeraig. But did I want to send her away again after only just rescuing her from Xital? In my heart I knew I wouldn't be able to keep her here, but she was the only family I had left. I didn't want to lose her as well.

"And this Maznar you returned with. I find her difficult to read. I am unsure as to whether she can be trusted. Watch her Anzig; watch her closely," the guardian said. The statue suddenly tensed and looked out through the thin veil that divided the ddraig's chambers from the rest of the lair. She let out a low hiss before turning to face me once more.

"A dragon approaches. Tend to them, and we will continue this conversation after it is dark and the lair is still," the guardian said. The corners of her mouth curved up in a smile, just revealing the tips of her silver fangs. "Before you leave, young ddraig, you may stop referring to me as 'statue' or 'guardian'. You may call me Mushussu. Go now, Ddraig, go with confidence, and know this; you have my protection now."

I blinked, and the statue was no longer standing in front of me. She sat in her alcove above the fire. It was hard to convince myself that the whole conversation hadn't been a dream, but the guardian's smug smile still lingered on the frozen statue; that, and the aching in my jaw. I shook my head vigorously. The entire ordeal felt so surreal now it was over. I took a few steps across the chamber and placed my paws on the wall, reaching up so that my head was almost level with the statue. There was no hint of any sign that would indicate that just moments earlier, this statue had been alive.

A sound distracted me, and I turned to see what the statue had heard. A shadow cast on the veil as a dragon lingered beyond. They had not been there long, and I was content to let them wait. Though my conversation with the statue, or Mushussu as I now knew her as, had dulled the edge of my grief, I had no desire to be in the company of other dragons. At the same time though, I knew I would be neglecting my duty as ddraig if I remained hidden from my clan. I had hoped for a little time to myself, but they had barely afforded me a night of undisturbed rest.

With a sigh I turned away from the statue and approached the veil. I shuddered as I felt the slight touch of Azlak's mind against my own. It wasn't the seer that repulsed me, but the magic that allowed me to feel his presence. I paused, holding a paw to my head as I heard the whispered thoughts from Azlak's mind. I could feel his trepidation, and that nervousness started to sink into my own mind. My heart raced as I leaped back with my breath coming in short, sharp bursts.

My head thrashed from side to side as I tried to rid myself of Azlak's thoughts and emotions, but it wasn't until I felt the touch of another's mind that I was able to calm myself. Even Mushussu's mind felt metallic against mine.

"Be calm, Anzig," the guardian said. Her voice resonated through my mind, blocking out the seer's whispers until I could hear them no more. The silence that filled my mind was blissful. My racing heart slowed and the rampant fear that had gripped my body receded. I took a deep breath and stepped out to meet the seer.

Azlak yelped as I roughly brushed the silk veil aside and strode out to face him. I could tell he did not know I was aware of his presence, as he felt he had approached with little noise. Coupled with his fear that I had shared, he was unsure as to whether he should disturb me.

"Ddraig Anzig," he gasped, lowering his head almost to the ground and remaining silent.

"What is it, Azlak?" I snapped. The seer seemed unwilling – or unable – to continue.

The seer averted his eyes, showing a hint of the insecure dragon that had been the omega of the clan. I hoped this hadn't been the dragon I had left in control of Laxtal, that he had instead been something closer to the dragon growing in confidence.

"Yalle hopes that you'll join him outside, by the edge of the gorge. He says he has matters to discuss with you. I believe it is about the wylax," the seer said timidly. I suppressed a groan. I had no desire to go and meet Yalle now, but I knew that the senior dragon would expect my presence no matter what I wanted. The duties of ddraig would not wait. As much as it pained me, I would have to put aside my grief for the time being and meet my clan.

"Tell him I'll be there soon," I said wearily.

Azlak dipped his head and retreated. He hurried back towards the main chamber and beyond to carry my message to Yalle and whichever other dragons wished to see me. I expected Marin and Saya. They were often the dragons Astar trusted to assist in ruling the clan. They would also be the most likely to challenge for my right to rule.

The thought of facing Laxtal was a daunting proposition, and that didn't even begin to consider how we could stand against the might of Xital and their human allies. We needed to take action, and fast. I had a few ideas already, but what I really needed was the steady voice of Carlee to assist and guide me.

"You have me now," Mushussu said. I closed my eyes and clenched my jaw tight, fighting back the new wave of grief that threatened to overwhelm me. The guardian was no replacement for the experienced veteran.

It wasn't until I swooped through the main chamber before I realised that I had allowed Yalle to summon me. I suppressed a stab of frustration at that thought. I should have demanded the albino dragon meet me in the ddraig's chambers, but given the mess I had left, perhaps it was for the best that I had not invited some of the more powerful dragons of Laxtal there.

A simmering of amusement ran through my mind. *"Should I return everything to its proper place?"* Mushussu asked.

I bit down on the snarl. It was bad enough hearing the errant thoughts of the dragons around me. I did not want the voice of the guardian commenting on everything I did. I struggled to shut her out, but I could still feel the metallic presence of her magic, lurking just beyond the range of my senses, like a shadow on the edge of my periphery. She remained mercifully quiet as I emerged into the daylight outside and banked up to climb out of the gorge. I quickly found Yalle and soared down to meet him.

Ellian stood with the albino, along with the expected pair of Saya and Marin. I could not see Azlak with them, so he had not remained after passing on my message. I wondered at that. The seer had been my chosen leader in my absence. Had he assumed he was no longer needed because I had returned with Ellian? I would need to discuss that with Azlak when I could, but I had other concerns to worry myself with.

I flicked my wings as I fluttered to the ground, deliberately kicking up a bit of dust and forcing the other dragons to look away. "Is there a reason for this?" I asked. If they had laid the first blow by successfully summoning me, then I made sure to get in the first word. These dragons needed a remainder on who their ddraig was.

"We have concerns," Marin spat out. His thoughts fluttered around the edge of my mind. I struggled to shut them out, but not before I caught a glimpse of his anger, frustration, and shame. I had no desire to pry deeper into his thoughts, but I found his shame unusual. What did he had to be embarrassed of? Did he recognise that he should not be positioning himself against his ddraig?

"Well?" I snapped, speaking into the silence. "What are they?" I looked around the four dragons, keeping their gaze in turn. Of them all, only Ellian was able to actually meet my eyes. She stood a few paces away from the others, an irritated snarl frozen on her muzzle.

Marin looked left and right to his companions. Neither of them said anything, so he stepped forward. He loomed over me. I struggled to lift my head higher, a futile effort given the advantage of size the older dragon had.

"Laxtal should remain pure from outside interference," Marin said, growling as he looked down on me. I noticed that he used no honorific when he spoke to me, nor did he speak with any respect. "There should be no reason why Laxtal should bow its head to any clan. We certainly should not be talking about alliances with Nixa, nor allowing Nixans and Xitals to gain any measure of control within this lair, like your choice of Azlak has allowed. He tried to justify his decisions by claiming you would support them. I would have you denounce them now and pledge that if you are to become our ddraig, then it will be for the betterment of Laxtal only."

Laughter burst out of me before I could hold it back. "Have you learned nothing from what has happened recently? Remaining apart is what has gotten us into this mess. Flying by ourselves lost us Ddraig Astar. If we refuse to accept the aid of our neighbours, then we face total destruction. Are these really your concerns, Marin? Do you share them too, Yalle and Saya?"

Yalle dipped his head. "We must preserve our way of life, yes."

"Our way of life?" I spluttered. I flicked out a wing and gestured out to the plains, where dozens of dragons flew, hunting or patrolling. "Our way of life requires us to be alive. Would your stubbornness allow you to oversee the death of our clan, just so you can claim with your dying breath that you accepted no Nixan aid?"

The three dragons bristled at my words. "Then it is true?" Saya asked. "You would rather dragons of Nixa and Xital to gain power than those of your clan?"

"This is ridiculous," I muttered. I turned away from the dragons and prowled towards the edge of the cliff. My tail whipped back and forth as I moved away. None of them came after me, giving me a moment to control my thoughts and wonder what purpose their complaints served. I knew what we needed to do. I had seen the army Xital had mustered. They had not. I knew what alliances the Royal Clan had already brokered. There would be no way of surviving if we did not do the same.

Marin raised his voice. "This clan needs a ddraig who will uphold the traditional ways of Laxtal. Your father had long hoped you would be that dragon, Anzig. Was he wrong?"

I hissed as I whipped around. How dare he invoke my father in this. "Laxtal needs a ddraig who will keep its dragons alive. I am that dragon. Haeraig Ellian will fly out and secure alliances with our neighbours. Together we will build an army that is unstoppable. Then, and only then, can we worry about the traditional ways of the clan. Survival is more important."

Saya inspected her claws. "Then you mean to delay the wylax even longer? I doubt there has ever been a time where Laxtal has gone so long without a formal ddraig."

"What do you mean?"

The ness snickered. "Did you forget? Your haeraig must be at the wylax. If you send Ellian away, then who will be your haeraig instead?"

I let out a low growl. She was right. I should have remembered that. Until the wylax concluded, I would need to keep Ellian by my side. Such a delay could prove critical in securing the alliances of clans like Axaatl. I would need to change plans, and quickly.

"Ellian, come with me," I said. "I would like to organise the wylax as quickly as possible. Your input will be valuable. You other three, I don't want to hear anything more about these insular ways. They did not help Laxtal in the past. They will be fatal now. Do you understand me?"

None of them said anything, despite my glares. Ellian hesitantly stepped forward. She flared her wings as I did so, and before anyone could protest, I took to the air. For a moment I was sure Marin or Saya would follow, but they remained on the ground.

I had no destination in mind. I simply wanted to get away from the lair and the irritating whispers that plagued my thoughts. I needed the space to breathe without the feeling that a dragon judged my every move.

Ellian's wingbeats kept me company. My unwanted magic fed me a small insight into her thoughts, bubbling away at the back of my mind. I struggled to shut that out. I sensed disapproval tinging her excitement, though the target of that emotion was not clear to me.

I stretched my wings and put on some pace, scattering a flock of starlings. Below me was a herd of deer, keeping a wary eye on the sky, but I was not interested in the prey. Not just yet. Nor were there any hunters close by to disrupt us.

We flew past the closest beacon to the lair, with two more visible on the horizon. Around the base of the beacon were the signs of occupation, around the small cave where the beacon keeper resided. That dragon would be crucial in protecting the lair, watching for signs from the more distant beacons. I caught a brief glimpse of the dragon, sat on the eastern slope of the outcrop upon which the beacon rested. They lifted a wing in greeting, before returning to their vigil.

I continued my flight a few minutes longer, until I reached the bank of one of the few small rivers that wound through Laxtal's territory. I fluttered down to the riverbank, the bubbling of water over stony ground a relaxing sound. A few fish darted beneath the murky surface.

"You should not dismiss their concerns so easily," Ellian said, taking to the ground by my side. She looked into the river, her lilac scales reflected back in the water. "They may be misguided, but they're just afraid about the future."

My shoulders slumped. I permitted weakness and uncertainty to show in my posture, something I would not allow were I in any other company. If Ellian were to be my haeraig, then I could trust her with my doubts. "What would you have me do?" I asked her, not expecting a true answer from her. "Their insular views put them in opposition to what we both know needs to be done. We can't survive this without help from other clans. If Marin gets his way, then we all die. We can't allow him to spread that idea through Laxtal."

"I'll see what I can do to make sure the clan is aware of our need to ally with Nixa," Ellian said. Her eyes tracked the movement of some fish beneath the water surface.

"We need this," I whispered. I curled my tail around my hindlegs.

Ellian fixated her gaze on the river, her head unmoving. She didn't even blink as she held one paw up. "We know it's right," she said, speaking slowly through her distraction. "Once we start making our moves, they will realise what we're doing is for the clan's benefit."

"When can we host the wylax?" I asked, looking up to the sky, though there was no sign of the moon above, having already set beyond the western mountains. There was no set time for a wylax, no designated day that we had to wait for, though a full moon was common. The next full moon was over three weeks away. There was no chance I would risk waiting that long. A different day would have to suffice.

Ellian lashed out with her paw, splashing into the water. Her claws snagged into the scales of a shimmering silver fish, flicking it out of the water to scoop it up into an arcing flight. Her teeth snapped out, blood on her jaws as she caught the fish between her teeth. Her blue eyes shone brightly as she crunched through bone and scale.

"We can do it beneath the thief," Ellian said, her mouth still full of fish. "That gives us three days to get everything prepared."

The thief felt like a poor choice of face for the moon, but also apt. I would be stealing control of the clan from those who deserved it. I looked up to the sky, absent of the moon for now.

Three days. I took a deep breath. Three days to ensure that my control over Laxtal was secure. Three days until I became the ddraig of Laxtal in all aspects. Three days until there would be no doubt that I was the true successor to Astar, the dragon everyone believed to be my father.

Three days until the lies consumed my life.

CHAPTER FOURTEEN

Ellian

I was glad to be home. Familiar scents. Familiar chambers. Familiar dragons. What was less familiar was the sense of unease in almost every shadow. The dragons of Laxtal were uncertain about something. Whether it was the coming war or the lack of an appointed ddraig, I couldn't yet be sure. I had heard many whispers, but no one had spoken of this discontent to my face.

I was glad to stretch my wings and soar through the clear sky, away from the tight confines and judging stares of the main lair. As the nominated next haeraig of Laxtal, I was not expected to patrol the territory, but it gave me the feeling of doing something worthwhile. Ever since I had returned to Laxtal, my wings had felt idle and still. Anzig struggled to control some of the more powerful dragons in the clan, who refused to act until we saw through the wylax. I knew my cousin worked hard to ensure the plans for the ceremony progressed, but it was a frustration that should not be taking up so much of our time.

As he had been for much of the last couple of days, Airil was by my side as we soared over Laxtal's sparse and empty territory. The beacon network provided some protection from invading forces, but a regular patrol ensured that Xital would not be able to surprise us with an invasion.

My eyes were often drawn south-east, no matter which direction I flew. Somewhere out there was the great army of Xital, and whichever clans they had already intimidated into joining them. I had seen their numbers. Tsona had bragged about them to me. I looked forward to the day I could silence that wretched, pompous excuse for a ddraig, but I feared that opportunity would never arise. If Laxtal refused to act, then we would never have the chance to fly against the traitor. Their forces would overwhelm us long before we could get close enough to Tsona.

"I know what you're thinking about."

Airil's bright voice cut into my thoughts. I glanced back at the Nixan, flying just behind my right wing.

"We have to do something, Airil," I said. My paws clenched as I kept them tucked up against my belly so they didn't slow down my flight.

"Have faith in Nixa. Ddraig Krateos won't let us down," Airil replied. He snapped at a small insect that dared to get close to his jaws. He took a moment to swallow the small snack. "The moment he unleashes Nixa's full strength, Xital won't have a chance."

I bit down on the immediate response to that. If Ddraig Krateos commanded such power, then he wouldn't need the alliance with Laxtal. I knew Nixa wasn't as powerful as some Nixans believed. I was sure Airil knew that as well, so I kept quiet for a little longer. I had no desire to feed into the delusion of grandeur brought about by their magic. It gave them a strength, just as Laxtal's fighting prowess was a strength.

We flew towards the southern borders of the territory, not far from the land held by the minor clan of Zestra. This part of Laxtal was lush and verdant, with large forests dominating the unpopulated land. A few narrow rivers snaked through the trees, providing refuge for herds of prey animals that largely ignored us.

Amongst the trees were the low mounds that gave a platform for the beacons. Airil had already shown an interest in the few we had passed over during our patrol, but he had politely not asked any questions about the network, the operation of which remained a Laxtal secret.

There had been no sign of any dragons who should not have been in the air. But for the occasional Laxtal hunter, the only dragons we had seen had been those occupying the beacons. If Xital was preparing their army to invade Laxtal, then they were not coming from the south.

I banked my wings and prepared to follow the assigned route towards the west and the distant Sxinix Mountains. As I did so, I caught sight of movement in the distance. Two dragons were in the air, flying towards us. There should have been no other patrol, and certainly not one flying counter to ours.

I immediately tensed. The two dragons were too far away to identify. I couldn't even determine which clan they might be from. Until I knew who they were, I had to consider them a potential threat.

I glanced back to Airil to make sure he had seen the unknown dragons, but his attention was elsewhere. He looked further left, to the south.

"Ellian, there," the Nixan said, gesturing with his forepaw.

Two more dragons, barely black specks against the pale blue sky. They flew north, converging on the other strangers with great pace.

I was unsure whether to fly faster or hang back. There was no way to know if the two groups of dragons were friends or enemies. If they represented a danger, then they outnumbered us. I quickly scanned the surrounding landscape, taking note of the closest beacon. The flames were not yet alight, so the beacon keepers had not recognised a danger.

"Do you think they've seen us?" I asked, musing the question more to put my thoughts to voice, rather than expecting an answer.

Airil gave me an answer anyway. "We've seen them."

I sucked my breath in. We had to assume that the other dragons had seen us. Normally, there would be nowhere to hide in the open air, not without taking a vulnerable position in the forests below us. No, we needed to act in a way no Laxtal dragon would expect.

"How high can you take me?"

Airil reached out with his paw, closing around mine. A moment later, reality unravelled around us, a dazzling array of colours ribboning into infinity. Within each speck of light I momentarily caught flashes of movement, of life existing in stunning diversity. Creatures I had no names for. Structures I did not understand. Barren landscapes and those of beauty. All of this within a single heartbeat.

I panted as senses flooded back, followed by a prickle of heat that filled every scale, radiating out from my paw. The warmth lingered even as Airil released me, the Nixan's wings faltering slightly as he recovered.

The chill, thin air quickly leeched at that warmth. We were not far below the wispy clouds that tore across the sky. A cold wind pulled at my wings, making it difficult to stay in one place. Rarely had I flown so high before. I had forgotten how hard it was to breathe with ease. Each gasping breath burned at my lungs.

The unknown dragons were now far below us, though slightly closer than they had been when I had first noticed them. I could see them a little clearer, framed now against the dark green of the trees, rather than the pale blue sky.

One of the dragons was brown-scaled, with their companion copper. The two dragons who flew in towards them from the south were green and red in colouration, but they were still too far away to properly make out their clan. The copper dragon beneath us was definitely a Xital.

I was about to declare all four dragons as enemies, before I realised the brown dragon was not Xital. They had long, sweeping horns to indicate a Laxtal dragon. Did we have a traitor in the clan?

I lost a little height to get a better look at the two. Neither looked up, so they were unaware of where we had gone. Nor did they look to the south. If anything, the two dragons appeared to only have attention for each other, flying with wingtips almost touching.

"Isn't that the Xital ness Azlak invited to stay in Laxtal?" Airil asked, breathlessly joining me. He gazed down with the intensity and focus of a hawk, eyes unblinking as he looked between the two groups of dragons.

"Tsona's daughter? Selane?" I furrowed my brow. It did look like the Xital ness, and the dragon with her did appear to be Ravet, her Laxtal mate. "Why is she out here?"

Airil had no answer. Instead, he circled in a tight motion, wings banked like he was a raptor hunting its prey. His eyes fixed on the two dragons from the south, while I kept my attention on the daughter of Tsona. I had not seen her while I her father had kept me imprisoned, so I had no insight into her betrayal. She had spoken nothing of her reasoning, not even to Ddraig Anzig.

The other two dragons from the south didn't slow down. They flew almost as fast as any dragon I knew, their wings beating with incredible power and pace. It was not long before their paths converged.

Selane's cry of alarm was loud enough to reach me. A moment later, her attacker thudded into her, almost knocking them both from the air. The second dragon grappled with Ravet.

It no longer mattered why Selane sought refuge in Laxtal. For right or wrong, Ddraig Anzig had upheld Azlak's decision to give her refuge, and she was under attack within our borders.

I trimmed my wings and began to plummet. The wind roared in my ears as I picked up speed, buffeting against my body as I tucked my legs as tight to my belly as possible. A shadow streaked behind me as Airil followed.

No one looked up until too late.

I extended my forepaws at the last moment, crashing into the red dragon and twisting him away from Selane. My momentum carried us lower. His wings struggled with my weight as well as his, unable to generate any lift. My claws dug into his scales, refusing to release my grip.

My foe butted his head into mine, the crown of horns surrounding his head cracking against my jaw. Xital, then. The questions would have to wait.

The Xital tried to butt against me again. I twisted my neck, pulling us both into a spiral as our weight shifted to the right. My teeth clamped down on his neck.

The trees were very close now, rising towards us at an alarming rate. But still I waited. The moment needed to be just right. The Xital let out a screech and tried to rip away from me. My grip held firm.

We were almost at the treetops when I finally released the Xital. I flared my wings wide, the sudden resistance dragging at my shoulders painfully.

The Xital crunched through the top layer of the canopy with a quickly truncated scream. My wings ached with the pressure of arresting my rapid descent, and the topmost leaves cracked against my paws as I skimmed the edge of the forest.

Beating my wings a few times to gain some height, I looked up to see Airil and Ravet had subdued the second Xital, pinning him between them. I hissed in pain, pulses of discomfort radiating out from my shoulders, as I slowly ascended.

"Airil, can you take him back to Laxtal from here?" I called out.

The Nixan growled, his claws digging into the tail of his captive. Ravet had control of the Xital from the front, both working together to keep the squirming dragon from flying away.

"I should be able to manage that," Airil replied. "I doubt I'll be able to come back though. Not for a few hours."

There was no other threat coming. The sky was clear of dragons, both friend and foe. Not even the closest beacon keeper had taken to wing to see what had taken place. I knew I would need to question that. Everyone controlling the beacons needed to be alert to any potential danger.

"We'll be fine," I assured the Nixan. "We'll fly back. Just take our prisoner to my chambers and tell Ddraig Anzig what has happened here."

"Of course," Airil replied. With a deafening crack of air filling a sudden void, he and the Xital dragon were gone. Ravet yelped, dropping in the air as the dragon he held vanished without a trace.

I turned my attention to Selane, swooping around to glare at the Xital ness, who had perched atop one of the nearest trees, the branches swaying under her weight. Close by was the scar left in the foliage where I had thrown one of her attackers. There was no sound coming from below the trees.

I ignored the Xital ness and fluttered beneath the trees, following the path of wreckage the falling dragon had created. A few broken branches were stained with flecks of blood.

In the shadows amongst the roots of the trees, I found the Xital dragon. Wings bent. Bones cracked. Chest still. He had not survived the fall.

I muttered a quiet curse as I suppressed the guilt and revulsion that burned at my throat, gorge rising. This was an enemy dragon, on an opposing side in war. I could have no opportunity to feel sorry for the life I had taken. A gentle prod with a paw confirmed what I already knew. There was no life left in the dragon's body, now a simple corpse.

Even for an enemy, I could not simply walk away. I turned and looked up to see Ravet and Selane both looking down at me, neither dragon having followed all the way to the ground. Instead, they perched in the branches like simple birds. Ravet held his wing around the Xital's body.

"Ravet, I need you to fly to the nearest beacon and get a firelighter. He deserves a proper burning, at least," I said quietly. I hung my head low. "Selane. You're to remain here with me. I want to understand what happened here."

"As you command, Haeraig," Ravet said. He touched his muzzle against Selane before he took to wing, dislodging a few leaves as he rose through the foliage. He soon disappeared from view, though his wingbeats were audible for a while longer.

Without any prompting, Selane opened her wings and glided to the ground to land a few paces from me. Her eyes lingered on the corpse of her clanmate. "I do not know what you wish to learn," she whispered. She kneaded at the ground, littered with uneven piles of browning leaves and broken twigs, some left behind by the devastation of the falling dragon, others from the deepening autumn.

"I want to know why you're out here, and I want to know why they attacked you," I said, sweeping a wing to the dead Xital.

"Gods preserve me," Selane said, turning away. Her tail swished through the old leaves, scattering them. "The first question is simple enough. Ravet knew a place where dragons of your clan frequently come to express their desire to be formally mated. We have committed to each other there. The second question is more complicated. I am not sure if I can answer it."

I tugged on Selane's tail, forcing her to turn back and face me. "If Xital is sending dragons to hunt you, then Laxtal needs to know why. As the proposed haeraig of this clan, I am asking if your presence is a danger to us."

Selane stared me in the eye for a few seconds. Her mouth hung partially open. Then she looked away. "Yes. My presence is probably a danger to you all."

"How? Why?" I would not let this Xital ness evade the truth. If she were to remain in Laxtal, no matter what Azlak or Ddraig Anzig thought, then we needed to know her intentions.

The Xital let out a snarl and stamped a forepaw down hard. She shook her head vigorously as she began to pace around in her obvious agitation. I simply sat back and let her work out whatever frustration built inside her. She had no authority to ignore my questions, and I was sure she knew that. It was a pleasant feeling. Xitals had always been far above my station. As a haeraig, even the royal clan could not claim authority over me.

"Because I know what they're planning," Selane finally said. She shrank in on herself, wings wrapped tight to her body. "I know what my father's next move will be. I know why he's doing all of this. If he thinks I'll tell your ddraig all of that, then he won't hesitate to have me removed. That's why they attacked me."

I found it hard to believe that the order to attack Selane could have come from her father. I knew already that Ddraig Tsona had abandoned many ways and traditions that dragonkind had upheld for generations, but I hadn't thought him to be so far gone. He had ordered his own daughter dead. Even if there were no other reasons to oppose Ddraig Tsona, then that would be one to unite most dragons against him.

Selane sat down and curled her tail around her hind legs. Despite the attack, she did not appear scared. I understood that manner of defiance.

"You need to help us stop him," I said softly. I approached her, tempted to reach out and touch her shoulder with a paw, but I refrained from contact.

"He's still my father," she whispered, voice hoarse with emotion. Her muzzle twisted into a silent snarl as she gouged out several deep trenches with her claws.

"Is he? He did just try to have you killed. No father does that to his daughter." It was not my intention to be harsh, but the Xital still flinched at my words. I stumbled as I tried to continue. "I mean to say, if he's decided you aren't his daughter, then you don't need to be loyal to him. You're free to choose your own family now. Free to choose Ravet."

Selane nodded. "I do choose Ravet." She paused and clenched her paw into a fist. "The humans have a weapon they intend to use on Nixa. According to George's friend, I believe they call him Rico, it will destroy the Nixan lair. I understand they also have a plan to recover the Axinstone, though I was unclear how they intended to do this."

I hissed slowly. "When?"

"I do not know. Believe me, I do not," Selane said. She looked up as wingbeats approached through the trees. Ravet swooped through the branches, carrying a firelighter in his paws.

The Xital turned her head and met me in the eye. She did not look away. "The rest I will tell to your ddraig. I do not betray the plans of my father lightly. I expect Laxtal to protect me as one of your own."

I hesitated. I knew what some of the dragons of Laxtal would say to that. She was not one of our own. She was from another clan. Worse, she was from Xital. We could not trust her. I growled away those imaginary conversations. I was not those dragons. Nor was Ddraig Anzig. We needed every dragon we could get.

"We will protect you. You have my word as haeraig."

Selane bowed. "Very well, Haeraig Ellian. You have my thanks. Let us do what needs to be done here and then return home. I would like to join Ddraig Anzig in questioning my other attacker, should he permit it."

Together, the three of us prepared a space to burn the body of the Xital dragon. I tried hard not to think too much about what I was doing. The strange pliability of the body. The way those eyes stared sightlessly. The small residue of guilt that tinged my every thought. I had meant to disable my enemy, not kill them.

Were Carlee still alive, I would have hoped for more lessons from the veteran to better hone my fighting skills. She had preached the importance of killing only when necessary. This had not been necessary.

My thoughts carried me through the entire preparation process. When we were done, I sat back and watched the flames burn until nothing remained of the dragon I had killed.

The smoke burned at my eyes. I did not look away.

CHAPTER FIFTEEN

Anzig

I was exhausted. I had barely slept since returning to Laxtal from Xital. Reality and fabrication overlapped, and I could never be sure what was spoken aloud and what were meant to be the hidden thoughts of the dragons around me. Every moment was torture, struggling to determine what I should answer to and what I should pretend I never heard. And through it all was Mushussu.

The guardian whispered to me throughout the day, attempting to guide my thoughts and offer advice. She ignored my pleas to leave me alone. Whether she refused my desperate demands or was unable to leave me be, she never said. I did my best to ignore her, but she made it difficult.

We were only meant to be one day from the wylax, the ritual ceremony that would confirm my heritage as the true ddraig of Laxtal, but I still felt so unprepared. I knew little about what the ceremony would entail. Despite that, I refused to listen to Mushussu's attempted explanations for it. If someone were to tell me, I wanted it to be a dragon of flesh and blood, not of her unknown magic and metal.

I knew I was being a fool for ignoring Mushussu and her advice, and her quiet whispers reminded me of this frequently. I simply feared that accepting the reality of the guardian was another thread unravelled in the world I had believed true. Hers was a magic more akin to Nixa, not Laxtal. Combined with the trauma of my own magic, and the realisation that I was not Astar's son, it all felt too much. What I needed most was the opportunity to get away from the clan, to be somewhere quiet where I could process everything, but I was about to become ddraig. That was not an option.

As much as possible, I claimed refuge in my new chambers, hoping that the clan would accept the excuses that I needed to prepare for the wylax, as well as forging plans for the war to come. In truth, I spent much of that time pacing restlessly, beating out a path with my paws that would surely start eroding the rock. No such track appeared, but my paws did grow weary. And yet still I walked, burning off the restless energy that filled my body.

"You must understand, I'm not Nixan," Mushussu said, cutting into my thoughts. "I am something far older than any of the clans. Something truly ancient, and yet merely a fragment of that old power."

"I don't recall asking," I growled. I had cleared up the chamber since my outburst on the first night as ddraig in Laxtal. It felt more like my home, with my scent present, especially having since moved most of my belongings into the cave from the haeraig's quarters, now occupied by Ellian. I still struggled to recall where I was when I woke in the mornings, for what little sleep I had managed, but I no longer felt like an intruder into my father's place. Or, Astar's place, at least. Once more I needed to remind myself he was not my father, and I was not his son.

"In blood only," Mushussu clarified. "You were his son in everything else that mattered."

"It won't matter to everyone else," I muttered. I then realised I had allowed Mushussu's comments to distract me from my mindless pacing. I let out another growl but did not give her the courtesy of looking towards her alcove above the fire.

I felt the guardian's disapproval radiating through me, though she remained silent. I knew what the clan would think if they knew about my magic and unknown parentage. Wylax or not, they would not tolerate me as ddraig. I knew from their thoughts that they already doubted me without that knowledge.

"You are untested. It is only natural there may be doubts," Mushussu said. "They will still give you a chance."

The immediate retort on my tongue died as a whiplash crack echoed through the chamber, coming from somewhere close outside. A muffled yell followed a moment later. It came from Ellian's chambers.

I moved without wasting time to think, shoving through the veil over the entrance and scampering down the narrow corridor to the familiar room that had once been mine. With Ellian away, it should have been empty. I did not expect to see Airil struggling with a strange Xital dragon.

I grabbed hold of the Xital by the throat and tore him away from the panting Airil. The Nixan dragon looked ready to pass out.

"Keep him away from me," the Xital dragon hissed, still scrambling to get away from Airil, even as my claws dug into his throat. The green-scaled Xital's eyes were wide as he looked over my shoulder. I didn't need to break into his thoughts to recognise his panic.

I kept the pressure firm on the Xital, but he wasn't attempting to escape me. "Airil, I need you to fetch Yalle or Marin for me," I said, speaking over my shoulder as I kept one eye on the dragon beneath me. "Can you do that?"

Airil said nothing, but he hurried out of Ellian's chamber, stumbling and swaying with each step. I knew his magic only allowed him to appear in places he was familiar with. I hadn't been aware he had come to Ellian's chambers. Curiosity warred with envy and disapproval, but I forced myself to ignore all of that for now. I had a prisoner in my paws, and I did not want to allow him to escape. Whatever had happened with Ellian and Airil on patrol needed an explanation.

The Xital dragon squirmed in my grip. "You let Nixans into your lair?" he hissed. His pulse thumped through his neck, twitching against my claws. He still breathed quickly. "Their magic is unnatural. You shouldn't allow them in like this. Why do you think Ddraig Tsona refused to ally with them?"

My growl silenced him. "Give me your name."

"Truda. It's Truda."

"I will give you one warning, Truda. You do not tell me how I should rule my clan again. I am the ddraig here, not Tsona. And especially not you."

Truda blinked. "You're the ddraig?" he scoffed, barely suppressing a laugh.

I resisted the urge to cuff him across the muzzle. I was glad I did so, as we were soon joined by larger, stronger dragons who were better able to pin down the Xital. Marin took over from me, his claws dimpling into Truda's scales and drawing a little blood. No one questioned how the Xital had appeared inside Ellian's chambers, but given Airil's presence, I doubted there would be much confusion.

"Get him to the dungeons and hold him there for me," I demanded, taking a step back to see who else had come. Yalle glared from the entrance, with Airil swaying behind him. I could see no one else, but I thought I heard more paws beyond the Nixan.

"Of course, Ddraig," Marin said, spitting out the words. "What will you do?"

"I'll follow behind you shortly," I replied. "First, I need to learn what happened with Ellian. Airil, if you could tell me on the way. Then you can get the rest you need."

Yalle turned his glare to me for a moment, before bowing his head and stepping back to allow Marin to drag Truda from the haeraig's chambers. The Xital went willingly, though he shrank away from Airil as they passed by in the narrow corridor outside.

I looked around my old chambers, now with unfamiliar rugs and blankets draped across the floor, with some new trinkets on the shelves around the cave. This was Ellian's place now. I wrenched my eyes away and forced myself to leave. I didn't want to leave Airil waiting for too long.

There were a great many questions to answer.

Ellian returned to Laxtal with Selane and Ravet before I could get much information from Truda, bringing with them knowledge of what Xital had planned. The captured dragon refused to confirm the accusations Ellian brought forward, but nor did he deny them either.

If we could believe Selane, then the knowledge she shared could be crucial. I could only hope we were not too late. I summoned Azlak, hoping the seer would be able to verify her story. While we waited, I arranged for a pair of guards to keep watch on Truda, ensuring he stayed imprisoned within the dark corners of the lair. We would not neglect him, but nor could I allow him to fly free.

I soon returned to the main chamber, sitting in a quiet corner and watching the activity around the clan. I clenched my jaw, struggling to contain the errant wisps of my mind, reaching out to every dragon who passed too close, bowing with deference. Hundreds of dragons were outside, going through military drills under the inspection of the few military leaders who had survived the ambush that claimed the life of Ddraig Astar. Those who remained inside processed the food gathered by the hunters, prepared the war paint that would adorn our scales in battle, and tended to those still sick and injured from Xital's brief but brutal rule, as well as the losses we had sustained in Astar's failed military campaigns.

I would not say Laxtal was thriving, there was still a fear and a weariness present that I could never recall witnessing before. There were no songs or revelry. Few dragonets were outside to play. For now, we survived. And that was enough.

A presence touched my mind. I looked up before Azlak had chance to announce himself. He recoiled half a pace and quickly lowered his head. Kaz had come with him. The Nixan tilted his head and flicked the tip of his tail, before he, too, averted his gaze in respect.

"You wished to see me, Ddraig?" Azlak asked, his voice small, but with some strength behind it. I was glad to see some lingering trace of the dragon I had left in control of the clan beginning to emerge again.

"Come with me. I don't wish to be overheard," I said, spreading my wings. Truth told, I also wanted to escape the crowd for fear I would become too distracted by the thoughts of those around me to properly focus on the conversation with Azlak. Not wanting the dragons of Laxtal to realise our powerful allies were at risk was merely a good excuse to hide behind.

Though I was tempted to return to the ddraig's chambers, I instead banked my wings and took to flight towards the upper corridors and the gorge beyond. I hoped I would feel better with the sun on my wings. Not only that, but I would be further away from Mushussu.

A spike of disapproval simmered through me, but the guardian said nothing. I was glad of that. It gave me fewer distractions as I picked my way through the familiar cave towards the surface.

I was disappointed by the bank of clouds that had rolled over much of the sky, robbing me of the sunlight I craved. I had been inside too long, and while the fires below had kept me warm, nothing gave energy to my scales like the sun. The days were already growing shorter and colder. I could not waste those days before winter came.

I fluttered down to land close to the head of the gorge, further away from the cliffs that overlooked the plains of Laxtal. Nearby was the small outcrop of stone that would be the place I would begin the wylax. From there I would address Laxtal as its true ddraig. One more day and that would become the truth. A truth that would hide the lies beneath it.

"What did you have to say?"

Azlak's question brought me out of my reverie. I shook my head to clear my thoughts, glad it was only mine that crowded my head.

I stared out over Laxtal, eyes towards the north, where the bulk of the clouds came from. "Selane told me what her father's plan is. He intends to attack Nixa, and soon."

Kaz snorted. "He won't succeed. No army can ever take Nixa."

I pawed at the soft dirt. "Selane seems to think he might have the means. Some humans have been developing new weapons. She isn't sure what they are or what exactly they're capable of, but the human creating them is confident that it can break through the magic defences surrounding your clan."

I could feel the concern radiating from the two dragons. I clenched my jaw and tried to focus on the copse of trees in the distance. In better times, there would be dragonets playing amongst them, darting across the grassland on agile wings. Now, it was almost completely empty. In the distance, I could hear the drills of the clan's remaining warriors, on the other side of the gorge.

I turned to face Azlak. The seer lowered his head to stare at my forepaws. "I need you to use your magic and See anything you can from Nixa to confirm Selane's information."

Azlak's tail quivered. He shook his head. "I can't do that, Ddraig Anzig. Magic doesn't work going into Nixa. If I were to have visions of what happens inside Nixa, I would need to be there myself."

So much for that idea. I growled softly and looked away from the seer. If Selane was right, then this would be a danger to the tenuous alliance I had worked so hard to achieve with Nixa. Any threat to the clan to the north would threaten us. I could not sit back with wings tucked tight while I knew about this plot against them. But nor could I do anything now and hope that my clan would allow another delay to the wylax. Already I had waited too long.

As much as I wanted to be the dragon to go to Nixa and warn them of the dangers to come, I would need to stay in Laxtal, even after the wylax. Ellian also couldn't be the dragon to go. We needed her elsewhere, securing our borders with further alliances. The seer made the obvious choice. Not only would he be able to use his magic to detect the dangers, his magic would not be seen as a curse in Nixa. With my authority behind his voice, they would listen to his warnings.

"You will leave after the wylax, then," I said, turning back to the seer and the Nixan. "Ddraig Krateos expects an emissary from Laxtal once I have been confirmed as the ddraig. You will go to Nixa and use your magic to confirm Selane's information. You will warn Ddraig Krateos of this."

"Of course, Ddraig Anzig," Azlak said, dipping his head.

I stared at the two dragons. They had been in each other's company almost exclusively. I sniffed their scent. They mingled. "You have been teaching Azlak how to control his magic?" I asked, addressing the Nixan healer.

"I have, Ddraig Anzig. He is proving to be a capable and eager student," Kaz replied, gazing at the seer with more than just admiration in his eyes. Azlak curled his tail and shrank down, a pale blush forming at the edges of his scales around his eyes.

I furrowed my brow. There was more here than I realised. I dared not use my magic to work out what. "Good, that is good," I said, distracted by the need to clamp down on my thoughts. "I would like to learn what you teach him as well."

Kaz blinked at me. He tilted his head. "Ddraig?"

I realised my mistake. I stammered. "If we are to have an alliance with Nixa. I would understand them. Know how Nixa controls their magic. How their strength works."

The Nixan slowly nodded his head. "I see. That is unusual."

I struggled to meet his curious gaze and keep my head held high. He couldn't know that I had anything to fear. No secrets to hide. I cleared my throat and struggled to control my voice, getting rid of the nervous stutter. "If I am to be a good ddraig of Laxtal, I must know my friends as well as my enemies. For too long have Nixa and Laxtal treated each other like strangers."

"A worthy goal, Ddraig Anzig," Kaz replied. He still sounded hesitant, but he did not question my slip. "But it is unnecessary. You do not need to understand how magic works to know that Nixa owes you a debt for returning the Axinstone. I do not presume to speak on behalf of my ddraig, but I doubt he will expect you to understand magic."

I did not dare argue. I could not give Kaz any reason to suspect why I should like to learn magic. Especially how to control it. I hoped Azlak would share some of that knowledge anyway, when we were alone and had a rare private moment. For now, I doubted I could extricate the seer from his tutor without raising some suspicion.

I resisted the desire to sigh. There would be no help here, but Azlak was not the only dragon I needed to see. There was another who could decipher the plans Selane had tantalised us with. "Do you know where Maznar is?"

Azlak and Kaz glanced to each other. The Nixan lowered his head and took a couple of steps backwards, leaving Azlak to answer my question. "No, Ddraig. I went looking for her this morning, but I wasn't able to find her. No one has seen her. The last anyone saw of her was when we returned from Xital. If my guess is correct, she slipped away that night, but no one knows where. Nor have I been able to See her."

"And no one thought to tell me this?" I hissed in dismay and lashed my tail against the ground, ignoring the pain it caused. "I have no time to search for her now. If she has gone back to the humans…" I growled softly and turned back to Azlak. "If you See anything of her, come to me right away. I am not yet convinced we can trust her, but this could still be innocent enough. She has no experience of living as a dragon. She could have just as likely gotten herself hurt while hunting as betray us."

"I understand, Ddraig Anzig."

I approached Azlak and put my paw on his shoulder. There it was again, the scent of Kaz on his scales. The two had been closer than a tutor and a pupil. A whisper of foreign thought tickled at my mind. I pushed it aside with a twitch of my neck. "Anything you can do, Azlak," I whispered through a tightly clenched jaw. "Anything you can See that can help us. We will need your magic until Nixa is able to commit their aid to us. Learn what you can and hone your magic to the best of your abilities."

"I'll do what I can, Ddraig Anzig," the seer said. "The moment I See something, I'll come to you."

"Please do," I said. I felt lost, unsure of what task I needed to do next. Everything relied on the wylax so I could become the ddraig of Laxtal, but after that was unknown. Despite the beacons and the scouts, we still had little idea what the movements of the humans or Xital dragons were. We didn't know their plans. How could we defeat an enemy without understanding them?

Lost in my musing, I only noticed Azlak and Kaz departing as their wings blew up gusts of wind into my face, swirling dirt and dead leaves around me. I was alone. As I was always going to be. No chance of a mate. No opportunity to feel close to another dragon, not with the responsibilities of ddraig on my wings.

I no longer knew what I wanted. No clear path before me. No wind pushing behind my wings. Everything was turbulent with storms approaching from every angle.

Temptation tugged at my wings. To unfurl them and let the wind lift me up, to glide wherever I might soar. To leave Laxtal far behind and never return, leaving my responsibilities and regret.

I shuddered and stamped a paw almost immediately, forcing those thoughts away. I could not abandon my responsibilities, or the legacy passed on to me from Ddraig Astar. Blood father or no, he had still chosen me to replace him on his death. A faint satisfaction radiated into my thoughts, emanating from the silver statue in my chambers. Mushussu's delight was clear to me, as though her emotions came from my own mind. The intrusion was not welcome, but I could not push her away.

It got worse. The guardian's voice echoed through my head, breaching through whatever mental walls I had constructed. *"You can't escape your destiny, Anzig. Sooner or later, you must face it, just as your father did."*

"Destiny?" I growled in disgust. Destiny and fate were things dragons like Azlak needed to worry about, concerns for seers and mystics. And yet, despite that derision, I still got the sense that I neared a critical day in my life. The wylax would come and I would either be uplifted to ddraig of Laxtal, or rejected and banished like the fraud I was.

Tomorrow, in the hills above the Laxtal lair, I would learn if I could control my clan or not. Only then would we be able to forge the alliance agreed with Nixa. Once the two ruling clans united, we would be able to move against the treachery of Xital.

One more flutter of wings until we had the strength we needed. It all seemed so easy. So much could still go wrong.

chapter sixteen

Nataik

The undergrowth rustled with the wind, carrying a scent I wanted little to do with. Humans had been here. Again. Their little raids into Nixan territory were getting aggravating to deal with, especially when I had promised the magical ddraig that I would be able to help keep them away. That had proven to be an unexpectedly difficult task. My pride would not let me return to the bizarre lair before I could at least find the tracks left behind.

Keeping low to the ground, I kept my ears alert for unexpected sounds while my eyes focused on the disturbed soil. Dragon and deer tracks criss-crossed the ground. I could see no sign of the humans, but they had been around here somewhere.

I suppressed a growl of irritation. Hush now. Quietly. It wouldn't do to draw humans to me before I knew exactly where they were. My scales were good for hiding, but they were not perfect.

How I longed for the marshes at home. There, a dragon could move with silence. Scales liked mine kept me hidden no matter where I was, but here I struggled not to make a noise. I had to take care where to put my paws.

Every day had been the same, for two weeks now. Tantalising glimpses and scents of the humans were all I had been able to discover. The Nixans were no closer to understanding what the humans were here for, but the failure still itched at my scales.

A momentary distraction pulled my thoughts from the hunt. I looked up in a futile attempt to find the presence that teased the back of my mind, the shadow that lingered in my periphery. Another suppressed snarl. Those nightmares were bad enough in my sleep. I didn't want them plaguing my waking hours as well. Nightwings could return to the ocean she had fallen into for all I cared. Her and Maznar. I still couldn't be sure how distinct the two were, if at all.

The strange spectre was nowhere around. No surprise, given she had followed Ddraig Anzig to Laxtal. She would not have returned to Nixa, no matter what my dreams might suggest.

One shadow that was real was the one that dappled my back, cast by the surrounding trees and lengthening across the ground as the sun began to set. Another day of failure.

Ashamed by the lack of success, I began the trek back towards the Nixan lair. The terrain around the low hills had become familiar to me over the past few days, my scent almost as strong amongst the trees as that of the humans. Few Nixans came out this way, preferring instead to fly over the canopy towards their traditional hunting grounds in the south. None flew now. Ddraig Krateos allowed no one to leave the lair unless they tracked the humans. Even hunters were carefully monitored.

Ddraig Krateos did not admit to it, but the Nixans were afraid. They had no control over the humans. We could not be sure what their plans were and how they would strike at the Nixan lair. It had been a couple of days since anyone had commented on how invulnerable the lair was.

I had almost made it back to the main entrance when I realised the scent of human had grown stronger in my nose. They had been here. Recently. All thoughts of returning to the safety of Nixa fled my mind. I paused long enough to cast a quick glance to the top of the nearest hill. No dragon waited for me up there yet. That gave me time to investigate this new scent.

I melted into the shadows, scales blending into my surroundings without a thought. There was not far to go.

Breaking through the trees was an artificial embankment of raised earth, dug up recently and piled up in a curved defensive shape. I knew it wasn't Nixan in origin. They didn't build defensive structures like this. And the protected side faced away from the lair.

No humans remained at their embankment, but they had left behind tantalising little clues. I sniffed out a small glass bottle discarded amongst the dirt, as well as a few metallic tools used to dig out the trench. A spade. A trowel. I didn't touch or move any of them, lest the humans recognise that someone had disturbed them when they returned.

Not wanting to return to Nixa without any further information, I continued my prowl. I heard nothing, so I knew no humans were close by, but even so I didn't let my camouflaged scales revert.

But for the tools and scattered junk, there was little of interest. For all my excitement of finally finding something the humans had done, I was utterly disappointed. If they had created something specifically to taunt and frustrate me, then they had done so perfectly.

Birdsong chirped through the trees. I sighed and looked up towards the rise of the Nixan lair. It was no bird that called out to the growing darkness. Meadus, the youngest son of Ddraig Krateos, had come to our meeting point so he could let me back into Nixa. I dared not linger, but as I turned to leave, my eye caught something flash in the twilight darkness.

I clawed at the scrap of metal partially buried in the disturbed soil to reveal a strange, blocky device of indeterminate use. It looked like it could be some sort of trigger or control, with several unlabelled buttons on one side. Thick wires connected the strange device to something further underground, well beyond my ability to pull out.

Stranger still, I found a socket that looked about the right size to fit something as large as a dragon's paw. In fact, it looked about the right shape for the Axinstone. That was curious.

I ran my paw around the indentation, before sharply looking up as another chorus of birdsong chirped through the forest. The sun had almost completely fallen. It would be dangerous to stay out any longer.

I brushed soil back over the strange device to hide that I had discovered it, then hurried out of the trench. The scent of humans faded as I retreated towards the lair. So, they had not come much closer than the fortification they had quietly dug. That might be useful information to the ddraig, but failure still weighed over my wings. I had promised the Nixans that I would help them understand this human foe. I was not enough. I needed help, but it was not a Nixan I needed to assist me.

Meadus showed no disappointment as I approached, deliberately shifting my scales to a reddish copper so that he would see me. It was only when I saw his raised eyeridge that I realised I had accidentally matched his colouration perfectly.

I lifted my head and met his eye. "What?"

The young Nixan snorted. "Nothing. Did you find anything?"

"Not quite nothing," I replied. "I need to speak to your father."

"He is no easy drake to see," Meadus said. He took a deep breath, swelling his chest, then utilised his intriguing magic. When he next spoke, it was not with his own voice, but the deep gruffness of his father. "I do not have time for simple frivolities. Nor can I meet any dragon who wishes a moment of my time. Ruling Nixa is no easy task, my young son. Consider yourself fortunate your wings will never know this burden."

I couldn't help but laugh, partly in amusement, but also in wonder at the sheer perfection of the mimicry. "Your father does not speak like that," I said, shaking my head.

Meadus shrugged his wings. "No. But he might as well sometimes," he said, reverting to his own voice. At least, I assumed it was his natural voice. For a dragon who could mimic any voice, dragon or otherwise, perhaps it was difficult to remember what natural was. Just like me. I no longer recalled what my natural scale colour was. They changed with my mood and surroundings so much that I simply couldn't remember what I had been before I had discovered my gift.

Realising I was standing still, gathering my thoughts and doing nothing useful, I shook my head again and focused my mind. Meadus was waiting for me, and the night was not a safe place for a dragon at the moment.

I hurried after the Nixan as he led me into their strange lair. The opening passage unnerved me as it opened far wider than it appeared, delving far down below the surface in a perfectly straight and even slope. The hill didn't seem large enough to contain such a passage, nor such a lair beneath, but any attempts at explanation simply gave me a headache. Nixan magic. That was enough of an explanation for me.

Being the youngest son of Ddraig Krateos, Meadus wasn't owed much respect by his clan. Few dragons even acknowledged his presence, with more eyes lingering on me. I was something new and interesting. From what I understood, it was rare that Nixa allowed dragons from other clans to stay within their lair for long. That I was the second such dragon permitted to remain in such a short time was highly unusual. The Laxtal dragon Vinzent was not well liked. I understood why the Nixans treated me with suspicion, but I longed for friendly eyes again.

Meadus led me safely through the tunnels and out through the central chamber of the lair, kept illuminated by the many crystals throughout the walls and distant ceiling. We flew directly for the ddraig's chambers. There was little activity so high up in the lair, with most of the dragons down at the distant floor. Despite the worries of the nearby human army, there appeared to be a celebration happening down there, with a great feast prepared. Though my stomach growled, I kept close behind Meadus. The consequences of travelling alone within Nixa had been vaguely, but firmly, impressed upon me.

The two of us ascended to the ddraig's chambers, towards the base of the sweeping dome that capped the lair. That ceiling didn't match any feature or structure I had seen on the surface, but once again I chose not to question it. Nixa. Reason enough.

There was no one on the wide alcove outside the sealed chambers of the ddraig. Carved from the same white stone as the rest of the lair, it gleamed in the eerie magical light. But for the paw-shaped impression in the stone at the deepest part of the alcove, there was nothing on the walls, though the floors were mostly covered with thick rugs. I flicked my tail, sweeping aside some dust as I sat down.

For all of Ddraig Krateos's willingness to let me stay and hunt out information about the human army, the Nixan had resorted to a series of power plays and games when meeting me. Sometimes he would be eager to hear what little information I had. Other times I would sit and wait most of the night for him to show up. Perhaps the presence of a feast would make him more eager to come out from his chambers.

Meadus looked back at me. "Wait here. I'll see if he's ready to talk."

The Nixan said nothing else before he simply vanished into the stone wall. I had tried to find a way in by myself before, but nothing worked. Not even when I put my paw in the controlling indentation they used to let me through. The entrance to the ddraig's chamber only worked for a Nixan. It was clever and incredibly defensive. I had to wonder if there was a way to break that magic, but I had the decorum not to ask Meadus or any other Nixan. I doubted they would look fondly on such questions.

To my surprise, I did not have long to ponder the defences around the lair before a gentle glow heralded the arrival of Ddraig Krateos and his son. I was not too surprised to see his only daughter as well. Haeraig Zeena was often her father's shadow as it was.

I bowed my head to the ddraig and haeraig, careful not to meet their eyes.

"Do you have anything tonight, Nataik?" Haeraig Zeena asked.

I stared at their paws. "I did find a device buried in the ground, though I have not been able to determine its purpose," I explained. I curled my tail to quell the urge to thrash it. "I believe it might be powered by the Axinstone in some way, though I cannot explain why the humans would build such a thing unless they had plans to reclaim it from your chambers."

Ddraig Krateos snorted in derisive laughter. "They stole it once. There will be no chance to take it a second time. If this device is truly powered by the Axinstone, then it will remain inert and useless to them. Anything further?"

I hesitated. This was a potentially dangerous bit. I knew what my skills were. I knew what I could provide Nixa and Laxtal, and all the other western clans. But I alone was not enough. I looked up. Lifting my eyes to look at the ddraig's throat. "I fear I am not enough to understand this army, nor will I be all needed to defeat them. I recommend sending an envoy to Xigax and request assistance from Ddraig Nunahra. If she knows the request comes from me, then she will answer it."

"You would have me invite more of your clan into my lair?" the Nixan ddraig growled. I didn't dare look any higher than I did, but I could see his wings shuffled against his back. I could hear the tap of his claws against the stone floor. "For what purpose would this serve?"

"You would refuse an army of Xigax warriors to help defeat these humans, Ddraig?" I asked.

Ddraig Krateos scratched a forepaw across the ground, his claws scraping against the stone. "We have no need of such things. Magic is enough."

"With all respect, Ddraig Krateos, magic will not be enough to win every battle. You will have need of our skills," I pleaded, regretting my initial blunt comment. I should have known the Nixan would bristle at such things.

"We have no need," Ddraig Krateos repeated. He lifted his forepaw, small sparks of crimson light crackling at the tips of his claws. "We have the Axinstone. We have all the power we could ever need. I see no reason to demean myself by seeking aid from Xigax."

I dipped my head low, almost with my muzzle touching to the ground. "Then should I prove my abilities are the match of yours, would you consider my request?"

I knew to expect it, but I could do nothing to prepare myself for the blast of magical energy that smashed into me. The Nixan's magic ripped me from the ground and slammed me into the wall. A twinge of pain snapped through my wings as he squeezed the breath from my lungs. I could move nothing, even with my paws suspended some distance from the ground.

Ddraig Krateos stared into my eyes. I could not look away, no matter how much I tried. The strength and power in those piercing green eyes captivated and terrified me.

"Magic is the strongest force there is," the ddraig said, eyes locked on me. "Nixa has no need of your clan's assistance. We have Laxtal as our shield. We do not require another."

I said nothing. I wasn't even sure if I was capable of speech. I simply waited until the ddraig's magic released me.

When he did, it was abrupt. My limbs were weak as I collapsed to the floor, wings draped helplessly beside me. I panted for breath and squeezed my eyes closed to control my spinning head.

The ddraig gently touched a paw to my chin. "Your offer of assistance was accepted, Nataik. Nixa does not require anything further from your clan. Your skills are nothing compared to our strength in magic."

I hid my smile. Ddraig Krateos had given me exactly the words I needed. Instead of showing that satisfaction, I shied away from his touch and stood up on shaky paws. That much at least was no feint. His magic was devastatingly powerful.

The ddraig turned to his youngest son. "Please guide our guest to the feast. She must be hungry."

I recognised the blunt dismissal. I said nothing to protest it. I needed the ddraig to think he had defeated me, that his display of power had definitively concluded our disagreement. I slunk past the ddraig and his haeraig without lifting my head, following after Meadus who opened his wings and prepared to launch from the platform.

I played the part of the cowed guest, leaping from the alcove and descending after the young Nixan dragon. I made sure to remain above him, out of his direct line of sight.

"You need to be careful with my father," Meadus cautioned. I wasn't sure that he recognised his voice matched mine. "He doesn't take kindly to those who threaten his authority and control."

I stayed silent. I had to pick my moment.

There were so few dragons in this part of the lair I knew I had a good opportunity. There was only Meadus to evade, for I had no intention of joining the feast below us.

I waited until we were halfway down the great chamber, Meadus babbling about what food he wanted to try first, before I made my move. I extended my wings a little wider, slowing my descent until the young Nixan was far enough away that I felt confident enough to quietly beat my wings and change my angle.

I veered towards the nearest wall and latched onto the strange white stone, glad to find some claw holds to grab onto. My scales melted to a perfect match of the wall as I folded my wings. Unless someone saw my eyes, no one would see me.

Though I could fly silently, I trusted my scales to keep me hidden better when I was close to the wall, especially when there was so much light. I began to climb, reaching slowly for the next claw hold, each movement carefully calculated so I made no noise at all. Somewhere far below, I could hear Meadus's confused calls, but I didn't look back. I just focused on the climb.

The young Nixan didn't raise the alarm. Nor did he fly back up to his father. Perfect. That just made everything so much easier.

One paw over the other, I gradually clawed my way back up towards the highest parts of the lair. I didn't stop moving, even when a dragon flew close by, trusting in my ability to stay silent and my scales to keep me hidden. No one cried out. No one even seemed to realise I had escaped Meadus. Had the young Nixan simply gone to the feast as though I was not his responsibility? I didn't look back to check, but it wouldn't have been the first time he had let me wander without supervision.

The climb felt good, putting exertion through my muscles, especially in my forelegs as they took my weight. I controlled my breathing, keeping it slow despite the effort, ensuring I didn't make too much noise.

I only stopped when I finally reached the underside of the ddraig's alcove. I closed my eyes and listened for any movement above me, but I could hear nothing. The ddraig and haeraig were no longer there. I had expected that, but it was still a little disappointing. Their scents were still fresh, though. They couldn't have gone far, and I expected they had simply retreated to Ddraig Krateos's chambers.

I hauled myself up onto the wide ledge, belly low to the ground and my claws safely sheathed. Even to my own eyes, my scales were practically invisible against my surroundings. I allowed myself a small smile, teeth safely hidden away behind my lips. The ddraig wouldn't expect this.

Pressed up against the wall, I waited, unmoving. I barely even breathed. Minute after minute I stared at the part of the wall where the ddraig would emerge through the magical portal from his chambers. And still Meadus didn't come to warn his father that I had slipped away.

I didn't once let my concentration slip. I focused only on my absent quarry. My muscles, trained for explosive movement and periods of stillness alike, never protested my statuesque vigil. I moved only to blink and breathe.

Finally, my moment came. The portal to the ddraig's chambers flared to life. Two shadowy shapes emerged from within. First came the haeraig, followed by her father.

"…foolish to let them stay so close, while we feast and celebrate," Haeraig Zeena said, continuing the conversation from within her father's chambers.

I crept closer. With my claws retracted I made no noise at all. Completely silent, I stalked my prey. The Nixan ddraig didn't so much as twitch in my direction.

I didn't give him time to react. I leaped for him, landing on his back and wrapping a foreleg around his neck, claws extending to dimple into his throat. To his credit, he didn't yell or thrash. He simply tensed.

"Tell me again how my skills are worthless?" I growled into his ear.

His daughter whirled around at my words, her eyes wide. She lifted a paw but did not unleash her magic on me.

The ddraig let out a low hiss. "I concede."

I paused a few seconds to let the satisfaction of those words sink in. Then I retracted my claws and slipped from the ddraig's back. My scales loosened their colour, reverting to a more common green.

The ddraig's eyes burned with anger. His paw quivered as he reached to feel at his throat, but I had been careful. I hadn't drawn a single drop of blood, nor pierced a single scale.

"You have made your point, Nataik," Haeraig Zeena said, filling in the silence while her father smouldered. "But the question still remains, what use do we have of stealth and deceit? There is little honour in the way Xigax wages war."

I now had the confidence to look the haeraig in the eye, if only for a moment. "There were many things Ddraig Anzig said in the council at Xital. One of them spoke true. There is no honour in war. Only victory or death. An alliance with Xigax will give you victory."

"I think it was Ddraig Aranat who said that," Haeraig Zeena whispered. She turned her head away, brow furrowed with thought.

I flicked my wings back. "It doesn't matter who said it. The words are still true. Will you send a messenger to Xigax and ask for my ddraig's aid?"

"What will Ddraig Nunahra demand for this?" Ddraig Krateos said, finding his voice again.

I shook my head. "I am not the ddraig. Nor am I her haeraig. I cannot speak for her thoughts, but she trusts my judgement. If you send a messenger on my behalf, then she will come. She will give you favourable terms. The defeat of these humans is what she will want. The honour of defeating them may well be enough, no matter the honour with which we fight with."

The ddraig growled low. He shared a quick glance with his daughter, then turned to bare his teeth at me. I refused to back down, though I did lower my gaze.

"Very well," the ddraig snarled. "I shall send a messenger to Xigax to open discussions with your ddraig. But in the meantime, I expect your behaviour to be exemplary. No more moving about alone, and no using your… abilities. I want you visible at all times when inside the lair. Do I make myself understood?"

"Perfectly, Ddraig Krateos. Thank you."

"Tchaa." The ddraig stomped his paw. "Now go. Join the feast. I will send that messenger at dawn."

I did not linger to test my luck any further. But as I flew down to the feast, I couldn't stop the smile on my muzzle. Xigax would join this war against the humans. An alliance between three of the ruling clans was a mere wingbeat away. No force could withstand the might of Xigax, Nixa, and Laxtal combined. My claws itched with desire. This battle could not come soon enough.

Meadus flew out with me the following morning under his father's orders. I chose not to question the ddraig's demand. He had, after all, fulfilled his end of his promise and sent out a messenger to Xigax almost before the sun's first light had breached the horizon.

The young Nixan was quiet as we flew out to the strange device I had found the previous day. Usually, I couldn't get him to shut up, but he didn't say a single thing until we landed amongst the trees.

I quickly found the trench and dug up the device, untouched since I had last seen it. No human had come here since the previous day. Their scents were faint and fading.

"Have you ever seen anything like this?" I asked the Nixan, hoping to draw some words out of him.

Meadus let out a sigh and approached. He stared at the strange device, then shook his head. His attention then turned back west, where the scent of human was slightly stronger. "Can we really win this?" the Nixan whispered, his voice so soft as though he feared his father might overhear his worries. He used a new voice this morning, one I hadn't heard from him before.

"What makes you think we won't?" I asked. My senses were all alert for any danger, but I turned my eyes to the youngster.

He looked away. "It's silly. I had a dream. More of a nightmare. Again. Every night for the last three nights. It's always the same one. Nixa destroyed and in ruins. My father and siblings all dead."

I snorted in surprise. Nightmares had plagued my sleep for just as long. "Three nights? Remind me, Nixan magic can't pass in or out of the lair, can it?"

"No. Dragons inside the lair can't influence anything outside it, or the other way around. Why?"

I let a little growl rumble at the back of my throat. Maznar's magic had been to control dreams, but if she wasn't in Nixa, then she could have no influence over my dreams or Meadus's. But had Isikian not once claimed that no other dragon in Nixa had magic that controlled dreams? It was a curious situation. I would have to disobey the ddraig's command and investigate the lair at night, to find out whether the strange spectre had returned to Nixa for some reason.

"Nataik?"

I blinked. I had allowed my focus to lapse, no longer taking in my surroundings. I dragged my mind out of its idleness. "No reason. Just a coincidence, I'm sure."

Meadus made a small noise in the back of his throat that indicated he didn't believe me. I didn't blame him. I wouldn't have believed me, either. But he said nothing to contradict or question me.

The thought of Maznar unsettled me. If she was back in Nixa then I needed to know why. She could be a threat, and if so, Ddraig Krateos would need to know. Just another added complication to the situation that none of us needed.

"Come on," I said, flicking a wing to my Nixan companion. "We should see if there are other trenches like this one. If we can understand what they're for, then maybe your father will understand there's a threat to worry about."

"Unlikely," Meadus muttered, but he spread his wings anyway.

We launched into the air together, cautious for any sound of humans, but the forest was largely quiet. A few birds screeched as they flew above us, the wings a cacophony of noise and feathers, but little else reached my ears. Certainly no humans.

I expected to scour the ground for hours to find any signs of further human activity, but we found it almost immediately. Meadus flicked out his wing to point towards a low ridge not far north of our position, close to the bottom of the slopes that made up the exterior of the Nixan lair. "That's new."

I trimmed my wings to investigate. A quick scan of the ground confirmed that there were no humans here, either. The ridge was an earthen mound much like the first, slightly curved to offer protection to those sheltered on the side away from the lair.

This trench and ridge was a little more exposed than the first, with no trees to overhang and cast shade on the ground. It made me wonder how the Nixans had failed to notice this during construction. I could only assume it had been done at night, when there were no dragons outside the lair. But Nixa prided themselves on their power and strength. This was a talon to the heart of those claims.

Meadus said nothing about such a thing as he landed. He put his head down low and sniffed out some of the scents, while I targeted the middle of the trench to see if there was a similar device dug just beneath the surface. The mound of disturbed soil was a good place to start, and it was only a few scoops with my forepaws before my claws touched something solid.

Sure enough, I found another of the strange devices, wired up to something else deeper underground. The only difference was the lack of a socket for something like the Axinstone to fuel the device. There was still nothing to give away the purpose. It was hard to know if this one connected below ground with the first, but I had a bad feeling they were.

Giving a sharp command to Meadus to follow, I took to wing again. A cold sensation settled in my gut as I flew further north. Now that I knew what to look out for, I easily spotted a third trench. And then a fourth. And a fifth. I followed the line of trenches around the five hills of the Nixan lair, forming a perfect ring. I did not need to fly to them all to know they would each have a strange metallic device in them. There was no chance this was benign.

Nixa was under siege. The dragons inside just didn't know it yet. And nor did I know what purpose it all served. I just knew the clan was in a far greater danger than they could possibly have anticipated.

"We have to find these humans. I have to know what they're doing," I said. I beat my wings to remain hovering in one spot, scanning the horizon for something, anything, that gave away their presence. If they were constructing trenches and installing unknown weapons so close to the lair, then they had to have some sort of base nearby. But all I could see was the untamed wilderness of draconic lands. If there were humans hiding there, then they did so well.

We had just one advantage over them, one lead to follow. They couldn't help but leave a scent. It would be difficult, and it could take a long time, but we could track that scent. I could only hope that I could find them in time.

A decision made, I turned to Meadus. "Go and warn your father that the clan is in danger. Try and convince him to evacuate."

The Nixan scoffed, his voice deepening to a low growl like the ddraig's. "Do you think my father would listen to that? Not without any evidence. Whatever you have planned, I'm coming with you."

I opened my mouth to argue, then snapped it closed again. I growled. The youngster was right. Ddraig Krateos would not listen to anyone, not even his son, that a great danger threatened his clan. Not without conclusive evidence. All I had right now was a hunch and a bad feeling. That was not enough.

"Then keep close," I said, banking my wings hard and flying back towards the first of the strange devices. There had still been a strong scent on that one. If I had any chance of following the humans, then that would be the place to start.

After landing, it only took a few minutes to find a trail left through the undergrowth with human scent. An occasional footprint lingered in the damp soil, not fully dry from the little rain we had over the last few days. I could see there had been at least three different humans, based on the size and shape of the footprints and the coverings they wore on their feet.

There was not much to track, but it was a start.

Meadus crunched through the leaves behind me, showing little aptitude to any stealth. Whereas my paws were silent and swift through the brown leaves that littered the forest floor, he blundered through with seeming no ability to plan where he put his weight. Almost every step brought a crunch or squelch through leaves, or the crack of a twig broken.

Until we got closer to the humans, I decided to say nothing. I led by example, making so little noise that I could ambush and stalk a squirrel, if I chose to.

For a while, I despaired. The scent of human was constantly there, but never increasing in strength. Never growing stronger and more recent. Their footprints moved in both directions down the trail. I even found a few drops of dried blood on a spiked vine. But nothing more recent than a day old. The humans had constructed their trench and underground device and then left. Their behaviour baffled me. Their hubris almost impressed me. They didn't expect dragons to find their work. Were it not for me, they would probably have been right.

Just as I was beginning to lose hope, fearful I had followed a false trail, I caught a strong scent on the wind. I froze. Meadus bumped into my hindquarters before he stopped.

From somewhere in the distance ahead of us, there came a human shout. Other voices followed it. They sounded static, not marching closer to Nixa for now. But they were still dangerously close to the lair.

I pointed to the nearest tree. "Wait for me up there," I said. I then added with a hiss, "And stay quiet."

Meadus was not quiet as he fluttered up to the tree and perched on a thick bough. His wings and claws sent leaves and fragments of bark to the ground, and he let out a little squeak of fright as he struggled to find purchase on the wood.

I sighed softly and shook my head. Nixans received no training for anything beyond their magic. They were useless when it came to claw and tooth combat and were worse than that when it came to stealth. If they wanted to win this war, then they needed Xigax. They needed me.

I felt no fear as I moved from the narrow trail and into the undergrowth. I moved slowly and with perfect care, ensuring I made as little noise as possible. My scales blended with the dull browns and faded orange of the rotting foliage around me. No human would see me, I was sure of that.

The reek of humanity assaulted my nose. I shivered and flicked my tail. It was like a switch had flipped. Suddenly their scent was all that I could smell. I glanced back, but could see nothing different in the air, but I suspected magic. Thoughts of the human-Nixans we had seen in George's castle added a little concern to my mind. Like I had no true defence to Ddraig Krateos's magic, I would have no ability to keep safe from magic wielding humans if they spotted me. I could make myself a difficult target to hit for a bullet. Magic was a different matter entirely.

As the scent got stronger and the sounds grew louder, I slowed my pace even more. My senses were all on high alert, making sure that no humans were moving through the undergrowth nearby. There were none. All of them were ahead of me. I thought I could hear around a dozen. So, this was not the full army that patrolled through draconic territory.

I pushed the tip of my muzzle through a thick bush to find a clearing on the other side. In the centre of the clearing was the charred remains of a firepit, with a fresh source of firewood a few paces away. Surrounding the firepit were half a dozen canvas tents. Eleven humans sat amongst the tents. One additional human paced in the centre of the group.

Hush now. This was a time for silence.

I crept forward, out of the relative safety of the undergrowth. Even my scales were not complete protection in the open clearing. But if I was to take information back to Ddraig Krateos, then I needed to get close enough to hear exactly what the humans were saying.

Two of the humans wore clothing I recognised as being associated with high-ranking officials in their army, though I couldn't recall the specifics of what the symbols meant. I could never remember why some had stripes and others wore stars. Both of those humans sat amongst the others who all wore military uniforms. Only the man pacing around the charred wood wore no such uniform. Instead, he wore what I had seen regular humans wear. A pendant hung from his neck, shaped like a clam shell.

I got as close to the humans as I dared, only a dozen feet away from the nearest of them. The canvas tents provided some cover, as did the packs of supplies: food and ammunition mostly, from the smell of them.

"Are you sure this will work, Rico?" one of the higher-ranked men asked the one pacing in the middle. He had three stars on his badge, above three diagonal stripes.

Rico. I recognised the name, but I couldn't place it. I resisted the urge to paw at the ground in thought. I had no time for distractions. I needed concentration so that no one could ambush or surprise me.

Rico's laugh was cold. "Why? Do the dragons scare you, Arnold?"

"It's not the dragons that scare me," the man called Arnold replied, shaking his head. "It's the power they wield in the Dragon's Head that concerns me. Why did you let them take it back?"

"Do you doubt me? Have I ever led you astray?" Rico asked, tapping his nose. Where his finger touched his face, small traces of pale red light lingered. There appeared to be a pattern to it, like ribbons of light that wound through his skin, but was so weak it could only be seen in response to the pressure of touch.

"With respect, sir," the second of the ranking humans said, raising his hand. He wore four diagonal stripes on his badge. Curious. "I think General Summers has a point. Under your orders, the garrison at Trevena was instructed to let the dragons take the Dragon's Head Rune, which they can use as their most powerful weapon. Not only that, but they lost Nightwings, who would have been a valuable asset in taking control of these lands."

Rico sneered. "If it helps put your minds at ease, then the Dragon's Head will soon be back in my possession. This was merely a necessary distraction to force some hands. Everything is still proceeding according to plan."

"Whose plan?" the second of the ranking humans said. "It seems there's your plan, George's plan, and the prime minister's plan. None of them seem to agree on what our objectives over here are. The prime minister wants land. George wants some sort of magical artefact. And you? You just seem to want to kill as many dragons as possible."

A wide smile broke across Rico's face, bringing out some more of those red lines that danced around his skin. "Let's just say I have some scores to settle against the dragons. Our goals may disagree on the strength of our action, but they are not opposed. We are all using each other as a means to an end, that is all."

"This still makes me uncomfortable," Arnold said, this General Summers. "I don't like campaigns that leave things to chance. You're risking a lot, especially when you won't even tell us what your goals are or who you answer to."

"None of that matters," Rico said, waving his hand. He paused to nudge some charred wood back into the firepit with his foot. As he did so, his eyes drifted over towards me. I didn't move. His gaze passed by without pausing. "Just keep following my orders and you'll achieve victory, no matter which goals you aim for. This world will be a better place for my vision."

An uncomfortable silence followed Rico's declaration. The other humans looked to each other. General Summers chewed on his lip, his brow wrinkled with thought lines.

Rico appeared to thrive on that discomfort. His smile grew wider, almost predatory. "Now, Sergeant Allen, are the troops in position at Dragon's Haven?"

"Yes, sir," the human replied. "If any survivors make it that far, they will be dealt with. But I still don't understand how you plan on breaking Nixa."

"Again, nothing to concern yourself with," Rico said. He turned to face the other humans and rubbed his hands together. "Very soon we'll be ready to act. Get the orders out to the main force at the haven to ensure they're in position."

I had heard enough. The attack on Nixa was imminent. Worse still, the danger would also take the refuge at Kxisila. Surely now, Ddraig Krateos had to act.

Quietly, I slipped away and found a place between the tents that obscured line of sight to the humans so I could take to wing. I was gone before the humans even knew I had been there.

Rico's voice shouted out from the clearing, a burst of joyful greeting. "And here we are. Didn't I promise you this?"

Damn it all. I should have stayed. Though temptation rose to bank my wings and fly back to see what had overjoyed the human with the strange red markings, I kept my course. If Rico had what he needed, then the attack on Nixa could be about to begin. Meadus needed to warn his father.

The young Nixan was right where I left him, his neck craning forward as he struggled to listen to the humans in the distance. He yelped when I soared down to land at his side, bowing the thick branch underneath my additional weight. Despite his focus, he still hadn't seen me coming. The pride at my stealth quickly subdued as the urgency of the situation established itself.

"Hurry back to your father. Warn him the attack is coming now," I warned the youngster. "He needs to know the Axinstone may be compromised or the target of theft, and the refuge at Kxisila is a trap. I won't advise him on what to do with this information, but he must understand that the threat is real and imminent. Can you do this for me?"

Meadus nodded. His eyes were wide as he looked over my shoulder. "What will you do?"

"Slow them down. However I can. Now go. Fly," I barked. I gave the Nixan a little nudge with my muzzle, almost pushing him from the tree. His wings snapped open, and he quickly gained height, flying just beneath the canopy of golden-brown leaves and bare branches.

I watched him leave, making sure he found his way back to Nixa, before turning back in the direction of the humans. There was a new scent mingling with their stench. Something different. More familiar. Another dragon had come somewhere close to here, but I couldn't work out who it was. It reminded me of Nixa, but not of any one dragon. Another curiosity that I could investigate later.

The humans were on the move already. Whatever Rico now possessed, it had been the signal for them to begin their march on Nixa. They had no more reinforcements. Twelve humans to take down the might of the Nixan lair? It hardly seemed credible, but there was something about this Rico that made me uncomfortable. There was a power in those faded red lines on his flesh that I could not understand. A malice in his eyes I could not comprehend. If he believed he could destroy Nixa, then I did not doubt that for a second.

Twigs snapped around me as the humans moved through the forest. They made no attempt to be quiet. I could track their movement without needing to see them. I marvelled at how I had not been able to discover them before now, but there had been some kind of magic protecting their camp. Now that protection was gone, as their scent was strong through the forest and their noises no longer muffled.

To my frustration, the humans spread out, so I couldn't follow them all together. They all moved in the direction of the lair, but which of them was the more imminent danger? I sniffed out Rico's scent and shadowed his footprints. The scent of dragon stayed with him.

Senses on alert, I tracked the humans a short distance behind them, looking for any opportunity I could take to intercept them. I had to slow them down, but while they had separated, they were still too close to each other to feel confident in attacking one and getting away before reinforcements came.

Time was quickly running out to strike. As the humans neared the low hills of the lair, they began to fan out further. I soon realised why. They were each going to one of the trenches dug around the lair.

I focused on Rico. Whatever it was the humans had gained would be with him, I was sure of that. He was the danger.

The other humans disappeared into the foliage. They were all far enough apart from each other, leaving their backs exposed. I crept a little quicker, closing the gap between myself and Rico. The human gave no indication he knew I was there. His focus was on the hill barely visible through the trees.

I pounced, silent wings giving pace to my attack, claws extended.

Rico spun. His hand closed around my throat. Heat flared through my scales like liquid fire.

His eyes were red. Inhuman. They burned with an anger beyond anything I could have imagined.

As I hung limply in the human's grip, I realised I could not breathe. The air drained from my lungs, just as the willpower to struggle sapped from my limbs. Looking into Rico's eyes was like receiving the judgement of the gods, and I did not have their favour.

"It's almost a shame you won't live to see what I have planned," the human hissed. His fingers squeezed tighter, and still I could do nothing.

A voice broke through the fog in my mind. A human voice. "Sir, there are dragons attacking. We need you!"

Rico snarled. He glared at me, fingers tight around my throat. Then he threw me away, my limp body crashing hard against a heavy trunk and collapsing to the ground. Pain erupted through my chest as the human stomped away, feet crunching through the leaves.

I struggled to draw breath. Pain lanced through my chest with each attempt. I feared my ribs had fractured in the impact.

Wings fluttered towards me. "Are you hurt?" an unknown voice whispered.

I looked up and blinked the blur out of my vision. Through the pain I recognised Meadus standing above me. He had been the one to call Rico away, mimicking a human. He gently put a paw beneath my head, coaxing me up.

"Did you warn your father?" I spluttered. I slowly rose to my paws, each breath a wheezing hiss. I slowly extended my wings and tested them. They still worked. Though the pain in my chest was severe, I thought I was lucky. Nothing was broken after all. Just bruised and painful.

"No, not yet. I thought you needed help."

I swore, then coughed as my stomach spasmed. I tasted blood on my tongue, but I spat it away. "We have to hurry."

I ignored the protest my body gave as I took to wing, my weight in the air straining my ribs and chest. I spat out blood again, all thought to stealth ignored as I pushed my aching body towards Nixa. Somewhere in the distance, humans shouted. Rico bellowed in anger. He had likely discovered the ruse.

Whatever little time Meadus had bought us was now gone.

My wings faltered as we burst from the trees, flying about halfway between two of the trenches. I didn't stop to look to see if the humans had reached their fortifications or not. All that mattered was warning

Ddraig Krateos that he was under attack. The Nixans would be able to repel the humans, just so long as they didn't activate their weapon.

I stumbled as I landed close to the summit of the tallest hill. Meadus ran ahead of me, preparing to activate the entrance to the lair. As he looked back to me, he froze.

I chanced a quick look behind. Two humans stood at the nearest trench. One was Rico. The other General Summers, who carried a small stone in a gloved hand. My eyes widened as I recognised the precious artefact we had struggled so hard to take from the grasp of humanity. The Axinstone. How and why didn't matter. All that mattered was survival.

"Inside, now!" I barked to Meadus.

The Nixan scampered away to put his paw on the entrance stone. Magic burst to life at his touch, the mystical tunnel forming from the stone and expanding far greater than it should.

I leaped for the entrance. Behind me, at the bottom of the hill, Rico laughed.

Magic erupted all around us. Heat seared my scales.

The hill vaporised.

CHAPTER SEVENTEEN

Azlak

I screamed in agony. A phantom claw had reached into my chest and was trying to rip out my heart. It came without warning, and an echoed cry told me I was not alone in my suffering. I struggled to breathe as pain, panic, and fear racked through my body. The emotion threatened to overwhelm me, yet I remained conscious through it all, writhing in agony on the ground. There was nothing I could do to lessen the pain.

A paw touched my chest, the gentleness of it still like fire against my scales. I screamed again. Someone called my name. I tried to answer but could only scream over and over, no words would form. My voice had fled; my thoughts slowing to stillness. Nothing existed but the agony. I writhed with my paws off the ground, wings spread wide.

Then it stopped. As quickly as it had assaulted me, and the torture ceased. I placed a paw on my chest to feel it pulse. Whether the phantom claw had been real or imagination, it had not stolen my heart. But something else was missing; I felt hollow, and with every rasping breath I took, it seemed to swirl around the void inside me.

With a great effort, I forced my eyes open and tried to focus them. I blinked and saw that the whole cave tilted at an angle; I realised then that I was lying on my side.

Kaz struggled to his paws, his wings draped limply over the ground. He had been teaching me to better control my magic while I searched the future for some hint of how to defeat the humans. We had been alone at the time, but as my mind started to clear once more, I sensed, more than saw, that at least two other dragons were now present. I groaned as I rolled over onto my belly, flexing each wing in turn, to make sure neither had been damaged in my pained thrashing. But beyond the echoes of the heart-wrenching agony and the curious sense of loss, I couldn't feel anything amiss.

"Are you alright, Azlak?"

I shook my head and looked up at the other dragons. I was somewhat surprised to see Keita and Okazuni standing there, both hesitant and unsure. I didn't trust myself to speak just yet.

"Something terrible has just happened," Kaz whimpered. We looked into each other's eyes; both aware that we had suffered the same harrowing experience, but neither of us yet understood the why, or the what. I ignored Keita and Okazuni as they asked what was going on, instead pushing past them to stand by Kaz's side, gently nudging his wings back into place.

"Have you Seen anything?" the Nixan whispered.

There was only one thing I could think of that could cause such agony. I didn't want to alarm Kaz unnecessarily, so I cast my mind out like he had taught me, focusing on Ddraig Krateos. If I was wrong – and I hoped I was wrong – I would not be able to See anything of his future. He should be safe in the Nixan lair, where my magic could not find him. With my eyes closed, I tried to consciously activate my magic, but saw nothing other than the inside of my eyelids. I sighed in relief, maybe I had been...

A bronze dragon led a force of around three hundred. Many carried terrible injuries, blood still on their scales. They flew to the mountains, seeking refuge at Kxisila. A small red ness flew at his side, her head bowed low in anguish. Then the gunshots punctured the evening calm. Already weakened, they began to fall from the sky, picked off one by one.

...wrong. I froze in terror, my mouth hanging in shock as I opened my eyes to escape the golden glare of my subconscious.

"What's wrong? What did you See?" Kaz asked urgently. He placed a paw on mine. To my side I could hear Keita and Okazuni whisper to each other.

I tried to speak, but no sound came out. My breath came in short, sharp bursts.

Kaz moved his paw to my face. I felt the cooling touch of his magic, but there was no healing for this. Nothing that could heal these wounds. "What is it Azlak?"

"N...Nixa," I managed to force out in a small voice. I paused to gasp for air again. My head bowed, looking down to the floor. My worst fears had come to pass. "Nixa has fallen. The survivors... They're going to be ambushed at Kxisila."

"What?" This time it was not the Nixan who spoke, it had been the Nyrian. I could feel Kaz's paw trembling. I doubted he was able to vocalise anything right now. I turned my head slightly so I could see Keita. She had her wing over Okazuni.

"You must tell Ddraig Anzig. He has to know about this," I told her.

To my surprise she nodded her head. "Of... Of course," she stammered. She took Okazuni with her, the two dragons scampering away to the upper reaches of the lair. Ddraig Anzig should be in his chambers. I knew he'd want to come and see me. The alliance he had worked so hard for was no more.

Kaz whimpered quietly. "Fallen? How?"

"I Saw something tear apart the ceiling when I was there. There was fire and rock... and death," I whispered, looking down at my paws. Should I have warned anyone? Could I have prevented this catastrophe? Surely Nixa had Seen this coming, there were dozens of seers in the clan. I couldn't have been the only one...

"How many survived?" The Nixan was shaking badly now, so much so that he was barely able to stand.

"About three hundred are making the flight to Kxisila. I don't know how many will survive the ambush there," I said. I didn't dare close my eyes, lest I See the devastation of Nixa once more. I had no desire to witness those visions again.

Kaz finally collapsed to the floor, his unsteady legs unable to support his weight any longer. "That's all?" He covered his face in his paws, hiding the anguish in his eyes, but his voice could not. I said nothing as I lay down by his side and put my wing over his body. I felt him tremble as his body shook with silent tremors of emotion. His eyes and cheeks were wet with tears. He leaned into me and tentatively sought out my paw with his. There was nothing else we could say to each other to ease the pain, but just being by his side was comforting. We didn't even move as distant wing beats announced the imminent arrival of another dragon landing just outside the cave entrance.

Kaz squeezed my paw as he started to relax more. A growl, a deep rumbling noise that I felt rather than heard, came from within him. "They won't get away with this. Nixa will never fall, not completely, not ever," he snarled.

"We will do all we can to assist," Ddraig Anzig said. His pained voice came from the archway leading out to the passages. We quickly stood to shaky paws and lowered our heads towards the ddraig. I was startled to see that he, too, had been racked with pain. Had he felt the death throes of the Nixan lair also? Keita and Okazuni had seemed unaffected, so it was not all dragons who had felt that magical shock.

"I thank you for your kind words of help, Ddraig Anzig," Kaz said, keeping his head bowed. "It is not the Nixan way to ask for help, but I fear that now Nixa needs all that can be given."

"Anything in Laxtal's power," Ddraig Anzig said. His eyes swept around the small chamber, before glancing back out towards the passageways. I couldn't be sure, but it looked like he was checking for any unwanted company. His paw tapped against the floor as his tail thrashed from side to side. His voice dropped to a mere whisper. "It felt like a talon to the heart. I fear for any survivors. Can you tell me everything you know, Azlak."

Kaz tensed. He looked towards me, his head tilted in confusion. I was sure he was questioning why the ddraig would have felt the agony of Nixa's destruction. I shook my head slightly. It was not my secret to reveal. The ddraig had asked for secrecy regarding his magic, and I would not betray that trust. At the same time, I was sure that it could not remain secret for long. Kaz's curiosity would only grow, and it would spread to other Nixan survivors soon enough. If there were Nixan survivors. I told the ddraig everything I had seen, reliving the worst of the visions. I couldn't know what had caused the destruction of the clan of magic, but I knew humans were to blame. There could have been no one else capable.

The ddraig listened to my report in total silence, his head bowed. When he moved, he was stiff and awkward, and his wings continued to droop a little. He had been badly wounded by the destruction of Nixa and his attempts to hide that pain were not convincing.

"We shall send scouts to hunt for survivors," Ddraig Anzig said, once I finished my horrid news.

"There will be few left if they are ambushed at Kxisila," I said bitterly. Now that the Nixans were outside the boundaries of their former lair, their futures would become apparent. Kxisila was so much closer to Nixa than Laxtal. Even our fastest dragons would not make it to the mountain in time.

Kaz flicked his wings. "Where is my brother? He could take someone to Kxisila to warn them."

"He was with Ellian, last I saw them," Ddraig Anzig replied. "Come with me, all of you. We need to understand what has happened and what to do next."

Following the ddraig's lead, we hurried through the lair as best we could, ignoring the lingering aches in our chests. Keita and Okazuni followed a short distance behind us.

Few in the clan paid us much attention, other than to show their respect to the ddraig. There certainly was no showing of grief or pain; no awareness that Nixa had fallen. Had it been my magic which linked me to the lair I had only visited once? That explained why Ddraig Anzig might also have suffered the way he did.

Yalle intercepted the ddraig in the main chamber. The albino dragon dipped his head. "My ddraig, we must start preparing you for the wylax. Already we have delayed too long."

Ddraig Anzig's jaw snapped closed. He pawed at the ground. "Can it wait a little longer? Azlak has brought some important news that cannot be ignored. I need advice from my haeraig first. Then I will come back and begin preparations."

Yalle let his breath out in a low growl, taking care to look away from the ddraig. "Any longer and we will have to put off the ceremony until tomorrow. Already the light runs short. The clan will not look kindly on any further delays."

I looked around the lair. The discontent Yalle warned of did not seem to be prevalent. In fact, few seemed to be paying us any attention at all. None showed aggression towards the ddraig, nor even disdain. There seemed little indication there would even be a ceremony that day. Everything about the clan looked perfectly calm and ordinary, a great contradiction to what I knew had just happened in Nixa.

"I will keep it quick," Ddraig Anzig said. Whether he noticed the discrepancy between reality and Yalle's warning, I could not tell.

Yalle bowed his head in submission to the ddraig. "Very well. I shall await your return."

No one else tried to stop the ddraig as he led us up through the highest part of the lair and towards the open sky. A thick bank of clouds lingered overhead, bringing with it cool air that threatened an early onset of winter.

We found Haeraig Ellian uphill of the lair entrance, close to the nearest river that gave water to the dragons of Laxtal. She stood over Airil, who crouched on the bank of the river, leaning down to lap up a drink from the cool water. His wings hung loose from his sides, his tail curled tightly around his hindlegs.

The haeraig turned as she heard our approach. Her eyes widened. "Oh, Anzig. I'm not sure what happened. I think Airil is unwell."

"He isn't," Ddraig Anzig said, touching down with his back paws first. He quickly explained what I had told him, what my visions had Seen.

Though Airil didn't seem to listen, he groaned and swayed when the ddraig finished speaking. "How could this happen?" he moaned.

"There is more to come," Ddraig Anzig warned. "We need you, Airil. You have to go to Kxisila and warn the survivors that there is an ambush to finish them off. I would like a representative of Laxtal to go with you, to offer our lair as refuge. I would go with you, but I am needed here for the wylax. As is Ellian."

"It is a long way to Kxisila," Airil gasped. Water still dripped from his chin, which he made no attempt to wipe up. "Carrying a Laxtal dragon so far will not be easy."

Ddraig Anzig swung his head to look at me. "Azlak has magic as well. That might make it easier for you."

I blinked in surprise. "Me, Ddraig?"

"You're the only other one I trust for this. More than that, I think Ddraig Krateos will be more likely to listen to you," Ddraig Anzig said. He looked back to Airil. "Will you be able to take him? Time is critical. We don't know how many survived the attack on your clan, but one thing Azlak is sure about is that there will be few survivors at Kxisila. Unless they are warned."

I almost spoke up to contradict the ddraig. I had not Seen how many survive Kxisila. All I knew was that an attack was coming. I closed my mouth again. Speaking against the ddraig's authority would be a bad idea. I didn't even know why I had come so close to speaking out.

"I can take him," Airil said warily. He eyed me up. "But I won't be able to use my magic to come back. We'll need to fly with the rest of my clan."

Ddraig Anzig nodded. "Just come back safely. Azlak will know what to do when you're there."

That put a lot of pressure on my wings. The ddraig had not even asked if I felt capable of performing this duty. Not only would I be responsible for rescuing the survivors of Nixa, but I would also be representing Laxtal as a diplomatic envoy. There was no chance I would reject that honour. No matter what had happened to the strength of our clan's alliance with Nixa, we still had a duty towards them. If the ddraig thought I was the best dragon for this, then I would do my best.

"Then come with me," Airil said, holding out his paw. I grasped it in mine and Laxtal vanished in an instant.

As fast as it took to blink, I stood close to the mountains, rain falling onto my scales as a light drizzle. To the west and slightly north I could see the sheer cliffs of Kxisila, the famed refuge of the Nixan clan. I could see no evidence of humans around it, but I still shivered. This was not far from where my vision had warned of the ambush.

A retching sound caught my attention. Airil staggered away, before collapsing into an undignified heap. He closed his eyes and trembled, pulling his wings up to cover his face.

"We can't stay here," I said, looking up to the grey sky. "We're too exposed. If there are humans here, they might see us first."

Airil grunted. "Give me a moment." His whole body trembled with spasms as he struggled to breathe. "That was a long way to carry you."

I grimaced as I kept watch, waiting for Airil to recover. The rain sapped the heat from my body, so I tried pacing around the stricken Nixan to keep warm. The drizzle obscured a lot of the scent in the air, so I couldn't be certain if there were any humans nearby. I couldn't see them, not even anything of their movement through the area, but I was sure my visions were accurate. They were watching Kxisila, waiting for the Nixan refugees to arrive. My goal was simple. Find Ddraig Krateos first. Divert them to Laxtal, not the ambush at Kxisila. It all sounded so simple.

Airil took a few minutes to recover enough to clamber to his paws. He was still unsteady and he kept his jaw clenched closed. He took a few heavy and deep breaths, snorting through his nostrils with each exhale.

"Which way is Nixa from here?" I asked. Though we had spent a night at Kxisila, I didn't recognise any of the landmarks enough to feel confident in knowing which way to fly.

Airil pointed with a wing, away from the mountains towards where the clouds were darker on the horizon and the rain looked heavier. There was nothing for it. We both flew into the bad weather, slowly at first, and keeping low to the ground to avoid any lurking humans spotting us.

The rain became heavier, going from drizzle to a full downpour. Thunder rumbled in the distance, but never close enough to feel uncomfortable or unsafe in the air. Airil struggled to begin with, falling back regularly and skimming the tops of the trees, but as the day darkened, his flight grew stronger. It wasn't long before he took the lead position, flicking water from his wingtips and tail as he pushed through the rain.

Then I saw the first evidence of humans. It was nothing but tracks in the mud, a few hundred footprints all with one direction in mind: Kxisila. I called out to Airil, and we banked away from the tracks, not wanting to risk any scouts or guards catching sight of us. I kept a wary eye on the forest below us, but there were not enough areas of open land to avoid the risk of flying into an ambush ourselves.

"Have you Seen anything?" Airil asked, slowing his pace and pulling back towards me. The air in front all looked clear and empty of dragons.

"Nothing yet, no," I replied. I had picked up nothing from the future since that first vision of the refugees. While I was airborne, I didn't want to risk reaching out with my magic, lest I lose my concentration on the present. I could only hope that my magic would warn me if anything significant was going to change.

Airil let out a low hiss. He kept his paws tucked close to his chest as he scanned the grey horizon. "It would be easy to miss them in this weather. Are you certain they'll come this way?"

"You know your ddraig better than me. You know the clan. They would come directly to Kxisila, correct?" I followed the Nixan's gaze to the south-east. A heavy curtain of rain swept across the plains far ahead of us, a black storm drifting to the south. Towards Laxtal. It would be difficult weather for Ddraig Anzig's wylax.

The Nixan sighed. He dropped a few feet, drifting a little closer towards the trees. "They would come to Kxisila, yes. It worries me that the humans would know to set up an ambush here."

It concerned me as well. I said nothing. With luck, we would avoid that trap. We could ask and answer all our questions about how the humans knew of Kxisila once the Nixan survivors were safe, and not before.

A dark shadow moved amongst the trees beneath us. I called out to Airil in warning, but before the Nixan could react, the shadow launched from the foliage. It was no human. A dragon crashed into the Nixan, sending them both spiralling to the ground. I trimmed my wings and dived after them, careening to my paws just after Airil and his attacker tumbled through the trees to land amongst the roots.

Airil was first to recover, leaping to his paws, ready to strike. He hesitated.

A moment later, I recognised his attacker. Lying on her back, wings flared wide, was Maznar. She grinned at me over Airil's shoulder, showing off her teeth. Her piercing red eyes met mine. "Well, this is a fortuitous meeting."

I trotted to Airil's side. Beneath the trees there was a bit of shelter from the rain, but the ground was still sodden underpaw. "What are you doing here?"

Maznar looked away. She rolled over onto her belly and tucked her wings against her sides. "Ah. Well, I went out hunting. Thought I'd surprise someone by catching something by myself. But I got lost, you see. Couldn't find my way back to the lair, so I've been flying around, hoping I came across another dragon to ask for directions. And here you are."

"Hunting?" Airil asked. He glanced towards me and shook his head.

Something about Maznar's excuse didn't ring true, but I saw no reason to doubt her for the moment. I looked up to the sky, barely visible through the canopy of partially bare branches. "Fly with us. We'll take you back to Laxtal. But first we need to find Ddraig Krateos."

"Ah, a rescue mission then?" Maznar said.

My eyes snapped back to the dark-scaled spectre. "What makes you say that?"

Maznar shrugged her shoulders, a very human gesture. "That pain I felt this morning must have meant something terrible happened in Nixa. Then you both are here looking for Ddraig Krateos, and there are humans wandering around the base of the cliffs over there. It's not hard to work out."

"No. I suppose it isn't," I said. I suppressed a growl as I was forced to look away from the spectre's red eyes, still too much a reminder of Nightwings. I forced myself to believe her, but I was sure Ddraig Anzig would like to have a conversation with her on our return to Laxtal.

Airil wrinkled his muzzle, but he said nothing to vocalise his obvious distaste. Instead, he just spread his wings and kicked off the ground. He quickly disappeared through the canopy, leaving me alone with the spectre.

"I was just hunting," Maznar said.

I ignored her and followed Airil. Her sigh was loud enough that I could still hear it, just before her wingbeats followed mine.

No one spoke as we continued to fly in the direction of Nixa. Maznar hung back from us, a few wingbeats away at all times. And yet, despite her position further back, she was the one who spotted dragons in the distance first.

"There!" The ness pointed ahead of us, just to the right, into the darkest part of the sky where the rain was strongest.

I squinted into the rain, trying to follow the direction of Maznar's forepaw. Then I saw them. A scattering of slow-moving dragons, some so close to the ground they almost grazed the trees. There were about three hundred of them at the most.

Airil cried out in dismay. I chased after the Nixan as he hurried forward, desperately closing the distance between us and the remnants of his clan.

I soon recognised Ddraig Krateos at the head of the refugees. He carried the Axinstone in his forepaws, the radiant heat of the magic within the precious artefact growing stronger as I approached. The ddraig did not look up. His eyes remained fixed on the ground as he focused on his laboured flight. Blood leaked from a couple of wounds on his sides, staining his scales crimson.

Haeraig Zeena followed just behind her father. My eyes scanned across the survivors, seeking out those few dragons in Nixa I knew. Isikian and Inilta were both there, the brothers flying towards the back of the refugees and largely unhurt. But Nataik was not amongst them. Her distinctive shape should have been easy to see. My stomach dropped away as decisively as though I had closed my wings.

Airil called out to his ddraig, but he was ignored. The ddraig flew past Airil without pause.

"Ddraig Krateos!" I shouted, beating my wings hard to slow my flight, hovering in place before he could reach me. "I come on behalf of Ddraig Anzig and Laxtal. We would like to offer you refuge in our lair."

"We have refuge," Ddraig Krateos replied. He pushed past me, almost knocking me from the air. "We fly for Kxisila. We have no need of further refuge."

"Kxisila is a trap, Ddraig," I said, angling my wings to fall into line just behind him and Haeraig Zeena. "There are humans waiting to ambush you there. I have Seen it. Ddraig Anzig sent me to warn you."

"The warning came too late," the ddraig snapped. He looked back to me, his fierce eyes boring right through me. I had to look away. "Ddraig Anzig's offer is appreciated, but the humans do not know of Kxisila. They have no access to the cliff tops. We will be safe there."

"With all respect, Ddraig, you won't," I replied, speaking quickly before my courage failed me. "If you lead your clan to Kxisila, you lead them to their deaths."

The ddraig snarled and powerfully beat his wings to accelerate, but I had an ally.

"Father, wait." Haeraig Zeena spoke up. "This is the seer who guided Anzig to reclaim the Axinstone. If he says there is an ambush at Kxisila, then we should believe him."

My wings sagged with relief, forcing me to sink a few feet below the ddraig and his haeraig. I struggled to regain the height. Behind me, I did my best to ignore the murmuring of the surviving Nixans. They had been through so much pain already, etched onto their scales and injuries, and I feared the announcement of an ambush waiting for them would bring more hurt. It would be worse if I allowed them to fly on to Kxisila.

Ddraig Krateos slowed his flight. His head moved back and forth, as though scanning the horizon for the humans I promised were there. His wings trembled, and he pulled the Axinstone up closer to his belly as he began to slowly turn. "How could this come to pass?" he hissed. I wasn't sure the words were meant for me.

"We were arrogant," Haearig Zeena said, speaking the answer I would never have dared utter, not to someone as powerful and proud as Ddraig Krateos. From his daughter, however, the Nixan drake barely even blinked. The haeraig was not finished. She swept her wings wide, rising through the rain. "We should not ignore the assistance offered from our allies. We are broken and hurting, and our refuge at Kxisila is compromised. We would be foolish to think we can do this alone."

"You are right, my daughter," Ddraig Krateos said, his voice cracking with dismay. "We must fly to Laxtal. We must accept Ddraig Anzig's offer of assistance."

I bowed my head, struggling to hide my relief and joy. The surviving Nixans would come…

A human with pale red markings on his face stormed to the base of the cliff and slammed his hand against the stone, which cracked beneath the force of the impact. Though blood leaked from between his knuckles, the human showed no pain as he turned to one of his companions. The second human cowered.

"How did you lose them?" the bleeding human demanded.

… to Laxtal and be safe. I shuddered as the force of the human's anger sickened me, even through time. If that was one of the humans controlling the army that had destroyed Nixa, then I longed to get to the safety of Laxtal. I could only hope that human didn't turn his attention to my home. I had no desire to meet him and discover the full force of his fury.

"Is everything alright?" Haeraig Zeena asked, peering at me. Rain mingled with blood as it dripped from her scales.

"We should hurry," I said quietly. "If you would follow me, I can take you to Laxtal."

I banked my wings and started to fly, eager to be home. I tried not to think that I took the lead position with both a ddraig and a haeraig behind me, and a host of three hundred surviving Nixan dragons. I could not entirely block out the sound of their wings, even as thunder rumbled and the rain pounded against my body.

Maznar flew by my side, a shadow in my periphery. A triumphant grin was plastered on her face.

I didn't dare question why.

chapter eighteen

Ellian

The clan waited with nervous anticipation. All around me, I could sense the excitement growing as the realisation that the wylax was upon us spread. Before nightfall, there would be an anointed ddraig of Laxtal once more, a successor to the beloved Ddraig Astar. That nervous excitement filled me as I paced around the great chamber. I would have my part to play, not only in preparing Ddraig Anzig to take on the mantle of his father, but I would succeed the new ddraig as his haeraig. Though we had both fulfilled our roles since the death of Astar, it was daunting to finally face the ceremony that would confirm our commitment to the clan.

Part of me was frustrated by the wasted time. We could have been securing alliances with our neighbours and preparing defences against the human forces, but instead we were grounded until we had held the wylax. My wings itched with impatience. The sooner today was behind us, the better.

A voice called my name. I lifted my head to peer through the crowd, finding Yalle struggling to push through. The albino bumped off a few dragons, growling and snarling his way through, until he stood before me. He bowed his head, wings fluttering, as he showed the respect due to a haeraig.

"Forgive me, Ellian. I was not able to track down Marin," the albino said. He was unable to meet my eye. "I cannot think where he might be, and I have no more time to spare. If Anzig wishes to be a ddraig tonight, then I must prepare the altar for the wylax."

I suppressed a snarl. "Do we need Marin for this?"

Yalle let out a little growl. Then his eyes widened and he snapped his jaw closed. He pawed at the ground. "Marin was a staunch supporter and powerful ally of Ddraig Astar. It would be a poor beginning to undertake the wylax without his support."

I rumbled in thought, tapping my claws against the stone. Then I sighed. We would have to find Marin, and we were running low on time. "Very well. I shall find him."

Yalle bowed his head again, then apologetically slunk away into the crowd. I sighed once more. Another thing I did not have the time for. Lashing my tail in annoyance, I stalked away from the centre of the great chamber, hunting down the scent of Marin. Amongst the chaos of the main chamber, that was almost impossible to find.

I would have no chance of finding Marin by myself. I needed an ally, but the dragon I trusted most was absent. Airil had gone with Azlak to warn Ddraig Krateos of the ambush on the Nixan survivors. An important task, but it robbed me of the dragon I needed. But perhaps that gave the opportunity for another dragon to come by my wing. I knew where I could find Kaz.

Sure enough, I found Nixan healer in the guest caves. The guest caves surrounded a small cavern, a diminutive replica of the main central chamber higher up in the lair. It even contained a central firepit for warmth and light, illuminating the narrow passages to the guest caves around the circular wall.

The Nixan seemed surprised to see me, and he was not alone either. He sprawled by the fire with Selane, the Xital ness, and her mate Ravet. All three hurried to their paws when they noticed my arrival.

"What can we do for you, Haeraig?" Ravet asked, bowing his head low.

"I was searching for Marin. I hoped you might be able to help me," I said, stepping into the guest caves. Despite the fire, the air was cool down here. Warmer than the majority of the tunnels that wound through the lair, but certainly colder than the main chambers nearer the surface.

Ravet and Selane both looked to Kaz. The Nixan scuffed his forepaw against the ground, kicking up some dust and soot. "He was here," Kaz said slowly. "He was searching for Azlak. I don't think he was pleased when he heard where Azlak had gone."

I flicked the tip of my tail. Marin's behaviour with his son confused me. I would have expected Marin to be proud of his son's achievements, especially given the lowly position the seer had held so recently. "Did Marin say where he was going?"

"He didn't," Kaz said, tightening his wings to his sides.

"I saw which direction he went," Ravet added. He took half a step forward. "I can show you, if you like, Haeraig."

"Please, if you would," I replied, glad for the offer of assistance, I swept a wing to the side, gesturing for Ravet to take the lead. Before I could leave, though, Selane stepped forward with her mate.

"Haeraig, if I may?" the Xital asked. She fell silent, not continuing until I nodded in indication that she could keep speaking. "My father became ddraig before I hatched. I expect I will never be allowed to Xital again. This might be my only opportunity to witness a wylax. Would you permit me to attend?"

I blinked in surprise. It had not been the question I had expected. "Of course you can. It is not just for Laxtal dragons to witness."

Selane's eyes brightened, and she quickly bowed low. "Thank you, Haeraig Zeena. I was fearful, given the attitudes of some dragons in your clan… I am grateful for this opportunity."

I rumbled in thought. What had some dragons been saying? A dozen questions welled up in my chest, but I had too little time. I would have to hold onto those questions for now. Instead, I dipped my head towards the Xital. "We shall begin the wylax soon. You may join us when you wish. The same for you, Kaz. You are both welcome."

"We shall see you there," Kaz said brightly.

I hesitated a moment longer, unsure if I wanted more information from them. Or if I wanted to warn them. If Laxtal dragons were warning them to stay away from the wylax, then there might be resistance from the clan at their presence. I resolved to deal with that if it flared up. For now, I needed to worry about finding Marin.

Ravet turned to go deeper into the caves, further beneath the surface. That surprised me. What purpose would the elder dragon have so far down, especially when he should have been helping with the wylax.

These caves and tunnels were often quiet. We were the only dragons down here, and while that raised suspicions within me, it also soon gave a new advantage. Scents were easier to pick apart with fewer dragons competing for my senses. Marin had been down here recently, and he was not alone. I fought to keep a growl within me. One of the scents I recognised was Vinzent.

Ravet didn't go far. "This is the way I saw him go, Haeraig," he said, dipping his head and standing aside, making sure the way ahead was clear for me.

"Thank you. I'll be able to find him from here," I said.

The dragon bowed again, then hastily retreated towards the guest caves. I waited until I could no longer see him, then turned to follow Marin's scent. And Vinzent's. What were they doing down here?

More recent scents made themselves known to me. It wasn't just the two dragons who had come here at the same time. Vinzent's parents were both here as well. Saya in particular concerned me, especially if she was with Marin. Perhaps six others joined them. They had chosen a curious place to meet, and at a worrying time. I shifted my weight back on my paws, lifting my claws from the ground to silence my walk.

I heard them soon after. They were in the cold caves, their voices hushed and echoing from inside the frigid part of the lair, where we stored our supplies of meat and other food for preservation. It was a brave dragon who spent more than a few minutes in there.

Creeping closer to the entrance, I tried to overhear what they discussed. If they were meeting in such a strange place, then I doubted it could be anything good.

"…besmirching the legacy of his father already. Allying and cosying up to other clans. Weakening our standing," Marin growled. It sounded like he stomped a paw on the ground.

I almost barged in on them right away. The very first thing I had heard spoke of their treason and disloyalty against Anzig. But I held myself still. Forced myself to listen. They outnumbered me. Confronting them here and now would not work. So I listened to them speak ill of my cousin.

"It isn't just his alliances," Saya hissed. "He is a weak dragon. That is why he must hide behind other clans. He has no confidence to lead, and he has no strength to act as he must."

Vinzent whined. "Mother, please. He rescued Ellian. He was brave enough to get the Axinstone."

A paw slapped against scales. Vinzent whimpered.

"He showed courage when fighting for Nixa," Saya growled. I could hear her pawsteps as she paced, but I didn't dare peer in to see what the traitorous dragons were doing. "I have seen nothing to suggest he will do the same for Laxtal."

"It makes sense," Marin added, a deep growl coming into his voice. "I have long had my suspicions about Azlak, and I fear Anzig might be the same."

A deep voice rumbled as Vinzent's father spoke. "Are you sure of this?"

"Sure? No," Marin spat. "But it would make sense."

"Another thing to be wary of then," Saya said. There was a short silence that followed.

"We have been absent too long," Marin said, a sigh of frustration punctuating his statement. "We should return before someone comes looking for us."

A grumbling of agreement passed through the conspirators in the cold cave. I took a couple of steps back, but they were not yet finished.

Saya continued speaking. "Remember, any sign of hesitation or doubt at the wylax, and we pounce."

"And if nothing comes of it today," Marin continued, "then we wait and watch. Anzig will fall. It is only a matter of time before he gives us a clear opportunity. A weak Laxtal only makes it easier for Vinzent to become ddraig."

"It only makes it easier for him to make Laxtal strong again," Saya added, a fiery pride in her voice. I thought I heard Vinzent whimper, but I did not stay long enough to hear anything further.

I hurried up the tunnels, claws off the ground, until I was sure Marin and his conspirators would never know I overheard them. My mind was a roiling mess of anger and confusion. I knew I would have to face Anzig soon. What did I tell him of the plot to undermine him?

I didn't have long to work it all out.

All I knew was that the wylax would have to go perfectly. Vinzent could have no opportunity to contest the leadership of the clan. Or, more precisely, Saya could have no opportunity to thrust her son into the position of ddraig.

I would do everything I could to stop that from happening.

Anzig whispered as though in conversation, though I could only hear the pawsteps of one dragon inside his chambers.

"…sure this is the right thing? What if they were to find out?"

I hesitated, once more finding myself listening in on a conversation not meant for me. I could hear no answer to Anzig's question, no evidence that he even had company in his chambers. I understood the desire to speak aloud to clarify thoughts internally, but Anzig's words suggested that he expected an answer.

The ddraig sighed. "What else can I do? I don't have any choice."

Were it not for the important task I had, I would have turned and left the ddraig to his vulnerable musings. But I could not. I carried in my mouth a leather strap that secured the pots of body paint necessary to prepare the ddraig for his wylax. The acrid scent of the paints tickled my nose, but they also reminded me of the role I had to fulfil.

A touch of panic came into Anzig's voice, rising to a higher pitch. "There is?"

The veil in the entrance to the ddraig's chamber parted. Anzig's wide eyes stared into mine. I tried to look like I had not overheard his one-sided conversation, instead lifting my head a little so I could show the clay vessels I carried.

"Is it time already?" he asked. He took a step back inside his chamber, holding aside the veil with a wing.

There was no one else there. The chamber was empty but for him. My eyes flicked up to the silver statue on the alcove beside the fire. Its blank eyes twinkled in the uneven light, making it look like the statue wore an oddly frustrated expression. I blinked and it was the same expressionless face it always had.

I gently put down the collection of pots in the middle of the chamber and stretched out my jaw. The pots were heavy and carrying them for even such a short distance was tiring.

"Please stand in front of the fire and I can get you ready to face the clan," I said, turning slowly to look at the ddraig, placing one paw on the closest pot.

He did not move. His wing, still partially extended from holding open the veil, quivered. His chest rose and fell rapidly with his breathing. "I don't know if I'm ready," he whispered.

I stood still on three paws. The ddraig failed to meet my eyes, looking more like a scared little dragonet than the dragon who was about to become the leader of one of the greatest clans. It struck me then just how much smaller he was in comparison to me, with his head barely coming to my shoulder. I had been taller than my cousin for a few years now, but not once had he appeared so small, like he had shrunk inwards on himself.

"You have been ready for this moment your entire life, Anzig," I said slowly. I hated seeing this scared dragon in front of me. It was a side of my cousin I had not seen before, but I also knew it meant he trusted me enough to be vulnerable around me. If I was to be a strong haeraig for him, then that trust was important.

The ddraig's doubts meant that I knew I could not reveal what I had overheard in the cold caves. That must remain a secret until after the wylax.

Anzig's head lifted sharply. His mouth hung partially open, his yellow eyes scared and wide. I didn't look him in the eye long enough to be sure, but I thought I saw flecks of milky whiteness in the yellow iris. Was he feeling sick? Or had he hurt himself in the way Keita had done, long ago?

When I chanced another quick glance, the whiteness was gone. A trick of the light, then.

I held my paw out to the ddraig. "Anzig, come here please."

Like a cowed dragonet, Anzig skittered closer. I touched my paw to the side of his head. "Your father prepared you for this day. Everything you have done has led you here, to this moment, where you take your rightful place as the ddraig of this clan. You have proven yourself time and time again. It is natural to feel fear, Anzig. But I know that you will never let that fear control you."

"But what if I fail?"

"I will not let you," I said, a growl coming to my voice. I touched my forehead to his, between his small horns. "As your haeraig I will always be the wind beneath your wings. Your strength when yours feels like it is not enough."

Anzig pulled away. He stared into the fire, the light reflecting off his green scales. "You don't seem to be afraid at all."

I opened the first pot of body paint, letting the clay lid clatter to the ground. "Of course I am. I already tried to lead Laxtal, when I feared you were dead. I expected to be where you are now, facing the clan at the wylax, ready to be their ddraig. I failed that time. Tsona dominated me and showed the clan I was not ready. I'm scared I'm still not ready. But I know I must try."

"Then so must I," Anzig said. His voice lifted as he tried to put strength into his words, but I could still see the fear in his posture, in the way his wings trembled and his claws scratched at the ground. His gaze fell upon the pots at my paws. "Do you know what it needs to look like?"

I nodded. "I've studied the patterns and I've picked out the colours based on tradition. Red for your father. Purple for your haeraig. Blue for Laxtal. White for yourself, washed clean to start anew as the ddraig." I opened each of the clay pots in turn, careful not to knock them over with my paws or tail. Tradition dictated that the haeraig must prepare the ddraig for the wylax, painting them with the war paints in a unique and distinctive pattern. Any mistake risked the ceremony, and with dragons already circling Anzig's leadership, I knew I could not afford anything to go wrong. My paw trembled as I dipped my claws into the white bodypaint.

Anzig took a deep breath, swelling his chest as he lifted his head to his full, diminutive height. He flared his wings wide, silent but ready for me to begin my work.

The ddraig was as still as the silver statue watching us from the alcove as my paw touched his scales. I could feel the steady beat of his heart, the swell of his chest as he breathed slowly, but otherwise he was as still and motionless as stone. He was my rock to paint, to decorate with these four colours so that he could stand before Laxtal and proclaim himself with the title he already carried.

I moved slowly and with care, desperate not to make a mistake as I painted his scales white, following the contours of his limbs to create an almost skeletal pattern, covering him from his forehead all the way to the tip of his tail. Even the leading edge of his wings were not spared, until I had exhausted almost the entire pot. The white represented the ddraig at the core of everything, the strength upon which the clan had to rest.

I paced around the ddraig, checking my work to make sure I had made no mistakes with the base white paint, using a claw to wipe away blemishes before it dried and set. Only once I was satisfied with that, did I reach for the second colour. Blue for the clan, represented by the azure gemstone he would also wear around his neck.

The blue went onto his scales with less rigidity, a more flowing pattern that swirled around and through the lines created by the white. Once more, I moved as slow as I could, ensuring that I covered every single scale with the correct paint. Blue and white streaked up my paw, but that didn't matter. I would wear that paint for days to come, a reminder to the clan that I had upheld my duties and declared my commitment to being haeraig.

Through it all, Anzig only moved when I asked him to lift a paw or raise his wing. I was sure he knew as much as I did that any mistake on his body paint would become a weapon against him. He would do nothing to increase the chance of a mistake.

Once I was sure that I had perfected the blue, I moved to the purple that closely resembled my scales. A ddraig always had to choose a haeraig. My colour mixed with and supported the blue and white, representing the strength I had to lend the ddraig and clan, to support and complement them both.

Last of the colours was red, the scale colour of the ddraig who came before. Ddraig Astar's crimson colouration represented the memories and traditions that the new ddraig must respect and uphold.

As the first touch of red paint went onto Anzig's scales, he moved for the first time. Just a quick, sharp gasp and a clenching of his forepaws, but it was enough for me to stop. Red dripped between my claws, splotching onto my paint-streaked paw.

"He left behind big pawprints," Anzig said. He closed his eyes then took in another deep breath. "I'm ready."

I waited a moment to be sure, but Anzig did not move again. He stared into the fire as though entranced. I added the first streak of red to his green scales. There was not much of his colouration left, and as I added crimson to the elaborate pattern, there became less and less of it. Even around his eyes was a mask of red, purple, and blue.

He was a masterpiece. I stepped back to admire my work, holding my paw out to the fire to dry the paint on my scales.

The ddraig remained still. His scales had not dried so quickly, and so he remained like a statue as I paced around him, checking my work for a final time. Little remained of his natural colouration, his dirty green covered almost entirely. The membranes of his wings displayed swirling patterns not to dissimilar to eyes, with irises of purple or red and pupils of blue. The patterns obscured the skeletal core of white by design, but the paint shone with an iridescent glow that still made it stand out from the distinctive colours that surrounded it.

Everything was perfect. A few minutes of inspections and waiting followed, until the ddraig was dry enough to move with confidence that the paint would not smudge.

I rested my clean paw against his shoulder. "You're ready," I said.

Despite the paint being dry, Anzig moved slowly with wide steps, his wings still outstretched. He peered into the reflective surface of a metal mirror, propped against the wall to admire my work. I watched on nervously, hoping he would approve.

"I barely recognise myself," he whispered. He wrenched his eyes away from the mirror. A shadow of a smile broke across his painted muzzle. "You have done everything perfectly. I wish I could have seen Astar like this. He would have looked mighty."

"You look mighty," I said forcefully.

He snorted with amusement. "I look…" He swung his head back to look at the mirror. His chest puffed out a little, his posture straightening. "I look like a ddraig."

I smiled. "Then let us show Laxtal their new ddraig."

Anzig looked up to the silver statue. Then he nodded. "It is time."

The wylax was about to begin. Anticipation thrummed through me, almost hiding my fear and apprehension. Everything had to go perfectly. Nothing else would suffice. Dragons like Vinzent waited for any opportunity to tear Laxtal apart.

If I wanted to erase the mistakes made that led to Ddraig Tsona ruling Laxtal, then I needed to play my part as much as Anzig. My painted paw was my reminder to that.

I led Anzig out towards the great chamber. The roaring voices of thousands of dragons met us, a wall of noise so strong that I felt physically struck.

I rose onto my hindpaws and flared my wings, roaring back at the writhing mass of dragons. They fell silent, awaiting the words that would begin the ceremony of the wylax.

"On weary wings we come from afar," I said, my voice echoing around the chamber. "We gather to share stories and strengthen the bonds that unite us all. Laxtal welcomes you all to the wylax!"

I stomped my forepaws to the ground and roared as loud as my lungs could allow. The response from the clan drowned out my voice.

It had begun.

CHAPTER NINETEEN

Anzig

I followed Ellian, the thunder of several thousand Laxtal dragons behind me, as we ascended towards the surface. The weight of the bodypaint lay heavy on my body, piling on the expectations and beliefs that those patterns indicated. Each wingbeat was a struggle, but somehow I found the strength to keep flying.

The procession made its way to the surface. Dark clouds and constant rain greeted us, a strong wind quickly sapping the heat from my scales. The paint did not run or drip, able to withstand the rain. I wished the rest of me could resist the weather so well. I did not dare look back to see if anyone considered the wylax not worth the conditions.

Our destination was the ceremonial altar higher in the hills surrounding the lair. On a clear day, a dragon could see for miles across the plains from the altar, but this was a miserable day where visibility would be difficult. At least the rise of the hills provided some shelter from the wind, but the sheets of grey rain were relentless.

One dragon waited for us. Yalle sat atop the stone slab of the altar, in the centre of a section of cleared land. Grooved platforms ran through the hills in a circle around the altar, providing an amphitheatre that might have been natural, or carved with unknown abilities long before dragons had ever settled in the lair.

I soared to the head of the altar, where I landed by Ellian's side so that Yalle could look down on us both from his perch on the stone. I then turned around to face the clan as they filtered into the partially enclosed space. There were many hundreds of them. Not all of the clan, the rain had turned some away, but a strong turnout. My heart swelled, relieved that the clan had not abandoned me, but also scared that I would have to perform in front of so many.

I waited, unmoving in the rain. Occasional thoughts drifted across my mind, those that weren't my own quickly ignored and pushed aside. I even managed to dismiss Mushussu's mental touch. Nothing could go wrong today. This was my chance to prove myself to the clan. My only opportunity. If I gave in to my fears and doubts, then they would cast me aside like the pretender I knew I truly was.

"You are no pretender."

Despite all my efforts, Mushussu's metallic voice rang through my head. My claws dug into the soft mud, water quickly filling the channels. I ignored the guardian as best I could, unwilling to give conscious thought to her presence within my mind.

The arrival of dragons seemed to take an eternity. The minutes stretched on, and still there was no end to them. I had not expected so many, not with the driving rain churning the ground into a sodden mud and the chill wind sapping away any lingering heat from the fires in the caves. As the rain poured from my scales, I certainly wouldn't have minded the offer of having the wylax inside the caves.

No such offer came. Instead, it was soon Yalle's turn to roar and get the clan to fall into silence.

"Weary wings have carried us far," the albino called out, deliberately echoing Ellian's earlier words. "We gather at the wylax to share our vision for the future of the clan and to ensure that we have a dragon capable of taking the mantle of ddraig."

I lifted my head higher. I knew the gaze of a thousand dragons were solely on me. If I gave in to the fear in my heart now, I would never be ddraig. My legs locked into position, and I struggled to ignore the itch on my scales from the paint.

Yalle continued to address the crowd, speaking loudly so that his voice could project through the rain. "Ddraig Astar was taken from us over a month ago, fallen in battle to the human threat on our borders. For many years he had been clear about who his haeraig was, about who should be the dragon to succeed him. His only son, Anzig, stands before us now to confirm his position as ddraig."

I didn't miss my cue. I spread my wings to fully show off the incredible patterns Ellian had painted on the delicate membranes. I still stood beneath the altar. I wasn't ready to stand upon the stone plinth just yet. That would come later, once I had proven myself to them through the ritual performance.

"My name is Anzig," I called out, silencing the few roars that had broken out after Yalle's words. I swept my eyes around the onlookers. As one, they all bowed heads to avoid meeting my gaze. Then I saw Marin, sat with Saya and Vinzent. The two older dragons kept my gaze. I almost stumbled over my words, before I found my place again. "I am the only dragonet of Ddraig Astar. I am his chosen haeraig and successor. By rights, I am Ddraig Anzig of Laxtal, and I shall prove this to my clan today."

There was no roar of support to my declaration as I had hoped, but nor was there any dismissal of my claim. I could not be sure if that was to be expected. I had learned what the wylax demanded I do, but nothing about how the clan might respond. Astar had already been ddraig when I hatched, so I had never witnessed a wylax before.

Yalle did not seem put off by the lack of vocal response. His shadow loomed over me as he stood on the edge of the altar, his body partially blocking some of the rain as it drove in from the north. "A ddraig is many things to a clan. They are a leader, a warrior, and a provider. They must always put the needs of their clan first. Are you capable of this, Anzig?"

I was not putting the needs of my clan first. Were I to do so, I would tell them what Carlee had told me, that I was not Astar's son. I should tell them of my magic. I should tell them of my fear. But I did not.

"I am capable," I found myself saying instead. There was a confidence in my voice I did not recognise, as though another had spoken through me. Mushussu's satisfaction was clear, and it was all I could do not to growl.

"Then prove you can provide for this clan. So that we can continue with the wylax, you must hunt for us, Anzig, son of Astar," Yalle said loudly, before dropping his voice so that only Ellian and I could hear him. "And please don't take long. This rain is getting colder by the minute."

I smiled and nodded, trying to hide my inner conflict. "I'll do my best," I said, before kicking off from the wet, muddy ground and taking to flight. Ellian took to wing behind me. She would follow at a distance to observe my hunt, to ensure that I did not cheat, but not to interfere at any point. I would have to ignore her.

Many hundreds of dragons watched me leave. I wondered how many would still be there when I returned after a successful hunt. I could see no easing of the rain on the horizon. It would be a nightmare to come back and see only Yalle waiting to complete the wylax, with no one else caring much about seeing me become their ddraig.

Movement flicked through the corner of my vision as I soared out of the natural arena. I did not look down to see who already left without even waiting for me to fly out of sight.

I had already worked out a plan of where to hunt, scouting during the morning before the rain had come. I could only hope that the prey animals had not retreated to safety so they could stay dry. The wylax was only meant to be ceremonial, performing no real purpose in proving the competence of a ddraig, but it would still be an embarrassment to bring nothing back. I banked my wings and angled towards the flat plains beyond the mouth of the gorge.

"Would you like my assistance in finding prey?"

Away from the eyes of everyone but Ellian, several wingbeats behind me, I allowed my shoulders to slump slightly. A sigh escaped my mouth. I already lied to the clan about my capabilities and right to rule. Did I want to deceive them by accepting Mushussu's assistance as well?

"If it makes you feel any better, almost every ddraig since the wylax took this form has accepted my aid."

"Aid, perhaps," I grumbled. "But what you did back there wasn't aid. You spoke for me."

"I merely reminded you of the confidence you already possess."

It had not felt that way to me. She had stolen my voice from me, even if for just a moment. I couldn't help but shudder.

"You should bank a little further to the left. Aim for the tall trees between you and the nearest beacon and you will have a good chance of a successful hunt. If you want my assistance."

I considered it for a moment. Then I tilted my wings and shifted a little further to the left, tail and wings both helping me change direction. I needed every bit of help I could get. Besides, who would know? No one else knew of the existence of the guardian. If she was right, then her purpose was to help the ddraig of the clan. It didn't make me feel any better, but I resolved to follow her guidance.

With Ellian's attention from above, I swooped down to the trees Mushussu had indicated, not far from the area I had scouted earlier. The rain had washed away any tracks and obscured scents, adding difficulty to my task.

Mud splattered over my decorated scales as I landed in the shadow of the trees, getting a little respite from the rain. Ellian stayed in the air, gliding in a circular route so she could keep constant watch on me. Even from a distance, I got a slight touch from her mind, her concerns and fears for me. I growled and struggled to keep those thoughts out.

"You may be pleased to know the rain will be easing soon."

"Can you predict the weather now?" I muttered, putting my muzzle close to the ground, hoping to pick up some hint of my prey.

"No. But I feel like my awareness has expanded. I feel stronger than I have in many long centuries."

I chewed on that thought but asked no questions. Mushussu's strength and magic were an unknowable mystery, but perhaps that was why she was so talkative today. I had not been able to shut her out.

"You could just ask. I may not be able to tell you everything, but there is some that can be shared."

I shook my head. "I don't want to know. Not yet. I have too much to do."

"Perhaps later. There is movement to your right, just a little further down the hill."

Aware of Ellian's watchful eyes on me, I kept moving. My paws splashed through muddy water as I scampered down the hill, following Mushussu's directions. The trees stood like silent sentinels, as though they too watched my progress.

I slowed as I approached a deep ravine and peered down to the small stream that flowed along its bottom. The water was brown, churned with mud. Despite the rain, life flourished down on the banks of the stream. A herd of deer sheltered beneath the trees, their thick fur a deep reddish brown. A large hart stood by the water, nostrils flared as he looked downstream. His heavy antlers were white and partially cracked in a few places.

Scampering amongst the deer were a dozen hares, noses twitching and ears alert. A couple of small birds flew from bare branches to snap at tiny insects around the herd of deer.

I crouched lower, eyes fixed on the large mammals. A deer would represent a fine prize. If I killed one of the beasts, I could send Ellian back to the altar for help in bringing the offering back to the wylax. I simply had to kill the animal by myself.

"I would make a poor guardian if I did not warn you, Anzig," Mushussu said, her voice breaking back into my mind. *"Deer are dangerous for a single dragon, and I can't keep you from harm if they strike you."*

"Some protector you are," I muttered. I then shut her out. She was right. I had never hunted a deer by myself before. I could not afford any distractions, but I needed to impress the clan. For the first time in my life, I had to bring down a deer as a sacrifice, a good omen to my rule as ddraig.

Keeping low to the ground, I moved through the mud and undergrowth. The bright paint on my scales kept me less hidden than my natural colouration, but the deer did not rouse as I slowly slunk around to a better place to attack. I had my eyes on an outcrop of stone that jutted partially across the ravine, the stream winding around the column of stone.

I peered down to the herd, then turned my focus up. I squinted through the rain, but I could not see Ellian above me. She must have still been close by, but keeping her distance so she didn't disrupt my hunt or distract the prey. I would be alone.

I eyed the hart. The big male made for a tantalising target, but he was also far bigger than any of the does in his herd. He stood at close to three times my height. A doe would be dangerous enough. I would need to inflict a killing blow quickly, scattering the herd before they could defend themselves, or else I risked a stampede and getting trampled in the process.

Claws tensing against the mud, I prepared myself to spring. I picked out the doe closest to me. She was smaller than the others, but still clearly a fully-grown adult. She would make a good offering.

I braced against the muddy ground as I extended my wings. Then I kicked off hard, launching from the outcrop and leaping towards my quarry.

The deer looked up. She bleated in warning and bucked away. My outstretched claws nicked her neck, but it was not the killing blow I had aimed for. I ripped out a gash of fur, spilling a small amount of blood.

I strained my wings to arrest my fall, twisting around to lash out at the doe a second time before sliding through the mud. She brayed and stomped her cloven feet, kicking up clods of wet dirt.

The herd partially scattered, the does screaming as they scampered away from the river. A bellowing roar told me not all the deer had fled. I leaped to the air. Too slow. A massive weight crashed into me, buckling my wing and ricocheting me into the ribs of the doe.

I tried to cling on, but she bucked and thrashed until she dislodged me. I fell away, leaving behind several lines of blood in her fur, as she scampered into the safety of the trees.

I had barely hit the ground before cloven hooves crashed down next to my head. I shrieked and rolled to the side, trying to get to my paws. The hart bellowed and slammed his feet again and again, forcing me to keep moving.

The hart was relentless and wild-eyed. One kick would be enough to kill a dragon. It was all I could do to roll, wings tucked tight.

I found my paws. I kicked up hard, spreading my wings and beating as hard as I could to get some air beneath them. The hart brayed and cracked his head into my back. I lost all control of flight, spinning back to the ground and crashing through the hares who had not fled. I rolled over the uneven ground, wincing from the impact.

Still the hart was not done. The aggressive male bellowed and lowered his head, antlers presented as he charged. I barely had time to leap to my paws again before he crashed into me. Pain exploded as my ribs took the full force of the impact. I weakly swiped out with my hindlegs, hoping to get a claw to the hart's eye as I clung on for my life.

The hart's heavy teeth snapped out at me, almost catching my tail. My forelegs hooked around the hart's antlers as I struggled to keep out of his reach. Each jolt and buck threatened to loosen my grip.

Then I crashed into a tree, pinned between trunk and frenzied hart. I couldn't breathe as I struggled to push back the beast, claws kicking out with no effect. There was no intelligence in those wild eyes, just pure aggression and rage.

Bone splintered. For a terrible moment I thought it was mine.

The hart screamed as his antler fractured, then tore free with a burst of blood and gore. The pressure released and I dropped to the ground with the hart's shed antler. The enraged beast kicked out once more, striking me across the shoulder, before fleeing deeper into the forest, leaving behind a trail of blood.

I kicked off the discarded antler and choked for some breath. I had failed in the hunt, unable to kill anything. With the pain in my chest and legs, I doubted I would be able to stalk anything else.

I couldn't find Ellian in the sky above, though I was sure she must have seen my failure. Was she already on her way back to Laxtal to inform Yalle that I was not suitable to be the ddraig?

"She is not far away." I groaned. The last thing I wanted to hear was the guardian in my head, but she ignored my discomfort. *"It may not be a deer, but there is something close by for you to return to the clan."*

I still couldn't see Ellian, despite Mushussu's assurances, but I pulled myself up to my paws to see what I might hunt. Ignoring the pain, I staggered in the direction the guardian's mental guidance pulled me, towards the stream. I coughed and spat up a couple of drops of blood, but I could not feel any significant injuries from the hart's attack.

It didn't take long to confirm Mushussu's directions. I almost trod on the body of a hare, partially hidden amongst the fallen leaves. Its neck had twisted unnaturally, broken either by me or the hart, I couldn't be sure. That didn't matter too much. All that mattered was that I had a dead animal to take back with me.

I ran my claws over the hare. Apart from the broken neck, there were no other injuries I could find. It had been a healthy male, close to half my height. I sighed. A hare was better than nothing at all, though I couldn't help but think of the adoration I would have received for bringing back a deer.

Turning away from the hare, I limped towards the stream and peered down at my reflection. Using some of the muddy water, I wiped away the blood on my scales. Hunting a hare would not have been a bloody struggle, especially not one with its neck broken. I removed all evidence of the fight with the hart and doe, glad that my efforts didn't wipe away any of the bodypaint.

Once I was satisfied, I returned to my prey. At least the rain had stopped, just as Mushussu had said it would. Dark clouds still lingered overhead, but the downpour had eased to a faint drizzle.

Digging my foreclaws into the hare, I cautiously took to the air, having to beat my wings much harder than usual to lift the hare with me. Almost the moment I cleared the tree line, I heard Ellian approaching. Mushussu had been right there as well. I almost rolled my eyes in response to the smug satisfaction the eased through me. Instead, I tightened my grip on the hare and flew a little faster, hoping to stay in front of my cousin. If she had something to say about my fight with the hart or the disappointment of my catch, then she kept it to herself. Even her thoughts were mercifully silent for the time being.

To my relief, there were still dragons waiting for me near the altar. Not everyone had remained. I could even see a few slink back towards the lair entrance as I approached.

Ellian stayed below me as I soared towards the central altar. She took to the wet ground, but Yalle stepped aside to give me space to land on the stone plinth. By his paws was the azure amulet that represented the might of Laxtal, the golden chain spooled beneath. The surface of the altar was pitted and grooved, with countless narrow channels pooled with water.

I placed the hare down at Yalle's paws. "A ddraig must provide for their clan. I vow to hunt and to ensure no dragon goes hungry."

The albino's eyes flicked down. *"Astar killed a great buck. This is…"*

Not here. Not now. I forced myself to shut out Yalle's thoughts. I could not afford to lose control now.

Yalle lifted his head and spoke no indication of his inner thoughts. "Anzig has returned with his hunt. Ellian, can you verify that this was Anzig's kill?"

I glanced down. Even I couldn't verify that I had killed the hare. It could have been me. It could have been the hart's trampling feet.

"I watched him kill it, yes," Ellian said, lifting her voice loud to be heard by all dragons present.

At least she was willing to lie for me. The thought sat uneasily in my gut. If she was going to lie for me, then at least that should mean she was more likely to keep supporting me. But it meant another dragon deceiving the clan.

"You don't know it's a lie," Mushussu reminded me. *"As far as you know, you did kill that hare. Just because it wasn't your intended target doesn't mean it's a lie."*

Yalle kept his focus on the onlooking dragons. "Anzig had the blessing of Ddraig Astar. He has the support of a haeraig. He has proven he can hunt for the clan. But does he have the support of Laxtal? Speak, dragons. Speak those who would have Anzig as their ddraig."

Despite the call for voices, no one moved. My eyes widened and I resisted the urge to take a horrified and scared step back. I needed to hold my ground and keep my head high despite the silence that lingered for a couple of agonising seconds.

Movement caught my attention. Saya came to the front of the clan, Marin by her side. Vinzent followed just behind them. I narrowed my eyes, wary at the smug look on Saya's face. The ness opened her mouth to speak. I knew it would not be in my defence.

Another voice shouted out. "I will speak for him!"

Surprised, I turned to see Selane standing apart from the other dragons on one of the higher platforms.

"You?" Saya barked. "Why should you get the chance to speak here? You are not Laxtal. Your opinion does not matter."

"She has every right to speak," Yalle retorted. He flared his wings and stared down the ness. Saya eventually bowed her head and retreated a couple of steps, returning to the crowd. The albino then turned back to the Xital, higher up and further away from the altar.

"You are right, I am not of your clan," Selane said, her voice regal and proud, showing no fear or indication that Saya had so vehemently spoken out against her. She kept her head held high and looked almost directly at me. "But I have seen the dangers that face you, and I know the type of dragon you need to rule. You need a dragon who is not afraid to change ways, who is not rigidly stuck in isolation. Anzig is a dragon who will seek out friends and allies. He will unite, not divide."

Another dragon shouted out. "I agree!" I stared as Okazuni moved forward, Keita by his side. The Nyrian likewise showed no fear. "I followed Anzig across the mountains with dragons from four different clans, including my own. He treated us all with respect, never once showing scorn to those not from Laxtal. If we are to fight these humans, then we need to put aside our differences. We need a dragon who will unite the clans. Anzig is that dragon."

My wings fluttered. Astar would never have tolerated such a thing. He was a warrior. A fighter. Forging alliances and friendships was not how he had ruled. Selane and Okazuni could not have known that. By focusing on those traits put me in direct opposition to the type of ddraig familiar to Laxtal.

"Anzig is strong," Keita said, lifting her voice. "He will not allow himself to be dominated by these alliances he seeks, but he is not so proud that he recognises we all need help. He is our best chance to fight these humans and to defeat Tsona."

I looked back towards Saya, expecting a further retort from her, but she had vanished amongst the crowd. Marin had gone with her, though Vinzent still lingered. The young silver dragonet looked like he was about to say something, before he snapped his jaw closed.

Others did not show the same restraint as Vinzent. Now that the silence had fractured, more voices rose to support my claim. They shared tales of my strength and kindness to show how I would make a good ddraig. I recognised few of those stories, exaggerated or misinterpreted from the truth. No one spoke against me.

Yalle flared his wings. Silence fell as he took the amulet gently in his claws. He lifted the golden chain, letting the azure stone glimmer in the light. "The clan is willing to speak for Anzig. His claim to be our ddraig is honoured."

I dipped my head forward as the albino reached for me. He slipped the chain around my head, letting it fall beyond my horns and down my neck until it sat comfortably at my shoulders, the stone itself sitting just above my forelegs. A small shiver ran through me. I was almost there.

Ellian jumped up onto the altar. She met my gaze for a brief moment. In her eyes was the same fear and apprehension I felt.

She placed her painted paw on my head. "With your claim honoured, I vow to fly beside you as your haeraig, until such a time as you choose another."

I said nothing. I was not supposed to speak. But I knew that I would be unlikely to choose another haeraig. Traditionally, the haeraig was the eldest dragonet of the ddraig, but I had no mate. The ness I wished to share my life with had chosen another. My eyes drifted, finding Keita with her chosen. Okazuni had spoken for me, speaking kindly of my leadership. My heart ached with conflicting emotion.

Her part done, Ellian stepped aside, but stayed atop the altar. There was just one final part to go. My pulse quickened.

Yalle took the body of the hare in his paws and dragged it into an indentation in the middle of the altar. He then slit the throat and let blood pool within the depression, mixing it with the water that remained from the downfall, even starting to trickle into the channels that branched across the surface. The albino dipped a paw into the blood, his claws coming away crimson.

"Blood of the ddraig who came before!" he bellowed, raising his bloody paw for the clan to see, before placing it on my forehead. I closed my eyes as I felt the hot liquid trickle between my scales. "May the spirit and wisdom of your predecessor guide you."

"His knowledge shows me the way ahead," I replied, doing all I could to stop my voice trembling. The hare's blood was all I could smell.

Yalle grasped the azure stone around my neck. I knew his paw would be bloody again, but with my eyes closed I did not see it. "The glory of Laxtal shines through your actions. May you bring honour and prestige to your clan."

"Your wind lifts my wings," I said. I opened my eyes again. Blood trickled down over my brow. I wanted to wipe it away, but I kept my paws still.

Yalle dipped his paw into the blood for a third time. This time he smeared the hare's blood onto Ellian's forehead, mimicking what he had done with me. "A haeraig is your eyes and ears, your claw and tooth. May you trust her to support you in everything you do."

I looked Ellian in the eye. She did not look away. "She is my haeraig, my heir and closest advisor."

For a final time, Yalle dipped his paw into the blood. He flicked it towards the onlooking dragons. While the drops fell barely beyond the altar, let alone on anyone else, it was the symbolism that mattered. "The dragons of Laxtal give you the right to rule. Without them, you command air and stone and nothing more. May they call you by your title."

I had nothing to say here. Instead, I turned to face the dragons, blood still trickling from my muzzle.

Keita was the first to speak. "You are Ddraig Anzig!"

The same four words were repeated again and again, scattered at first, but soon growing into a united roar. Though in truth I had been since the moment Astar had died, now the clan honoured that by calling my name. I was Ddraig Anzig, ruler of Laxtal.

Had I given up my control, I could have cried. Instead, I stood on the edge of the altar and took in the roar of the clan. With Ellian by my side, I had taken the mantle of the dragon I had called father. The pawprints he had left behind were massive, too large for my diminutive frame to fill. But Laxtal expected no less from me. I would do everything I could to live up to the title of ddraig.

Now that they had confirmed my right to rule, I could begin the long and terrifying task of protecting Laxtal from human and Xital threats.

I flared my painted wings and waited for silence to fall. Before I could start issuing orders, there would come my first words as ddraig. The first words every ddraig of Laxtal had uttered after the wylax.

"Let us feast!"

The roar that followed was the loudest of the day.

CHAPTER TWENTY

Azlak

Laxtal was a welcome sight. After three nights in the wild, sleeping wherever we could find shelter and constantly fearing a human ambush, the promise of a warm cave to sleep in encouraged the Nixan survivors. While wounds had been healed from the attack on Nixa, our wings were weary and the mental scars were still fresh. Throughout the days there had been little conversation, with the Nixans lost in their grief.

As we passed over Laxtal territory, the beacon fires lit to warn the central lair of our approach. Sure enough, there were dragons waiting for our arrival as the lair came into sight. Ddraig Anzig was amongst them, his green scales still partially obscured by paint, far more complex than the war paint worn by warriors in the clan. I felt a little relief at the sight. He had been through the wylax. Now no one in Laxtal could deny that he was the true ddraig.

I drifted towards the back of the Nixans as we came to land, staying close to Airil, Isikian, and Inilta. Not far from us flew the spectre of Maznar. Like the Nixans, she had been quiet during the long flight from Kxisila, refusing to explain further how she had come to be out there. I had caught no lies in her claims that she had gotten lost when hunting, but something about her story didn't quite work.

Ddraig Krateos approached his Laxtal counterpart. "If we are imposing…"

"You and you clan honour ours with your presence," Ddraig Anzig said, interrupting the Nixan. "Our lair is yours, for as long any Nixan requires sanctuary or sustenance. There is no imposition occurring here, Ddraig Krateos."

The Nixan ddraig bowed so low his muzzle almost touched the ground. "Then Nixa is forever in your debt, Ddraig Anzig of Laxtal," he said. He kept his head low. "We have been humbled by these humans, who have access to weapons we could not even dream of."

Ddraig Anzig glanced around the surviving dragons. "Perhaps we should discuss what happened in private. I can have food and drink prepared in my chambers."

The Nixan bowed again. "That would be most welcomed, thank you."

Ddraig Anzig turned his attention to the lilac ness by his side. He whispered something to his haeraig, before he addressed the Nixan refugees with a loud, powerful voice. "Haeraig Ellian will ensure you have food and shelter. Laxtal welcomes you and sympathises with your loss. Together, we will ensure the humans who committed this atrocity will come to justice."

Muttered and muted cheers followed, coming from the few Nixans who could muster any sort of emotion. While the two ddraigs soon disappeared below the surface, the haeraigs stayed together and began to organise the refugees. Airil quickly left my side to approach Haeraig Ellian, a flutter of wings and excited trill from the Laxtal haeraig showing her excitement for all to see.

My own excitement grew when I saw someone familar amongst the Laxtal dragons. Kaz bounded towards me, and he gently pressed his muzzle against mine. There was a slightly haunted look in his eyes as he looked around at the gathering of Nixans.

"I know you said there weren't many, but seeing them…" he said, voice quivering. He took a deep breath and trembled. "We need to do something, or else Laxtal could be the next target."

I didn't need to use my magic to know what crossed Kaz's mind, or to predict what he was about to say next. His attention had turned to linger on Inilta and his brother. "We should see what is in those deep caves."

"What is this about?" Inilta asked, clearly aware of the attention Kaz was giving him.

"Azlak Saw something below the lair here. Something of incredible power," Kaz said brightly, turning to his clanmate. "You were with us in his vision, so we knew we had to wait until now."

While Kaz spoke, a silent snarl grew on Inilta's muzzle. "This again."

I shrank back as Inilta's gaze turned to me. Because of my visions he had followed Ddraig Anzig into human territory and back. I doubted he was keen to follow them once more.

"I trust him."

I looked up again to see Isikian, standing behind his brother's shoulder. The emerald-scaled healer nudged Inilta and smiled.

"It's not a lack of trust," Inilta growled. To my surprise, his shoulders sagged as his gaze swept around the survivors of his clan. "I'm just tired, Isi. We just watched our clan burn. Something we were told was impossible just happened. We were defeated and we didn't even have a chance. How can we fight that?"

"Whatever is down there will help us."

"We don't have to go today, if you don't want to."

I spoke at the same time as Kaz. The two brothers looked between us. Isikian's eyes were bright, while Inilta's were dull and weary.

"No," Inilta said with a sigh. "We shall go now. If your visions told you this was important, then I must treat it so. If I learned anything across the mountains it was that I should listen to the dragon who can See the future."

My tail curled around my hindlegs as I sat back, unsure what to do with the compliment. I couldn't meet the Nixan in the eye, instead staring down at his grey paws.

"I'll stay and help everyone get settled here," Isikian said, sparing me from an uncomfortable decision. I had not seen Isikian in my visions, so I was glad he decided to remain. The healer looked towards the lair, before his gaze lifted to the low hills that rose beyond the gorge. "I have never been to Laxtal before. It is a shame I am not here in happier circumstances."

"We will defeat them," Kaz said, moving between the brothers. He sat back on his hindlegs and put a paw on each of their shoulders. "We know what they're willing to do now. We won't be caught unprepared again. Ddraig Krateos and Ddraig Anzig will make certain of it."

Inilta shrugged away Kaz's touch and prowled a few steps towards the gorge. He then looked back at the two healers. "Then let's see what you've found. If it can do anything to save another clan from destruction, then we'll want to get it to the ddraigs as soon as we can."

Though I was reluctant to leave Isikian and the Nixans behind so soon, I spread my wings and took to the air. The two haeraigs paid no attention to me as I led Kaz and Inilita into the gorge and then through the narrow entrance of the lair. There were not many dragons flying through the gorge at the moment, most were either staying in the caves, or already outside helping the Nixans. I was sure it would not be long before the caves were much busier as Haeraig Ellian organised places for the refugees to stay. The guest caves were surely not large enough for everyone.

We flew through the main chamber quickly, ignoring the gazes that met us. There was no sign of Ddraig Anzig or Ddraig Krateos. The two must have quickly flown on to the private chambers above the great fire. Small clusters of dragons gathered around the flames. My father was amongst them, his conversation with Saya and Vinzent interrupted by my brief presence. I didn't even slow down as I did my best to ignore them. Not that they tried to call me down.

"You were never mine to begin with!"

The green dragon stamped both forepaws on the ground as his tail lashed out. His eyes were wild.

I shuddered. The fury from the future seemed to simmer in the present as well. Something was coming from my father. Something soon. Some small part of me craved that confrontation, even if I feared what revelations were to come. I was sure he had long wished that I was not his, but never had I known him to put that desire to words.

Kaz soon took the lead position from me as we flew towards the deeper caverns of the lair. I marvelled at how he could remember the way. He stopped only once we reached the limit of the torches and illuminated caves. He fluttered to the ground and peered ahead into the total darkness. Even now I could hear the soft roar of the underground river and the gentle breeze coming up from those pitch black depths. Once again, I believed every story about the ghosts that haunted these deep caves.

"Down there?" Inilta asked, landing by my side.

I could only let out a small squeak as I nodded.

Kaz looked around, twisting his body as he searched the shadowed tunnel. "We'll need a torch."

Inilta scoffed as he stepped forward into the darkness. A moment later his magic engulfed into blue flame, illuminating the way ahead from a spiralling conflagration that centred around the Nixan. Despite the light, the darkness seemed to swell ever blacker and deeper.

Kaz followed Inilta. For a moment, I lingered. I considered if it would be worthwhile turning back and returning to the lighter parts of the lair where there were fewer ghosts.

"Are you coming or what?" Kaz's voice echoed out of the darkness. I cursed my visions and darted in after them.

It was still a long walk to the deep fissure at the very farthest reach of the caves, which we took in almost complete silence. But for our claws scraping against stone, the only sound was the ever-growing roar of the mysterious underground river.

Inilta's magical light barely penetrated that darkness at all, so I was surprised when I found we had reached the fissure at the very deepest part of the Laxtal caves. As far as I knew, no dragon had ever set paw beyond this point, scared away by the legends told of these depths. I dreaded to think how much rock was above our heads now; the path had been nothing but a steep downwards descent ever since we left behind the torches.

A tiny ball of blue flame split apart from the storm of flame Inilta controlled. The small offshoot of light passed through the fissure and into a cave that I was sure had not seen light in an eternity. What had just been impenetrable darkness, now became an array of colour and reflections. What ghosts would we find in this new light?

One at a time, with Inilta leading, we stepped through the fissure. We were on a small ledge that clung to the edge of a gigantic chamber that seemed to stretch on forever. It was large enough that Inilta's flame failed to reach the far side. About fifty feet below was the surface of the river. The black water churned and frothed as it rushed over the uneven rocks. For now, I couldn't feel the eerie magical presence, but was sure it wouldn't be long before it revealed itself.

Kaz ran a paw along the cavern wall before calling out. His claws had traced an engraving in the rock. "Gaxaga," he read out, before frowning in concentration. He hissed in frustration. "I don't know what that means."

"It could mean danger," Inilta huffed, but he leaned over Kaz's shoulder to peer closer at the engraving. "What language is that?"

"It's draconic. That means these words are six hundred years old at least," Kaz said proudly. He slowly worked his way further down the ledge as it started to slope downwards. Other words were written into the rock every few feet, but Kaz wasn't able to identify any of them.

I glanced up to the flickering ball of flame that shone along the narrow crevice we had squeezed through. Up there was warmth and comfort, and most of all, safety. I couldn't See anything specific, but I kept feeling the sensation that there was something down here that we shouldn't disturb. I couldn't be sure if we were walking into danger or not. While Inilta may have shared some of my doubts, Kaz was completely unconcerned. He had descended even further and rounded an outcrop in the wall, vanishing from sight.

"Hey, this one's different," Kaz called out from the darkness. Inilta moved down to join the other Nixan, and for a moment I was left without any light to see by. I yelped in terror and quickly ran down the ledge, not stopping until I ran into Inilta. The larger dragon snorted in amusement.

Kaz ignored both of us as he continued to study this new word. I edged around Inilta to get a better look, and right away I could also see that these symbols were different. The other words had all weathered away from the inexorable passage of time and were almost gone, but these cut deep into the stone. They were fresher.

"It looks like a name. Definitely not draconic," Kaz said, backing away half a step before reading it aloud. "Bri'An."

I shrieked as a pulse of white light burst out from somewhere off in the darkness, assaulting me not only with its brightness, but also a wave of pure magic. Heat tingled along my scales and I staggered to the side as I became disorientated, almost stumbling off the ledge.

Only the quick-acting Kaz saved me from the dark depths below as he pulled back on my tail.

"What was that?" I asked in horror. I shook my head and blinked several times in a futile attempt to rid my mind of the white afterimages that remained burned into my eyes. It wasn't the white light that concerned me, but the shape it outlined. It was the shape of a human.

If the light startled either of the Nixans, they did their best to hide it. Kaz just grinned. "What we came here to find. Magic," he said with an excited hiss. He looked up to Inilta. "Ready to go on?"

Inilta's paws smouldered as flames started to build up around them. He took a step forward, burning away eons of dust that crackled and fizzed where his paws touched the rock. "It was the name that triggered the magic," he said. I didn't like his mischievous smile, as he looked in my direction. "Now, what was it again?"

"Don't say it," I said, knowing what he was about to do.

He ignored me. "Bri'An."

Again, the light burst forth from the dark distance, a lot more intense, but this time it wasn't only white. There were more colours than I could have ever imagined, but in too short a moment, it vanished once more. Darkness returned to the cavern again, all but for the comparatively dim glow from Inilta's magic.

"I think that's where we need to go," Kaz said, nodding his head in the direction from where the light had emanated from. I didn't understand how he could still be so positive about everything. How could he still be so courageous? The display of light and magic had stripped me of my confidence. Only a token sense of pride pushed me into motion, to follow the two Nixans. That, and not wanting to be alone with nothing but the darkness for company. Fear warred with pride as I began to regret this journey.

Other than the sound of the river, which increased the more we descended, there was nothing else to make a noise. No bats or other cave animals sounded their presence in the black cavern. This was a dead, ancient place. But for whoever – or whatever – had carved the name Bri'An into the wall, I wouldn't have been surprised if we were the only living things to walk this narrow ledge in centuries. We were not too far from the lowest reaches of the lair, but the isolation I felt down here was almost suffocating. Even the air felt heavy. Every step we took the air chilled more, and the darkness grew darker, more intense.

I could feel the magic now, a constant throbbing in the back of my mind. I tried to ignore it, as I tried forgetting the darkness that seemed intent on extinguishing Inilta's light. It was there, pushing close but never quite able to touch us. But Inilta's magic was no longer the only light. A faint golden glow emerged from the darkness, the source of which was unclear. Each step we took, the glow battled against the black void around us. The light was almost directly ahead.

Kaz bounded on with obvious eagerness, pausing only to inspect scratches in the rock. He found no more words carved into the wall, but that did nothing to dampen his excitement. Behind him, Inilta plodded without enthusiasm, but grim determination. He showed no fear as he followed his fellow Nixan. I scampered some distance behind, taking care not to stay out of the shadows but never confident enough to walk by the side of the Nixans.

The mysterious glow afforded us wondrous sights; high above us the rock glistened as Inilta's light mingled with it, revealing massive stalactites hanging down, each dripping with water. I had never ones so big before, as almost reached all the way down to the river below. Then something metallic caught my eye. I ran ahead and placed a paw heavily down on Inilta's tail.

He leaped into the air, pulling his tail free, as he snarled, spinning around with claws ready to strike me. "What?" he growled as he lowered his paw. Was he more scared than he was letting us know?

"Up there, look," I said, pointing with my wing up to the metallic structure, almost completely walled in by the mass of stalactites. Shrouded in shadow, I couldn't make it out, but Inilta's eyes were sharper than mine.

"It's a torch sconce," the Nixan said, tilting his head to the side. "But it's massive. I've never seen one that big before. It could hold a whole tree."

"Uh, you're going to want to look at this," Kaz said from further down the small path. For the first time his voice quavered as a touch of fear was evident. Curiosity, excitement, as well as fear, forced me forward, to see what had caught Kaz's attention. What I saw was unexpected. Carved out of the rock on the other side of the river was a giant edifice of stone, inset with metal. It looked almost like a human castle, even down to the wide bridge that crossed the deep chasm over to it. A gaping black hole served as a doorway and must have been some thirty or forty feet high, and double that wide. On the lintel above the great doorway were a more lines of writing, burnt into the rock in reddish-gold, like lava bubbling on its surface.

"Aysh saagrax Laxtal. Kxi siletta jy tso ddraggn," Kaz read out.

"And what does it mean?" I asked, looking up at the burning letters in wonder. Their constant movement entranced me, watching as they never once lost their meaning or form.

"I... I have no idea," Kaz admitted. Like me, the Nixan couldn't tear his eyes away from the fiery lettering.

Inilta hissed in alarm. I tore my gaze from the mysterious words to see him point with his wing. "There's someone down there."

My eyes drifted down to where the Nixan was indicating. In the shadows at the bottom of the edifice was the shape of a human, slumped again the wall. It didn't appear to have seen us, but we all shrank back and Inilta dimmed his magical flame-ball. Still there was no movement, nothing at all to indicate the human knew we were there. We had not made any effort to hide our presence before; surely the human must have heard us?

Kaz crept forward again. "Hello?" he yelled out. His voice echoed around the vast chamber, returning to us several times before drifting away into the black abyss.

"What are you doing?" I hissed, pulling the Nixan back. I panicked as I looked down towards the human, expecting it to turn and face us. Still, nothing. No movement at all.

"I think the human is dead," Kaz said, grinning widely.

Inilta sniffed his displeasure, but he started to move forward again. Once more the ball of fire above his head blazed brightly as his fears diminished.

The bridge that crossed the dark river was part of a stone road. I had no idea where it led to as I had not seen anything similar in Laxtal. Maybe it never surfaced, or had collapsed further down. These lands were meant to be untouched by human influence, but I could think of nothing else to explain this. Only pitch darkness met my eyes as I looked away from the mysterious structure. The road was a different type of stone than that of the cave. It was lighter grey in colour, and whilst it was generally smoother, I could see large grooves in the side of every slab.

"Claw marks," Inilta said, placing his whole paw inside just one of the grooves.

"How is that possible?" I whispered. There was only one creature I knew of with claws that big. This place was ancient, so surely Nightwings had nothing to do with this?

Inilta shook his head and turned away. It was a puzzle for another time. First, we needed to find the source of the magic and see if it could aid us in some way. Kaz had already crossed the bridge and was starting to sift through some of the debris there. By the look of it, a rock fall had occurred at some point, as small boulders littered the wide shelf between the bridge and doorway.

I slowly approached the great doorway, neck craning to look up to the lettering. The darkness between the pillars was untouched by Inilta's magic, resisting like there was a physical veil in the way. I crept closer. My scales tingled with growing magic until I was almost through the archway. I reached out with a paw, then backed away when I realised the other two had turned away to approach the slumped figure. I hurried after them.

Now that we were closer, I could see, but not smell, that the human was dead. It was a female, that much was clear, made obvious from her garments and hair. She was lying twisted against the rock, with a small knife impaled through her clothes to her heart. On her skin were faded patterns, like yellow strings of light that had been painted onto her flesh. Her open eyes stared listlessly into the darkness.

I followed her dead gaze to look upon a small opening in the rock just beside the massive doorway. It appeared to lead through to a small antechamber. As Kaz and Inilta quietly talked to each other, discussing whether or not to go on or turn back, I padded across to the antechamber and poked my nose inside. The roughly hewn walls certainly weren't natural, but this chamber was marked by small chips from human tools, not from the claws of dragons or other such creatures. Initially, I thought the square room was empty, but then something caught my eye. Lying in the middle of the floor was a small shard of jagged rock. My first thought was of the impossible; how could the Axinstone be here? Coming to my senses, I quickly realised it couldn't be the Nixan artefact. Ddraig Krateos had that in his possession, far above us.

I reached out to touch the small stone and felt a pulse of magic as my paw came into contact with the rough stone. I yelped and jumped back, causing the stone to flip over, revealing a burning symbol of a leopard's head carved into the shard.

Kaz and Inilta came running when they heard my cry, and in just a moment they had come into the small chamber.

"Is that the...?" Kaz asked.

I tentatively picked the stone up in my paw, feeling none of the power that the Axinstone possessed. But for the slightest tingle, it was without magic. "No, it's not the Axinstone. It doesn't have a dragon's head," I explained, showing my companions the fiery leopard head that distinguished it from the Nixan artefact. This was something altogether different.

"What is it then?" Inilta asked, gently taking the shard of rock from me, turning it over and over in his paws. He found nothing of interest and passed it back to me.

"I don't know, but there's nothing else in here," I said. I was almost disappointed. This small shard of rock was not the source of the waves of magic that had blinded us so, but I was convinced it had to be close by; I could still feel the pressure the unknown power was exerting on my mind. While Inilta and Kaz went back to searching the wide shelf, I sauntered back towards the mysterious body of the woman, keeping the shard of rock in my paw. There was something strange about this woman, but I couldn't place what it was.

I put the rock just to one side, where I could still see it, and edged closer to the woman. A slight heat came off her. That couldn't be right. If she was dead, then why was her body warm with life? And why was there no trace of any blood around the knife embedded in her heart? Without realising what I was doing, I reached out to touch her chest.

"What are you doing Azlak?" Kaz called out. I pulled my paw away as though shocked. In the brief contact I had with the corpse, I had felt power beyond anything I had experienced before. The might of the Axinstone paled to insignificance compared to the strength of magic within this human's body.

"It's her. The human is the source," I called out.

I only half-heard Inilta's and Kaz's confused voices as my attention focused on the human. I hesitantly touched the knife. The black handle felt as though it made from heavy stone and was ice-cold to the touch. My body tensed as I prepared to do something foolish.

"Are you sure, Azlak?" Kaz asked uncertainly.

"No," I replied, before pulling sharply on the knife.

I fell back onto the floor as the obsidian knife came free of the human's chest. For a moment I just lay there, waiting for something to happen. Nothing did. The body just slumped over a bit more.

"Well that was…" Inilta started to say, before he was interrupted by a howling wind. The noise was deafening. The erupting storm centred on the human's body; the shadows seemed to be pulled closer as swirls of light and darkness were dragged into the growing vortex.

I scrambled to my paws and tried to stand up, but the strength of the magic was too strong, and I tumbled over onto my side. I fell sharply onto the shard and felt it slip under my scales.

As suddenly as it began, with one last thunderclap of noise, the vortex vanished. It left no trace of its presence. All was calm and still again. The only sound was the river.

"What was that?" Inilta snarled. His wings were unfurled, and he was looking back to find the ledge we had come down.

I hadn't moved. This wasn't over yet. I could feel that the shard hadn't gone too deep beneath my scales, but something stronger than pain distracted me. Magical energy grew all around us.

A light started to flash, just above the human's head. First it was white, but then it started to change to other colours. I shuffled back a few steps, plucking the stone from my side. Whatever it was, I wanted to keep it if I could, even if just to find out what it was. I winced slightly as it came free, but was more intrigued about what was going on in front of me.

The light grew and expanded until it filled the whole cavern. It was fierce, but never blinding or painful. The light flashed and swirled, creating a mesmerising mixture of colour and energy. I tried to find patterns but failed. There seemed to be no source; it emanated from nowhere yet danced off every surface it touched. I glanced back at my companions. They were glowing and radiating with the same magical energy. I was sure I was, too.

We all took a few more steps back. If any of us had hoped to find the darkness, we failed. Each step we took caused the rock beneath our paws to smoulder with new colours.

As the aura of magic grew and expanded, a new sound echoed out. A voice. "Bri'An?"

A shadow moved in the light. A human form stood, arms held out wide as they took in the brilliance of the display. She seemed to be absorbing the light, feeding from it.

She screamed and fell to her knees as the last of the magic absorbed into her body, leaving the cavern in almost total darkness. Her haggard breaths rasped over noise of the river. A soft, yellow glow enveloped her body, created by the threads of light on her skin.

No one dared to speak.

No one dared to move.

Slowly the human rose to her feet. "You are not Bri'An," she said in a hoarse whisper. She staggered forward a few steps until she was just a wing's breadth away. Still my paws would not respond, freezing me in place.

She stumbled down to her knees again in a fall that was half intentional. She sat back, bringing her head almost level with mine.

"Who... who are you?" I asked, my voice finally returning.

Her eyes stared into mine. Her blazing eyes of liquid gold.

"I am Esperance."

CHAPTER TWENTY-ONE

Anzig

Ddraig Krateos was silent as he flew close to my tail. A few curious glances came in our direction, quickly replaced by deference and respect, clearing the space for us to fly through unimpeded. Despite the intrigue of the Nixans arriving, many hundreds of dragons remained beneath the surface, with several dozen lingering close to the firepit in the main chamber, speaking quietly in the dancing shadows cast by the roaring fire. We stopped only long enough to arrange food and drink, before heading directly for my personal chambers, where we would have privacy to discuss what had happened in Nixa.

Mushussu was grooming her silver scales as I pushed aside the veil separating the passageway from my chambers. The statue rose and bowed her head towards Ddraig Krateos.

"It is a relief to see you well, Mushussu," Ddraig Krateos said, much to my shock. I had believed that I was the only one who could see the guardian. This misconception was good news. It removed any lingering doubts that Mushussu had been a creation of my deluded mind. I managed a small, subtle smile to myself, contrasting with the mental equivalent of an eye roll I got from the guardian herself.

The guardian did not address my silent relief. Her attention remained on the Nixan ddraig. "I felt the eruption of magic in Nixa as it happened. How did my other self fare?"

Ddraig Krateos lowered his head and looked away. His wings wrapped tight against his body, making himself appear even smaller than his already diminutive frame. "There was no time to think of anything other than survival. My chambers were destroyed in the explosion. I do not believe she survived," he said.

"A guardian is not so easily slain. There is hope yet," Mushussu replied. From her mind I learned that every clan had a statue like her. I had seen some of them before and disregarded them as a trinket, but they were all guardians. All of them were Mushussu, an ancient magic come to life to protect the ddraigs of the forty-two clans.

"Hope," Ddraig Krateos said dully. He opened his paw and let the Axinstone drop to the floor, where its hot vortex of magic warmed my scales. It itched deep inside me, a new sensation. Did the artefact also mourn the loss of Nixa? I furrowed my brow and stared at the stone, paw twitching. So great was my distraction, that I almost missed the Nixan continue to speak.

"What hope have we got? We were destroyed in minutes. We had no defence."

Mushussu crept close to the Axinstone. Her silvered scales, usually blank and pure of any reflection, shone with a red light my eyes could not see. "It is possible the humans have unleashed something they did not intend. Ever since your clan was destroyed, my magic has become more powerful. It is possible all guardians have felt the same. I know this will do little to ease your pain and suffering, but that need not lead to despair. There may yet be a way to turn this into our advantage."

"I just don't see it, Mushussu." Ddraig Krateos stared at the Axinstone between his forepaws. The artefact that I had done so much to return, buying the alliance that should have been enough to topple the tyranny of Tsona. The magic prickled at my scales.

Ddraig Krateos batted the Axinstone in anger. The stone skittered across the ground, throwing up small red sparks. I scampered aside as it almost struck me, but Mushussu's silver paw lashed out and stomped on the magical artefact. Crimson fire engulfed the reflections in her scales. As she stepped away, she stared down at her paw, her brow etched with confusion. The tendrils on the sides of her muzzle quivered as though in a breeze felt only by her.

Keeping a wary eye on the Axinstone, I stepped around it and the motionless guardian. "There must be something we can do. I will send Haeraig Ellian to forge alliances with our other neighbours. We will not stand alone here, and nor will we give up the fight. Nixa must be avenged."

Ddraig Krateos looked me in the eye. *He has no idea what it is like. No way of knowing. How could he?"* The Nixan looked away before I could react to his unspoken thoughts. "What can we do in the face of such power?"

I glanced to Mushussu, but her focus was still on her paw. I sighed. "I don't know. Not yet. But what I do know is that we can't give up now."

The Nixan looked a shadow of the powerful dragon I had met just three weeks earlier. Not only did he still have blood on his scales where his wounds had not healed properly, but there was little spark in his eyes. His shoulders slumped and his wingtips dragged to the ground. "They defeated us in an instant. There was no warning, not even one our seers could give. I do not mean to belittle your offer of assistance, Ddraig Anzig, but right now it seems right that Ddraig Tsona has gathered to him the strongest army. I see no way that we can preserve our opposition to him."

I had no answer to that. Words stuttered and died on my tongue as I tried to think of something we could do, some way to counter Tsona and his human allies. We did not understand this magic they wielded, their Human-Nixans controlling abilities beyond anything the dragons of Nixa possessed. It did feel hopeless, in stark contrast to the hope I had felt in the days before the wylax.

Mushussu placed her paw back to the ground. A red tint still lingered on her leg. "I think…"

What the guardian had to say remained unsaid as her head snapped towards the archway. Her form shimmered, and in the time it took to blink she had returned to her usual place in the alcove above the fire. *"Someone comes."*

"Father?"

I turned at the unexpected voice. Haeraig Zeena had nosed her way into the chamber, the translucent purple veil snagging slightly on her blunt horns. The Nixan haeraig then noticed me and turned, bowing her head as she addressed me. "Forgive me Ddraig Anzig, I was looking for my father. May I enter?"

"You may, and be welcome," I said, taking a step back to move into the space vacated by Mushussu, ensuring my hindpaw didn't knock the Axinstone.

The Nixan haeraig swiped her paw at her horns, disentangling herself from the veil without tearing it. Despite the healing she must have received in the days since the attack on Nixa, she still limped slightly, favouring her right forepaw with each step. She stepped to the side to allow three other dragons to follow her, carrying a platter of charred meat and a jug of imported wine between them. Though my stomach roused at the smell of food, the Nixan ddraig barely lifted his head.

The three Laxtal dragons bowed their heads and retreated, quickly exiting my chamber to leave me alone with the Nixan ddraig and haeraig. I swept a paw to the platter of food. "Would you care for something to eat?" I asked Haeraig Zeena.

The red-scaled ness fluttered her wings. "I would be grateful, Ddraig Anzig. I have barely eaten since the attack on our home. Your haeraig is seeing to my clan, but I wished to ensure my father was well. He has not taken this defeat well."

I blinked in surprise, biting down the immediate response. I gave myself some time by pouring the wine into a wide bronze bowl for us to drink from. It was unusual for Haeraig Zeena to speak so candidly of her father to me, even more so that she spoke as though he was not sat next to her.

"I am the ddraig," the older Nixan snapped. He ignored the food and drink entirely as he clenched his paw at slammed it against the ground. He spoke with a fierce venom, a grimace locked onto his muzzle as though each word burned his tongue as they forced their way from his throat. "I was supposed to protect the clan. Not only did I fail, but I brought this upon us. It was my arrogance that blinded us to this threat, but more than that, this was retribution for the crimes of my past. I did not deserve to be ddraig of Nixa, and this is the price I pay."

I took a half-step forward. I was reluctant to interfere, but his words had piqued my curiosity. "How could it have been your fault, Ddraig?"

Ddraig Krateos growled as his daughter tried to pull on his shoulder so that he faced her. He shoved her aside and covered his face with his wing.

Haeraig Zeena pulled back. Her shoulders slumped as she hobbled away from her father. Though her eyes focused on the floor, I could see that her spirit was not as crushed as her father's. *"There is something he's not telling me."* The haeraig's thoughts growled her displeasure. When she spoke, this time aloud, her voice was sombre and slow.

"My brothers were all killed in the attack. My father blames himself for their deaths, as well as the thousands of other lives lost to the humans," she said. She sat gingerly and stretched out her injured left paw, before reaching for a chunk of meat. By the smell, it was rabbit or hare. The haeraig kept her head raised high as she slowly ate. Pride still coursed through this haeraig's veins.

"And Nataik? Is she with you?" I asked, hoping the Xigax ness had survived the attack, but I could sense immediately that she had not.

The haeraig couldn't meet my eye. She swallowed her mouthful and let out a low sigh. "She went out with Meadus the morning of the attack. They had gone to scout the humans' movements. We saw no sign of either of them, but I fear they both died in the attack. I'm sorry."

I whimpered in dismay. How could I explain this to the Xigax ddraig?

"It was my fault," Ddraig Krateos repeated. He slammed his forepaw down so hard he almost spilled some of the wine in the bowl nearby. He grimaced in pain as he tried to stagger upright, no longer able to place much weight down on all his paws. His eyes burned with a wild light, reflecting the flames in the fireplace. "I brought this upon us."

"Please, father, do not say such things. You did not inflict this onto our clan," Haeraig Zeena protested with a quick flare of her wings.

Ddraig Krateos staggered away to the fireplace, still not putting any pressure on his right foreleg. He stood, half-turned from us staring into the hearth, where the charcoaled wood still gently smoked, the dragon seemingly searching for solace within its dying embers. Was he thinking the same of his clan? Did he think his clan was dying too?

I didn't dare reach out with my magic to learn that answer. Nor did I approach him, staying still with his daughter. We both waited, barely daring to make a sound, waiting for the ddraig to continue. When he eventually did speak, it was in little more than a cracked whisper. "Meadus was not... he should not have been the youngest."

"I don't... I don't understand father. Meadus was the youngest. How could he not be?" Haeraig Zeena words were as pained as her expression.

"Meadus was barely one year out of the egg, when your... when your mother died. You must have been eight. I don't know if you remember her at all," Ddraig Krateos said, smiling gently to himself, deep in the memories of an earlier, happier time for him. Still he didn't look around, instead concentrating on the gentle wisps of smoke rising from the blackened wood, his head bowed with the weight of his perceived failure. "At that time, I was haeraig. I had lost my mate and had four sons and a daughter to care for. My father was in poor health, so I was assuming more and more of his duties as ddraig. I thought... I did what I thought was the right thing to do at..." His words trailed off, as though wisps of smoke themselves.

"What did you do?" Haeraig Zeena demanded. I couldn't help but gasp aloud as I felt her frustration and her horror building. Without realising, my mind reached out to touch hers. It was a roiling storm of emotion, with anger and fear writhing, snapping, and clawing for dominance. I felt her terror at learning what her father had done, but at the same time, the desperation for the truth. The secret could not remain with Ddraig Krateos any longer. I hastily withdrew from Zeena's mind, as the haeraig looked in my direction with nervous curiosity.

"As if five dragonets weren't enough, before your mother died we had one more clutch on the nest; three more eggs. I... I knew I couldn't raise eight dragons on my own, so I carried the eggs away in the middle of the night. I abandoned them and left three unhatched dragons to die in the wilderness," the ddraig said. He spat out the final words as though it was poison in his mouth. He choked as he suppressed a pained howl.

To my horror, tears splashed from his eyes, but neither ddraig nor haeraig seemed ashamed by the display of weakness. I took a step back, second-paw shame burning behind the scales of my face as I watched the Nixan ddraig, one of the most powerful dragons across all forty-two clans, openly sob in my chamber.

Instead of showing any shame herself, Haeraig Zeena slowly approached her distraught father and put a paw on his shoulder, nosing her muzzle beneath his. She said something quiet, something that I could not quite hear.

My mind turned to the ddraig's shocking declaration. Three eggs? The words ignited a spark deep within my mind. Like the sleepy stirring of an awakened beast, a memory came alive; glowing brighter and brighter... Maznar! Manzar had told me her egg had been found with two others, abandoned in the wild. Surely not...

Before I could give voice to my realisation, Ddraig Krateos looked back towards his daughter and spoke. "I truly believed it was necessary to save the five I already had. But I was wrong. I have paid the price, and thousands have died because of me. I was not worthy of becoming ddraig of Nixa."

Haeraig Zeena shook her head. "Don't be ridiculous, father. No matter what mistakes you made in the past, no matter what happened to my brothers or sisters, that does not change the present. Those actions had nothing to do with this."

"How can you be sure my daughter?" Ddraig Krateos said. He sighed and looked away from his daughter again, half raising his wing to hide behind. "I apologise that you brought out this food for me, but I fear I am not hungry. Are the usual guest chambers free, Ddraig Anzig?" Ddraig Krateos addressed the depths of the hearth.

I nodded pointlessly. I didn't yet trust myself to speak. How would Ddraig Krateos react to the news that one of those eggs had survived, and that his daughter, his youngest daughter, was present in this lair? The news that she had been a victim of human magic and torture for all her life would also add to his grief and guilt. I vowed to hold my tongue, for now. The ddraig needed to grieve for the lives lost from his clan. *"That is a good idea,"* I heard Mushussu say directly into my mind.

I said nothing as Ddraig Krateos turned without a word and left for the sanctuary of the chambers set aside for the Nixan when he visited. Haeraig Zeena followed close behind, more as a confused daughter than a concerned haeraig, I feared. The moment they had passed through the veil, Mushussu leaped down from her alcove and circled around me so her tail almost touched her own muzzle. "I know what you are scheming, young ddraig," she said, staring into my eyes. I couldn't meet those blank orbs for long; there was nothing to focus on. Not even my reflection.

"I have to go to her. I have to know," I replied. I had no idea what impact it could have, but surely things would change if Maznar was Ddraig Krateos's daughter. Not only that, but I needed to get out of my chambers. I felt incredibly hot, though the fire only smouldered faintly.

"It will only bring grief to Ddraig Krateos," Mushussu growled.

I tried to nudge past the guardian, not wanting her advice, but she remained as firm and unmoving as a statue should be, refusing to let me go. I snarled and struck out repeatedly at her, but only succeeded in hurting a paw against her silver body.

"I do not entirely trust Maznar yet. If Krateos knows that she is his daughter, then he would have to bestow a position of some power on her. Are you certain she will only use that power for the good of dragonkind?" she asked.

Begrudgingly, although I didn't want her advice, Mushussu had raised a valid point, and for that alone I relented my pathetic attack on her unflinching silver scales. Could we trust Maznar, or was she Nightwings still? I sat back on my haunches and fanned my wings wide, trying to cool down as Mushussu eased away to give me a little more space. She remained standing between me and the archway out to the rest of the lair, but at least she gave me the room to move.

"I just think she deserves..." I started to say, before something caught my eye. Neither of the Nixans had remembered to take the Axinstone with them. The dragon's head on its surface burned brightly as I approached it.

"Be careful young ddraig," Mushussu said.

I ignored her and reached out a paw to touch the magical stone. The heat that emanated from the Axinstone tingled through my scales. Whispers filled my mind. *"Bri'An, where are you Bri'An?"* Other voices spoke. Some I recognised; most I did not. The Axinstone faded from my sight, along with the rest of my chamber, as my vision was overtaken by flashing images of dragons; many, many dragons. Before I had a chance to identify any I saw, or even where they were, my vision had moved on to another.

I tried to focus on one particular dragon that kept flashing before my eyes, a large red drake who was lying down in front of the great fire. I didn't know his name. No, what was I thinking? Earus was his name. How could I forget that? He tilted his head to the side and stared at me. "Kyeara, are you alright?"

"Who?" I replied...

I blinked, my head twisting. I couldn't recall ever hearing that name before, but no... of course I had. She was my mate and had been for many years. I pawed at the ground. That shouldn't be something I could just fail to remember.

The ness shook her head and fluttered her wings. "Sorry, I felt funny for a moment," she said. She slowly edged closer and pressed her head to mine. "Something strange came over me. It almost felt like I was another dragon for a moment." As my mate leaned against me, I briefly caught the eye of a green-scaled ness, Sierra, from across the other side of the chamber.

Vertigo spun the cave for a moment...

I quickly looked away from the larger dragon, not wishing to confront him. I hadn't intended to meet his eyes, but he had glanced up from his mate unexpectedly. I growled before grabbing the strings of the salt bag, tightening it up with my teeth so nothing would spill. Taking the weight in my paws, I spread my wings and laboured my way up to the top of the grand chamber. My shoulders strained with the effort, but I slowly ascended towards the surface. I couldn't take a straight route – dragons were flying in almost every direction, and I had to weave my way around them as they wouldn't move out of my way. I still needed to hurry though. If I took too long the hunters would start complaining. They needed the salt to preserve the fresh venison they had caught. Winter was coming, and the cold caves would empty quickly with all these new dragons from Nixa.

The smaller passage that led out from the grand chamber was easier to fly through. I stayed right on the tail of another ness as she unknowingly cleared a path for me.

The salt bag knocked against a protrusion in the ground, unbalancing me. I only just caught my flight in time and avoided the humiliation of falling from the air, but in that moment my head felt like it split apart...

A ness bumped into me as she flew out towards the open sky. I snarled at her, but she didn't even seem to realise I was there. All her focus was on the bulging bag of salt she had gripped in her claws. I could have gone back to berate her for her inattention, but I had more important matters to deal with than a ness who couldn't control her burden.

I looked up to the small opening beyond the unlit firepit. I shivered in anticipation. I had never been up there before, but now I had the perfect opportunity. The Nixan haeraig was up there, and I had a message that only she must hear. Then a puff of smoke drifted over me. I coughed and squeezed my eyes closed as the scorched scent of burned wood filled my nose…

I coughed and grimaced as I slowly walked away from my father. He was not coping with the decimation of our clan. There was nothing I could say to him that could help, so I had decided to leave him with his grief. I could only hope that he would once more become the leader Nixa so desperately needed.

I paused for a moment and put a paw against my head. There was an odd pressure there and I thought I could detect the faint scent of magic, not just the lingering burn of phantom smoke. Its touch was unfamiliar though, and there were few Nixans left alive whose particular magic I did not recognise. I shook my head. It was something I could worry about later.

I felt bad for leaving Ddraig Anzig so suddenly; he had graciously opened his clan to us when we needed it most. I was sure that with Clan Laxtal's assistance, and the power of the Axinstone which we had thankfully saved, we would begin to recover.

The Axinstone! I had left it in Ddraig Anzig's chambers. I shrieked in dismay and horror. A Laxtal dragon could not touch a thing of such power and hope to be unharmed. I sprinted back to the ddraig, hoping I would be able to stop him before he came into contact with it.

"Haeraig Zeena," a large red Laxtal dragon called out, his wings fluttering as he landed.

"Not now," I snarled, barging past him and knocking him from his paws before he could properly find his balance. I ignored his cry of protest. I had no time for common dragons right now.

I burst unannounced into Ddraig Anzig's chambers to find that I was already too late. The ddraig had hunched over, the Axinstone gripped tightly in his forepaws. His wings twitched fitfully, and though I couldn't see his face I knew he was in pain.

A flash of silver streaked across my vision as I dived forward and shoved at the ddraig with all my strength. He was smaller than me, and I was able to push him hard enough that he flew back several feet. The Axinstone spun out of his paws as he smacked against the wall, a lot harder than I intended.

I opened my eyes groggily. Everything hurt. My wings felt like I had flown for days without rest. My head was nothing but stabbing barbs of light; I was in agony. I couldn't even see anything but for the piercing white lights.

"Ddraig Anzig?" Haeraig Zeena asked tentatively. A red mist started to form in the field of white. "Are... are you alright?"

"I saw..." I started to say, before biting down on my tongue. What had I seen? I had been inside the mind and body of other dragons. Was this the true range of my magic? Could I really see and feel what others were experiencing, and not just hearing their thoughts? If this really was the case, then Haeraig Zeena could not know the truth. She obviously presumed that I suffered from injuries inflicted by the Axinstone.

I groaned and rolled over to my front, wishing the Nixan haeraig had been a little less forceful in pushing me away from the Axinstone. My sight was starting to clear. Haeraig Zeena was nervously standing a few feet away. She clutched the Axinstone to her chest, seemingly keeping it as far away from me as I could. *"His eyes... why were they white?"*

Paralysed with fear, I could do nothing as that thought echoed through my mind. Azlak's eyes turned white whenever he peered into the future.

"You said you saw something? What did you see?" she asked in a tone that was a little harsher than was polite to use towards a ddraig.

I still couldn't move, let alone speak. What was I going to say? She had seen my eyes turn white – surely a sign of magic. There was nothing I could say to deny that. I felt nauseous. I pushed my tongue against the inside of my teeth in an attempt to quell the feeling. Thinking it would be better to stand, I hauled myself upright and faced the Nixan. She had backed away as though in fear. Haeraig Zeena had nothing to be afraid of, not like I did.

"I..."

A large red dragon interrupted us as he came bursting in unannounced. I almost whimpered with relief as the dragon ignored me and placed his paw on Haeraig Zeena's shoulder. The Nixan snarled and cuffed the dragon across the face, but he was not cowed so easily.

"Haeraig Zeena, I beg you to hear me. Isikian has requested your urgent attention," he said not waiting for her answer, but bowing his head to look at the Nixan's paws.

"Did he say why?" Haeraig Zeena growled. The dragon quickly shook his head and backed away. The Nixan growled again, this time turning her ire on me. "I think it is best if you wait here for me, Ddraig Anzig. Something isn't right here, and I want to know what."

Before I knew what I was saying, I found myself agreeing to the haeraig's demand. I stayed silent as I watched her leave with the Laxtal dragon, who no doubt could not believe he had heard his ddraig submit to the demands of a haeraig. I knew I would still be here when she returned, no matter how long she took.

Fear took hold of me, and I turned to the bowl of wine, untouched by either of the Nixans. I lapped up the sweet liquid, drinking far quicker than I knew was wise. I tore at the strips of charred rabbit meat, attempting to use both drink and food to settle my uneasy stomach. Neither worked, and I soon resorted to pacing the length of my chamber, back and forth so many times I was surprised I did not leave behind a worn track.

All the while, Mushussu watched me from her alcove, saying nothing. I could feel her blank eyes upon me, but for the time she kept her mouth closed, I did not break the silence.

Eventually, the guardian spoke, evidently unable to keep her silence any longer. "I think there is more to this than you realise."

I stopped my pacing and looked up. I couldn't be sure how long I had been moving, how long since Haeraig Zeena had left. The air had grown cold in the absence of the Axinstone, despite the fire that still smouldered. I couldn't even be sure if it was still daylight, or if night had fallen. No one had come with more food, but perhaps the dragons responsible for that had thought the platter of rabbit enough. The arrival of several hundred refugees had likely shaken up a lot of routines.

I growled at the guardian when she said nothing further. "I am not in the mood for riddles, Mushussu. Either speak what you have to say, or be quiet."

The guardian jumped down from her alcove. Now it was her turn to pace. Not only did she not reflect the firelight, but I noticed she didn't leave a shadow either. "I cannot speak plainly, as I am bound by the promises I made to your predecessor. But these eggs are important. It is up to you to learn why."

I sighed. "Maznar said she was found by a dragon and given to the humans."

"Which leaves the identity of the other two eggs a mystery," Mushussu prompted.

I pushed past the guardian and peered out through the veil. There was no movement beyond my chamber and little noise. If Haeraig Zeena was coming back, then it seemed unlikely that she would do so until morning. For a moment I wondered what business had pulled her away, but then I shook my head and turned away. The wine had left my steps feeling unsteady, and the irritation with Mushussu made me more likely to snap out. My pile of furs was looking more attractive an option by the moment.

"How do we even know they survived?" I asked, reluctantly turning my mind back to the guardian.

"They did." That was all Mushussu said.

Though I looked to her for more information, the guardian stayed silent, as though another dragon had come into the chamber with us. Realising I was not going to get anything more from her, I growled in frustration and curled up on my nest of rugs. Their warmth provided a good respite from the chill air. I couldn't be sure if that was reality or illusion from the absence of magic, but I was grateful for the thick rugs.

I did not intend to sleep. I wanted to be alert in case the Nixan returned to continue the awkward conversation, but as I closed my eyes for just a moment, my dreams ambushed my mind and pulled me under.

A pair of piercing red eyes opened in the shadows. "Aah, Little One. I've been waiting for this moment for a very long time."

The darkness receded, and with it went the eyes.

I found I was standing in the snow atop a tall mountain, far higher than I could ever hope to fly. The snow was cold, wet, and unfamiliar beneath my paws. I had seen snow before, I had played in it during a particularly fierce winter when I had been a dragonet, but never had I seen it so deep. I had to leap just to be able to move, as I sunk in almost to my chest.

To my left was a jutting spire of rock that reached up to the sky, with a dark crevice that ran down its centre, almost splitting it in two. On my right there was a giant precipice that dropped away as far as I could see as I tentatively looked down. I was stunned to see clouds below me. Just how tall was this peak? There should not be air at this height, but I was able to breathe just fine.

I knew I was here for a purpose, and I looked around for some evidence of the spectre's presence. Sure enough I found it, a shadow amongst the shadows with just her gleaming red eyes to give her away.

"Where have you brought me?"

Maznar stepped out of the shadows, moving through the snow as though it wasn't there. "We are in mountains to the distant east of Laxtal, not far from the draconic territory of Vatrea. There is a human village and a city built by creatures known as the kaur somewhere down below us, beneath the clouds."

I had seen these mountains once before. They were indeed a long way from Laxtal, but I had never heard of a village in those peaks. I hadn't known humans dwelt beyond our eastern borders. I growled softly, frustrated by the spectre. This was not what I wanted. I wished simply to lie in blissful peace and silence to try and forget my worries.

"Does this have to be now?"

Maznar snickered. "My dear Anzig, of course it has to be now. After what you have seen and heard, surely you must be approaching the truth?"

I snarled and struck out at the snow, but the soft mush splattered easily, doing nothing to lessen my anger. "Speak plainly, for once. You remind me of... of someone I know." Even in this dream I could not mention the name of Mushussu. The spectre ignored my demands and laughed again.

"Where is the fun in that?"

I turned my back on her, but that had about as much effect as attacking the snow. This may have been my dream, but Maznar had full control over it. Sure enough, the spectre appeared in front of me again, and I cried out in terror as she became the monstrosity of Nightwings. Memories of the agony she had caused me ruptured through my body, causing me to double over in pain.

"You know who my father is," Nightwings roared. She launched into the sky and started to circle overhead like an eagle hunting its prey. I was conflicted, trying to both keep my eyes on her and cover my head with my wing and cower. "Three eggs, Anzig. I told you that. One was mine."

Like a shimmering mirage, a bronze dragon crossed in front of me. It was Ddraig Krateos, but he looked significantly younger to how I knew him. Clutched in his paws was a single off-white egg. Two others lay nearby, semi-translucent in the snow. Nightwings was showing me his dreams. His nightmares. His hidden shame.

Ddraig Krateos rested the third beside the other two. His paw lingered as though frozen to the eggs themselves. They couldn't be far from hatching as only a few black specks blemished their surface. "Forgive me." The ddraig's parting words drifted away on the wind as he spread his wings and took to the sky, passing beyond the realms of the shimmering scene Nightwings had shown me. Only the three eggs remained.

"Why are you showing me this?" I cried out to the circling spectre. She had started to fly ever higher until she became little more than a dark blot against the sun. Her voice remained as strong and loud as though she was standing right beside me.

"Those eggs didn't die, Anzig. They were found, and they all hatched. Who do you think they are?"

"Just tell me!" I shrieked, but again the spectre laughed.

"Three lost children of Nixa," the spectre sung. "Three dragons who bear the gift of that clan, without knowing their heritage. Three dragons with impossible magic."

I froze. The snow no longer chilled just my scales. It seeped into my heart.

Nightwings landed in front of me and shrunk back to Maznar, though her smile never seemed to diminish. Her teeth and fangs were all I could see. "Aah, there it is. Realisation."

I wrenched my gaze up from her mouth, meeting her ferocious and gleeful eyes. "No, you're lying to me..."

"Time to go, Anzig. Someone is trying to wake you."

The dream ended with a wrenching pull. I woke gasping and shivering, the phantom cold dripping from my scales until the firelight could warm me again.

I knew who had hatched from the abandoned eggs. I knew which dragons possessed the impossible.

I stared up at Haeraig Zeena as she stood above me, concern in her eyes.

I ran my tongue over my teeth. How could I tell her what I now knew?

How could I tell her she was my sister?

I had some serious explaining to do.

END OF BOOK 2

The Destiny of Dragons continues in book 3: Fate of Three.

ABOUT THE AUTHOR

J.F.R. Coates was born and raised in picturesque Somerset, England, but she moved to Brisbane, Australia as a teenager. She grew up reading from a young age, starting with Enid Blyton's *The Famous Five* and *Secret Seven*, before finding her calling with J.R.R. Tolkien's *The Hobbit*. Speculative Fiction has gripped her ever since, and now she calls amongst her favourite authors Maggie Furey, Robin Hobb, and Neil Gaiman.

She still lives in Brisbane, where she lives with her husband and – as seems ubiquitous for authors –two cats.

You can follow her on your social media of choice: Twitter, Facebook, Mastodon, Instagram, and Bluesky. Just search for jfrcoates.

She also has a Patreon, which allows for sneak-previews of what's to come, as well as additional stories that fit in around her novels. All support is always gratefully received.

https://www.patreon.com/jfrcoates